Ali McNamara lives in Cambridgeshire with her family and her beloved dogs. In her spare time, she likes antique shopping, people watching and daydreaming, usually accompanied by a good cup of coffee!

Ali has the chronic illness M.E./CFS and is a disability and invisible disability advocate.

To find out more about Ali visit her website:
www.alimcnamara.co.uk
Follow her on Instagram: @AliMcNamara
Or like her Facebook page: Ali McNamara

T0384122

Ali McNamara

A Secret Cornish Wish

SPHERE

SPHERE

First published in Great Britain in 2024 by Sphere

3 5 7 9 10 8 6 4 2

Copyright © Ali McNamara 2024

The moral right of the author has been asserted.

A CIP catalogue record for this book
is available from the British Library.

ISBN 978-1-4087-2706-5

Typeset in Caslon by M Rules
Printed and bound in Great Britain by
Clays Ltd, Elcograf S.p.A.

Papers used by Sphere are from well-managed forests
and other responsible sources.

Sphere
An imprint of
Little, Brown Book Group
Carmelite House
50 Victoria Embankment
London EC4Y 0DZ

An Hachette UK Company
www.hachette.co.uk

www.littlebrown.co.uk

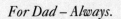

For Dad – Always.

A Note from Ali

Another St Felix book! Who would have thought when I wrote about a Little Flower Shop by the Sea back in 2015 that I'd be sharing my fifth St Felix story with you all.

In this book I've loved writing about Frankie and her friends, through their lives from teenagers to mature and successful women, and the little Cornish town of St Felix from the 1980s to the present day, and I really hope you enjoy their story too. There are lots of mentions of characters from past St Felix books – I do hope if you've read my other St Felix stories you manage to spot them all!

As always, I have a few people to thank who have helped me grow this story through its own unique life, from the seed of an idea to the finished novel you have before you now.

So, a huge thank you to the following:

Hannah Ferguson my *always* wonderful agent.

Rebecca Roy my *always* enthusiastic editor.

The *always* efficient team at Sphere and Little, Brown with special thanks to: Zoe Carroll, Brionee Fenlon, Henry Lord and Lucy Malagoni.

My *always* wonderful family – Jim, Rosie, Tom and our lovely dogs, who *always* make me smile!

Why am I using the word *always* so much? You'll have to read the story to find out!

Enjoy *always*!

Ali x

'If a mermaid's treasure washes up on the shore
Return it to the waves and be happy forevermore.'

Prologue

Autumn 2024

It never really changes, does it – the sea?

The seasons change, the weather changes; the light that bounces on the waves and makes them look either an invitingly turquoise blue or a bitterly cold grey – that changes. But the sea, with its rhythmical waves washing in over the sand, time and time again – it doesn't change. It simply remains a constant. You can rely on the sea to do its thing, day after day, year after year, without any fuss or worry. It's always there – just like it always will be.

Sitting high up on the rocks that overlook the beach and the little Cornish town of St Felix, I gaze out over the sea while I watch the gulls soaring above, and I remember . . .

I remember us all standing together down there on the rocks as the waves splashed below. Six school friends with our whole lives in front of us. We had no idea back then how the world would change over the next thirty-five years, or how we would, too. We were young and full of hope and anticipation at what our futures might bring.

Back in 1989, we'd rush home every day from school to watch *Neighbours*; Harry had only just met Sally on the big screen, but you could giggle at Baby and Johnny dirty dancing on the small screen if you were lucky enough to have a machine and a local video rental shop; Kylie and Jason, and New Kids on the Block, topped the charts; telephones were something plugged into the wall and computers were something you learnt about once a week at school.

I had no idea back then that I'd be sitting here in St Felix once more when I reached, what seemed to me at the time, the incredibly ancient age of fifty. No idea that my teenage friends would be here with me again – well, most of them would. Sadly, this time, there would be one of us missing.

But on that magical evening, when we stood on the rocks together, we each wished for something different, and we each kept it a secret. All except for the wish we made together: that we'd be friends for ever, no matter what happened in our lives, that we'd keep in touch and try to be together, and, amazingly, all these years later, we've managed to do just that.

Unlike the sea, every one of us has changed over the years. We've grown older, some of us wiser, but we've kept the promise we made to each other.

The promise we'd always be together.

One

July 1989

'No,' I insist again when Eddie asks the same question he's asked me at least five times already. 'It's not my thing.'

'Is it any of our things, really?' Eddie replies, trying to look innocent. 'But we're still stepping up.'

I turn around from where I've been painting scenery for the dance – a seascape not unlike the one we might see once we return home from school this evening.

'Yeah, right,' I say, brandishing my paintbrush at my friend. 'This is right up your street and you know it!'

'All right.' He gives a good-natured shrug. 'You might be right. I am quite looking forward to performing. But I need three backing singers, or it won't look right.'

'I thought you had three already – Claire, Mandy and Suzy?'

'Suzy's dropped out.'

'Why? She's got a great voice.'

'I know,' Eddie says with an anguished expression. 'I really need her, but she says she'll embarrass herself.'

'And the rest of us won't?'

'You know what she's like – always changing her mind at the last minute about everything.'

He was right. Our friend Suzy is quite erratic and prone to second thoughts, which is a shame really, because her mind can be incredibly sharp and focused, especially when it comes to issues she's passionate about, like the environment.

'*Save me*, Obi-Wan Frankie – you're my only hope!' Eddie says in a high-pitched voice, as he clasps his hands together in a praying motion.

I've known Eddie since our first year at secondary school, when we were put in the same form together. And even though he is a pain sometimes, especially when it comes to things like this, he is also one of my best friends – there's no way I'm going to let him down.

'All right, Princess,' I sigh. 'I'll do it. But I want to be hidden at the back, OK?'

'You're a dream!' Eddie hugs me, and I hurriedly hold the paintbrush away from him. 'Thank you. The choreography wouldn't have worked with just two.'

'Wait, you didn't say anything about choreography!'

'See you at the harbour at seven tonight,' Eddie sings as he hurriedly makes his way down the steps from the stage and across the assembly hall. 'We're rehearsing on the beach tonight.'

I shake my head as he exits through the door at the back of the hall. It was bad enough being on stage and singing, let alone dancing as well.

I'm about to turn back to the scenery and finish up my art-work for tonight, when a girl carrying a violin case enters the hall, followed by a group of other boys and girls all carrying various musical instruments, some of them in cases, some of them not.

'Don't let us stop you, Frankie!' Jenny, one of my classmates, calls, as she lifts a chair from where they're stacked at the side of the hall. 'We're just going to rehearse for a while.'

'No worries,' I reply, about to turn back and finish off my waves – one of the parts of my scenery I'm most proud of – when I notice Robert Matthews enter the room behind the others. He's carrying a guitar case and he looks a little lost.

'Over here, Rob!' Jenny gestures to a chair she's just laid out. 'I've saved you a place.'

Robert, looking a tad embarrassed, nods and heads over towards Jenny. He glances up at me standing on the stage staring down at him.

'Hi,' he says with a half-smile. 'Nice waves.'

'Th ... thanks,' I reply, for some reason waving my brush at him so a little of the blue paint flicks down onto my face. I hurriedly wipe it away with the back of my hand, and I know it will have left a smear on my now flushed cheeks, so I hurriedly turn back towards the huge backdrop I've been working so hard on this week and try to remember what I'm supposed to be doing. But for some reason I've not only forgotten what I'm working on, but how to paint too.

I pretend to be mixing some paint while I gather myself.

Robert Matthews has just spoken to me! Not only that, but he also noticed my artwork – he said, 'Nice waves.'

Ever since Robert came to our school as a new pupil at the beginning of this term, my heart has felt like it's going to burst out of my chest every time I see him. Either that or my stomach begins doing all sorts of complex gymnastics whenever he's near.

It's so embarrassing that my body decides to behave this way around a boy. I spent most of my fifteen years on this planet

5

detesting them, but he's the first one to make me feel this out of control – it is very annoying.

But Robert is different to all the other boys at school – his short sandy hair is soft and shiny-looking. He has the most amazing pair of dark-brown eyes – and the longest eyelashes I've ever seen on a boy, or a girl for that matter. He's sort of quiet, but not too quiet. He's smart – I know this because he's in a lot of the same classes as me – but he's not a swot.

He fitted in right away, and the other boys appeared to accept him into their groups with very little resistance. I was quite jealous – I've spent my whole time at this school trying to fit in, trying to find my place in the right crowd, and Robert seemingly managed to do it within a few days.

I'm not the only girl to notice his presence, of course. There are often a lot of dreamy looks and overly long gazes when he's around, followed by much giggling. Robert quickly became the best-looking boy in our school by a long shot, and it didn't come as any surprise that a lot of other people seemed to think so too.

Finally, my hand remembers how to paint again and, while the musicians practise their pieces for the show behind me, I continue working on the set.

The 'Enchantment Under the Sea' dance that I'm painting a backdrop for is to be our school's official leavers' event this year. At fifteen, me and my friends won't be leaving school until next year, but the tradition is that we, as the year below, are allowed to attend as a sort of transition to becoming the oldest in the school. But to earn our place, we provide the evening's entertainment.

The theme was a popular choice, after the success of *Back to The Future* a few years ago, where there was a school dance of the same name. All sorts of committees were formed to organise the event, and I found myself volunteering to paint the backdrop for the evening – this year, a talent show of sorts, where all the acts had to have a sea theme to gain entry.

I love to paint and draw, and to be allowed to create something on a large scale such as this is very exciting. I am probably just as excited about creating my backdrop as most of the other girls are about creating their outfits for the evening.

I've always been a bit of a tomboy, happier in trainers, jeans and a baggy sweatshirt than a pair of fancy shoes and a dress. But even I'm making an effort for the dance – that's if I haven't first been laughed off the stage for my singing, and now it seems my dancing ability too.

The musicians practise for about an hour behind me, while I carry on with my painting. I try not to make it too obvious that I keep sneaking the occasional glance in Robert's direction. I make sure I only do it when I load my paintbrush up with more paint or change the colour on my pallet.

Eventually, as I'm just about to finish up for the afternoon, the musicians decide to call it a day too. As chairs are replaced and instruments packed up below me, I do the same on the stage with my art equipment.

After gathering all my dirty brushes in a pot, so I can wash them in the sinks in the girls' toilets afterwards, I jump as I realise Robert is now up on the stage behind me. He's holding his guitar case in one hand, while he admires my backdrop.

'It's very good,' he says, not looking at me but at the sea in front of him. 'Did you do all this yourself?'

'Yes.' I'm trying desperately to stop myself – and my voice – from shaking. 'Yes, I did.'

'I wish I could paint, but I'm pretty rubbish at it.'

'I'm sure you're not.'

'Frankie, we're in the same art class. You must have seen how awful my work is. Miss Simpson never offers to hang any of my paintings on the school walls, does she? Whereas they're covered in your work.'

I'm not sure if I'm more shocked he knows my name, or that he's noticed my artwork displayed around the school.

He turns to me and smiles, and I almost pass out on the spot.

'Right ...' he says when I don't speak. 'I guess I'd better let you get on.'

'No!' I cry suddenly. 'I mean ... I've finished now ... a ... a bit like you have. With your rehearsal.' I wave my hand in the direction the musicians were a few minutes ago. 'You sounded good.' I'm desperate for him not to leave now he's actually here talking to me. 'Are you entering the talent show?'

'Couldn't you tell by the songs we were practising? They were all sea-based.'

'Oh ... oh, yes, of course they were. I wasn't really thinking about it to be honest. I was just enjoying the tunes while I painted.'

'Great, then we can't have been too bad.' He grins, and I hurriedly smile back at him.

'I didn't know you played the guitar,' I say, keen to keep this conversation going. I've dreamed about the day this might happen. I didn't quite envision standing here in my dungarees, covered in acrylic paint when it did, but I don't care about that now, only that it *is* actually happening.

'Yeah, I took lessons at my last school. I haven't bothered with them since I came here, but when Jenny and the others found out I played, they asked me to join their group for the show.

I bet they did! Jenny has had her eye on Robert since he arrived.

8

'Are you doing anything? Anything apart from painting brilliant backdrops, that is?'

'Thanks,' I reply shyly. 'Er, I've sort of been roped into singing with my friend, Eddie, and some other girls.'

'You sing?' Robert looks surprised.

'No, but someone dropped out, so I said I'd help. I'm sure it will be a disaster though.'

'You can't be good at everything.' Robert glances at the seascape next to us again. 'I guess I'll see you at rehearsals and stuff this week, then?'

'Yes, yes, you will. I'll be there!' I triumphantly punch the air in front of me, and then immediately regret it.

Robert stares at my fist still hanging in mid-air. Hurriedly I pull it back down to my side.

'See ya then, Frankie,' he says, grinning, probably at my ridiculous behaviour.

'Yes, see ya, Robert,' I murmur, knowing my cheeks are likely giving my embarrassment away for me.

'Rob,' he says. 'My mates call me Rob.'

'Rob it is, then,' I say, trying desperately to be cool, but failing miserably as usual.

Rob simply nods and makes his way quickly down the steps and through the school hall, while I stand on the stage, covered in paint, quietly dying inside.

And that Monday was the first time I ever spoke to Rob.

Two

'Two, three, four and … Frankie, why haven't you moved?'

'Sorry,' I say for what feels like the hundredth time tonight. 'I told you I wasn't good at this kind of thing.'

Eddie looks at me with a mixture of frustration and pity. 'Why don't you sit this one out and watch the others?' he suggests. 'Maybe it will help if you see what you're supposed to be doing.'

'Sure.' I shrug, happy for any excuse to stop this torture.

We've been rehearsing down on Morvoren Cove, one of the quieter beaches in St Felix. We've tucked ourselves in among some large rocks for a little privacy, and we've been going over and over Eddie's planned routine for our spot in the Enchantment Under the Sea talent show.

It's all right for Eddie and Mandy; they are natural performers – neither of them ever one to shy away from the spotlight when it's on them. My other friend, Claire, is naturally quiet and shy, so I was surprised to hear she was going to be a part of the performance. But Eddie can be very persuasive, and I have no doubt he's sweet-talked her into this somehow.

Sitting cross-legged on the sand, I watch them move around

in front of me to a track I'm already sick of hearing played over and over again on Mandy's portable cassette player, and I can't help but smile at their very different ways of performing.

Eddie is the life and soul as always; his moves and gestures are pronounced and over the top – just like he is.

Mandy somehow manages to make Eddie's choreography look feline and sexy as she moves her curvy figure around and bats her long black eyelashes.

And Claire – well, she's just Claire. As always, trying her absolute best, but somehow always managing to scuttle around in the background like a little mouse.

'Yes!' Eddie claps his hands triumphantly when they complete the routine reasonably successfully without me. 'That's it – we've nearly got it!'

'Have we, though?' Mandy asks, throwing herself down on the sand beside me. She opens a can of Fanta and takes a long slurp. 'It still seems pretty sloppy to me.'

Claire also sits down beside us. She too opens a can, but she sips delicately from it while she neatly arranges her legs underneath her.

'It's only sloppy when I'm involved,' I reply, smiling. 'Without me it's ten times better.'

'Oh, no!' Eddie fiddles with the cassette player again, no doubt rewinding it ready to play yet another rendition of the Beach Boys' 'Surfin' USA'. 'You're not getting out of it that easily, Frankie. You'll pick it up eventually.'

I look desperately at the others for help while Eddie is turned away.

They just grin back at me.

'If we have to do it, you do too!' Mandy whispers. 'What I wanna know is how Suzy managed to get out of it so easily.'

11

'Claire?' I whisper, and I clasp my hands together as though I'm praying. 'Help me – you know I have two left feet when it comes to dancing.'

Claire thinks for a moment, then she nods. 'You know, Eddie,' she says suddenly, making us all jump. Claire is always quiet and rarely speaks up unless she has to. 'I was wondering about something.'

'Yep?' Eddie is still trying to set up the track.

'If we're supposed to be dressed as mermaids on stage, then how are we actually going to be able to dance?'

'What do you mean?' Eddie asks, turning around.

'Well . . . mermaids have tails, don't they, not legs. How can we dance if our legs are hidden in a fishtail?'

Yes, Claire! I think euphorically. *Brilliant!*

Eddie's face suggests he hasn't considered this small, but important, fact.

Claire continues. 'What about if we sat on a wall or something and just sort of swayed in time with the music – would that work? It would be a lot easier for all of us.'

I'm grateful she hasn't said, 'Easier for Frankie.'

'Yeah, Eddie,' Mandy joins in. She jumps up and goes over to him. 'I mean, we all know you are the star of the show, aren't you?' She puts an arm around his shoulders and then gestures as though they can see a mock-up of the stage in front of them. 'We're just there to make up the numbers – and of course look totally and utterly lip-smackingly gorgeous! Couldn't we be perched on some sort of rock or a shell or something?' She encourages us to put this into practice now on the nearby rocks.

Claire and I hurry over to the nearest one and begin to arrange ourselves on top with our legs pressed together as though we have long mermaid tails.

'I'm sure our budding Picasso over there could whip some-thing up for the stage, couldn't you?' Mandy asks, looking at me.

'Oh, yes, I could paint a large shell or a rock – whatever you like,' I hurriedly say, suddenly envisioning a much less embar-rassing time for myself on the stage.

Mandy lets go of Eddie and joins us on the rock, then we begin to make up some impromptu moves by swaying our hands to and fro like a hula dancer describing the sea.

Eddie watches us.

'It might work, I suppose ...' he says a little reluctantly. 'I still get to be a surfer dude, though, don't I?'

'Of course,' I tell him keenly. 'You're the main man, Eddie. You will be ...' I try to think fast. 'The Jason Donovan to our Kylie Min ... No, wait, our Kylie Mer ... *maid*.' I thank my brain for coming up with this analogy so fast. One which I know Eddie will appreciate.

Eddie nods, clearly enjoying this thought. 'All right, let's try it with the music.' He goes back to the cassette player to press play.

I breathe a sigh of relief. 'Thanks, guys,' I say quietly. 'You've saved me.'

'I think we've all saved ourselves from a lot of embarrass-ment,' Claire whispers. 'But most importantly we managed to do it and not let Eddie down.'

'We'll be the best mermaids St Felix has ever seen!' I say as the intro of the song begins to float once more over the sand.

'And the best-looking too!' Mandy says, as always full of the confidence that both Claire and I lack in our own appearance. 'The boys won't know what hit them!'

*

13

A few days later, our rehearsals are going much more successfully.

While Eddie struts his stuff around the front of whatever our makeshift stage is that day, Claire, Mandy and I sit at the back on whatever we can find to be our rock. We work out our own choreography to fit in with Eddie's, and although I'm still not overly happy about being on the stage dressed as a mermaid, I'm a lot happier now I don't have to dance dressed as one.

Suzy, we find out, in exchange for not performing with us, has offered to help Eddie make our costumes. Which I don't actually mind, because I hate using a sewing machine even more than choreographed dancing.

It's a weekend in St Felix, and it's even busier than usual as I take my lunch break from the florist I work in every Saturday, and sometimes after school.

The shop, appropriately named the Daisy Chain, is run by a lovely lady called Rose, and I enjoy working there with her. Rose makes up all the bouquets; I just help behind the counter selling flowers and taking orders, but it's fun, and it gives me a bit of extra money.

I treat myself to a pasty from Mr Bumbles, the baker's a few doors down, and head off to look for somewhere quiet and preferably shady to sit and eat. But everywhere is heaving with people – they are either milling around along Harbour Street, where the bakery and flower shop are, or sitting in the sunshine along the harbour front watching the boats and doing what I'm trying to do – sit and eat my lunch.

But the benefit of being a local is you know all the quiet, and often hidden, places to sit. I head up and across the town, through the streets of old fishermen's cottages to a grassy hill that overlooks one of the many beaches St Felix has to offer. But instead of trying to find a free wooden bench, I head up over the grass to a set of steep steps, cut into the rocky headland, that lead down to the beach.

Halfway down the steps, I climb back onto the surrounding grass and make my way carefully across the tufts towards a natural little shelf worn into the rocks, which I'm overjoyed to find is empty. It's slightly hidden from view and gives me not only a shady place to eat my lunch, but also an uninterrupted view of the sea. I make myself comfortable on a large flat rock that's been worn smooth over the years – probably *decades* – by the many people sitting right where I am now, looking out to sea, and I sigh happily.

Peace at last.

I've always liked my own company. Unlike a lot of people my age who seem to crave being in a crowd or a gang, I'm not afraid to be alone – in fact, I really enjoy it. It gives me a chance to think, work things out in my head, and simply *breathe*.

Don't get me wrong, I love my friends, but none of us ever set out to become a part of the tight-knit group we are now. We were all drawn to each other randomly, simply because none of us are what is considered a 'normal' teenager.

There's Eddie – the only male of the group – who is what my mother politely calls 'a little eccentric', or 'full of life', or 'a flamboyant young man', depending on her mood. What she doesn't ever call him is what he actually is: gay.

Eddie was teased a lot at school when he first came here to St Felix. He got called names because he was different from the other boys and didn't want to do the kind of things they did. Where most of the boys want to kick a ball around after school or hang out in gangs trying to look cool, Eddie is most likely to be found hiring an old musical from the video-rental shop or practising his latest dance moves. Boys occasionally try to bully him because they think he won't attempt to defend himself, but they're always in for a shock. Eddie's older brother, James, is a highly skilled boxer, who's been tipped to go to the Olympics, and, before he left St Felix to go and train in Ireland, he taught Eddie how to defend himself. I witnessed many a boy, much bigger than Eddie, scuttle away with a bloody nose or arrive in school the next day with a black eye after trying to pick on him. And because Eddie is Eddie, none of them want to admit that he got the better of them.

Then there's Mandy, the oldest of our group by a few months. Mandy has a reputation for being *easy*. This makes me really cross, because she isn't at all. But Mandy never seems that bothered by it. She's confident and brash, and she doesn't care who knows it. Mandy likes attention from boys, and she wears clothes and make-up that only encourages their attention. But underneath all her short skirts, jewellery, eyeliner and mascara, Mandy has a heart of gold, she's deeply loyal and there's nothing she won't do for her friends.

Suzy is probably the smartest and most virtuous of all of us. She's incredibly ethical and all about saving the planet. If there's a campaign, you can be sure Suzy is a part of it. She was all over Band Aid a few years ago, raising money to help those poor starving children in Ethiopia, and she's a huge campaigner for both animal rights and the environment. Heaven help you if Suzy sees you miss the bin when you throw a can or a ball of paper towards it. You will be picking up that litter moments later – have no doubt about that.

Suzy isn't a misfit as such, she's just a little different and painfully shy. When most girls our age are worrying about their hair

16

or the colour of their nail polish, Suzy is worrying about something called global warming, and she's recently been banging on about some sort of hole in the ozone layer. I'm not really sure what that is, but Suzy seems quite concerned about it.

Oh, and her other issue – well, it seems to be an issue for some, not us – is she comes from a mixed-race family. Her mum is white and her dad is black. Probably quite common if you live in a big city, but down here on the tip of Cornwall it's fairly unusual, making Suzy different, and, at our age, different is too often seen as bad.

Claire I've known since we were at primary school and, before that, playgroup together. According to our parents, both of us were quiet toddlers, so I guess we must have bonded over our love of keeping within the lines when colouring with our crayons or something like that. Claire isn't really different, she's just quiet, and not everyone gets quiet people, do they?

And then there's me – Frankie. I like my own company, but I'm not quiet like Claire – I speak up if I need to. I don't like wearing dresses or skirts or anything girly, and I get called a tomboy by those same people that call Eddie, Mandy and Suzy names I choose not to repeat. I'm happiest when I have a paintbrush or a pencil in one hand and a sketchbook in the other. I don't think I'm really all that different – I'm just me.

But our differences are what brought us together, and, although we rarely tell each other, I know we are all secretly very glad they did.

My pasty, as it always is when it's bought from Mr Bumbles', is delicious. I brush the crumbs from my lap, hoping one of the little birds that flit around St Felix looking for scraps manages to get to them when I've left, before the huge seagulls that rule the roost around the harbour find them.

I open a can of Diet Pepsi and watch the waves rhythmically rolling onto the sand of Morvoren Cove below while I drink. Little kids try to jump over the white spray, squealing with delight when they don't succeed and the cold seawater splashes up their little legs.

I can already see several pink-looking bodies, where sun worshippers haven't used a strong enough sun cream, and a few dogs run about the beach happily chasing balls and frisbees.

I look past them further out to sea and note the differing hues today – turquoises and mint-greens vie for prominence over the usual navy blues and purples. All encouraged by the strong sunshine cascading down onto the waves.

Just as I'm feeling almost hypnotised by the waves, something catches the corner of my eye, making me jump – a splash of salt spray in the water, breaking up the perfect rhythm.

What was that – a fish jumping in the waves?

No, it was too big to be a fish's tail – must have been a dolphin. We often get schools of dolphins around the St Felix coastline.

It happens again, and for a couple of seconds I see the flick of a large fishlike tail in amongst the waves, and then nothing. The waves go back to their usual rhythmical rolling pattern.

Even though I only saw it for a brief second or two, I knew it wasn't a dolphin's tail, or even the moon-shaped tail of one of the basking sharks that occasionally make their way closer to the shore at this time of year. No, this definitely looked like a fish's tail, but it would have had to have been an incredibly large fish to have a tail that size. The mackerel that are so profitable for the local fishermen's nets are never as big as that.

I check my watch and realise that it's already time I headed back to the shop. So, forgetting all about the fish's tail for now, I pick up my rubbish and climb back along the rocks to the steps and then up the hill and across town back to the florist.

'Did you have a nice lunch, dear?' Rose asks as I return.

'Yes, thank you. I managed to find a shady spot to eat overlooking Morvoren Cove.'

'How lovely. Will you be all right if I just pop out for a bit and get myself something to eat? It's been pretty quiet in the last hour.'

'Of course, Rose. I'll be fine.'

Rose smiles. 'I know you will. You've been such a blessing to my little shop since you came to work here, Frankie, I can't thank you enough for all you do.'

'Oh,' I say, completely thrown by her kind words. 'It's nothing. You know I love working here.'

'If my granddaughter, Poppy, turns out anything like you when she's older, I'll be a very proud grandmother indeed.'

'Thank you, that's very kind of you to say. How are your grandchildren – it's Poppy and . . . William, isn't it?'

Rose nods. 'They're very well. They're coming to stay in a few weeks with their mother. I'm sure I'll be exhausted having a four-year-old and a six-year-old running rings around me, but I can't wait to see them again and give them a big cuddle.'

'If you need me to cover any more shifts, I'm sure I can.'

'Won't you have school, though?'

'School holidays begin in a couple of weeks! I'll be as free as a bird all summer!'

'Ah. Yes.' Rose nods. 'What a wonderful situation to be in. When is the dance you were telling me about?'

'Next Saturday.'

'Do you have your dress yet?'

I shrug. 'I'm not really a dress person, so I'm finding it a bit difficult to be honest.'

Rose nods knowingly. 'Just between the two of us, I was a bit of a tomboy too when I was younger. However, I did bloom – no pun intended!' she says, looking at the pots of flowers surrounding us. 'When I got to about eighteen or twenty.' She looks me up and down. 'You know you're about the size I was back then. I'll get some of my old dresses out for you. Pop round to the cottage one night and you can have a look. No pressure!' She holds up her hand. 'I know you're probably thinking what's an old bird like me going to have for a youngster like you, but you never know. I won't be offended if you don't like anything.'

'Sure,' I reply to be polite. I simply can't turn up at the dance in one of Rose's old cast-offs though, I'd be the laughing stock of the school. But I haven't found anything myself so far that I either like or that suits me, so I guess it might be worth a try.

'Right, I'll be off to get that lunch, then,' Rose says. 'See you in a jiffy.'

I wait for her to leave the shop, then I look around for something to do. There's always something, whether it's refilling the big silver buckets that Rose keeps all her flowers in, or sweeping the floors of stray leaves and greenery. I know that if someone came in wanting something more complicated than a few stems of flowers, like a bouquet or a wreath for instance, then all I have to do is take their details and either ask them to come back when Rose is here or tell them she will call them. As I look around, I notice Rose has been making up a bouquet for someone in the back of the shop, so I grab a broom and begin to sweep the floor.

The bell over the shop door rings to signal that someone is entering, so I leave the back room and return to the main shop.

'Hello,' I say, then stop when I see who it is.

'Oh, hi.' Rob looks equally as surprised to see me as I am to see him. 'I didn't know you worked here?'

'Yes, every Saturday and sometimes after school, too.'

Rob nods and looks awkwardly at some of the displays.

'Was there something in particular you were looking for?' I ask, still in automatic shop assistant mode.

'Yeah, it's my mum's birthday tomorrow and I thought I'd get her some flowers.' He fumbles in his pocket and pulls out a five-pound note. 'This is all I have right now, though. Can I get much with it?'

'Yes, I'm sure we can find you something,' I say, looking around for inspiration, and I begin to pick out a few stems from the silver buckets. Flowers that I knew if they were still here at the end of the day, Rose would offer to me to take home for my own mother. Rose always begins a new week on Monday morning with fresh flowers. Anything not sold by four-thirty on a Saturday afternoon is always given away.

'How long have you worked here?' Rob asks to make conversation while I gather various buds and arrange them in my hand into a posy of sorts.

'A few months now. I really enjoy it.'

'That's good. I wish I could get a part-time job.'

'Why can't you?'

'My parents won't let me. They say it would interfere with my education too much.'

'Oh.' I'm not really sure what to say to this; my parents were really pleased for me when I got a job and started earning some money for myself.

'Couldn't you help out round the pub – you know, clearing tables and stuff?' Rob's parents bought the Merry Mermaid

21

pub on St Felix harbour when it went up for sale – that's why they moved here in the middle of the school year. I only know this because Mandy's mum has a cleaning job there and is always full of gossip about the pub and the people who go there, which Mandy delights in passing on to us if it involves anyone we know from school or their parents.

'I'd like to, but because they bought the pub at this "critical time in my education" – that's what my mum says, anyway – and I had to move school and stuff, they want me to concentrate on that for now, until I've done my GCSEs, anyway.'

'That's fair enough, I suppose. What about these?' I ask, showing Rob the bouquet in my hand. 'I'll tie it up with some ribbon. Rose – that's the lady who owns the shop – she always likes to use white ribbon. Is that OK?'

'That's great. Are you sure I can get all this for five pounds?'

'Yes, some of these flowers will only go to waste if we don't sell them before we close, so you're doing us a favour really.' As expertly as I can, I wrap some of Rose's special white ribbon around my bundle of flowers, immediately transforming them into a small posy. 'Here.' I pass them to him, at the same time taking the five-pound note in his outstretched hand. 'I hope your mum likes them.'

'I'm sure she'll love them – thank you. I don't really know much about flowers, but they look pretty.'

'You've got roses in there.' I point to them. 'And these are alstroemeria. Those little white ones are gypsophila, and the big ones are gerberas.'

Rob nods. 'Mum will be impressed if I know the names.'

I ring the five pounds up in the till and turn back towards him again. 'Well . . . ' I say, not knowing what to say or do next.

He looks just as awkward as I feel. 'Well . . .'.

'How's the pub doing?' I ask at the same time as Rob asks, 'How's the mermaid rehearsals going?'

'How do you know about that?' I stare at him. 'I didn't think it was common knowledge we were going to be mermaids.'

Rob flushes in embarrassment. 'I've seen you,' he admits. 'Down on the beach, or on the school field practising. You look good. I mean you all look good – you know? Well rehearsed.' His cheeks redden even more.

I grin. 'I'll take well rehearsed as a compliment.'

'Good. Your act looks much more interesting than the one I'm in.'

'You sounded good the other day when you were rehearsing.'

'Thanks, but even though we can play all the tunes, I think it's a bit dull. At least you're singing and dancing. It will be much more entertaining.'

'Entertaining might be a bit generous.' I grin. 'But I appreciate the encouragement.'

Rob nods. 'I better be going, I suppose. Put these in some water for tomorrow.'

'Yes.' I wish I could think of something else to say to keep him here a little longer. But what?

'Why did you agree to be in Jenny's group?' I ask suddenly as Rob is about to turn towards the door.

'What do you mean?' He looks confused.

'I ... I mean ...' *What do I mean? Come on, Frankie, think!* 'Guitar is quite cool, isn't it?' The words barely have time to form in my brain before they're tumbling out of my mouth. 'And Jenny's group ... well, they're not cool, are they? They're more of a formal orchestra – although they're very good!' I add, in case he's offended. 'But I always see a guitar as being more at home in a group ... you know, like a rock band?'

To my enormous relief, Rob smiles.

'Now it's my turn to thank *you* for the compliment. I wish I was cool enough to be in a rock band. I've not had many offers though.'

'I'm sure you're cool enough,' I say before I've thought it through. 'Perhaps St Felix isn't the best place to get offers though – Bon Jovi doesn't often pop into the Merry Mermaid for a pint, does he?'

To my delight, Rob laughs.

'No, sadly he doesn't. Neither does Freddie Mercury.'

'I've heard Guns N' Roses sometimes take a cottage here over the summer, though ... '

'Yeah, right – I wish!' Rob grins. 'You like rock music?'

'Yeah, I do. My parents soon bought me headphones when I started playing AC/DC full blast in my bedroom.'

'Nice. Who else?'

To my surprise, Rob and I begin to have a very detailed conversation about rock music, who we like, and who we don't, and it feels like the most natural thing in the world. I almost forget who I'm talking to and where I am. So that when the bell rings again over the shop door and Rose returns with her lunch, I almost jump out of my skin.

'Don't mind me,' she says as we both stare at her like she's caught us up to no good. 'I'll just take my lunch out the back.' She raises her eyebrows good-naturedly at me as she passes.

'I ... I'd better go,' Rob says, looking at his flowers. 'Water ... you know.'

'Yeah, that's a good idea. I ... I hope your mum likes them.'

'I know she will. Thanks again, Frankie.'

'You're very welcome.'

'See ya around.'

I nod.

As he leaves the shop, my legs actually buckle underneath me as my knees give way, something I thought only happened in romantic novels, and I have to hold on to the shop counter to stay upright.

'Nice-looking young man!' Rose's voice sounds from the back room, clearly having heard the door open and close.

'Yes,' I can only murmur as I begin to regain the feeling in my legs again. 'He is.'

Rose pops her head back into the shop.

'Ah,' she says, smiling at me. 'Young love, the most powerful and yet often the most painful love of all.'

Three

'Louder!' Eddie calls across the sand as we go over the song once again in our now favoured rehearsal spot hidden in between the rocks in Morvoren Cove. 'They won't hear you singing otherwise.'

'I'm sure there's going to be a microphone, Eddie,' I say as we sway together on the rock. 'The audience will hear *you*, and that's the most important thing.'

'Yeah,' Mandy adds, grinning. 'We're just here to look pretty!'

'Cut!' Eddie shouts dramatically, waving his arms above his head. 'Enough! You've ruined it now. Go again, please.'

We sigh and roll our eyes at each other. 'Now, you've done it,' Claire says, looking worried. 'Eddie looks awfully cross.'

'I don't care.' Mandy hops down off the rock. 'I've had enough. I need a break.' She begins to rummage about in her bag.

Suzy, who's been watching us rehearse, gets up from where she's been sitting cross-legged on the sand and walks over to us.

'I thought you were all really good,' she says with encouragement. 'The outfits I've made for you are going to look great.'

'Yes, about the costumes,' I begin, but I notice that Mandy, instead of pulling some sweets or a drink from her bag as I expected her to, has actually pulled out a packet of cigarettes, and, cool as a cucumber, she proceeds to light one up while Claire, Suzy and I just stare at her open-mouthed.

'What?' she asks nonchalantly. 'Stop gawping at me like three goldfish gasping for air.'

'Why are you smoking?' I demand.

Mandy shrugs. 'Just felt like trying it.'

'But where did you get them?' Claire asks, eyes wide. 'You're not old enough to buy cigarettes.'

'The old fella in the corner shop sold them to me,' Mandy says, pretending, I notice, to take a drag, but not actually in-haling. 'He doesn't care who he sells to as long as he gets his money.'

Eddie doesn't say anything as he arrives next to us. He simply pulls the cigarette from Mandy's fingers, throws it down on the beach and kicks some sand over it, so the cigarette rap-idly extinguishes itself.

'Hey!' Mandy says. 'I paid good money for that.'

'I don't care if you paid in blood,' Eddie says, glaring at her. 'Smoking will ruin your lungs and therefore your voice.'

'You can't just extinguish cigarettes on the beach.' Suzy kneels down in the sand, attempting to uncover the cigarette with her hands. 'Apart from being terribly bad manners, it's terrible for the environment and it's littering too!'

Mandy glares at Eddie and pulls the packet of cigarettes from her bag again.

'Don't!' Eddie warns.

'Or you'll what?' Mandy says defiantly. 'I'm sick of you boss-ing us around, Eddie, and telling us we're no good. I think I can speak for all of us mermaids when I say none of us wants to be here doing this on a Sunday evening. We're doing it as a favour to you. You'd do well to remember that!'

Eddie continues to stare at Mandy for a moment, then very slowly he turns to each of us. 'Is that true?' he asks. 'You don't want to do the talent show with me?' He waits for our reaction but when we don't speak, he asks, 'Frankie, is that how you feel?'

'Er ... you know performing isn't my favourite thing in the world,' I answer diplomatically. 'But I know you love it.'

'Yes,' Claire joins in. 'We wanted to support you, Eddie. You're our friend.'

Eddie turns to Suzy. 'Don't look at me,' she says. 'I was honest, I told you I didn't want to do it. That's why I offered to make the costumes.'

Eddie's chin drops to his chest, and I glare at Mandy.

'What?' she mouths silently, shrugging. But she has the good grace to push her packet of cigarettes back into her bag.

I'm about to step in and try to build bridges when I hear something.

'What's that?' I ask, tilting my head to one side to hear it better.

'Sounds like someone playing a guitar,' Suzy says, looking around.

We all turn, trying to spot the invisible guitarist playing the Beach Boys song we are all far too familiar with by now.

'There!' Suzy points along the beach. We look in the direction she's gesturing and see a lone guitarist appearing from behind some rocks. As they walk towards us, they are lit from behind by the setting sun, so we can only really make out their silhouette.

'Isn't that Robert Matthews?' Claire squints into the evening sunshine.

'Yes, I think it is,' Suzy replies, holding her hand above her eyes. 'I didn't know he played the guitar.'

'He can play my strings any day,' Mandy says, watching the silhouette getting nearer.

Both Eddie and I are silent as we watch the familiar figure of Rob getting closer.

'Sorry if I'm interrupting,' Rob says as he stops playing, his guitar hung by a strap around his neck. 'I heard the song and felt like joining in. Do you mind?'

'No, not at all.' Mandy immediately goes over to him and loops her arm through his. 'By all means, come and join us.'

Rob glances at me as Mandy leads him over to the rock we were sitting on. 'Also, I think I should mention you've got some spies in your camp,' he says, glancing upwards before he sits down.

'What do you mean spies?' I ask, following his gaze.

'Up there.' Rob points. 'Tucked up on the hill.'

Everyone now follows Rob's hand and we see a group of girls younger than us giggling up on the hill that looks over the bay.

'You little . . .' Mandy begins, her brow furrowing with rage. 'That's my bloody sister and her silly mates.'

She storms over to the edge of the sand. 'Bugger off, you lot!' she shouts, gesturing at them. 'Wait till I get home, Hetty!'

'Wait till I tell Mum what you've been up to,' Hetty calls back, and she pretends to smoke an invisible cigarette. Then Hetty and her giggling friends scuttle off up the hill and disappear down the path on the other side.

'Bloody Hetty!' Mandy fumes as she returns to us. 'She's such a little shit.'

'Aren't you worried what your mum will say if she tells her?' I ask.

'Nah, she won't say anything,' Mandy says. 'I've got stuff on her that she won't risk me telling Mum about if she dobs me in first. Thanks for letting us know though, Rob. I hadn't spotted her. Eddie's been running us ragged rehearsing down here.'

Eddie opens his mouth to protest but Mandy continues. 'Now.' She sits down next to Rob on the rock before anyone else can. 'I'm sure we'd all love to hear you play some more. Wouldn't we?' She looks up at us for encouragement.

'Only if you want to, Robert,' Claire says. 'We don't want to force you or anything.' She raises her eyebrows at Mandy.

'What about our rehearsal?' Eddie asks. 'We haven't finished yet.'

Mandy glares at him.

'Perhaps Robert can play for us while you rehearse?' Suzy suggests diplomatically before it all kicks off again. 'He clearly knows the song.'

'Would you like to?' Eddie asks casually.

'On two conditions,' Rob says, looking at us all. 'You call me Rob and not Robert.'

'Ooh, yes,' Mandy says. 'That suits you much better.'

'What's the other?' Eddie asks a little suspiciously.

'You all stop arguing. I've seen you guys rehearsing a few times; you're really good. Be a shame to spoil all your hard work by falling out.'

Mandy and Eddie look sheepishly at each other.

'Soz, Ed,' Mandy says first. 'I know this show is important to you.'

Eddie nods. 'I'm sorry too. I'm being harsh on you all, I know, but I just want this to be perfect.'

They give each other a hug.

'Right, then,' Rob says, smiling at me. 'Shall we give this a go?'

After we've rehearsed our routine a few more times with Rob playing his guitar as accompaniment instead of the original track, we decide to call it a night.

For some reason, once Rob became involved, everyone tried that little bit harder and behaved that little bit better.

He could certainly play the guitar, and had no trouble playing 'Surfin' USA' over and over again.

'Thanks, guys,' he says as he zips his guitar back into its case. 'I really enjoyed that tonight. It was a lot of fun.'

'You know, Eddie,' Suzy says, giving me a look that suggests she might need some backup in a moment. 'If he was open to it, might it be a good idea to ask Rob to continue to play with us – even make him a part of the act ...'

'Yes!' Claire says eagerly. 'You played wonderfully tonight, Rob. Come and be a mermaid with us!'

Rob had looked initially pleased at Suzy's suggestion, but now looks a little worried.

'You don't have to do either if you don't want to,' I say hurriedly. 'I mean, you might like to play, but you don't have to dress as a mermaid or anything. That's just what we backing singers are going to be dressed as.'

'I don't know, though.' Mandy looks Rob up and down. 'I'm sure he could rock a fishtail ...'

'You could be a merman!' Claire says joyfully. 'Then you would match us. Could you do a merman's outfit, Suzy?'

'Whoa!' Eddie says, holding his hand up. 'Everyone is getting a little carried away here.'

We all look at Eddie. Was he going to reject our idea?

'No one has asked Rob yet,' he says, turning to him. 'Firstly, Rob, thank you for playing for us tonight. Your presence,' he looks across at us knowingly, 'has certainly focused the girls on their performance.'

'And it has made *no* difference to you, I suppose?' Mandy asks, smirking at Eddie.

Eddie bats his eyelashes coyly back at Mandy. '*Anyway . . .*' he continues. 'If you're open to the idea, Rob, I would formally like to offer you the chance to come on board with us – no pun intended – and become an honorary mermaid. The costume, I should make clear, will not be necessary should you choose to accept.'

Rob looks around at us all, and his gaze rests on me.

'I would love to,' he says sadly. 'Really, I would. But, as Frankie knows, I'm already part of an act. I'm playing in Jenny Meadows's orchestra next Saturday.'

There are groans and whines of disappointment.

'Ah, don't be minding about Jenny Meadows,' Mandy says airily. 'She's a stuck-up cow, anyway.'

'Mandy,' Claire says admonishingly. 'That's not fair. Jenny can't help the way she is.'

'If she pulled that clarinet out from where it's wedged up her arse, she might possibly be bearable, I suppose,' Mandy says, making Rob laugh.

'Can I do both?' Rob asks. 'I wouldn't want to let anyone down.'

We all look at each other. 'Is there a rule for that?' Suzy asks. 'Can you perform in two acts?'

'Dunno,' Eddie says. 'Perhaps no one has tried before?'

'We could ask?' Claire suggests. 'It wouldn't do any harm.'

'I'll check tomorrow with Miss Kelly,' Eddie says. 'She's in charge of the show. But if she says it's all right ... Then, Rob, may I be the first to welcome you into our gang. And may I also wish you the very best of luck too – you'll need it with this lot!'

'Are you all right?' Robs asks as we walk up the hill that leads up and out of St Felix.

We all left the little cove and walked up through the town together like we always do. As each of our houses or streets came along, one of the gang would depart, leaving the rest of us to continue on our way. I always hated being the last one left, as my house was a little bit further from the centre of the town than the others, but I quickly realised that tonight I wouldn't be alone as I walked the extra few minutes to my house, as Rob would be with me.

'Don't you live above the pub?' Mandy asked Rob as we passed the Merry Mermaid on the harbour front, still full of holiday drinkers spilling out onto the wooden benches in front of the pub as they enjoyed the last few hours of the warm Sunday evening.

'No, there's not enough room for all of us. There's five of us altogether, so my parents are renting a house on the new estate as you head out of town. You couldn't get more different from a new build to a pub that's stood on the harbour for hundreds of years.'

Claire, who was walking with me slightly behind the others at the back of the group, nudged me excitedly.

'What?' I asked.

'You'll be the last one walking with Rob,' she whispered, her eyes bright.

33

'So?'

'I think he likes you.'

'Don't be silly!' I hissed, slowing her up a little so the others didn't hear us. 'What ... what makes you say that?'

'Suzy said that, while we were rehearsing, he kept looking at you.'

'He was probably looking at how bad my singing and dancing was.'

'Not the way Suzy said it, he wasn't.'

'What are you two gossiping about at the back there?' Eddie turned back towards us.

'Nothing!' I quickly replied. 'Hurry up, Claire, we're dropping behind.'

We caught up with the others and nothing more was said. But as we walked along Harbour Street and up through the town, and our party of six diminished one by one, I couldn't help thinking about my conversation with Claire.

Now I realise I've been thinking a little too much, because now we've said goodnight to Claire, and it's just me and Rob, I've barely spoken in the last few minutes.

'Yes, yes, I'm fine,' I reply to his question.

'Good, you've just been a bit quiet since we left the beach, that's all.'

'Not much to say. I'm not one to chat away about nothing.'

Rob smiles. 'That's good to hear. Most of the girls I know chit-chat and gossip all day. My sisters are terrible for it.'

'Nope, not me.' I shrug, suddenly worrying I might sound a little rude with my abrupt answers.

'I wondered if the reason you were quiet was because the others had asked me to be part of your act?' Rob looks genuinely worried, which surprises me.

'No! No of course not,' I assure him. 'I'm pleased you're going to be one of the mermaids – sorry, we're not really called that. But until we – or Eddie – think of a better stage name, we've kind of called ourselves that temporarily.'

'Eddie and the Mermaids!' Rob says, waving his hand in front of our faces as though he's reading our name up in lights. 'Doesn't really have much of a ring to it, does it?'

'No, that's why we have to think of something better.'

'I was genuinely pleased when Suzy asked me, you know?'

'Were you?'

'Yeah, I've not really found any good friends since I came here to St Felix, and you guys always look like you're having a great time together. I have to admit I've been quite jealous.'

I stare at him and almost stop walking.

'What?' he asks.

'But I've always thought how well you fitted into the school since you came here – how easy it seemed for you.'

'No way.' Rob shakes his head. 'I may have made it seem easy, but I can assure you it hasn't been. Because of what Mum and Dad do, I've changed schools a couple of times before, and it's never easy being the new kid. Maybe I've just got better at it.'

'So the boys you hang around with – they're not really your friends?'

'Mates, maybe, but nothing like you and your friends seem to have. Without sounding weird, I've seen you all together loads of times. You're a really close little gang, aren't you?'

'Yes, I guess we are. But we never set out to be a gang – we all just kind of ended up together cos we're all a bit different.'

'How do you mean?'

'We just are.' I shrug. 'I've always called us a gang of

35

misfits – that's why we all get on so well. We all know how it feels to be a bit different.'

'The Misfit Mermaids.' Rob smiles.

'What?'

'The name for your group. You should call yourselves the Misfit Mermaids.'

I think about this for a moment. 'Yeah, the Misfit Mermaids, I like it. It works.'

'As long as Eddie is happy to be called a mermaid, of course.'

'Are you kidding? Eddie will love it! Thank you, Rob, it's a great idea. Er . . . this is me.' I awkwardly point down the road we've arrived at the junction of as we've made our way up the hill out of town.

'Oh, right. Our house is a few streets further on. Do you want me to walk you to your door?'

I desperately want to say, 'Yes, please!' but I'm worried it will make me seem far too needy. 'No. I mean . . . thank you, but I'll be fine from here.'

Rob nods and, feeling incredibly awkward once more, we stand in silence for what is really only a few seconds but feels like minutes.

'Well . . . goodnight,' I say eventually.

'Yeah, goodnight.'

I turn to walk away.

'Frankie?' Rob asks suddenly.

'Yes?' I turn back.

'Can I ask you one more thing?'

'Sure.' I can feel myself trembling inside. Is Claire right? Is Rob going to ask me out? What if he asks if he can kiss me? My mind runs rapidly over what I've eaten today. Will my breath be rank?

36

I suddenly realise Rob is already talking.

'What I mean is, if I'm allowed to play guitar with you for the show. Would it be all right if I hung out with you too? I mean, like, all of you,' he hurriedly adds.

And it's then, just when I want to say something cool and interesting, that I utter one of the silliest sentences ever to come from my lips.

'Erm, that depends ... Are you misfit enough to be a mermaid, Rob?'

Four

'Tell us what you said again,' Mandy asks, grinning across the grass at me while we eat lunch on the school field the next day.

'No, you heard me the first time,' I reply firmly. 'It's bad enough I actually said that, let alone having to keep repeating it!'

'I know, but I still can't actually believe you asked Rob Matthews if he was mermaid enough to be a misfit.'

'*Misfit* enough to be a *mermaid*,' Eddie corrects her, finishing off his bag of Wotsits.

'I know what it was.' Mandy's grin widens. 'I was just seeing if it sounded any better the other way around. And you know what ... it didn't!'

'Oh, God!' I bury my face in my hands. 'I'm such an idiot.'

'I'm sure you're worrying over nothing, Frankie,' Claire says gently, putting her hand on my shoulder. 'He probably thought nothing of it.'

'Yeah.' Suzy nods. 'I mean, what did he say after you said that?'

'Not a lot.' I say, lifting my head from my hands. 'He sort

38

of nodded and said something about he'd try, and then he left and carried on to his house.'

'See,' Claire says, trying to be helpful. 'He said he'd try; that's good, isn't it?'

'*Try* to stay away from the Looney Tune more like . . . *What*?' Mandy asks when we all glare at her. 'I'm just being realistic.'

'I've blown it, haven't I?' I say, sighing deeply. 'Why I should have expected anything more of myself, I don't know. But it all happened so fast – first it was the scenery and the nice waves thing, and then the flower shop and the rock music – and suddenly he was there walking me home! I wasn't ready. I didn't have time to prepare for that sort of pressure.'

'Wait just a minute!' Eddie sits down next to me. 'What are you talking about? Are you saying there's more to this than him stumbling upon us on the beach rehearsing, then offering to play for the group?'

'Yeah, what do you mean "the nice waves thing" and "the flower shop" and what was the other stuff?' Mandy asks.

'Rock music, I think,' Suzy answers.

I glance at Claire. She was the only one I confided in about the other stuff, because I knew she would keep quiet about it.

'You might as well tell us everything,' Claire says diplomatically so as not to drop me in it with the others. 'You've started now.'

I nod and tell them everything that's happened so far with Rob, from never speaking to him one minute, to everything else. Which, now I'm saying it, really doesn't sound all that much.

'So?' I ask them when I've finished. 'What do you think?'

'It certainly sounds like he's been trying to be places you might be, doesn't it?' Suzy looks at the others. 'I mean, he may have genuinely wanted to buy flowers for his mum's birthday, but he could have got some at the Co-op up on the hill, couldn't he, and they'd have been much cheaper than from a florist?'

'I think so too.' Claire nods enthusiastically. 'And what are the chances he'd be on the beach at the same time as us last night?'

'Although,' Suzy says, 'that is a bit creepy if he's been watching you, Frankie, and following you around … What do you think, Eddie?'

'Sadly, I think this means he's straight,' Eddie says, sighing. 'I had hoped not. But the others are right, Frankie. It's a bit too much to just be a coincidence.'

'Mandy?' I ask when she doesn't join in. 'You're awfully quiet. You always have an opinion on everything.'

'Are you sure you want to know?' Mandy looks serious.

'Yes, just tell me. I can take it …'

Mandy grins. 'Oh, he fancies you all right.'

'What?'

'He fancies you – clearly. The signs are all there.'

'B-but why would he do that?' I look down at my loose T-shirt, and my baggy, pale-blue denim jeans held up with a wide leather belt. 'There are so many other girls in the school that wear skirts and make-up and do their nails and stuff … Like you, Mandy. You try really hard to look good all the time. Why would he like me? I'm just a tomboy.'

Mandy shrugs. 'I dunno … It's a mystery to me … No, you daft thing, I'm kidding. *You*, Frankie, are gorgeous! We can all see it. But you for some reason can't.'

'Maybe that's the attraction,' Eddie says. 'He likes her *because* she doesn't know how pretty she is.'

'Yes, that's probably right,' Suzy says. 'You're giving off the right pheromones, Frankie.'

'The what-a-mones?' Eddie asks.

'Pheromones are substances that are secreted by a person, then picked up by a second individual of the same species,' Suzy replies. 'It's a well-known fact in the animal kingdom, it's how they attract a mate. But how it works within humans is not quite so well documented.'

This is nothing unusual – we are all pretty used to Suzy dropping scientific facts and figures into conversation with us.

'Well,' Mandy says. 'Whatever you're doing, either consciously or unconsciously—'

'*Sub*consciously,' Suzy says.

'What?' Mandy asks.

'It's *sub*consciously. You said *un*consciously.'

'OK, *sub*consciously. Whatever you're doing, Frankie, it seems to be working.'

'You don't think I've messed everything up then with what I said?' I ask anxiously.

'Dunno.' Mandy glances over my shoulder. 'But we're about to find out . . . '

I turn around to see what she's looking at, and to my horror see Rob walking across the grass towards us.

'Act casual!' Mandy instructs.

'What do you mean, casual?' I ask as the others all pretend to be talking about something or hurriedly eating their lunch again.

'Hey, Rob,' Eddie calls as Rob approaches. 'How's things?'

'Good. Yourself?'

'Yeah, great. Just chilling and having lunch, you know?'

Rob nods, but looks a little confused.

'So, I just wanted to let you know I've spoken to Miss Kelly and she says it's never been done before, but she can see no reason why I can't compete with two different acts on Saturday. So if you'll still have me, I'd really like to play guitar for you all.'

'That's amazing news!' Eddie claps his hands in excitement. 'We can have matching outfits! Can we have matching outfits, Suzy?'

'I'll see what I can do,' Suzy says calmly. 'The mermaid tails are taking me longer than I thought they would.'

Rob looks worried. 'I don't want to put you out or anything. I'm sure I can find something of my own to wear.'

'Nonsense!' Eddie says. 'You are now officially a Misfit Mermaid, Rob! Welcome to the gang. Ooh, it's going to be completely amazing on Saturday night – I can feel it!'

'You told them, then?' Rob asks, looking across at me for the first time. 'About the name for the group?'

'And the rest,' I hear Mandy mutter behind me.

'Yes,' I reply quickly, hoping Rob didn't hear her. 'And we all think it's a great idea – don't we?'

Suzy nods. 'Yep – fab idea.'

'I love it!' Claire says enthusiastically.

'The Misfit Mermaids it is, then.' Rob grins. 'And, yes, Frankie, I am.'

'Sorry?' I ask, not getting his reference.

'You asked me last night was I enough of a misfit to be one of the mermaids? Or something like that?' He smiles. 'And I'm pleased to tell you that, yes, I definitely am.'

Rob sits with us for the remainder of our lunch break, then, as the bell sounds across the field to tell us it's time to head back to our various classrooms, we gather up our things and begin to make our way back to the school building.

'Are you rehearsing later?' Robs asks as we both find ourselves hanging at the back of the group; the others have allowed us to drop back a little, and I can only imagine the nudges and whispers up ahead as we all meander across the grass in two distinct little packs.

'No, not tonight. Eddie is letting us have a night off for once.'

'Ah, right ...' Rob hesitates. 'It's just I was wondering if you'd like to hang out with me for a bit?'

'Yes ... that would be fun.' I try to reply as casually as I can. But my insides are doing somersaults again. 'Oh, no, wait,' I say as I remember something. 'I have to go somewhere after school.'

'Oh ... oh, no bother, then.' Rob doesn't look at me.

'I could make later though,' I say hurriedly, blowing my cool. 'Say after dinner, about seven?'

Rob smiles. 'Great! Where shall we meet?'

'Er ... what about at the end of the harbour?' I have no idea why I suggest literally the first thing that pops into my head.

'You mean right at the end, near the little lighthouse?'

'Er, yeah.'

Rob shrugs. 'Sure, why not?'

We're back at the school building now, and I see Claire waiting for me by the door because we have double French together.

'See you later, Frankie,' Rob says as he peels away and turns towards the sports block.

'Yeah, I'm looking forward to it already,' I say, far too keenly, the words barely leaving my lips before I regret them.

I turn away from Rob as he heads across the playground and I grimace at Claire.

'Why did I say that?' I'm whining.

'That you were looking forward to seeing him?' Claire asks.

'I'm guessing that's what the two of you were discussing – a date?'

'No, not a date. We're just going to hang out tonight, that's all.'

'So what's wrong with saying you're looking forward to it, then?'

'I'm trying to be cool about it, that's why. Instead of saying the first thing that pops into my head every time I'm near him.'

'Frankie,' Claire says, pausing as we walk down the school corridor together. 'Has it ever occurred to you that maybe what Rob likes about you is the fact you're not cool, and you always say what you think?'

I think about this for a moment and I'm about to reply, telling her she doesn't get it, when Claire continues.

'It's one of the things *I* like about you. I don't want a friend who's trying to be cool all the time, I want one that's honest and fun to be with. Perhaps Rob feels exactly the same?'

Five

When the school bell rings again later, this time to signal the end of the school day, I walk with my friends back down through St Felix as usual. But, instead of stopping at a shop for some snacks or an ice cream before heading home as we often do, today I leave them and walk up into the part of the town that contains the many fishermen's cottages that once upon a time would have been home to the population of St Felix. Now, however, the narrow little houses are fast becoming accommodation for the many holidaymakers who visit the town in the spring and summer months.

But not the particular house I'm looking for – Snowdrop Cottage – where my boss from the flower shop, Rose, still lives.

Ah, here it is, I think, pausing for a moment outside a pretty cottage in one of the last rows before the sea. I do hope Rose is as relaxed about me turning down her offer of dresses as she seems to be about most things. I really can't imagine she'll have anything I like.

I lift my hand to reach for the knocker, but the door opens before I can get there.

'Ah, Frankie,' Rose says, smiling at me. 'I'm so pleased you came. Come in.'

Inside is a pretty little kitchen with pale blue units, a black Aga stove and a small, round table with four chairs.

'I'll make us some tea in a moment.' Rose gestures to the table where she's already prepared a tray with some cups and saucers. 'I've laid out the dresses upstairs for you. The light is so much better up there in the sitting room. We're a bit topsy-turvy here, because of the view you see.'

As I follow her up the stairs, I realise that, unusually, the sitting room is in the upper part of the house, and immediately at the end of the room I can see why. Past a rocking chair and a plump, scarlet sofa with patchwork cushions, is a pair of French windows, and, beyond that, a small balcony.

'Gosh.' I walk over to the windows and gaze out. 'You have a beautiful view here.'

'Yes, I'm very lucky. St Felix Bay is very picturesque what-ever the weather outside. I spend many happy hours up here looking out at that view. Now, I'll just make us some tea and then we can have a look at the dresses.'

While Rose pops back downstairs to make tea, I wander out onto the balcony to take in the view.

Today, the sky is cornflower blue, broken by just a few white clouds floating calmly by. Seagulls ride the gusts of wind in front of me, and I can just see the beach below where holiday-makers sit protected from the breeze by colourful windbreaks, while dogs run around on the beach, chasing balls and knock-ing down sandcastles with their excitable tails.

'Now then,' I hear Rose say behind me, and I turn to see her putting down the tea tray on a little coffee table. 'Milk, one sugar, right?'

'Yes, please.' I walk back through into the sitting room. 'This is such a lovely house, Rose.'

'I'm very lucky here. Being one of the last rows, we all have this incredible view of the bay. When I'm not in the shop, I spend as much time as I can out there.'

'I would be painting that view if I lived here,' I say without thinking. 'In all weathers. Each picture would be so different from the last as the skies and the colours changed.'

Rose smiles and gestures for me to sit on the sofa. 'I didn't know you painted?'

'I don't very often. Mostly at school, really. I occasionally sketch, though, when I have time.'

'I guess it's a busy time for you right now preparing for your exams next year?' Rose passes me a cup of tea.

'Yes, we don't get much free time – it all seems to be taken up with homework.'

'It will be worth it when you're done, though. Do you still want to go to art college?'

I'm impressed Rose remembers me telling her this during my interview for the shop.

'I would like to. Whether I'm good enough is a different thing.'

'Oh, I'm sure you are. And if you're not, then it's not meant to be. I'm a great believer in things happening when they're supposed to.'

'I don't know what I'll do if I can't go.' I take a sip of my tea. 'I'm not really interested in much else.'

'Life has a funny way of showing us what we *actually* need, rather than what we *think* we do,' Rose says, nodding slowly.

I'm not sure what to say, so I sip again on my tea.

'Now, shall we have a look at these dresses?' Rose asks. 'I'll

47

bring them through and if there's any you like, you can try them on. I have a long mirror in my bedroom.'

'Sure.'

Rose puts her tea down on the table and heads across the landing to her bedroom, returning with several dresses on hangers. She lays them over the back of the sofa and proceeds to lift them up one at a time.

I smile and nod, and say how pretty or lovely they all look. But even me, with my limited knowledge of fashion, can see the dresses all look like they're from the 1950s, which, thinking about Rose's age, they probably are. They all have fitted bodices, narrow waists and full skirts, some with several layers of net underneath.

'This one,' Rose says, holding up a white dress with black polka dots, 'was made by a lovely lady who used to have a shop here in St Felix ...' She thinks for a moment. 'I think it was where the wool shop is now – you know, Wendy's Wools?'

I nod.

'That shop was owned by ... oh, what was her name ... Clara! Yes, that was it. She was a very talented seamstress who used to make all the latest fashions for us to wear. Not like it is now where you can easily go to a big department store to buy a dress, or one of those high-street boutiques you youngsters like.'

'We could probably do with something like Clara's shop now,' I say, looking at the dress, which is probably the best Rose has shown me so far. 'We have to get the bus to Truro to find anything remotely fashionable in one of those boutiques you're talking about.'

'Nothing in Penzance?' Rose asks.

'Not really – they have more shops than here in St Felix, but they don't really sell anything that people my age would wear.'

48

'That's a shame. So, yes or no to this one?' Rose holds up the dress again.

'Maybe?' I reply diplomatically. 'I'll certainly try it.'

Rose lowers the dress. 'This isn't working for you, is it?' she asks, looking me directly in the eye, so I have no choice but to tell the truth.

'I'm really sorry, Rose. It's so kind of you to have me here and to offer me your dresses. They're all very beautiful, and I'm sure would have looked amazing on you back then.'

'But they're just not your cup of tea?'

I shake my head.

'Not a problem, dear. Not a problem at all. Let me just go and hang them back up again.'

Rose lifts all the hangers from the sofa and, with a rustling of net petticoats, escorts them back to her bedroom.

I feel awful. I didn't even try one on.

I get up and go over to the French windows once more and look out at the view. The tide is coming in and the waves are strong and high as they roll into the bay.

Wait, what's that? I see something splashing about in the sea a little way out from the beach. There it is again! It's the same thing I saw on Saturday when I was having my lunch – a large fishlike tail flipping about in the water.

I'm about to step out onto the balcony to see if I can see it any better when Rose returns.

'I was just hanging the dresses up in my old wardrobe, when I noticed this at the back,' she says as I turn away from the view back towards her. 'This dress was my mother's, so it's not from the same era as mine. It's from the late 1920s, I think, possibly early thirties? I wondered if it might be more your thing?'

I look at the dress she's holding up – it shimmers in the

sunlight coming in through the window behind me. The dress is covered in rows and rows of overlapping blue, green and turquoise sequins, which make it look like the scales of a fish as it catches the light.

'It's a flapper dress – I think.' Rose frowns. 'I was always a bit too … I like to call it *curvy*, to wear it. But you would be able to carry it off much better than I ever could.'

Rose is clearly referring to my figure, which, unlike Mandy's voluptuous curves, is fairly straight up and down. So a dress like Rose is holding would likely hang on me like its hanging on its silk, padded hanger right now.

'I can see by your expression that you like this one a little more,' Rose says while I gaze at the dress. 'Why don't you try it on?'

'It's like a fish,' I say, walking towards her. 'A fish's scales, I mean – the colours are beautiful, especially when it catches the light.'

'I've always thought so too.' Rose looks at the dress with me. 'Go on, try it, Frankie. What have you to lose? My bedroom is just across the hall there.'

I take the dress from Rose and head into her bedroom. I slip off my uniform, then I unzip the back of the dress and pull it up over my legs and hips. Finally, I place my arms through the delicate narrow straps, pulling them up onto my shoulders, where, to my surprise, they sit perfectly.

In fact, the whole dress seems to fit perfectly. It's neither too big nor too tight anywhere. It's as if it was made for me.

Rose knocks on the door. 'Are you decent?'

'Yes, come in.'

'Well.' She pauses in the doorway as she sees me. 'Don't you look a treat!'

'It does seem to fit quite well.'

'It fits you perfectly, Frankie. Turn around for me?'

I spin slowly around so Rose can see the dress from all angles.

'You look simply beautiful,' Rose says, looking pleased. 'It's like there's a beautiful mermaid standing in my bedroom.'

I stare at her for a moment. I've not told Rose anything about our act at all – let alone the name.

'Oh, have I said the wrong thing?' she asks anxiously.

I shake my head. 'No, you've said the best thing actually. Not only does this dress fit me perfectly, but it will also be perfect for the entire evening.'

I look in Rose's antique walnut mirror again.

Enchantment Under the Sea dance . . . I think, turning to and fro. *You might just have found your first mermaid of the evening.*

Six

'Hi, sorry I'm a bit late,' I say as I arrive at the end of the harbour to find Rob waiting for me.

'No worries.' Rob turns around from where he's been leaning on the railings looking down into the waves. He looks gorgeous this evening. Even though he's only wearing black jeans and a black Guns N' Roses T-shirt, he looks effortlessly casual and relaxed.

'Hey, you look nice,' he says, noticing that, for once, I've made an effort. 'I like your T-shirt.'

After a lot of thought in a short space of time – I've been in a permanent rush since I left Rose's cottage with my borrowed dress – I wolfed down my tea, then dashed upstairs to my bedroom to find something to wear to meet Rob. After throwing nearly everything I owned onto my bed, the only thing left hanging in my wardrobe was my newly borrowed mermaid dress. I decided eventually on blue jeans, a smart black jacket and my white Bon Jovi T-shirt with the band's emblem on the front – a red heart with a dagger vertically though the middle, and two angel wings at the top. I pulled my curly hair up on one side with a comb, and at the last minute I whipped on the black pixie boots, instead of my usual trainers.

'Thanks. I like yours too.'

'Great minds think alike, obviously!'

'Great minds that like rock music,' I remind him in case he's forgotten we have that in common.

'Yes. So, what would you like to do?' Rob asks.

I shrug. I'm not entirely sure what you actually do on a date? This is the first one I've ever been on. But I don't tell Rob that. 'I don't mind. What would you like to do?'

Rob looks like he might be as much in the dark as me. Even though I don't think he's been out with anyone since he came to St Felix, I can't imagine it was the same at his previous school. 'Shall we go for a walk on the beach?'

'Yes,' I reply keenly. 'I'd like that. Which one?'

We're spoilt for beaches here in St Felix. There's the busy harbour beach just below where we are now – at high tide we'd only be able to walk along that for about a minute, but at low tide the sand extends right around the side of the harbour to another much longer beach on the other side of Pengarthan Hill, very popular with holidaying families. Then there's St Felix Bay where the surfers hang out, waiting to catch the huge waves that often roll into the bay there. Rose's house looks out over that bay. Just around from that is Morvoren Cove, where we've been rehearsing our performance for the dance, and, finally, Porthaven Bay – a tiny cove that is often fully covered at high tide.

'How about St Felix Bay?' Rob suggests. 'We could go across the town then down over the beach. If we went up over the hill, we could stop for a drink or something at that little café that's always open on Morvoren.'

53

'Oh, yes, and I know a really lovely little place to sit there.'

'Tucked up on the cliff face?' Rob asks. 'Looking out over the sea?'

'Yes – you know it too?'

'I often go up there for a bit of peace and quiet when it's busy in the town.'

I smile at Rob.

'What?' he asks. 'Have I said something odd?'

'No, not at all. I think that sounds like the perfect way to spend the evening.'

We walk together across the town and along the soft sand of St Felix Bay. We stop for a few minutes to watch the surfers attempting to catch the early evening waves.

'Have you ever tried surfing?' Rob asks as we watch yet another wave crash over the top of a wetsuit-clad surfer.

'No, not really my thing. I'm much better off on dry land. Have you?'

'I'd like to, but I don't think I'm strong enough – these guys are really muscly.'

'I think it's more about technique than muscles,' I say to try to reassure him. 'If you want to, you should try it. I think they do taster sessions for beginners.'

Rob shrugs. 'Maybe one day. Shall we walk again?'

We walk across the beach, chatting about school and the competition on Saturday and what possible costume Suzy might come up with for both Eddie and Rob to wear.

'It's all right for Eddie,' Rob says as we come up off the beach and take the little path up and over the hill that leads to Morvoren Cove. 'He can carry off something bold and bright. He has the personality for it.'

Contrary to what I expected, Rob isn't confident and

self-assured at all, but actually quite shy, and he definitely lacks confidence in himself and his abilities.

'When you're on stage, it's not about whether you have the personality in real life, it's whether you can pretend to have it long enough to convince your audience,' I tell him.

Rob smiles at me. 'You're right, of course. But I've never done anything in front of an audience before – what if I'm rubbish? What if I freeze when I get up there?'

'What if we all do? Luckily, the others will cover if one of us goes wrong. We're not going solo. We all have each other.'

'I know I said this the other day, but I really am so pleased to be a part of your little gang, Frankie. I've always been quite envious of you guys.'

'Can I be honest?' I ask.

'Er . . . yes. I guess so.'

'I was really surprised when you told me that.'

'Why?'

'Because you always seem so confident and at ease with everything. Like I said to you, it was me who was envious of you coming to the school and fitting in so quickly. I've grown up here and I still don't feel like I fit in properly. You seemed to find it so easy.'

'Maybe I'm better at pretending than I thought after all, then. Because that's far from how it felt.'

'Maybe you are. Perhaps you'll surprise yourself when you get on that stage on Saturday night – you might even enjoy it!'

We stop at the little kiosk at the front of the café that sits at the top of the beach and buy a can of Diet Pepsi each. Then we make our way up to the cliffside hideaway where I sat and had my lunch on Saturday.

'I'm so pleased Mum and Dad moved here to Cornwall,' Rob says as we gaze out at the view. 'I really like it here.'

'Where did you live before?' I ask.

'Cambridgeshire. They ran a little country pub there. It was OK, but the scenery is so much lovelier here. Have you ever been to Cambridgeshire?'

I shake my head.

'It's very flat. The view here is much prettier.'

I turn to look at him and realise to my surprise he's now looking at me, and not the view in front of us.

I don't know what to do – apart from flush a ridiculous shade of red. Rob looks similarly uncomfortable, so I turn away, pretty certain my cheeks must be on fire, they're that hot.

'Whoa, what's that?' Rob's sudden cry makes me turn back, and I see him looking down into the waves.

'What?' I ask, relieved the awkward moment has passed so quickly. 'What did you see?'

'It looked like a huge fish's tail,' he says, still staring at the sea. 'What fish do you have here in Cornwall with tails that big? It definitely wasn't a dolphin or a basking shark. It looked like … a huge goldfish tail. You know the sort – all soft and feathery.'

'Yes, I know exactly what you mean. I saw something similar myself sitting here the other day.' *And also when I was at Rose's cottage. That's three times the tail has been spotted in the last few days.*

'Did you? What do you know about it?'

'Nothing. I've never seen it before either. It's very odd, though. Like you said, it's far too big to be a regular fish, but it's not shaped like a dolphin or anything like that.'

'Strange! We'll have to do some investigating then and find out more about it.'

I like that he says 'we'.

'If you want to that is?' he adds.

'Yes, I'd like that. I like a bit of a mystery.'

Rob grins. 'Funnily enough, me too. Shall we watch for a bit longer in case it appears again?'

'Yeah, we probably should.'

We sit up on the cliff edge for another half an hour, but we don't see the tail again. As the evening draws to a close, the wind that was warm and light when I left my house earlier this evening now has quite a chill to it as it blows up off the sea.

I feel myself shiver, and Rob turns to me. 'Are you cold?'

'A bit. I think the wind has changed direction.'

'Do you want to go back?'

That's the last thing I want to do. I'm really enjoying spending this time with him – just the two of us.

'No, it's OK, I'll be fine.'

'I … I could put my arm around you?' Rob asks, looking down immediately after he's spoken. 'To try to keep you a bit warmer?'

Again, I'm lost for words. So I just nod.

Rob slides a bit closer to me along the smooth rock, then puts his arm around my shoulders.

'Is that any better?' he asks.

I'm still freezing, but of course I don't say.

'Yes, thank you,' I whisper, barely able to get my words out now I'm this close to him. This has never happened to me before, and inside I'm completely panicking. What happens next? What should I do? What if he tries to kiss me?

Again, we sit for a bit longer watching the waves below us. Well, I think this is what we're still doing. Both of us sit in complete silence staring at the sea, me completely paralysed by my nerves, and Rob as still as the cliff face behind us.

To my annoyance, I begin to shiver again.

My movement seems to awaken Rob. 'Oh, God, you're still cold!' he says with anguish, as though it's all his fault he hasn't been able to warm me up.

'No, I'm not, honestly.' I turn to look at him and I suddenly realise how close our faces are.

'Honestly?' Rob repeats, staring at me in an odd way.

I shrug. 'Maybe a bit ... '

It's possibly the strangest, and at the same time most awkward, situation I think I've ever found myself in as we continue to stare at each other. If this were a romantic movie, we'd be gazing longingly into each other's eyes, but the truth of the matter is we're staring, both of us seemingly wondering what should happen next.

Suddenly, among the noise of the gulls and the swirling wind, I hear a splash down below. Rob hears it too and we both turn away from each other to look.

Below us is the tail again, nothing more than that, simply what appears to be a huge fish's tail flapping around in the water. Its green, blue and turquoise colours are almost iridescent as they catch the evening sunlight.

Now, instead of staring at each other, we stare at the tail, but, try as I might, I can't make out a body beneath the waves to try to figure out what species this could be. And then, after only a few seconds, the tail dips down beneath the waves and is gone again.

'It is real, then?' Robs says, still looking down into the waves in case it makes another appearance. 'We didn't imagine it?'

'Seems that way. I wonder what it is?'

'I think we should probably head home soon.' Rob turns away from the sea. 'You do seem quite cold now, Frankie.'

'OK.' He's not wrong; I am freezing. But I don't want this night to end yet.

'Come on, then.' Rob holds out his hand and I take it gladly as we climb down from our viewing position.

We walk back through the town and then up the hill that leads out of the old part of St Felix towards the newer end of town, where most of the new-build houses are in little estates.

Unlike the last time we were here, Rob insists on walking me right to my door.

'I had a great time tonight,' he says as we pause on my doorstep. 'Thank you.'

'I had a great time too,' I reply, hoping desperately that Mum or Dad don't appear and open the door. 'I . . . I'm glad you saw that fish thing too. I wasn't sure if I might have imagined it before.'

'Yeah, that was odd. Like I said before, maybe we can do some investigating and try to find out what it could be?'

I nod. 'The library might have some books? We could take a look one night after school.' As I'm saying this, I'm actually cringing inside. *What are you babbling about, Frankie? You've just been on a date with the boy of your dreams and you're talking about going to visit a library with him!*

'Good idea,' Rob says to my relief. 'Let's do that.' He glances at the lounge window just behind me. 'I think your dad might be keeping an eye on us,' he whispers.

I turn around and see the top of my dad's head swiftly disappearing behind the patterned curtains.

'Sorry,' I whisper back. 'I think he's gone now.'

'It's fine. My parents would probably be doing the same

59

thing if this were my house. They're usually a bit busy at night with the pub, though, to worry too much what I'm up to. Right then, I guess I'll see you at school tomorrow?' Rob begins to back away.

'Yes.'

He takes another quick glance at the window, then, before I know what's happening, he leans forward and kisses my cheek.

Then looking almost as surprised as I am, he turns and heads quickly down the path, pausing only at the bottom to turn back briefly and lift his hand to wave goodbye.

But I'm in so much shock, I can't even lift mine to respond, let alone notice the flushed look on Rob's face that so closely matches my own current expression.

Rob Matthews kissed me ... OK, it was only a peck on my cheek, but, still. He actually kissed me ...

Seven

'You all look amazing!' Suzy says as she surveys the costumes for our performance. 'I knew it would work.'

My fear that we would end up in bikini tops made of shells and long fish tails covered in scales was completely inaccurate. Instead, Suzy has created outfits that aren't too revealing at all, but at the same time manage to make us look very mermaid-like.

It's Saturday night and Claire, Mandy and I are all wearing swimming costumes in different shades of blue and green. Attached to these are layers of matching sea-green chiffon fashioned into long skirts that taper in at the ankle. Our tail fins are attached to our flip-flops, so when we sit on our papier mâché rock they look exactly like the tail fins of a fish as we swish them to and fro, but we can still walk.

Around our necks we have long necklaces made of shells, which Suzy tells us she collected off the beaches around St Felix, so we must put them back when we're finished, or it will mess with the ecosystem. And on our heads, each of us has pinned one side of our long hair up with a comb covered in fake shells, which Suzy says she found really cheaply in one of the many beach gift shops.

Eddie and Rob are wearing colourful Hawaiian shirts and matching long shorts with the Fat Willy's Surf Shack insignia. Suzy's brother works part time at the shack in St Felix and managed to source them from some old stock kept out the back of the shop. Suzy also managed to obtain a broken surfboard at the same time to complete our 'set'.

'You've done so well, Suz,' I tell her as I admire our outfits. 'Considering your budget was the little bit of money we could all scrape together, I think you should take up costume design when you leave school.'

'Thank you, Frankie, it's lovely of you to say, but I don't think so. I want to make a difference to the world when I get a job. I don't want to sew for a living.'

'I'm sure there's more to costume design than just sewing,' Eddie says. 'But Frankie's right – you really have done an incredible job. I can't thank you enough.'

'I'm just pleased I got to be a part of this, but I didn't have to sing. I can't bear the thought of getting up on that stage in front of everyone and making a fool of myself. But I'm sure you guys won't,' she adds quickly when she realises what she's said. 'I've seen you rehearsing, remember – you will all be wonderful!'

'We'll know in about an hour, won't we?' Mandy looks at her watch. 'We're due on around seven.'

'I can't wait to see you all together up on the stage,' Suzy says. 'I'll be cheering you on from the audience. But right now, I have to go and find Miss Johnston. I said I'd help with seeing people to their seats. The hall looks amazing, by the way – wait until you all see it. Frankie, your backdrop is the *pièce de résistance*; it sets everything off beautifully!' She hugs us all before she goes. 'Break a fin!' she calls as she leaves us in the drama studio that is being used as a temporary dressing room for all the acts.

'So now what?' I ask as we watch Suzy go. 'Do we just wait?'

'Nah, I've found somewhere we can secretly watch everyone else,' Mandy says, beckoning us over into a huddle. 'I want to see what the competition is like.'

'Is that allowed?' Claire asks, looking worried. 'Miss Kelly said we were to wait here until we're called.'

'Sod that,' Mandy says. 'I ain't staying here cooped up with all these losers. Have you seen Jenny Meadows? She keeps giving me daggers.'

'I'm pretty sure it's me she's aiming those dirty looks at,' Rob says. 'She hasn't forgiven me from dropping out of her orchestra.'

It had quickly become clear that it was going to be impossible for Rob to take part in both acts. Due to a 'scheduling conflict', as Miss Kelly called it, there wasn't going to be enough time for Rob to change from the black suit and tie he was due to be wearing in Jenny's orchestra into his surfer-dude outfit. Because of the varying sets all the acts were using, it was necessary for our two groups to perform one after the other.

Jenny didn't take it too well when Rob informed her that he was going to be performing with the Misfit Mermaids, and not the Octopi Orchestra, as Jenny chose to call her group, and she's been bad-mouthing us ever since to anyone who would listen.

'It's not even Octopi,' Suzy said when Rob told us. 'That comes from there being Latin involved in the original meaning of the word. Some people think because there's Greek origins it should be Octopodes, but actually Octopuses is correct because the word is English.'

We all listened politely to another of Suzy's explanations.

'Technically there shouldn't even be a plural involved at all,' she continued when none of us responded. 'Octopuses are solitary creatures; they'd hate to be in a group of any kind.'

'Let alone one run by Jenny Meadows – eh?' Mandy quipped. 'Don't worry about it, Rob. You're better off with us mermaids.'

Now, Mandy sighs impatiently. 'Come on, Claire! Do something daring for once in your life. I'm going to watch the others and see what competition we have.'

Reluctantly, we follow Mandy out of the drama studio and along the school corridor until we're on the other side of the school hall and on the far side of the stage.

'Look,' Mandy says, as she begins to climb up a ladder. 'This leads up to the lighting rig, but there's a little viewing area where we can watch from above what's going on down below on the stage.'

'Mandy, we're wearing flip-flops!' I say in disbelief. 'I'm not climbing a ladder in flip-flops with a huge great fish tail attached to the front.'

'What about the rest of you?' Mandy asks, already pulling off her flip-flops so she can climb the ladder. 'Are you game?'

'I'll do it,' Rob says. 'Why not?'

'Eddie?' Mandy is already halfway up.

'You know I don't like heights,' Eddie says stoutly. 'I'm staying down here. Actually, I think I'll just go and check Kevin has definitely got our music prepared. I don't trust him at all. Why Miss Kelly put him in charge of sound, I have no idea. He can barely turn on a Walkman without help, let alone provide the accompaniment for a whole show!'

While Eddie heads purposefully down the corridor, I look at Claire, but she anxiously shakes her head. 'I'm not going up there; we might get in trouble.'

Rob is already climbing the ladder. 'Come on, Frankie. It might be fun?'

'Usually, I'd already be following you because I'd be in jeans and trainers,' I say, watching him climb. 'But I've got an incredibly tight long skirt on. I'm finding it difficult enough to walk in this outfit, let alone climb a ladder!'

Rob hesitates, and I wonder if he's debating whether to go or whether to stay with me.

Since our 'date' on Monday evening, Rob and I have only managed to see each other alone a handful of times. We've seen each other at school plenty – when I'd catch him glancing at me across the classroom and I'd smile shyly back at him. Or when we managed to sit next to each other in a school assembly and Rob slipped his hand into mine, so they were clutched together hidden between our chairs.

We didn't think anyone would notice, but, the following maths lesson, someone wrote on the whiteboard *Rob 4 Frankie* inside a heart with an arrow through it. I flushed the exact shade of red as the marker pen the words were written in. But our dates – if you could call them that – when it was just the two of us were perfect, and I loved spending time with him. Rob was kind and funny and he made me laugh. We actually had quite a lot in common, as well as our love of rock music. As I spent more time with him, I realised that Rob really was a bit of a misfit like the rest of us. Having moved schools so many times, he always felt like an outsider, which gave him a vulnerability that made him even more attractive.

One night, we were down on the beach at dusk when Rob drew a heart in the sand with a piece of driftwood. Like the heart on the whiteboard, he wrote inside *FH 4 RM Forever* and I almost cried. How could this be so perfect? Something surely had to go wrong. I was only fifteen and even I knew life was never this easy. Usually, my life felt like I was trudging along through thick mud, but right then it felt like I was floating along on a fluffy white cloud.

And just when I thought it couldn't get better. It had.

As we stood on the sand together, holding each other's hand and gazing at the heart, Rob gently squeezed my hand so I turned to look at him.

As quick as a flash he leaned in and kissed me – but not on the cheek like he had before. This time, it was fully on my lips.

As he pulled away, I stared at him. Partly in shock, partly in awe at how quickly my heart was beating – who knew it could go quite so fast and beat quite so hard?

'Was that ... OK?' Rob asked.

Speechless, I nodded.

'Only, I've never kissed a girl before. Not properly.'

'Really?' I managed to gasp.

Rob, looking worried, nodded. 'Could you tell?'

I shook my head.

'Should I do it again then?' he asked.

'Yes, please,' I said, already leaning forward.

And that moment, standing on the sand of Morvoren Cove, as the sun began to set, was where Rob and I shared our very first kiss.

Sadly, the rest of our week had to be split between school, homework and rehearsals. But now it was finally showtime, then shortly after that the end of the school year, so I was looking forward to six weeks of summer holiday, hopefully filled with lots of Rob.

'You go!' I say, waving my hand at him, confident he'd be quite safe with Mandy. Mandy is my friend and even though she likes a handsome face, I know I can trust her. 'I'll see you in a bit.'

'Sure?' Rob asks, still hesitating.

'Sure.' I nod.

Rob smiles then he continues up the ladder behind Mandy.

I turn to Claire. 'Shall we go back to the drama studio?'

Claire shrugs. 'I don't think we have a lot of options dressed like this, do we?'

We begin to walk – or waddle might be a better description – back towards the drama studio.

'Is everything all right with you and Rob?' Claire asks as we wander slowly down the school corridor together.

'Why – do you know something?' I ask a bit too quickly.

'No? I just meant how's things going, that's all.' Claire looks puzzled.

'Ah, I see. Yes, it's all good ... I think.'

'What do you mean "you think"?'

'I'm just not sure there is a me and Rob. Not yet, anyway. We've only had a few dates. That doesn't exactly make us a couple ... or does it?'

'You're asking the wrong person,' Claire says calmly. 'I've never even been on a date with a boy.'

'None of us apart from Mandy had until Monday,' I tell her. 'That's why I'm a bit confused. He seems keen enough and everything, and we get on well when we're together. But what if I mess it all up?'

'Why are you going to mess it up?'

'I don't know. What if I'm not interesting enough? What if he goes off me and decides he likes someone else better? He seems to enjoy being a part of our group as much as anything. Maybe that's what he really wants, and I'm just a way in.'

Claire pauses at the door of the drama studio. 'We've all seen the way he looks at you, Frankie. I think he really like you. But maybe he likes being a part of our gang as well.'

I think about this. 'You might be right. He did say he was quite jealous of our relationship before he got to know us.'

'There you go then. He likes you and he likes us – nothing wrong in that. I really think you're over thinking everything.' Claire stands back a little to let another girl come past us into the drama studio.

'Thank you, Claire,' the girl says. She turns and smiles at me as she passes. 'Hi, Frankie,' she says in a soft Irish lilt.

I smile politely back. She's tall and slim, and dressed in long white trousers with wide bottoms, a white short-sleeved blouse and a pale-blue knitted tank top. Holding back her long blonde hair is a matching blue scarf tied elegantly at the bottom of her head, so it hangs down with the rest of her hair. She looks like a 1930s movie star as she wafts elegantly into the room.

'Who's that?' I whisper.

'That's Marnie,' Claire says. 'She's Rob's replacement in Jenny's orchestra.'

'Jenny got a replacement? I didn't know that. Does she go to this school? I don't remember seeing her before.'

'Apparently she's starting properly next term. She's moving from Ireland, but she's having a few days here before the summer holidays as a sort of taster, I think?'

'Oh, right. Bit odd, isn't it, though? New pupils usually just start at the beginning of term.'

'Don't ask me. I just heard that Jenny was super pleased to find her. It's completely revamped their act apparently.'

I look through the door of the drama studio and see Marnie laughing with some of the other 'Octopi Orchestra'.

'Bet they're not as good as we are – even with her,' I say. 'Now, we must keep an eye on the time. If it gets near our slot to be on stage and Mandy and Rob aren't back, we'll have to go and find them.'

Luckily, Mandy and Rob seem to have some idea of time, as they arrive back in the drama studio just as Miss Kelly is rounding us up to go and wait in the wings at the side of the stage.

'Here they come!' I say to Miss Kelly as they dash through the doors of the studio. 'I told you they'd just gone to the toilet.' I glance at Mandy as we're ushered along the corridor. 'You're cutting it fine,' I say.

'Nah, we knew what we were doing.' Mandy is, as ever, completely oblivious to any panic or stress. 'We had a great view of everyone who's gone so far. And you know something, I think we might have this in the bag.'

'Don't get too confident,' I tell her, lowering my voice as we approach the stage. 'We haven't been on yet.'

'Funny,' Mandy whispers, as we enter through the door and crowd into a tiny area on the side of the stage. 'That's exactly what your boyfriend said.' She looks ahead of us to Rob, who's towards the front of our little group with Eddie.

'Rob's not really my boyfriend. We've only been out a handful of times.'

'He seems to think he is.'

'What makes you say that?' I ask immediately, keen to know more.

Mr Stevens, the drama teacher, who's also acting as the stage manager, turns to look at us. 'Girls! Quiet, please. The next act is about to go on.'

'Sorry, sir,' I whisper back. I wait until Mr Stevens has

turned away from us before I speak again. 'Why?' I ask Mandy in the lowest voice I can manage. 'What did he say?'

'He couldn't stop talking about you.' Mandy grins like she always does when she has a secret she wants to share. 'Asking me all sorts of questions, he was.'

'Like what?'

'Frances and Amanda!' Mr Stevens raises his bushy eyebrows and gives us a stern look this time. 'I really must insist you remain silent, or I shall have to ask you to leave.'

I have no choice but to stop with my questioning. But it's so frustrating. I want to know what Rob said to Mandy about me.

Eddie, Rob and Claire shuffle forward a bit so Mandy and I can see the stage too, and the small movement means I find myself standing next to Rob.

He smiles at me. 'Nervous?' he whispers as the Octopi Orchestra begin to play on the stage.

'A bit,' I whisper back.

Rob reaches out his hand and takes mine, and for a moment I forget all about where we are and what we're about to do. Rob Matthews is holding my hand again. *Does life get any better than this?*

I float back down to earth as I listen to the music, and I notice that rather than the formal attire the Octopi Orchestra said they were going to be performing in, actually they are all wearing jaunty white sailor suits, with little navy ties around their necks, as they play their various instruments.

And then I realise that I recognise the music they're playing too.

'This isn't what we were rehearsing before,' Rob says, listening intently. 'It's completely different.'

'I think it's from a musical,' I reply. 'It sounds like ... Yes, it's from *Anything Goes*.'

As the orchestra finish their overture, Marnie floats effortlessly onto the stage from the wings opposite and begins to sing the musical's title song, in a voice that not only fills the whole of the stage, but the entire school hall too.

'What has this to do with the sea?' I hear Mandy whisper behind us.

'*Anything Goes* is set on a cruise ship,' Eddie informs her. 'The songs aren't really sea-based, but I guess the show does go with the sea theme. Blimey, this girl can sing, can't she?'

'Yeah, but who is she?' Mandy asks. 'I haven't seen her at school before.'

'Starting next term apparently,' Claire replies.

Although I can hear all this going on behind me, I'm not really focused on what they're saying, I'm more concerned with what's going on both in front of me on the stage, and also right next to me.

Marnie only sang for a few bars when I felt Rob's hand loosen its grip on mine. Now she's well into the chorus, his hand has dropped mine completely while he stares at the vision of effortless elegance on the stage in front of him.

I stand completely still next to him, trying not to feel hurt by his actions, while at the same time trying desperately not to hate the girl singing so beautifully on the stage.

Marnie sure can hold a note, I have to give her that. If Whitney Houston was standing on the stage right now, I don't think her voice would fill the school hall any better than Marnie's. But why does Marnie have to be so pretty as well? A fact that has clearly not missed Rob's attention either. It's just not fair.

I glance at Rob. His eyes are wide and a little glazed as he watches Marnie, who, now there's a bridge in the music, is not singing, but tap-dancing instead, and her dancing appears to be just as good as her singing.

I look out into the section of the audience I can see from the wings. Rob is not the only one gazing in awe at Marnie, the audience too seem enchanted by this vision in front of them.

I turn to the Octopi Orchestra and Jenny Meadows meets my gaze. She smiles triumphantly back at me – and suddenly I realise how professional they all look in their crisp white matching outfits, and how silly we probably look with our cobbled-together costumes.

I want to turn around and run. Off this stage, out of this school, to anywhere that isn't here – standing next to the boy who has only just noticed me, and yet who now apparently only has eyes for someone else.

The performance ends with Marnie giving one more rendition of the chorus. The audience immediately begin to applaud enthusiastically, a few people rise to their feet and there are cheers and whistles. Rob is clapping with them – a bit too keenly for my liking.

Marnie waits for the rest of the orchestra to join her at the front of the stage and then they all take a carefully rehearsed bow together. Then Marnie gives a little wave to acknowledge her admirers, before they all leave the stage together, exiting into the wings opposite.

Mr Stevens pulls the curtains from a rope at the side, and pupils wearing black clothes rush onto the stage and quickly change the Octopi Orchestra's set for ours. Then before I know what's happening, my friends are pushing out onto the stage, and I am carried along with them.

'Places!' Eddie hisses as I stand dumbstruck on the side of the stage. 'Frankie! What are you doing? Get on your rock!'

I jump at his voice and see Claire and Mandy already waiting for me in their positions on our papier-mâché rock. I hurriedly dash over and perch myself next to them on top of the grey paint.

Then I look out front, and to my far right I see Rob getting his guitar ready at one end of the stage and, in the middle, Eddie waiting behind his microphone stand.

'Are you all right, Frankie?' Claire whispers as the stage lights go down and everything goes very quiet. 'You seem a bit out of it. Have you got stage fright?'

'No, I'm fine,' I whisper just as the curtains are pulled back again and the bright stage lights come on above and in front of us.

The familiar music begins to play, and we launch into our performance.

I feel like I'm in a dream as I perform our carefully practised routine. I can see Eddie loving every minute of being our front man, and Rob to his side enjoying his role as lead guitarist.

Then I realise that the audience, many of whom are parents, know our song well; they begin clapping along and tapping their feet to the music, which only encourages our front man to become even more animated.

While Claire and Mandy perform with smiles on their faces, I feel like I'm on automatic pilot as I sway to the music along-side them. And as we come to the end of the song, and Eddie does a big flourish with his mic stand, it feels to me like we've only just begun.

The audience applaud and Eddie encourages us to all take a bow just like the act before us did.

As we line up, I spot Marnie at the side of the stage clapping along with everyone else, but she's smiling at Rob as she does, and Rob, I'm gutted to see, is smiling back at her.

Leaving the stage, everyone around me is in high spirits, so I excuse myself by saying I just need to pop to the toilet.

After a few moments of trying to collect myself, I emerge from the cubicle, wash my hands and look at my reflection in the mirror, and for the first time ever I see everything that Marnie is and I'm not.

Marnie is pretty. I'm not.

Marnie is elegant. I'm definitely not that.

Marnie is curvy and womanly. I just look like a boy.

Why would Rob ever choose me over Marnie?

And as I stand there, I begin to cry.

'There you are!' Mandy says as she bursts through the toilet door. 'We wondered where you'd gone. Shit, Frankie, what's wrong?'

'Nothing.' I sniff, furiously trying to wipe my eyes on my bare arm.

Mandy goes into the cubicle and pulls off what seems like half a roll of toilet paper. 'Here,' she says, passing it to me. 'I wouldn't rub yourself too hard with it, though – that stuff is like sandpaper.'

I dab gently at my eyes with the crunchy paper. 'Thanks.'

'Wanna tell me what's wrong?' she asks gently. 'Is it Marnie?'

'How do you know that?'

'The way Rob went after her when we came off stage. It was like he'd been hypnotised or something. Completely in a trance he was.'

I look miserably in the mirror at myself. My mascara has now all smudged under my eyes, adding to the 'mermaid in a horror movie' look I'm currently sporting.

'Why do you think he did that?' I ask in a pitiful voice.

'Dunno – he's male, isn't he? Most of them are a waste of

space. That's what my mum says and I'm starting to agree with her.'

I turn to face Mandy. 'But I thought you liked boys ... I mean, men ... well, the male of the species anyway.'

Mandy shrugs. 'They have their uses. But my girlfriends are far more important to me. You want my advice?'

'Maybe?' I reply hesitantly.

'Sod him! If he wants to fawn over some blonde bimbo, then so be it. You, Frankie, are worth a hundred of him ... no, make that a thousand. Don't let him ruin your evening. We were fabulous out there tonight. Pretty sure we won't win after the turn the octopuses put in, but even if we don't, I'm gonna enjoy the rest of the night. I've got an amazing dress and I'm going to live it up and I suggest you do too. You don't need a boy to make you happy, Frankie. Only you can choose to do that.'

Mandy's unexpectedly wise talking-to does me the world of good. I wash my face as best I can with water, then I go back with Mandy to the drama studio, where I properly remove all my mermaid make-up, replace it with something a little lighter and get changed into my dress for the dance.

'You lookin' good, girl!' Mandy says with a low whistle as she takes my arm ready to head back into the main hall. 'The singing mermaid has transformed into one hot mumma of a mermaid! Where did you get the dress?'

I tell Mandy about Rose and her vintage dresses as we walk arm in arm back to the party together. The school hall has now been transformed from a theatre into a magical underwater venue for the Enchantment Under the Sea dance. The chairs and the audience members have disappeared, and in their place are fifteen- and sixteen-year-old pupils all milling around looking a little awkward with their friends.

We quickly find the other mermaids, and, after we've all admired each other's outfits, including Eddie's electric-blue tuxedo and bow tie, we help ourselves to non-alcoholic fruit punch.

I try hard after Mandy's pep talk not to look around for Rob, but occasionally I find my eyes moving around the room wondering where he is. I can't see Marnie either, and I can't help wondering if they're somewhere together.

'And so, without further ado,' Mr Evans, our headmaster, continues his welcome speech from behind the microphone on the stage. 'It's time to announce the winners of the Enchantment Under the Sea talent show. Our audience were all asked to complete a voting slip as they left the hall tonight and I now have the results of their vote.' He pauses to open a gold envelope and quickly scans the piece of paper inside. 'In reverse order, third place goes to Jane Edwards, Melissa Jenkinson and Louise Roland for their very unusual and some might say unique performance of a traditional sea shanty to the *Blue Peter* theme tune!'

There's applause as the girls hurry up onto the stage to receive their prize – a box of seashell-shaped chocolates each.

'And in second place we have . . .' Mr Evans pauses for effect. 'The Misfit Mermaids with their splendidly sea-themed rendition of the Beach Boys' "Surfin' USA"!'

There are some cheers along with applause, and we all traipse up onto the stage to receive a similar box of chocolates with the addition of a sea-scented candle. Rob reappears to claim his prize with us, and I try desperately hard not to look at him.

Then we stand at the back of the stage in front of my back-drop with the other runners-up while Mr Evans announces the winners, who I think most people have guessed already.

'And the winners of this year's talent show are ... the Octopi Orchestra with special guest, Miss Marnie Morrissey!'

So Marnie gets her own billing now, I think sourly. This evening just gets better and better.

The Octopi Orchestra literally skip up onto the stage to receive their prizes – chocolates, candles and a voucher for ice cream donated by one of the ice-cream shops on the harbour.

I can't help but glance at Rob as the winners claim their prizes, and as I suspected I find he's gazing doe-eyed at Marnie as she collects her prize from Mr Evans.

'And I have a wonderful bonus for you all this evening,' Mr Evans says as I'm desperate to escape the stage. 'Marnie has agreed to perform for us again this evening, along with some of our leavers. So, without further ado, I wish you all a wonderful evening of dancing, music and laughter, and I pass the microphone over to Miss Marnie Morrissey accompanied by,' he quickly checks his card, 'the Friday Rock Project!'

The prize winners are all encouraged to leave the stage by the wings. I glance back and the last thing I see is some of the older boys, carrying guitars and a drum kit, hurrying onto the stage, and Marnie, now wearing a long shimmering dress in turquoise blue, looking far too beautiful, preparing her microphone to sing again.

'Hey,' Rob says as he pushes past me out of the wings and down a couple of steps into the school corridor, presumably in a hurry to get to the front of the stage to see Marnie again. 'Fancy a dance later, Frankie?'

I'm about to say, 'Yes, that would be wonderful!' when I remember what Mandy had said.

'No, thanks.' I stop at the top of the steps so I'm that little bit higher than he is, as he looks back at me with a confused expression. 'I'll be spending this evening with my friends. My real friends, that is.'

Rob stares at me for a moment, absorbing what I've just said.

'Sure,' he says, looking a tad bewildered. 'If that's what you want?'

'It is.'

'Right, then.' He nods. 'I need to get to the stage. I really want to see the show.'

I bet you do, I think silently. *I can't believe you're actually admitting it to my face.*

Rob's about to leave when he pauses and reaches into his pocket. 'I almost forgot. Did you drop this?' he asks, holding out a shell in the palm of his hand. 'I assumed it came off one of your costumes. I found it on the stage just now.'

The shell looks like a cross between a conch shell and a horn shell, but, instead of being rough and spiky on the outside, it's incredibly smooth and its mother-of-pearl appearance sparkles under the fluorescent light above us.

'I don't think so. It's a bit too big to have come off any of our outfits.'

'Well, you might as well have it,' he says, hurriedly pressing it into my hand. 'I've no use for it any more ... Have I?' He looks hopefully up at me, as the front of his sandy hair falls over his dark eyes, and for a moment I almost give in to his forlorn gaze.

But I hold my ground, and don't say anything.

'Fine. I see how it is.' Rob gives me one last look, then he turns smartly and walks purposefully away down the corridor.

And all I can think about isn't how jealous I am, or how upset he's made me, but only why I hadn't wished for something different ...

Eight

Two nights earlier ...

'So that's it, then,' Eddie declares proudly. 'Our last rehearsal. In two days' time, we'll be up on the stage about now.'

It's Thursday evening and we are at Morvoren Cove. Suzy is with us to watch our last rehearsal, and there's an air of relief mixed with apprehension as we complete our final run-through.

'We're gonna be great!' Mandy says with her usual confidence, flopping down onto the picnic rug next to Suzy. 'We'll whop the others. No one has an act like ours.'

'How do you know?' Claire asks from the rock we mermaids have been perched on until now. 'We don't know what everyone is doing yet. I've only heard a few rumours.'

'Have confidence in yourself for once, Claire!' Mandy props herself up with her hand behind her head. 'If you believe we'll be the best, then we will.'

I climb down off the rock and sit on the second rug we've brought with us, and I'm pleased when Rob comes and sits next to me, after putting his guitar safely away in its case to protect it from the sand.

'Drink, anyone?' Mandy asks, leaning over and pulling a large bottle of cider from the carrier bag next to her. 'I have glasses too!' She pulls a stack of clear plastic cups from the bag.

'How did you get that?' Eddie asks, kneeling on the rug next to Mandy and Suzy.

'I have my ways.' Mandy taps the side of her nose. 'Be a dear and hold the cups, Eddie, so I can pour without spilling it.'

'But we're not old enough to drink,' Claire says, looking worried. 'We'll get in trouble if anyone sees us.'

Mandy opens the bottle. 'Claire, look around you. The beach is deserted, it's only us here and now the tide has turned, the chances of anyone joining us is unlikely. You know how small this cove gets when the tide is in; there's hardly any sand, unless like us you know where to go.'

Claire nods, but still looks concerned.

'Right, who's for cider?' Mandy says as she begins to fill the plastic glasses one by one and Eddie hands them out.

We all take one, even Claire.

'Now, who is going to make the toast?' Mandy asks. 'Eddie? This performance was all your idea.'

Eddie, always one for a grand gesture, stands up.

'Hmm, now let me see ... I would like to thank you all for coming on board in the first place. I know I had to pester some of you ... ' He raises his eyebrows at me. 'But I think you'll all agree now we're just forty-eight hours away from the show, it's all worked out really well. I'd also like to say a special thank you to Suzy, who, even though she probably has the best voice of all of us, has made a wonderful job of our costumes.'

'Yes, hear, hear!' We all raise our glasses to acknowledge Suzy.

'You haven't seen them all finished yet,' Suzy says, grinning. 'You might hate them!'

'Nonsense, I've seen them and they're amazing,' Eddie says. 'Now, where was I? Ah, right, here's to the Misfit Mermaids! Not only an amazing act, but the best bunch of friends I could ever ask for!'

'The Misfit Mermaids!' We all cheer together, and we begin to drink our cider, which to my surprise actually tastes rather nice.

After we've all sat chatting and finishing off our drinks, Mandy begins to refill our plastic cups, and as she pours the last drops from the bottle into Eddie's glass, Claire looks relieved. 'Oh, is that the end?' she says, not sounding all that upset. 'What a shame.'

'Nah, got another bottle, haven't I?' Mandy says, pulling a second bottle from her bag. 'Now pass over your glass, Claire.'

Claire glances at me as she stands up to hand Mandy her plastic tumbler.

'Claire, you don't have to take a second one,' I tell her as she watches Mandy prepare to refill her cup. 'No one is forcing you.'

Mandy looks up at Claire. 'Yeah, don't take it if you don't want to – all the more for the rest of us!'

'I will pass if you don't mind,' Claire says. 'I already feel quite lightheaded after my first helping.'

'Nothing wrong in that, Claire,' Rob says kindly as she sits back down again. 'My parents say it's a good thing to know your limits with alcohol.'

'Another, Rob?' Mandy asks, lifting the bottle.

'Of course!' Rob stands up. 'I haven't reached my limit

yet! Frankie?' he asks, holding out his hand for my tumbler. 'Another?'

'Yes, please,' I say, handing him my cup, even though Claire isn't the only one to feel a little lightheaded after her first glass. 'Fill it up!'

The rest of us all take a second serving of cider.

'Look how amazing the sky is this evening,' Suzy says, as we all relax on the picnic rugs, the little bit of alcohol we've drunk making everything seem beautifully hazy and warm. 'I bet there's going to be an incredible sunset over St Felix Bay tonight.'

'I'd go and take a look if I could be bothered to move,' Eddie says, stretching on his back. 'But I'm so comfy here.'

'Me too,' Rob sighs. 'Why can't life always feel as relaxed as this? Right now, I'm not worried about anything. I'm just happy for once.'

He looks over at me and smiles. *I know just how you feel*, I think, smiling back.

'I'm sorry to pop all your lovely, chilled bubbles,' Claire says. 'But we might have to move in a minute; the tide is getting very close to the rugs.'

'Nah, Claire. You worry too much!' Mandy grins. 'The sea never comes in further than this point.'

'But it looks like it might today.' Claire, who is still perched on the rock, is watching the waves ripple over the sand. 'It's been getting closer for the last few minutes.'

Eddie rolls over on his stomach to look at the sea.

'You might be right,' he says, his eyes at beach level. 'But I kind of like the jeopardy of it right now. Jeez, what was that?' He immediately sits up.

'What?' I ask.

'I dunno, I thought I just saw a really big fish flip over in the sea. Well, I only saw its tail, but it was massive!'

'Me and Frankie have seen that.' Rob pulls himself up to look. 'Like a really big goldfish tail, only more colourful?'

Eddie nods. 'Yeah, exactly like that. It's not the alcohol, then? I thought for a moment I might be seeing things.'

'You've only had two glasses of cider!' Mandy says mockingly. 'You've hardly been downing shots.'

We all watch the waves for a bit, but we see nothing else unusual.

So we settle back down on the rugs. This time Rob manages to move closer to me, so he now has his arm around my shoulders as we lie back and look up at the pink-and-peach-coloured clouds moving across the tangerine sky.

'What do you all want to do when you leave school?' he asks. 'I mean, I know we have another year yet, but do you know?'

'Make lots of money!' Mandy pipes up first.

'How?' Rob asks.

'Dunno, but that's what I want to be – successful and rich.'

'I want to make a difference,' Suzy says. 'Probably environmentally in some way.'

'Ah, Suz, now you're making me look bad!' Mandy grins. 'Always the noble reply.'

'It's the truth. I do want to make a difference. This earth won't last for ever, you know. Not if we keep treating it like we currently do. Take your empty bottles of cider there and your plastic cups. When we leave the beach, we'll just throw them in the bin – and we're good for even doing that. At least we clear our litter away – too many people just leave it.'

'What else can we do other than throw it in the bin?' Mandy asks.

'Recycle it,' Suzy says. 'So it can be made into something else. But it's not that easy here when there's no facilities for collecting recyclable items. We have no choice but to bin them. But if we keep throwing all our rubbish in landfill, eventually it's going to give off toxic gases that will affect not only the ozone layer, but eventually our environment too, and in the long term cause global warming.'

'Is global warming like the Ready Brek advert?' Eddie asks, grinning. 'So in the future we'll all have a warm glow around us!'

'Laugh if you want, Eddie,' Suzy says, not seeing the funny side. 'But it won't be far from that. The whole earth will heat up, and eventually if we don't do anything it might explode.'

'Bit dramatic, even for you, Suz.' Eddie raises his eyebrows at the rest of us.

'It's not dramatic, Eddie, it's the truth. And the sooner more people realise it, the more likely things will change.' Suzy sighs and folds her arms determinedly across her chest. 'Burying your head in the sand and making jokes is what the ignorant do, not the informed.'

Eddie glares at Suzy and there's an awkward silence.

'It sounds like you know exactly what you want to do, Suzy,' Rob says in an attempt to defuse the situation. 'It's clearly a cause that's important to you.'

Suzy nods.

'So what about you, Eddie?' Rob asks. 'What do you want to do? Something theatrical, I bet.'

'However did you guess, darling?' Eddie says dramatically, forgetting his annoyance with Suzy for the moment. 'The whole world is a stage – and I want to be on it in some form or another!'

'I can't imagine you won't be.' I smile at him. 'You were born to be a performer! Unlike the rest of us who need a little persuasion.'

'What about you, Claire?' Rob asks. 'What do you want in life?'

'Oh, I just want to be happy,' Claire says contentedly, completely comfortable with her answer. 'I don't want to be rich or famous or anything like that. I just want to be happy.'

We all look at Claire and smile. As she so often does, in her own quiet way she's hit the nail on the head. 'Well said, Claire. I guess that's all any of us want really, to be happy in life. What about you, Rob?' I ask, turning to him. 'You asked the question – what do you want to do?'

'Oh, I dunno, really. Mine's a bit like Claire's. I want to be happy, I want to have a job that I enjoy and I want to have a relationship like my parents have – one that lasts a lifetime. I see them together and I think that's what I want to have when I'm their age.'

'*Man*, can you get any cuter?' Mandy looks at me. 'Frankie, you've fallen on your feet with this one!'

I blush furiously.

'What about you, Frankie?' Suzy asks, trying to rescue me from my embarrassment. 'What do you want?'

'Oh, I really don't know yet. I just want to pass my exams and then see what happens next. I don't have any plans or goals or anything like that.'

'Frankie wants to be a professional artist one day,' Claire announces from her rock. 'She'd like her own gallery like the ones dotted around St Felix. Don't you, Frankie?'

I frown at Claire.

'What?' she asks innocently. 'You told me all that, and you

said you wanted to go to art college, but you aren't sure if you're good enough.'

'Are you kidding?' Rob is looking down at me while I lie on the rug wishing the beach would open up and swallow me. 'You're an amazing artist. You'd have no problem getting into art college.'

'See, I told you he was a good 'un!' Mandy grins.

'Maybe,' I say, trying to play it down. 'We'll have to see what this next year brings, won't we? As long as the Misfit Mermaids are still all together, then I'll be happy.'

'Hear, hear to that!' Eddie lifts his empty glass.

'Where are you going, Suzy?' Claire asks as Suzy gets up and begins to walk across the sand.

'Flotsam and jetsam!' Suzy calls back over her shoulder. 'Back in a mo.'

'What does she mean?' Rob asks.

'Flotsam and jetsam are things washed up from the sea,' I explain. 'That's what Suzy calls them, anyway. It means she's going to collect some rubbish she's seen floating in the water or lying on the sand. She often does it if she sees something on the beach that shouldn't be there.'

'We should probably all do that,' Rob says. 'Maybe there wouldn't be so much if everybody picked up rubbish from the beach.'

'I feel bad about what I said earlier,' Eddie says, watching Suzy. 'I'll go and help her.'

Eddie gets up and jogs across the little bit of sand that the sea has left us.

'We sometimes have our fallings out, but we never stay mad with each other for long,' I explain for Rob's benefit. 'Do we?' I look over at Mandy and Claire.

'Nah!' Mandy says. 'Life's too short.'

But Claire is intently watching Suzy and Eddie.

'What's up, Claire?' I ask.

'I'm not sure, but I think Suzy and Eddie have found something interesting.'

We all sit up and look over at the two of them standing together on the edge of the water. They seem to be examining something.

I call out to them. 'What have you found?'

They both look back at us.

'Not sure,' Eddie replies. 'We'll bring it over.'

Suzy and Eddie walk back over to the picnic rugs carrying something made of wood. As they get nearer, it looks very much like a small beer barrel with rusted metal hoops holding the wood of the barrel together.

'Is that a barrel of beer?' Mandy asks as they put their find down on the sand next to us.

'It feels a bit light to be full of beer,' Eddie says. 'But it's still sealed, which is a bit odd.'

'It looks more like a cask that would have held whisky,' Rob says, examining it. 'There were some at the pub when we moved in. The people that owned it before us had used them as decoration in the bar. This one is old, though, by the look of the wood – is there a date stamped on the outside anywhere?'

We all crowd round to look at the barrel.

'There!' Rob points as Eddie turns the barrel around. 'On the bottom. There's some numbers.'

'I think it says ... something 1824.' Eddie squints at the barrel. 'But some of the letters and numbers have rubbed off, so it's a bit difficult to see properly.'

He lifts the barrel again to get a better look, and something rattles inside.

'What was that?' Suzy asks. 'It doesn't sound like liquid.'

'I'm out!' Mandy says, sitting back down on the rug. 'If there's no alcohol left inside, what's the point?'

'Can we prise it open, do you think?' I ask. 'Then we could see what's inside. I don't suppose anyone has a penknife or something similar on them?'

'Funnily enough, no.' Eddie grins at me. 'Knives aren't something I usually carry.'

'Don't touch it!' Claire suddenly announces this in a commanding voice, very unlike her usual tone.

We all turn to look at her.

'What's wrong, Claire?' I ask. 'You look like you've seen a ghost!'

'Not a ghost,' Claire says, her voice trembling now. 'But I think we might have seen a mermaid . . .'

Nine

'What on earth are you talking about, Claire?' Suzy asks. 'There's no such thing as mermaids.'

'Claire, come and sit down,' I say gently. Claire is looking very pale and I'm quite worried about her. Perhaps she's had a bad reaction to the alcohol?

Claire does as I suggest and sits herself down on the same rock we were rehearsing on only a short while ago.

'Now what do you mean you think we've seen a mermaid?' I ask, sitting down next to her.

'Not seen exactly, more been in the presence of one.' Claire still looks shocked. 'Haven't any of you heard the story about the Mermaid of St Felix?' she asks, looking round at us all. 'No? Not even you, Rob?'

Rob frowns. 'Why would I know anything about it?'

'The Merry Mermaid is called what it is because of this story. I thought you'd know it since your parents run the pub now.'

Rob shakes his head.

'I can't believe none of you know this,' Claire says, looking surprised.

Mandy folds her arms. 'For the love of St Piran, will you just tell us, Claire!'

'I'm just about to, Mandy!' Claire gives her a look. 'If you'll just give me a minute!' She takes a breath. 'So, the story is, that one night a maid who worked at Tregarlan Castle – that's the big house up on the hill above St Felix Bay,' she explains for Rob's benefit.

Rob nods. 'Yes, I know it.'

'The maid stole some jewellery from her bosses. She was stealing to order for a gang of pirates, and she was supposed to float the stolen jewellery out to the pirates' boat in an empty whisky barrel in exchange for payment. But the story goes she couldn't find an empty barrel, so she stole one that was half full from the local public house, rolled it down to the beach, then drank the contents so it would be empty enough to float the jewellery in.'

'Why didn't she just tip it out?' Suzy asks, ever practical. 'If she was by the sea, why didn't she just tip it out instead of drinking it all.'

'*That* would have been such a waste,' Mandy says. 'She probably did the right thing – double bubble for her.'

'Hardly,' Claire says stoutly. 'She drowned.'

'Oh no!' I'm totally caught up in Claire's tale. 'Really?'

'Well, technically she didn't, but – look, just let me tell you the rest of the story.'

'Go on, Claire,' Rob says encouragingly.

Claire is clearly enjoying having us all hanging on her every word for once. 'So, as you can imagine, the maid got pretty drunk, or should I say *merry*, as a result of drinking all this alcohol, and when she went to throw her barrel full of jewellery into the sea, she slipped and fell off the rocks into the waves and was never seen again. But . . . ' Claire holds up her finger to keep our attention. 'And this is the really interesting bit – it's said she didn't actually drown. The story goes she was actually rescued by a passing merman, who took her down to the bottom of the ocean along with her treasure. The maid fell in love with the merman and was transformed into a beautiful mermaid and was never ever seen again on the land.'

We all stare silently at Claire for a moment.

'That's where the Merry Mermaid of St Felix came from?' Eddie asks, looking puzzled. 'Not much of a story to name a pub after, is it – a woman who drowned?'

'That's not quite the end of the story,' Claire says, 'and this is the bit I can't believe none of you know – there's a proverb!'

'Which is?' Suzy asks, looking doubtful.

' "If a mermaid's treasure washes up on the shore. Return it to the waves and be happy forevermore." No?' Claire asks when we all look blank. 'None of you have ever heard it? My mum told me it years ago when we were on the beach one day.'

'There's an engraving saying that in the pub,' Rob says. 'It hangs just above the door inside.'

'See?' Claire says. 'I told you the two were linked. Mum said it means if you ever find the mermaid's treasure, you must throw it back into the sea and the mermaid will grant you one wish.'

'Is it some sort of test?' Eddie asks. 'Because the barrel is supposed to be full of treasure?'

'Yes!' Claire says keenly. 'If you throw it back to the mermaid, it signifies to her that you are worthy of a wish.'

We all turn and look at the worn-looking barrel.

'But what makes you think that's the same barrel?' I ask. 'There could be loads of empty whisky kegs floating around in the sea just waiting to be washed up on shore?'

'The year the maid went missing was 1824,' Claire says. 'The same date as on your barrel over there.'

'She's right,' Rob says, confirming this. 'It says that date in the pub too.'

'So you're saying we should throw it back in the sea?' I ask.

'Yes,' Claire says. 'That's what the proverb says we should do.'

'But it could be full of treasure!' Mandy says, not sounding that convinced. 'If what you say is true, Claire, there could be jewellery in there.'

Again we all stare at the barrel.

'If that tale is true, and this is the barrel, then we could make a wish,' Eddie says quietly. 'All of us, if we all returned the barrel to the sea.'

'I'd much rather have a wish than some treasure,' Suzy says wistfully.

'I'd rather have the treasure,' Mandy says, practical as ever. 'Or the money that the treasure is worth.'

'It won't be our money, though, if that barrel did contain anything valuable,' Suzy tells her. 'We'd have to hand it in to the authorities and then it would belong to them or the original owner. I collect things off the beach all the time; there are laws covering anything valuable.'

'She's probably right,' I tell the others. 'If that jewellery was stolen from the castle, then technically it would still belong to them.'

'But that old fella lives there now, doesn't he?' Mandy says. 'What is it my mam calls him? Oh, yeah, Mad Stan the pasty man! I doubt he'd even know it belonged to his ancestors if he's a bit doolally.'

'I think you're all getting a little carried away,' Rob says.

'The chances of that story actually being true are low to begin with, let alone there actually being treasure in the barrel. I think we should open it.'

'No!' We all shout at once.

Rob looks surprised at our outburst.

'You haven't lived in Cornwall very long, have you, Rob?' Suzy asks. 'The one thing you learn when you've lived here a while is that this area is brimming with myths and legends. Some of them might be made up or embellished over time, but some of them ... well, you just can't explain.'

'Suzy's right,' I tell him. 'St Felix in particular has many myths that surround it.'

'Like the place you work,' Claire says to me. 'The flower shop has its own special magic, Rob.'

'Does it?' Rob asks, looking at me.

'Yeah,' I say, feeling a bit embarrassed. 'It's supposed to, anyway. Something to do with special bouquets made up with white ribbon.'

Rob nods, but doesn't mention the bouquet I made up for him and his mum. 'So what do you want to do then – throw it back?'

I look at the others.

'We are the Misfit Mermaids,' Eddie says, smiling. 'It seems quite appropriate we should be entrusted with a mermaid's treasure like this.'

'What about if we climb up on the rocks and throw it back?' Rob asks. 'If we try to roll it back into the sea, it will probably just wash ashore again.'

'Yes, I think we should do that,' Claire says, nodding. 'To give the treasure a good chance of being returned to the mermaid.'

'You don't really believe this is a mermaid's treasure, do you?' Suzy is looking with concern at Claire. 'You know there's no such thing?'

'You don't know that, Suzy,' Claire says. 'Just because you think you know everything about the sea and the beach. There are some things that can't always be explained.'

'Yes,' Suzy says. 'I know science has a lot yet to teach us about nature. But whether mermaids are real or not isn't one of those things.'

'What about that tail Eddie saw a little while ago?' Claire says defiantly. 'Frankie and Rob have both seen it too. The way they described it sounds exactly like a mermaid's tail to me.' She looks to me for backup.

'It could be, I suppose?' I reply carefully, keen to remain impartial. Suzy and Claire are both my friends – I don't want to side with one over the other. 'It did appear to be what you might imagine one would be like.'

Suzy shakes her head. 'Rob?' she asks. 'Surely you don't think it was a mermaid's tail you saw?'

Rob stares at Suzy with wide eyes, then he looks across at me and at Claire. He's now caught in the same quandary. Whatever he says, it's going to cause trouble.

'Do I think it was a mermaid we saw – no, probably not. But if you're asking me if it looked like a mermaid's tail might – then I'd have to say yes, it did,' he answers very diplomatically.

'You see?' Claire says. 'It's the mermaid's treasure. If we throw it back, she will grant us a wish.'

'All of us, or just one?' Eddie asks.

'If we all push it back, then I guess we are all worthy of a wish being granted,' I say, looking at the barrel again. 'Anyway, it looks pretty awkward to lift, so it will probably take all of us to get it up on the rocks. I say we give it a go.'

With difficulty, we all manage to hoist the barrel up to the top of one of the clusters of rocks that surround Morvoren Cove.

'Ready?' Robs asks as we all balance a little precariously on the rocks, with the waves splashing at our feet.

'Does everyone know what they are going to wish for?' I ask, looking at the others.

'Can I wish I don't have a little sister?' Mandy says, grinning. 'Hetty has been a pain in the arse recently. I wouldn't mind being an only child for a while!'

'Mandy, you must take this seriously,' Claire says with a stern face. 'It isn't a joke.'

Mandy nods. 'Sorry, Claire. I'll behave. So how are we going to do this, then? Do we all do it one at time, or all together?'

'We have to keep our wishes secret or they won't come true,' Claire says, wobbling a little on the rocks.

'Careful, Claire,' I tell her.

'We're not cutting a birthday cake,' Eddie says. 'Why do we have to keep them secret?'

'Guys!' Robs calls from below me, where he's taking the majority of the weight of the barrel with Eddie. 'Can we hurry up and do this, please, or I might be washed away like the maid was soon. This barrel is heavy!'

'Right, after three, then,' Mandy says. 'We all push the barrel and wish at the same time, and we all do it in secret. OK?' She looks at Claire.

Claire nods.

'Right, one, two, *three*!' Mandy shouts as we all brace ourselves.

With one mighty push, the barrel rolls over a little, then goes toppling back into the waves. While at the same time, standing on the rocks, we all close our eyes for a moment and make our own special wish.

'Now,' Claire says, as one by one we all open our eyes and stare into the waves at the barrel floating away. 'Let's make a wish all together.'

'For what?' Mandy asks.

'Let's wish ... No, let's *promise* each other that whatever happens in our futures that we'll always try to be friends.'

'Of course we will!' Suzy says brightly. 'Why wouldn't we be?'

'Please, can we just do it?' Claire asks again. 'I love you all so much, I want you in my life for ever.'

'If we're going to do it, we should do it sooner rather than later,' I say as a wave licks the toe of my trainer. 'Otherwise, I've a feeling we're going to get very wet in a moment or two.'

'Close your eyes again.' We all do as Claire says. 'Now make the wish in your heads.'

And right there, on Morvoren Cove, as the waves cover us in their salty spray, we make our promise to each other.

Ten

August 1994

Stunning.

That's how I always describe the view as I arrive back in St Felix via train. As it winds its way around the pretty Cornish coastline, I, along with all the other passengers, get my first glimpse across the sea of the little harbour town I still call home.

And that view, after all this time, still makes my heart leap with joy, especially now I spend most of my time in Glasgow. It's a warm summer's day and St Felix looks picture-postcard perfect as the bright sun shines over the town, highlighting its quaint beauty against a vivid azure sky.

As I alight from the train with the other passengers on this Wednesday lunchtime, I too carry my luggage along the platform, then up some steep steps towards the town.

But unlike most of the other passengers, I won't be staying in a rental cottage or a B&B. Tonight, I will be sleeping in the familiar surroundings of my old bedroom, in my old single bed, with posters of Bon Jovi, Michael J Fox and Rob Lowe looking down on me from the walls.

This is a journey I've made many times over the last few years, as I travelled back and forth from art college. In my first year, I lived in halls of residence, and I had no choice but to return home during the holidays. In fact, I was quite glad to come home and be spoilt by my mum for a few weeks. But last year I moved into a shared house with some of my student friends, so trips home became less frequent and worked around when I could get time off from my part-time job in the Sauchiehall Street branch of HMV.

Next month, in September, I will enter my last and most important year at college, but for now I'm home for a very special occasion.

After I've spent some time with my parents – and been fed to bursting by my mum – I unpack a few things in my room and decide to take a walk down into town.

'Will you be back for dinner, love?' my mum asks as I tell her I'm heading out for a while.

'You've just fed me enough food to last three days, Mum! You can't possibly expect me to think about dinner yet?'

'You know I worry about you up there in Scotland fending for yourself,' Mum says, looking genuinely concerned. 'I like to make sure you have plenty to eat when you come home.'

'I know,' I say gently. 'But I live in Glasgow city centre, Mum, not the remote Highlands. There are plenty of shops and markets. I do eat when I'm away from home, you know?'

Mum gives me a reproving look. 'Wait until you have children of your own, Frankie, then you'll understand. Talking of which . . . how's that nice boy you brought home at Easter?'

I roll my eyes. 'That nice boy is certainly not marriage material, if that's what you're thinking. And if you must know, Paul and I have broken up.'

'Oh, Frankie.' Mum pulls a disappointed face. 'Why? He seemed such a nice boy.'

'He was a nice boy, until I caught him cheating on me.'

'Oh.' Mum's expression is now one of concern. 'Are you absolutely sure?'

'Of course I'm sure. I found them in bed together at a party! I think that's proof enough!'

Mum nods. 'Fair enough, then.'

I'm about to turn and leave, but I can't help myself. 'Why did you ask if I was absolutely sure?'

'No reason.'

'*Mum?*'

Mum sighs. 'It's just you seem to use that excuse quite a lot when you break up with your boyfriends.'

'What do you mean *that excuse*?'

'That they've cheated on you.'

'Do I?'

Mum nods.

'Perhaps I'm just unlucky, then?' I say quickly. 'Look, I appreciate your concern, Mum, really I do, for both my feeding habits and my love life. But I can assure you I'm absolutely fine on both counts.'

Mum just nods in that way mums do when they think they know best but don't want to tell you so.

'I'll be back later. I said I'd meet up with Claire this afternoon and catch up on all her news before Saturday.'

'Ah, lovely. She must be so excited. Do you know Jonathan well? I've seen him about the town, but I don't know much about him and his family.'

'Not really.' I wonder why Mum is asking this. 'I met him at Easter when I was here. Why?'

'Oh, no reason. Now you get off and enjoy yourself.'

'Right ... OK, I'll call you if I think I might be late back. Is there still a phone box on the harbour?'

'Yes, but it's quite often out of order now. They really should get a more reliable one installed. What if people need to call someone while they're out?'

'They'll probably phase all phone boxes out if mobile phones take off,' I tell her. 'From the things I've read, they reckon we'll all be carrying them soon.'

'Nonsense,' Mum says. 'Who would want to carry one of those brick-like things around with them all day? It would be ridiculously heavy.'

I'm about to inform her that the yuppie-style phones she's referring to are already getting smaller and much more common, and it's not only city workers carrying them now either, but I know it's not worth it. Mum has never been one for technology.

'I think they have a public phone in the Merry Mermaid if you need to call us,' Mum suggests.

'Great. Is the pub still owned by the Matthews family?' I ask casually.

'Yes, Helen and Don still run it.'

'What about their son ... is he still at university in Cambridge?'

'You mean Rob?' Mum gives me a knowing look. 'I think he is. To be honest, I don't have much to do with Helen now she's not a member of the Women's Guild. Why don't you ask Claire; I think they kept in touch. He'll be at the wedding, won't he?'

'I have no idea.' I shrug innocently. 'Right, I'll be off. See you later.'

'Bye, love, have fun with Claire. Just like the old days, eh?'

'Perhaps,' I say to Mum. 'Or perhaps not,' I mutter under my breath as I leave the house.

How could we possibly have much in common any more? Claire is getting married, whereas I couldn't think of anything worse to be doing right now.

As I walk down the hill into town, I think about what Mum said about me using cheating as an excuse to break up with my boyfriends. I haven't exactly had a lot of relationships in my twenty years on this earth, and I *definitely* haven't had the experience I had six weeks ago with Paul before, but have I been cheated on that often?

I definitely ended relationships when I suspected a couple of my boyfriends of messing me around, but Paul was the first I actually caught doing it. But I certainly wasn't imagining the others, and, even if I was, why would I do that?

I wonder if the others are all going to be here on Saturday. It would be good to see everyone again. Even though we tried to keep in touch, it became more and more difficult after we all went our separate ways and left St Felix.

I walk along the familiar cobbles of Harbour Street, pausing outside the florist. I glance at my watch. I still have plenty of time before I'm due to meet up with Claire, so I open the door and the familiar sound of the bell rings above my head.

There seems to be no one in the shop as I enter, but then a little head pops up from behind the counter.

'Hello,' I say to a little girl with long dark hair, who looks familiar.

'Hi,' she replies shyly.

'Is Rose about today?' I ask as another head pops up next to the girl; this time it's a slightly older boy and I know

101

immediately who the children are: Poppy and William, Rose's grandchildren.

'She's on the phone out back,' the boy says. 'Can we help you?'

I smile. 'That's kind of you, but if it's all right with you I'll wait for Rose. I don't know if you remember me, but I used to work here. I remember the two of you coming to visit your grandmother for your holidays.'

'Yes, I remember you,' Poppy says. 'Your name is Frankie.'

'That's right, and you are Poppy and William.'

'I'm Will now,' the boy says with a serious expression.

'Sorry, Will it is. You've both grown a lot since I last saw you. You could barely see over the counter the last time I was here.'

'I'm nine now,' Poppy says.

'And I'm eleven,' Will says proudly. 'I'm going to secondary school in September.'

'Oh, how exciting,' I tell him. 'I hope you enjoy it.'

'Frankie!' Rose calls as she comes into the shop. 'How lovely to see you again!'

Rose hurries around to the front of the desk to give me a hug. 'I didn't know you were coming back; how long are you here for?'

'Just a few days. I'm back for my friend Claire's wedding.'

'Ah, yes. I'm doing the flowers. Of course you'd know Claire; she's about your age. Do you know Jonathan, her fiancé, too?'

'Not really, only Claire. We were best friends at school.'

Rose nods. 'That makes sense. Have you met Jonathan?'

'Only briefly.'

'And what did you think of him?'

I haven't really formed any opinion of Jonathan. He seemed

OK – a bit uptight maybe, not really my type at all – but Claire seemed to like him, and that was all that mattered.

'He seems like a good chap.'

'Good, then I'm sure he is.'

I'm slightly puzzled by Rose's comment, but I'm not sure why.

'I'm so pleased you're doing their flowers,' I tell her. 'I know you'll make a great job of them. I see you've got two new assistants helping you out in the shop.'

Rose looks proudly at her grandchildren. 'Yes, they're doing wonderfully. Almost as good as you were.' She winks at me.

'I bet they'll be even better in time.' I smile at Poppy and Will still looking up at me from behind the shop counter.

'Have you time for a cuppa?' Rose asks. 'I was just about to put the kettle on. I'd love to hear all your news.'

I glance at my watch again. 'Oh, I wish I had, but I'm supposed to be meeting Claire in a few minutes.'

Rose looks disappointed.

'How about I try to pop in another time while I'm here?' I suggest. 'Then we can have a good catch-up and a gossip?'

'I'd like that, Frankie. I'd like it a lot.' Rose pauses and looks me up and down. 'You're looking well. University really suits you.'

'It's art college, but thank you.'

'Yes, you're definitely finding your own style; I can see that. I'm pleased for you.'

'Thanks,' I reply, knowing that Rose means this as a compliment. My mother has long given up commenting on what I wear when I return home. Discussions about appropriate clothing for a young lady fall on deaf ears these days, and she knows it. 'Right, well, I'd better go. It was good to see you again, Rose, and you too, Poppy and Will.' I smile at them. 'Look after your Granny Rose, won't you?'

'I prefer Grandma,' Rose says, smiling. 'I'm not sure about looking after me, but they keep me young, that's for sure!'

I leave the shop and head down to the harbour. I'm due to meet Claire at the tea rooms on the harbour front and, as I approach, I see her already sitting at one of the outside tables.

'Frankie!' She waves at me. 'Over here!'

We greet each other with a hug.

'Oh, it's so good to see you again,' Claire says, sitting back down at the table. 'It feels like ages since I saw any of you guys.'

Claire is the only one of us mermaids who hasn't left St Felix for work or university or college. Instead, after her A levels, Claire took a job at the primary school in St Felix as a teaching support assistant. There, she met her first and only boyfriend, Jonathan, who is a teacher and now her fiancé too, and that's where she stayed.

'I was here at Easter,' I tell her. 'It's not been that long.'

'I know, but I didn't see you that much then. Besides, so much has happened since.' She places her hand carefully on her stomach.

'Oh my God, are you telling me you're pregnant?' I ask, staring at her.

'Shush, it's early days,' Claire says proudly. 'I barely knew at Easter, I only suspected. We've not even told our parents yet. We're telling them after the wedding.'

I stare at Claire. How can she be this happy? She's the same age as me, and yet she's getting married and expecting her first child – in my eyes that's the worst thing I could imagine happening to me right now. I have so much I want to do before settling down.

'I ... I'm pleased for you,' I say, trying to sound happy. 'That's amazing news.'

Claire smiles. 'I know you don't understand why I'm so happy about this. I'm sure my situation would be a complete disaster for you and all the other mermaids. But I love Jonathan, I can't wait to marry him on Saturday, and then in approximately six months have his baby.'

Claire looks so genuinely happy that I can't feel anything other than delighted for her.

'If you're happy, then so am I,' I tell her, smiling. 'Would I want to be doing what you are right now? Absolutely not. But if this is what you want, and I can see it is by the look on your face, then I wish you and Jonathan the very best of luck.'

'Thank you, Frankie. That means a lot. Really it does. Now, I want to hear all your news?'

A young boy waiting tables comes out and takes our order.

'I don't really have any news,' I say, trying to think of something to tell her.

'How's Paul?'

'Paul and I broke up.'

'Oh, I'm sorry to hear that. Jonathan and I thought he was great.'

'Yeah, well,' I reply. 'You know, it happens.'

'Anyone new on the scene?'

I shake my head. 'Nah, I think I'm done with men for a bit.' I stare out at the harbour at the fishing boats bobbing about on the waves.

Claire waits before speaking again. 'You know, Rob is coming to the wedding on Saturday?'

I look back at her across the table. 'Is he?' I try to sound unfazed by this news. 'That's nice.'

'He's not bringing anyone.'

'What do you mean?'

'Like a plus one.'

'Neither am I. So?'

'Nothing.' Claire shrugs and looks at the waiter bringing our drinks to the table. 'Thank you,' she says as he puts them down in front of us.

'Let me know if you want anything else, won't you?' he says, before he moves on to another table.

'What did you mean before?' I ask. 'Come on, Claire. I know you, remember?'

Claire sighs. 'Yes, you do. And I know you too, Frankie?' She raises her eyebrows at me.

'What?'

'It's just . . . it always seemed like such a shame that the two of you never got together, not properly, anyway.'

'That was a long time ago now,' I say with as much indifference as I can manage.

'Only five years,' Claire insists.

'A lot can change in five years, Claire. Besides, we were just kids then. He was simply a schoolgirl crush.'

She shrugs. 'Maybe. He's at Cambridge now, isn't he? Do you know what he's studying by any chance?'

'History and modern languages, I think?'

Claire smiles. 'That's very specific.'

'What is?'

'That you should know the exact degree he's taking.'

'*No* . . . ' I insist. 'I think my mum must have mentioned it, that's all.'

She nods in the same knowing way Mum did earlier.

'Claire, leave it,' I tell her. 'Just because you're about to get married and have a baby, it doesn't mean everyone has to be partnered up too. Don't turn into one of *those* people.'

'What people?'

'The ones who, once they're married, spend all their time trying to get everyone around them hooked up with someone. I'm happy as I am right now. I've got an important year coming up at college with my final show; the last thing I need is to be worrying about relationships. It will be nice to see Rob on Saturday, that's all, in the same way it will be great to see all the other mermaids. Who else is coming?'

'Mandy should be arriving tomorrow from London; she's not bringing anyone, either.'

'How is Mandy? Is she still working in the city?'

'Yes, I think she's doing quite well at her company.'

'I didn't expect anything less. Mandy was never one to mess about when she had something she wanted to do.'

'Er . . . ' Claire thinks. 'Eddie is arriving Friday; he *is* bringing someone.'

'Ooh, who?'

'New boyfriend, apparently. He met him in a bar in Newcastle.'

'He's still working with the theatre company, then?'

'I think so. He was pretty gutted when he didn't get into drama school, though.'

'Yeah, he was really down for a while. I was quite worried about him when we spoke on the phone. But he seems happy now. I think he gets to move around quite a lot when they're touring and stuff. Sounds fun seeing lots of different places.'

'Yeah.' Claire doesn't seem to share my enthusiasm. 'If you like that sort of thing.'

'What about Suzy?'

'She's going to try to get here – she has a gig on Friday night in Bath, but she's going to drive down straight afterwards.'

'I still can't believe that Suzy, out of all of us, is the one who ended up on stage,' I say, thinking about how Suzy changed after the night of the Enchantment Under the Sea dance. 'She was the one who wouldn't perform at that dance and made the costumes instead.'

'I know, she really blossomed after that girl encouraged her up on the stage to sing. What was her name again?'

'Marnie,' I say, annoyed I have to think about her once more. She didn't even come to our school in the end; we only ever saw her that evening. But in the course of one night, she not only ruined mine and Rob's blossoming relationship, but she changed Suzy's life for ever.

'That's it – Marnie. Yeah, she really had an impact on Suzy by getting her to sing that night. We never found out what she said to her, but thank goodness she did. Suzy was a changed person after that.'

'She sure was.'

It was a complete surprise that evening, back in 1989, when Suzy suddenly appeared on the stage to sing, first with Marnie, and then afterwards on her own. We already knew Suzy's voice was amazing, but to suddenly hear her perform in front of everyone that night was incredible, and that first performance at the Enchantment Under the Sea dance not only completely changed the direction her life took over the course of the next few years, but gave her so much belief in herself too. Whereas before Suzy only shared her views with us, afterwards she became much more confident in sharing them with others too.

I have no idea what Marnie said to her that night to get her up on the stage, or even how she knew about Suzy's voice, but she did Suzy a huge favour, one that was still paying dividends now.

'You know, she nearly got on *Stars in Their Eyes*?' Claire says.

'Did she? I didn't know that.'

'Yeah, she auditioned to be Sade, I think, but they went with someone else in the end.'

'Imagine one of us mermaids on television. That would have been amazing.'

'You'd have thought it would have been Eddie if it was going to be anyone.'

'Yes, Eddie was always the theatrical one.'

'I still am, darling!' A familiar voice behind me makes me turn around.

'Eddie!' I say as he approaches our table. 'Claire said you were coming Friday.'

'I was.' Eddie gives first me, then Claire, a hug. 'But Joe and I broke up, so I couldn't wait to get away for a few days.'

'Oh, Eddie, I'm sorry,' I tell him.

Eddie shrugs. ''Tis what it is,' he says matter-of-factly. 'Now, tell me all your news, and what's been going on? Then,' he looks excitedly at Claire, 'I want to hear all about the wedding – what you're wearing, who's coming, every little detail, darling!'

Eddie and I spend the next hour or so sitting with Claire listening to her talk with enthusiasm about her forthcoming wedding and catching up on all our news.

'Then we shall be each other's plus one,' Eddie says, taking my hand when I tell him about Paul. 'We definitely won't let each other down!'

'I've sat you all around the same table,' Claire says. 'So you can all have a good catch-up. I've called it the mermaid table. Well, in my head I have. It's actually table three on the plan.

I'm quite jealous of you all. I'll miss out on all the fun sitting at the top table.'

'Don't be silly, it's your wedding day – you'll have the best time.' I squeeze her hand. 'I'm sure nothing exciting will happen and we'll all just be chatting about old times.'

'Exactly!' Claire says. 'I miss that. I want to be a part of it again.'

'Couldn't we all meet up before the wedding?' Eddie asks. 'When is everyone else coming?'

'Mandy should be here Thursday evening,' Claire says. 'But Suzy isn't coming until late Friday, possibly Saturday morning, because she has a gig Friday night.'

'Ah, I see. And I guess you'll be wanting an early night on Friday?'

Claire nods.

'What about Rob?' Eddie asks, giving me a quick sideways glance.

'I think Friday,' Claire says. 'He wasn't too sure.'

'Do we still count him as one of the mermaids?' Eddie looks at me again.

'Why do you both keep looking at me when you mention Rob? He's nothing to do with me any more.'

'But he was, darling, for a while.'

'Briefly. *Very* briefly one summer, that's all. If he hadn't been a part of our Misfit Mermaids performance that night, no one would even be mentioning him now.'

Claire and Eddie exchange a glance.

'Look, as I was saying to Claire earlier, we were at school then. A lot has changed in the last five years. We've all moved on. We only went on a few dates, and after that summer his parents sent him to private school. We hardly saw him.'

'We did,' Claire insists. 'Sometimes at weekends, and in the holidays. He always made the effort to catch up with us, even if he was at another school.'

'Didn't do him much harm, did it?' Eddie says. 'Going to private school. He ended up at Cambridge University. I bet he's right hoity-toity now.'

Claire shakes her head. 'He's not. I've bumped into him a couple of times when he's been back visiting his parents. He's still Rob.'

Claire hadn't told me she'd seen him.

'If Rob wants to be a mermaid still, then he can be,' I say airily. 'It makes no difference to me.'

'Perhaps we should try to have a little get-together Friday night, then?' Eddie suggests. 'Nice and early so that Claire can get her beauty sleep. We'll have to catch up with Suzy at the wedding. How exciting.' He lifts his glass of juice in a toast. 'The mermaids all back together again. Just like the old days!'

Eleven

The next couple of days I spend chilling around St Felix.

The beautiful weather holds and I decide to do some sketching along the harbour and up in the cliffs. I'm overjoyed to find that the little hidden nook I loved so much as a teenager is still accessible, so I sit for a while on Friday afternoon partly sketching seabirds – mainly gulls and cormorants – and partly just gazing out at the never-ending seascape that always manages to calm yet energise me at the same time.

As I'm heading back to my parents' house down through the town, someone calls my name.

'Frankie! Hey, Frankie!'

I turn to see Mandy rushing towards me along the narrow street.

'I thought that was you!' she says, catching me up. 'How are you?'

We give each other a hug.

'I'm great, thanks. How are you?'

I haven't seen Mandy since she left school part way through sixth form. She became fed up with education and decided, against advice, that she was going to go to London and get a job – and that's exactly what she did. She took a very junior position in an up-and-coming tech firm, and over the last few years has been working her way up the corporate ladder. We tried to get together once when I was down in London on a college trip visiting the many art galleries, but Mandy came down with the flu so she had to cancel.

'Fabulous! Feels a bit weird being back here again.'

'Don't you come back to visit your mum and dad?'

'Yeah, not as often as I should, though. How about you?'

'I was last here at Easter.'

'Ooh, check you out, doing the right thing as usual.' Mandy smiles.

'And check you out,' I say, standing back to look her up and down. 'Little Miss Corporate. I like your hair like that. It suits you.'

Mandy's long, wavy dark hair is now cropped into a sharp pixie cut, and, unlike her schoolgirl attire that was always a bit too short and a bit too low cut, today she's wearing a pair of loose navy trousers, a crew-neck striped top and white plimsolls.

'Thank you,' Mandy says, putting her hand to the back of her head where her hair used to sit. 'I've only had it done recently, I'm not that used to it yet. I'm not that corporate, though, am I?' she asks, looking worried. 'I thought I'd toned it down for the seaside?'

'You look very chic,' I tell her. 'Unlike me!'

'But you're an art student.' Mandy grins. 'They're supposed to be a bit grungy and unwashed, aren't they?'

'Hey, less of the unwashed. You sound like my mother!'

Mandy laughs. 'Oh, it's good to see you again, Frankie. It's been too long!'

113

'Yes, it has. Where are you heading right now, back into town?'

'Yeah, I was just taking a wander, seeing if the old place has changed much. And I'm very pleased to report it hasn't!'

'Shall we walk back together?' I ask. 'Are you heading to your parents' house?'

'Sure am! It will be just like the old days – you can drop me back at my house before you carry on up to yours.'

We begin to walk side by side, back through the fishermen's houses down into the town.

'Are you coming to the pub tonight to catch up with everyone?' I ask as we pass yet another terraced house up for sale. I've noticed so many For Sale signs in the town on this visit.

'I am indeed. Seven o'clock, isn't it?'

'Yeah, so we don't keep Claire up too late before her big day.'

We give each other a knowing look.

'Bit young to get married, don't you think?' Mandy asks.

I nod. 'Yeah, but she seems happy.'

'She does. Were you surprised that Claire didn't ask us to be bridesmaids?'

'A bit, I suppose, but I don't really mind. Claire told me she'd had to ask Jonathan's sister and two of her nieces, and if she'd asked us she'd have had to ask all of us, not just one, and then she thought Eddie would feel left out.'

'That's true. I don't mind, either – dressing up like a meringue isn't really my scene these days, as you can probably tell.'

'*Four Weddings and a Funeral*,' I say, getting the meringue reference. 'Yes, you are very Fi-like from that movie.'

Mandy thinks about this. 'I suppose, and you would be . . .'

'Scarlett!' We both say this at the same time, thinking of the bohemian flatmate of Hugh Grant's character.

'I do dress a bit like her, I have to admit,' I say, shrugging. 'But when you're an art student, I feel you're obliged to dress a little quirky.'

'And you do it very well!' Mandy says. 'I didn't think I'd like that movie, but I did. It was really good.'

'Me too. I saw it at the cinema last week. It made me think of Claire while I was watching it. I wonder if the wedding tomorrow will be anything like those weddings?'

'Hopefully a bit less drama!'

'And a little less comedy!' I grin. 'I'm sure Claire doesn't want anyone forgetting the rings or the vicar messing up the ceremony. She's very excited about the whole thing.'

'So she should be. I only saw her very quickly this morning. I didn't arrive until late yesterday after I got the last train down from London, so I haven't had much time to catch up with anyone properly yet. The bonus is my sister is here for a few days too, so I get to catch up with her as well as my parents.'

'How is little Hetty?'

'Not so little any more. She's actually fallen for some local guy, so she's always back here now. His name is David and he was in the year above us at school, so you might not remember him. My parents are over the moon – at least they get to see one of their offspring regularly.'

'It's hard to keep coming back, isn't it? I mean, I love it here; it's still so beautiful. But Cornwall is such a long way from Glasgow, it's a really long journey for me to do regularly.'

'It's not too bad from London on the train, but it's not just the distance, we're all moving on with our lives. St Felix is our past, not our future. It feels like going backwards every time I'm here. Do you get that?'

'Not really. I mean, don't get me wrong, I have plans for my future – lots of them. But I don't think I'll ever stop returning to St Felix. Even if my parents moved away, I think I'd still visit. It sort of resets me when I spend time here. I feel energised, like I'm ready to tackle whatever comes next.'

'Nice. I wish I felt like that. It just makes me feel glad I left when I did.'

'Really?'

Mandy nods. ''Fraid so. When I look around here, I have lots of memories – some good, some bad. But I also have regrets too.'

'Like what?'

Mandy shrugs. 'It doesn't matter. Like I said, that's in the past. My life now is in London.'

We've reached the top of the close where Mandy's parents live. 'I guess I'll see you later, then,' I say, pausing.

'Sure will, I'm looking forward to catching up with everyone again. It will be like the old days.'

I nod and smile, then I carry on up the hill.

Why does everyone keep saying, 'It will be like the old days.' Will it? How can it be when we've all moved on with our lives? We may only be a few years older, but so much has changed.

Can it really ever be the same as it once was?

It turns out it can.

As close as is possible, anyway.

When we all meet up in the bar of the Merry Mermaid that night, to begin with the conversation is polite, and sometimes a tad stilted, as we all enquire how each other is and catch up on everyone's news.

It's just the four of us to begin with: me, Claire, Eddie and

Mandy. But around eight o'clock, Suzy surprises us by arriving early.

'My gig was cancelled due to a flooded toilet,' she explains. 'Sadly for the pub, the water escaped into the bar, so they had to close. After the call, I jumped straight in my car and drove as fast as I could get away with, all the way down here.'

Suzy looks so different now. She really has blossomed. Not only is she a taller, slimmer version of the Suzy I used to know, but now she simply oozes both elegance and confidence. Her dark curly hair is smoothed tightly back into a chic ponytail, and she wears a plain and simple outfit of a cream T-shirt, caramel-coloured jeans, and long brown suede boots. She immediately turned a few heads when she walked through the door, and I can imagine she has that same effect wherever she goes. But Suzy being Suzy, she doesn't appear to notice anything unusual, and even if she does, she doesn't show it.

'And guess who I bumped into outside the pub?' she says, her eyes shining. 'He wasn't sure he'd be welcome tonight at our mermaid reunion. But I assured him we'd all welcome him with open arms.' Suzy gestures towards the door and a tall young man appears, carrying some empty glasses from the tables outside.

'Rob!' Eddie says first. 'Why didn't you tell us you were already here? You could have joined us earlier.'

Rob smiles. 'Let me just put these on the bar,' he says, lifting some glasses. 'Then I'll be with you. The pub is really busy tonight, so I've just been helping out for a bit.'

I'm suddenly aware that the four joyful faces around the table are all turned towards me.

'What?' I ask. 'It's only Rob.'

'How are you all?' Rob comes over to our table. 'It's good to see you again.'

A part of me thinks Rob hasn't changed a bit since we were at school, and a part of me thinks he looks very different.

Like Suzy, he's a little taller, and he's definitely 'filled out'. His slight frame is now more muscular and broad underneath his white T-shirt, and I can see a shadow across his face where he clearly has to shave away a dark beard. But his hair is still the same – the warm sandy colour I remember admiring so much at school, and his eyes are of course the same deep shade of chocolate brown. And, I'm pleased to see, still look kind and gentle as he casts his gaze around the table at us all. His eyes rest upon me.

'Hello, Frankie,' he says quietly. 'It's been a while.'

'Yes,' I reply, not liking how my stomach is reacting to this interaction one bit – it seems to think now is a good time to take up internal gymnastics once more. 'It has been. Are you well?' I hear a polite voice enquiring, making me sound like I'm in a Jane Austen novel.

Rob smiles. 'Yes, very well, and you?'

'Yep, I'm great, thanks.'

There's silence while we make this short exchange.

'Rob, come and sit down.' Mandy gestures to an empty chair next to her. 'Are you happy perching on that stool, Suzy?'

'Let me get a round of drinks in first,' Rob says. 'On the house!'

Once Rob has got us all a drink, we settle around the table.

There's a quick update on what everyone has been up to for those who have arrived late. Then it's not long before the formalities end and we all fall into our past roles once more.

'I still can't believe one of us is getting married,' Suzy says, looking at Claire. 'I still feel like I did when I was fifteen.'

'You don't look much like you did back then,' Claire says, once again deflecting talk about her wedding. I get the feeling she doesn't want to seem different to the rest of us this evening. 'You look amazing! Being a singer obviously suits you.'

'Thank you, kind friend,' Suzy says. 'But I'm not sure I'll be doing it much longer.'

'Why?' I ask 'You're so good. What's changed?'

'I have. It's time I started making a difference – using my voice for something other than singing.'

'What are you going to do?' Rob asks.

'I've been offered a job working for Tony Blair,' she says quietly.

'The politician?' Eddie asks.

'The new leader of the Labour Party – yes. It's only a very junior position. But I hope it might be the start of a career in politics.'

'Wow, politics is a bit different to singing,' I say. 'But that's what you said you always wanted to do – make a difference.'

Suzy nods.

'They think he might be the new prime minister, don't they?' Mandy says. 'I've got a mate who works at the Houses of Parliament. They reckon he's a shoo-in if he plays it right at the next election.'

'That's a while away yet,' Suzy says. 'But that's the plan, I've been told. It's a very exciting prospect.'

'Gosh, you're all doing so much with your lives, while I'm still at art college,' I say. 'I feel a bit left behind.'

'I'm still at uni too,' Rob says, holding up his hand.

'Even you're at Cambridge University.'

'But you're at the Glasgow School of Art,' Rob says. 'Home

119

of the famous Charles Rennie Mackintosh. I heard it's a pretty big deal in the world of art colleges.'

I'm surprised he knows which college I'm at. I only talked tonight about being based in Glasgow.

'Some say,' I reply bashfully. 'I like it there.'

'I'm hardly flying high in the world of business.' Mandy grimaces. 'You should see where I live. My block of flats is pretty grim.'

'Travelling the country with a small theatre company isn't exactly glamorous,' Eddie admits. 'We stay in some dreadful digs. But it's fun most of the time.'

'And none of you think I should be getting married tomorrow,' Claire pipes up. 'I know you all think I'm far too young to be settling down – so I think that trumps all of you!'

There's a chorus of 'No' and 'Of course we don't think that!' around the table.

'Come on.' Claire is shaking her head. 'Just be honest. I know Frankie thinks I'm too young – she told me so the other day.'

I feel my cheeks flush red as the others look at me. 'No, I said I wouldn't want to be doing it. But it's clearly making you very happy – and that's what matters, not what I think.'

Mandy nods. 'Exactly. It wouldn't be for everyone. But then we're all different. We may have been friends at school, but our lives are clearly all taking very unique paths right now. Claire, your wedding has given us a reason to meet up again. If it hadn't been for you, we wouldn't be here now.'

There's silence around the table as it dawns on all of us that this might never happen again. What reason would we all have to meet up again like this in the future?

'Then we should enjoy what time we have together both

this evening and tomorrow!' Eddie says, raising his glass. 'In case it's our last time!'

'No, don't say that, Eddie,' Claire says forlornly. 'I like to think we'll always have a reason to get together again in the future. Maybe not as often as we'd like, but we should at least try.'

'She's right,' Suzy says. 'I'd hate to think I'd lose touch with any of you. If only there was some way we could keep in touch without having to physically meet up. That would be great.'

'The company I work for thinks within ten years or so everyone will have access to the internet,' Mandy says. 'You've heard of the internet, right?'

Rob nods. But the rest of us look blank.

'It's a new thing that's going to work through computers,' Rob says. 'I have a mate at uni who's into all this tech stuff. There's going to be all sorts of pages you can look at and get information and stuff – like a massive great encyclopaedia.'

'It's to be called the World Wide Web,' Mandy explains. 'It's going to be huge. It will launch officially later this year. But it's already there if you know where to find it.'

'It all sounds a bit like *War Games*,' I say. 'You know that movie with Matthew Broderick we all rented from the video shop one Saturday night, and you all came round to my house to watch it because my parents were away.'

'Oh, yeah, about the guy that hacks into the Pentagon's computer and nearly starts World War Three?' Claire says. 'I liked that one.'

'You liked Matthew Broderick, you mean,' I say, teasing her. 'You got your brother to rent *Ferris Bueller's Day Off* after that, and you insisted we all watched it at your house.'

'We didn't all have posters of rock stars on our wall when we were teenagers,' Claire good-naturedly reminds me. 'Anyway, I don't remember any of you complaining too much? Especially Eddie – he made us play it again that night, if I remember rightly.'

Eddie nods. 'I did. Matthew Broderick was very cute – still is, actually. But I thought that first movie was about a computer that developed its own personality and messed with its owner's life?'

'No, that was *Electric Dreams*,' Rob says. 'I remember my older sisters renting that one and letting me watch it with them.'

'*Anyway*,' Mandy says, shaking her head. 'When you've all finished your trip down memory lane ... ' She smiles. 'The internet is what will let us keep in touch with each other in the future. There's going to be something called email, where you can write and then send the equivalent of letters, but on a computer instead.'

'But that would mean everyone having a computer,' Eddie says. 'They'll have to be a lot cheaper than they are now for that to happen.'

'The people at my company seem to think they will be,' Mandy assures us.

'How do you know all this?' I ask. 'It sounds like a lot of it is classified information?'

'Maybe Mandy is this decade's Matthew Broderick?' Rob says, grinning. 'Just don't start World War Three, will you?'

Mandy grimaces. 'Funny! No, I've just listened and read a lot since I've been in this job. You learn a lot of interesting stuff that way. Not only do they think everyone will have a computer, they reckon within fifteen to twenty years we'll all be carrying phones that can do virtually the same thing as computers too.'

'Will we all be riding hoverboards as well?' Eddie asks. 'Like in the second *Back to the Future* film – another of our video rentals! And will we be talking to each other over screens like Marty McFly did?'

'It's a definite possibility,' Mandy says.

'I'll believe it when I see it,' Eddie concedes. 'Well, guys, if that's the case we won't have to worry about meeting up, it seems we'll be able to do it all remotely.'

'But until then,' Suzy says, 'we should try to make an effort to keep in touch with each other. Even if it's just the occasional phone call or letter.'

'Yes, let's toast to that,' I say and we all raise our glasses. 'To keeping in touch with each other for a long time to come!'

'And to making sure it doesn't take one of us to get married for the Misfit Mermaids to remain friends,' Claire adds before we can take a drink.

'To friendship!' Rob says, and as we all take a long drink from our glasses. I can't help but notice his gaze remains steadily upon me.

As we leave the pub that night, we're all in high spirits.

Claire reluctantly left us earlier in the evening. Sensible as always, she knew a late night in the local pub was not the best way to prepare for your wedding the next day.

The rest of us all stayed on until closing time, reminiscing about old times and passing on any gossip we knew from our various siblings or parents about people we used to know.

We realise we've fallen into our old habit of walking everyone to their house one by one. As we say goodnight, we're all looking forward to another day spent with our fellow mermaids, both at Claire's wedding in the afternoon, and afterwards at her reception at a hotel in St Felix.

Without Claire in our posse, after we say goodnight to Mandy, it's just me and Rob.

'That was a fun night,' Rob says as we walk up the hill together. 'Great to see everyone again.'

'Yes, it was. I'm so glad Claire could make it. She'd have been gutted if she'd missed out.'

'Do you really think she's too young to be getting married?' Rob asks.

'Yes, I suppose so. But she's happy and that's all that matters, isn't it? Not what we think.'

'Indeed. You've met Jonathan, haven't you?'

'Yeah, at Easter. He seems like a nice guy, and you can tell he loves Claire.'

'Can you? How?'

I hadn't expected this question, so I'm momentarily caught off guard.

'Er ... you just can. He can't keep his eyes off her for one thing, and she seems so happy when he's around. Like he makes everything complete for her. It's quite lovely to witness actually.'

There's a moment of silence before Rob says, 'Good, then I'm pleased for her.'

'Me too.' I pause for a moment. 'Why did you ask that?'

'I just wondered, that's all. So, is there a budding Mr Right in your life yet?' Rob asks, and I feel like he's changing the subject.

'No, not right now. What about you?'

'No Mr Right.' Rob grins.

'You know what I mean.'

'I broke up with my last girlfriend a few months ago. I quite like being single right now, to be honest. I've got a lot on this last year of uni, with exams and my dissertation.'

'Me too. We have a big final show of our artwork that's quite a large percentage of our final grade. Not really any time for relationships. Right, this is me.' We've arrived at the top of our road.

'I do remember,' Rob says, glancing down the street. 'I remember a lot of things from back then.'

'Good times,' I reply quickly. 'Happy memories.'

'Very happy . . . It's been really good to see you again tonight, Frankie. Really good.'

Rob looks into my eyes, and I'm shocked at how I feel when he does.

'So . . . I guess I'll see you tomorrow, then, at the wedding?' Rob says when I don't speak.

'Uh-huh . . . ' I whisper, as I just about manage to take control of my voice once more. 'I'll be there.'

I stand awkwardly on the pavement, not really knowing what to do. How is Rob having this effect on me again, after all these years?

Pull yourself together, Frankie! 'Goodnight, Rob.' I manage to say in a voice that sounds vaguely normal.

'See you tomorrow, Frankie.' Rob winks.

I manage to reclaim control of my legs now, and I begin to walk down the road towards my old house – a small part of me feeling like I don't really belong here any more, but, quite unexpectedly, a much larger part of me feeling like I'm fifteen again, and I've never been away . . .

Twelve

The next morning, I have a bit of a lie in. And as I snuggle under the duvet of my single bed, with Jon Bon Jovi looking down at me from the wall, I think about the previous evening.

Our little get-together was a lot of fun, and it was great to catch up with everyone again. Although I was used to seeing Claire when I came home to visit, for lots of reasons – but not for a want of trying – I hadn't seen the other mermaids in a long time.

And I hadn't seen Rob in about three years, I decide, as I try to remember our last encounter. I think it was probably in our first year of sixth form, when Rob had been home from his private school for the holidays and we bumped into each other on the beach one day when I was early meeting Claire and Suzy.

It was a little awkward, as it often was after the night of the school dance. Neither of us ever spoke about what happened that night; our 'relationship', if you could even call it that, simply faded away, and we were both happy to keep it that way. At least, that's how it seemed.

Rob would still, occasionally, hang around with us when he

was home from school, but as our little gang slowly thinned out with the departure of Mandy to London, then Suzy to follow her singing career, followed by Eddie and then myself after our A levels, our encounters became fewer and far between, until they never seemed to happen at all.

I thought about Rob more often than I cared to admit, and wondered how he was getting on. As casually as I could, I would try to get information about him from Mum or Claire when I was back in St Felix. But really Rob was just my teenage crush from school, who I was lucky enough to be with for a few fun days one summer, until he messed everything up at the dance with that girl.

However, if it wasn't for Marnie, Suzy might never have had the confidence to showcase her voice. We all knew she could sing, but she never had the confidence to share her talent with anyone else. Now, it seemed, the confidence she gained from performing was about to get her foot in the door of her dream career.

I envied her.

Although I got into art college and I loved being in Glasgow, I still have no idea what I'm going to do when I graduate next year. Being a professional artist, as many of us on the course already acknowledged, was a dream that was incredibly hard to achieve.

'It's all right for you,' I murmur, looking up at the poster of Jon Bon Jovi. 'I bet you always wanted to be in a band. I bet you never had any of these problems, and I bet you never had a patchy love life, either?' I grin at the poster silently smiling back at me. 'No, of course you didn't. Just look at you!'

Eventually I get up and grab a cup of coffee and a piece of toast from the kitchen. Mum and Dad have gone to do their weekly big shop at the local supermarket so I have the house to myself.

I work out roughly how long it will take me to get ready to be on time for Claire's wedding at three o'clock. I need to shower, wash my hair, blow-dry my hair – I hate blow-drying my hair as it takes ages to dry, but it will have to be done today – then I need to do my make-up and actually get to the church.

I decide I've got just enough time to take a walk to freshen up both my mind and body after last night. In comparison to some of my student nights out, last night was fairly tame alcohol-wise, but I still want to look and feel my best for the wedding later, and a blast of fresh sea air will be just the job to blow away any alcohol-induced cobwebs.

I pull on some jeans, an old T-shirt and my burgundy Doc Marten boots, which I virtually live in at uni. I pull my unwashed hair back into a loose ponytail, then I wrap a checkered shirt around my waist in case the sunshine through the window is a decoy, and, as so often happens in St Felix, the wind is blowing in off the sea and it's actually quite chilly – even in August.

I lock up the house, then walk down the hill into town.

St Felix, as is inevitable on a sunny Saturday in August, is filled to the brim with holidaymakers as I wind my way through the town. In their hands they carry a mixture of buckets and spades, bags filled with pasties, and melting ice-creams. It's quite the art getting through them without getting ice cream in my hair or Cornish pasty in my face as they dawdle around on 'Tourist Time' or 'Holiday Hours' as we locals call it – i.e. slowly with all the time in the world.

I wonder if they've discovered my little hideout yet? I head up to my favourite place tucked high up in the rocks. When I was there yesterday it was late in the day; now it's lunchtime – peak time for someone looking for somewhere quiet to sit and eat their lunch.

As I begin to climb the path, my heart sinks as I see a couple sitting high up on the side of the cliff-face in the spot I cherish so much.

But as I get nearer, they rise, and begin to climb back down the hill together hand in hand, helping each other as they descend the rocky ground.

I pause and wait for them to reach the much easier and smoother route of the little tarmac path I've just come along. While I'm doing so, I pull my shirt from around my waist and pop it over my T-shirt. Although it's not cold, I can already feel the wind blowing in off the sea, and I know it will only get stronger as I get further around the side of the hill. The couple smile as they pass me, and I'm just about to continue my climb when I notice someone else hurrying to take their place.

No! I groan internally, watching them. I only wanted to sit up there for a while and breathe in the air to clear my head.

But then I notice the figure climbing towards my favourite spot is a familiar one. I squint behind my sunglasses to try to see more clearly.

Yes, if I'm not mistaken, that's Rob clambering up the grass towards the little viewing area.

I stand for a moment wondering what to do. If I go up there now, will he think I'm following him?

No, don't be daft, I tell myself. *Why would he think that?*

But do I really want to sit up there with Rob, making polite conversation? After all, this was the place we came to on our first date.

While I'm thinking about this, Rob sits down. Now that his back isn't to me, he's spotted me just as easily as I saw him.

He waves, and the choice is made for me.

'Hey,' I say as I catch up with him. 'Fancy seeing you here.'

'You still remember, then?' he says, and I wonder if he's referring to our date. 'I mean, you still come up here when you're home?'

'It's one of my favourite spots in St Felix.' I sit down next to him on the little ledge. 'But I fear a few more people are finding it now.'

'Sorry,' Rob says. 'Do you want some peace? Shall I go?'

'No, I don't mean you,' I reply hurriedly. 'I mean, there's quite often someone up here now – especially in the peak summer months.'

'Ah, right. Yeah, I think it's since they tarmacked the path around the hill; it makes it easier to get up here. The more people that come, the more people who notice our little spot.'

I notice he says 'our little spot', and again I wonder if he's referring to the fact we came here on our date, or simply – and more likely – that we both enjoy sitting here.

'The tarmac does make it easier to get up here, but the climb around the edge is still challenging – as long as they don't put a path around there, we'll be fine.'

'How's your head after last night?' Rob asks.

'Not too bad, thanks. What about you?'

Rob shrugs. 'I've had heavier nights.'

'Me too. University teaches you many things – and how to handle large amounts of alcohol is one of them!'

'Absolutely. How's your course going?'

'Good, thanks. I have my final exhibition and degree show at the end of next year. What I'll do after that, I don't know.'

'Me neither. It's been a great course, but what it will lead to I'm not sure.'

'You've enjoyed it, though?'

'Oh, yes. Actually, the thing I've enjoyed the most has been the social side of uni – I recently joined the Footlights and I've really enjoyed being a part of that.'

'What's the Footlights?'

'It's like an amateur dramatics society – they mainly do comedy sketches and stuff like that.'

I look at Rob.

'What's that look for?' he asks, smiling at me.

'I just never saw you doing am-dram, that's all.' I grin. 'When we were at school, you were really worried about being on stage with us that time, and back then you were into your rock music and your guitar.'

'I can do both, can't I?' Rob says, still smiling.

'Do you still play?'

'Of course. Not as much as I'd like, but I still have my guitar with me at uni – except it's an electric one now, which I have to play with headphones plugged in or I get complaints from my housemates.'

'Fair enough.'

'And you've clearly not noticed my T-shirt.' Rob sits back so I can see the emblem on his black T-shirt a little better. It's a yellow smiling face with its tongue sticking out.

'Nirvana,' I say knowingly.

'It is indeed.'

I open up my shirt and show him my T-shirt.

'Ha ha! Great minds!' Rob says, seeing my own T-shirt with the same emblem, but in black on a white shirt. 'Things don't change that much, then?'

'Look at me.' I gesture to my clothes. 'Do I look like I've grown out of being a rock chick?'

'Bit more grunge in there now, though.' Rob grins, looking me up and down. 'Mixed with a tad more art student.'

'I'm going to take that as a compliment,' I say. 'I'm never going to be elegantly strutting my stuff down the catwalk in a designer dress like Cindy Crawford now, am I?'

'Do you want to be?' Rob tilts his head a little. 'I've always liked the fact you're you, and you don't try to be anyone else.'

My cheeks pink a little at his compliment.

'Thanks,' I murmur, feeling suddenly embarrassed. 'And I like the fact you can be rocking out on your electric guitar one minute and prancing around on a stage the next.'

'I don't do much prancing.' Rob winks. 'But I'll let you off.'

We stare at each other, and for a brief moment it feels like we've never left this spot, this town or each other.

There's a splashing sound in the waves below, but we don't turn to look at it. We still only have eyes for the person opposite.

The splashing sound intensifies and we both turn to look down into the sea below us.

'Did you see that?' Rob says, staring hard into the waves, which are now rhythmically rolling into Morvoren Cove again as if nothing has happened. 'It looked a bit like . . . you know . . . Do you even remember?'

'Of course I remember.' I turn my gaze back from the sea to look at him. 'Like you, I remember *everything* from back then. It looks like it might have returned.'

'Or . . . ' Rob says slowly, looking into my eyes once more. 'Perhaps it never went away . . . '

And I'm pretty sure neither of us are talking about the splashing in the waves any more.

132

Thirteen

Claire looks so pretty as she walks down the aisle of St Nicholas, the tiny, but quaint little church in St Felix, that I feel quite emotional.

Her dress is pure white silk, has a fitted bodice, long leg-of-mutton sleeves and a voluptuous full skirt with layers of tulle underneath to push it out even further. On her head she wears a delicate ring of flowers framing her face, and her light auburn hair is pinned up at the sides and styled in loose ringlets. Her huge bouquet of flowers only makes her tiny frame seem even smaller as she walks on the arm of her father, beaming happily at all her guests.

The pews both sides of the aisle are packed full of Claire and Jonathan's friends and family, and it's halfway down on one side of the church that the mermaids sit squashed together on one of the wooden pews.

'Oh my,' I hear Suzy say as Claire walks past us on the arm of her father. 'She looks beautiful.'

I turn to look at Suzy, who is a couple of seats away from me, and I see she's hurriedly searching for tissues in her bag. Eddie next to her reaches into his jacket pocket and gives her a small pack after taking one for himself, and Suzy smiles gratefully at him.

Mandy, sitting between me and Eddie, glances at them, then she turns to me looking equally as moved. 'Can you believe one of us is getting married?' she whispers.

I shake my head, then I turn to my right and smile at Rob, who's sitting on the other side of me.

Rob is one of the reasons we're so squashed up.

He came into the church later than the rest of us and there weren't many seats left. Mandy waved him over and we all shuffled along the pew as much as we could to fit him on at the end. He had to put up with a few Hugh-Grant-based, *Four Weddings and a Funeral* jibes about him arriving late.

I've never seen Rob look quite as smart as he does today. He's wearing a navy-blue suit with a waistcoat, a white shirt and a blue paisley tie. Quite different to how he looked this morning up on the rocks overlooking Morvoren Cove.

But then I guess I look a fair bit different too.

I'm wearing a three-quarter-length, sleeveless purple silk dress, a bargain I found in a vintage shop in Glasgow. I've teamed it with long beaded earrings and a matching choker necklace I bought from a craft market, and around my shoulders I have a colourful silk pashmina that I borrowed at the last minute from my mum. On my feet I wear purple silk slingbacks – again a second-hand find, this time from a charity shop near my college. And even though I spent ages blow-drying my long hair, in the end I chose to pin it up loosely on top of my head with a few loose strands framing my face.

When Rob wedged himself in next to me, he was quick to tell me I looked beautiful, and I was equally complimentary about his own outfit.

The service seems to fly by; we sing hymns and listen to Claire and Jonathan exchange their vows. Just before they go off to sign the register, we're surprised when Suzy stands up and excuses herself. But as Claire and Jonathan disappear to the back of the church, we realise why. Suzy appears in front of the pulpit and proceeds to sing the most beautiful rendition of 'Ave Maria', while the whole of the church sits spellbound.

By the end, we're all reaching for Eddie's packet of tissues. Rob, who has a little more room now Suzy has gone, turns to me and I see he too has misty eyes.

'How amazing is our Suzy?' Rob says, blinking hard.

'Incredible.' I dab at my face to mop up the tears. 'I knew she could sing, but that was something else.'

Claire and Jonathan walk back down the aisle a married couple, and we all follow them outside into the fresh air again. The warm, dry weather has held for the wedding and their photos are taken in the most beautiful bright light, that makes everything, and everyone, look perfect. We all mill about outside the church, waiting for the moment we're dismissed and can head off to the reception.

'My mermaids!' I hear Claire call after the photos seem to have gone on for ever.

'Er ... can I have the *mermaids*?' the photographer asks hesitantly.

We gather, some of us a little reluctantly, in front of the church around Claire and Jonathan, and have a couple of photographs taken.

'Now just the bride and her friends,' the photographer says, and Jonathan steps aside to talk to a group of his own mates. 'Can you all squeeze a little closer together, please? That's it, arms around each other.'

As we move closer to Claire, I feel Rob's hand around my waist as we pose for the photograph. Then, as we all smile for the camera, I feel his fingers delicately caress my side with the gentlest of movements – and I'm pretty sure as the photographer clicks the shutter, that this photograph will capture the biggest smile I've ever had in front of a camera.

The reception is held in one of the larger hotels in St Felix, one that sits high up on the hill as you exit the town.

As Claire promised, we all sit together at one big table for a three-course meal, with a couple of Jonathan's cousins and their partners, then, after the speeches, we gather in the hotel bar while the main reception room is prepared for the evening, when there will be a disco and a private bar, and yet more guests arriving.

'It's been a good day,' Mandy says contentedly as we relax on a couple of sofas. 'Better than I thought it might be.'

'Why do you say that?' I ask. 'Didn't you think you'd have a good time?'

'It's not that. I just thought it might be weird being back here again with all of you. I know Claire has never left and you visit all the time, Frankie, but I hardly ever come home now. Like I said to you, I should, but I don't.'

'I have no reason to come back any more,' Eddie says. 'Now my mum has remarried and moved away, other than Claire I have no ties here.'

'How is your mum?' I ask. We all knew Eddie's mum well when we were teenagers. She was extremely protective of Eddie, and therefore protective of his friends too.

'She's really happy, thanks. Colin has been so good for her. She loves living in Brighton with him now. It's weird, though, knowing my house is still there, but that someone else is living in it.'

'My parents are going to be selling up soon too,' Suzy announces. 'The real-estate market here has boomed recently – they've decided to cash in on people wanting holiday homes in St Felix.'

'I've noticed a lot more For Sale and Sold signs around the town on this visit,' I say. 'I don't blame your parents at all for selling up if the market is good, but how do you feel about it?'

Suzy shrugs. 'A little sad, I suppose. But I didn't really live here as long as some of you did when I was growing up, so it's not quite such a tug on the heartstrings.'

'I guess it will all come to us eventually,' Rob says. 'Mum and Dad are happy in the pub at the moment, but I guess they won't run it for ever.'

'Why are you all looking so sad?' Claire is walking towards us. 'This is supposed to be a happy occasion!'

'We're not sad, beautiful,' Eddie says, taking her hand and giving it a little squeeze as she joins the group. 'We're just talking about people moving away – our parents specifically. Do you want to sit down for a bit and take the weight off your feet?'

'Yes, please,' Claire says gratefully. 'These shoes are killing me.'

'Here, take my seat.' Rob stands up. 'I'll perch here.' He sits down on the arm of the sofa next to me, and I can't help notice a few wry smiles and raised eyebrows. But I pretend not to notice.

'Thanks, Rob.' Claire adjusts the many layers of tulle under her dress as she sits down. 'Ah, I can relax for a bit here with you guys. I feel like I've been on show all day.'

'Jonathan seems like a good guy,' Rob says. 'I spoke to him for a bit earlier.'

'Yes, he is. He's lovely. I'm very lucky.'

'No, *he's* the lucky one,' Rob says, smiling at her.

'You're very sweet, Rob, thank you.'

'This must have all cost a pretty penny,' Mandy says, looking around her. 'Is Jonathan loaded or something?'

'Mandy!' I exclaim while the others laugh.

'His parents did pay for much of our wedding,' Claire says, not seeming to mind. 'And my parents helped out with a few things too. There's no way we could have afforded all this without them. We've just bought a little house up the road, so our mortgage is huge with the prices in St Felix now.'

'I didn't know you'd bought a house,' I say. 'You never said.'

'Yes, we're moving in after the wedding – Jonathan's parents are quite traditional.'

'You don't live together yet, then?' Mandy asks in surprise.

'No,' Claire says, beginning to look a little uncomfortable.

'But how do you know if you'll get along?' Mandy continues. 'You have actually done the deed, Claire, haven't you? I mean you're not going into this without road-testing his equipment?'

We all laugh and Claire flushes. 'Yes, of course,' she whispers, looking around her in case anyone has heard. 'And I'm pleased to say he passed his MOT with flying colours!'

'Good,' Mandy says surprisingly seriously, while the rest of us are still smiling at this exchange. 'Cos, you never know what you'll find out until you do.'

We all look at Mandy, waiting for her to continue, but she doesn't.

'Right, is that bar open again yet?' she says instead, looking across at the bar. 'I could do with another drink.'

'Yes,' Claire says. 'It never actually closed.'

'Then what are we waiting for?' Mandy stands up. 'I'll get the drinks in.'

'Do you want a hand?' Eddie asks. 'I'll be asleep soon if this room gets any warmer.'

Mandy and Eddie take our orders and head off to the bar.

'Mandy's right, it is pretty warm in here.' Rob takes off his jacket, 'I might get some fresh air – anyone?' He looks at Claire and Suzy first before his gaze falls on me.

Claire and Suzy stare at me with such force it feels like they're actually pushing me with their eyes. 'I'm fine, thanks, Rob,' Suzy says. 'Claire?'

'No, I'd better go mingle again,' Claire replies, standing up. 'I'm sure Frankie will go with you, though.' She smiles deliberately at me.

'Yes, all right,' I say, trying to look with annoyance at them both, but in a way that Rob can't see. 'Why not?'

Rob and I make our way outside through some French windows onto a large terrace which has seats, tables and sun loungers on it. From our position high up on the hill we can still see the sea and the coastline a little way in the distance.

'Do you want to walk around the gardens or have a seat?' Rob asks.

I look around. There's quite a few people milling around outside, mostly chatting in small groups. A tall, elegant woman wearing a bright sea-green dress and razor-sharp black stilettos watches us with interest while she sits at a table smoking a cigarette. I noticed her in the church earlier – then she'd been wearing a huge black hat that looked like a flying saucer perched on the side of her head.

'A walk would be good, I think. Too many people out here.'

We take a slow meander around the large gardens that surround the hotel. Everywhere we go is lit by tiny little lights set into the paths and borders.

'Did you think when we were fifteen that we'd all be back here again when we were twenty for someone's wedding?' Rob asks as we walk.

'I never really thought about it,' I reply honestly. 'Too many other things on my mind when I was fifteen.'

'Like what?'

'Oh, I dunno, my hair, my skin, my schoolwork – fitting in, you know?'

'I don't think any of us ever really fitted in, did we? That's why you christened yourselves the Misfit Mermaids.'

'*You* christened us the Misfit Mermaids, if I remember rightly.'

'Did I?'

'Yeah, when you wanted to join us on stage that time?'

'I don't remember giving you the title, though.' Rob stops walking, so I do too.

'You did. Don't you remember it was after our first date, when we were walking back to my house?'

Rob doesn't say anything. He simply turns towards me.

'Of course I remember, Frankie,' he says in a low voice. 'How could I ever forget that night.' He reaches out his hand and his fingers gently tuck a stray piece of my hair behind my ear.

'Just like in the movies,' I joke, feeling unsettled by his closeness.

'What is?' he asks, still in the same hushed voice.

'They always do that hair thing in films before . . . '

'Before?'

140

I shrug.

'Before they kiss?' he asks.

I nod.

Rob leans in towards me and as I feel his lips on mine for the first time in five years I don't resist. But unlike when we were two school kids having their first nervous dalliance with the opposite sex, we're both older now. We're both more experienced.

Rob's arms move around my waist, and I allow him to pull me closer, so I'm now pressing up against his firm torso.

'You look amazing tonight,' Rob murmurs, beginning to kiss my neck now. 'Incredibly sexy too. Quite unlike I've ever seen you before. Why do you hide your beauty, when you can look this good?'

'What do you mean?' I ask, my brain only just managing to override the intense feelings stirring inside my body right now. I pull back just a tad so I can look up at him. 'What do you mean, why do I hide my beauty?'

'Nothing,' Rob says, obviously keen to continue more physical rather than verbal explorations.

But I don't budge.

'I just mean you look utterly gorgeous today, and I'm not the only man who's noticed. You must have seen all the looks you've been getting?'

'No, not really.' That's not exactly true. I did notice I was getting a little more attention from the opposite sex than I usually did. 'I'm more interested in why you think I should dress like this all the time, though. What's wrong with how I usually dress?'

'Nothing, nothing at all.'

I stare hard at Rob.

'What do you want me to say?' he says, letting go of me. 'You must know you look better like this. More ... feminine.'

'Feminine – really?'

'What's wrong with feminine?'

'Nothing's wrong with feminine – but women shouldn't be forced to dress a certain way if they don't feel comfortable like that.'

'No one is forcing you – I just said you looked great in a dress. When did that become an insult?'

'It's not. But I don't want to be a stereotype.'

'Who said you're a stereotype? Not me.'

'What do the girls dress like in Cambridge?' I ask. 'Are they all prim and proper in dresses and white gloves?'

'What *are* you talking about?' Rob asks, quizzically tilting his head to one side.

'I don't know,' I reply honestly. I know what I want to say, but I'm not sure how to word it properly. 'I didn't mean that about the gloves and stuff. I just meant what I wear on the outside isn't me – well, it is, it's a reflection of me. Today I'm conforming because it's Claire's wedding and I don't want to let her down. But if this,' I gesture to myself, 'if this is the sort of woman you want, one who dresses *prettily* all the time, then you've picked the wrong person.'

'Why are you pushing me away again?' Rob's confused eyes scan my face for an answer. 'Like last time.'

Now I'm the confused one.

'What do you mean?'

'You're doing the same thing as when we were at school. There's nothing wrong here but you're pushing me away again.'

'I didn't push you away when we were at school. You were all over that girl.'

'What girl?'

'Marnie – the one who sang with the act that won the competition. The one who encouraged Suzy to sing that night.'

Rob looks genuinely puzzled.

'I wasn't all over her. Yes, she was pretty – I remember that, and, yes, she could sing. But she wasn't a patch on you, Frankie.'

As I stare at Rob, I have such mixed feelings. Part of me is annoyed with him for talking about my appearance like he did, and I want to challenge him more about what he said and why. But part of me needs to clear this up.

'So why did you rush away to see her on the stage after we'd got our prizes?'

Rob frowns. 'Did I?'

'Yes. Remember, that's when you gave me the shell, too.'

Rob puzzles this for a moment. Then his eyes light up and he smiles.

'Now I know what you're talking about! I wasn't rushing off to see Marnie sing, I wanted to see the band that was performing with her.'

'I don't understand?'

'The group that was performing with her was made up of a few older boys in the year above us. They were a sort of rock band – they played electric guitars and had a drummer. I thought they were pretty cool at the time. Christ, what were they called now . . . oh, I can't remember. But that's the reason I was dashing off so fast after we got our prizes.'

Oh, no . . .

'Is that the reason you ditched me that night?' Rob asks when I don't immediately respond. 'Because you thought I was lusting after another girl?'

143

'No ... yes ... I mean. It's just Mandy said ...'

'Mandy? Mandy said what? Are you telling me that we broke up because of something one of your friends said to you?'

I shake my head. 'No. Well, yes. Oh, I don't know, it was a long time ago – a lot has happened since.'

'The way I feel about you hasn't.' Rob moves closer to me again. 'It wasn't until I saw you again yesterday that I remembered just how strongly I felt back then. Yes, we might only have been fifteen, and, yes, we weren't exactly a couple very long, but I really liked you when we were at school, and I really like you now. The question is, Frankie, how do you really feel about me?'

Fourteen

Claire and Jonathan's evening reception is amazing.

Not because of the disco – although the DJ does play some great tunes that we all dance to, including some from the eighties that really take me and the other mermaids back to our school days. Not because of the delicious buffet, either – that appears halfway through the night and we all hungrily help ourselves. And not even because of the bar – that is free for the first part of the evening, allowing us to get even more tipsy than we were after the champagne and wine from earlier in the day.

All of the above only adds to my enjoyment of Claire's wedding day. But the main reason the evening is so amazing is because I get to spend so much of it in the arms of Rob.

After our tête-à-tête outside in the hotel gardens, I decided to give him the benefit of the doubt and, after another rather enjoyable interlude of our lips pressed together, we walked hand in hand back into the hotel, much to the amusement and delight of the other mermaids. We then spent the next few hours, with more drinking, more kissing and a new addition to the proceedings – bopping away with the others on the dance floor until late into the night.

At approximately 11 p.m., I'm in a hazy state of happiness and euphoria brought on by the events of the evening, the mostly free alcohol, and the joy of spending time with my old friends once more.

'Quick, you two – Claire is going to leave soon!' Eddie calls and I feel a tap on my shoulder. 'Put him down for a minute, Frankie!' Eddie says firmly, attempting to prise Rob and me apart. 'Your friend is leaving for her honeymoon!'

Eddie, Rob and I hurry to join the others already gathered to see the happy couple off outside the front of the hotel. The guests have all formed a makeshift walkway for Claire and Jonathan to leave through, and we join it towards the end of the line near their car – with the traditional tin cans attached to the bumper and a *JUST MARRIED* sign in the back window.

Claire and Jonathan, now changed into their going-away outfits, make their way happily through the middle of all their guests, stopping to hug the occasional person and to receive everyone's good wishes.

When they reach us, Jonathan goes over to his own friends, some of whom are standing opposite us, while Claire comes over to see us.

'Have you had the best day?' I ask her happily as she hugs each one of us in turn and comes to me last.

'I have, Frankie – it's been amazing. The happiest day of my life! I know it's a cliché, but it really has been.'

'I'm so pleased for you, Claire. You look radiant and so happy.'

Claire glances at Rob. 'And I see we're not the only couple for whom love is in the air ... I'm so pleased the two of you have got it together at last, and at my wedding too – it's just the best end to my day!'

146

Jonathan comes over and takes his bride's arm. 'Time to go, Claire,' he says gently.

'Wait, I haven't thrown my bouquet yet!' she says, winking at me.

'All the single girls come forward!' she calls. 'And we'll see who's going to be next ... '

More desperate women than I think I've ever seen suddenly surge forward, pushing me and the other mermaids back a little.

I don't mind. The last thing I want to happen to me right now is getting married.

'Ready?' Claire turns her back on the group. 'One, two, three!'

Claire's bouquet flies through the air across the heads of all the women, some of whom jump in the air trying to intercept it as it passes them. It comes far too close to me for my liking, but has just enough oomph to pass me and land in the hands of the person standing next to me – who just happens to be Eddie.

Eddie glances with shock and a tinge of sadness at the flowers in his hands, and then quickly shoves them at me. 'I don't think I've much chance of getting married!' he says bravely, winking at me. 'You have them!'

Claire turns around to see me standing with her bouquet in my hands, about to argue with Eddie. But she blows me a kiss and looks so pleased that I have her bouquet, I don't have the heart to do anything else but wave at her and hug the flowers close to me.

Then Claire and Jonathan climb into their car and we watch them drive away, waving through the back window to their guests, as they start their new life together.

'Don't worry,' I say to Rob as the car disappears around the corner at the end of the hotel drive. 'I'm not intending to get married anytime soon!'

'It's fine,' Rob says. 'I saw Eddie catch them and press them onto you.'

'Good. So what now?'

'Apparently the disco is carrying on and the bar is open until twelve. So I guess it's back for some more of the same!' He puts his arm around my shoulders and we walk back into the hotel with the others.

'My round,' Rob says as we get back to our table and I lay Claire's bouquet carefully in the middle to protect it. 'Same again, everyone? Where's Mandy?'

'I don't know. She was with us when we were outside seeing Claire off,' I say, looking around with the others.

'She was talking to a woman outside,' Eddie says. 'Well dressed. American, I think. She had that big black hat on in the church.'

'Oh, yeah, I know the one.' I pipe up. 'It looked like a flying saucer.'

'Yeah, it did.' Eddie giggles.

'I'll just get her the same as she usually has then,' Rob says. 'Back in a mo.'

'I see the two of you have been getting on very well this evening.' Eddie is grinning at me as I watch Rob walk across the dance floor towards the bar.

'Maybe?' I try to say this as enigmatically as I can.

'No maybe about it,' Suzy says, smiling too. 'It had to happen sometime. I just didn't think it would take five years apart to ignite the flame of love!'

'It's hardly love, it's only been a few hours tonight.'

Eddie laughs. 'Lust, then! It's very definitely that! Someone isn't going home alone tonight . . .'

'It may have escaped your notice, but both Rob and I are staying with our parents. Hardly the ideal setting for an illicit night of passion.'

'You could find a way if you wanted to, I'm sure.' Eddie winks. 'I bet that's what you two wished for, didn't you?'

'What do you mean?'

'That night on the beach, when we found the mermaid's barrel. We all made a wish, didn't we?'

'Oh, yes,' Suzy says. 'I'd almost forgotten about that.'

'I hadn't,' Eddie says. 'I was down in Morvoren Cove this morning, and it all came back to me when I saw a fish jump in the water.'

'You saw a fish jump?' I ask carefully. 'Did you see the whole fish, or just its tail?'

Eddie tries to remember. 'Just its tail I think – why?'

'Because that's what we saw last time, wasn't it, Frankie?' Suzy asks. 'Just the tail. A really big tail.'

I nod. 'Rob and I saw it the other day too when we were sitting up on the cliffs overlooking the bay.'

'The mermaid of Morvoren Cove is back!' Eddie says, holding up his hands and wiggling his fingers. 'Ooh, spooky!'

'Or maybe she never left?' Suzy says. 'Perhaps it's not only us that sees this tail?'

'I think we'd have heard something about it if anyone else saw it,' I say. 'My mum is always full to the brim of the local gossip; if this was a regular occurrence, everyone would be talking about it.'

'It's like we've got our own Loch Ness monster, here in St Felix,' Eddie says. 'They'll soon come from near and far just to spot the Morvoren Mermaid's tail!'

'Not if we keep quiet about it, they won't,' Suzy says. 'Which I really think we should.'

'Why?' Eddie asks.

Suzy leans forward and speaks in hushed tones. 'Because my wish has already come true.'

'Ooh, really? What did you wish for?' Eddie asks.

'I can't tell you that.'

'But you said it's already come true. It's not like a wish that hasn't been made yet and if you tell someone it won't happen.'

'True ... '

'You don't have to tell us if you don't want to, Suzy,' I say hurriedly. The last thing I want is to get into a discussion about what we wished for that night – not now.

'Don't have to tell us what?' Mandy asks, appearing back at the table with a tray of drinks.

'Oh, it doesn't matter,' I say, looking at the drinks. 'Why have you got these? Where is Rob?'

'He's talking to Jenna – she's a woman I met outside just now. Really interesting – she works in casting in LA.'

'Like plaster casts?' Eddie asks, lifting his drink from the tray. 'Is she a doctor?'

We all laugh.

'What?' Eddie asks. 'What did I say? My brain has had far too much alcohol. It's not thinking straight.'

'Not casting as in plaster casts, you numpty,' Mandy explains. 'Casting as in parts for movies and TV.'

'Wow, really?' Suzy says. 'How exciting.'

'But why is Rob talking to her?' I ask.

'He came up to the bar just now where I was waiting for drinks, and I introduced him. You'll never guess, but Jenna had only seen him before, in some lights show in Cambridge or something.'

'Footlights,' I say. 'It's a theatre company for students there.'

'Yeah, that's the one. Anyway, now they're talking acting and stuff – so I said I'd bring the drinks over.'

While Mandy dishes out everyone's drinks, I can't help but keep looking towards the bar to see if I can see Rob. But the bar is on the other side of the dance floor, so my view is always masked by people dancing.

Eventually, after about twenty minutes, Rob comes back to join us.

'Sorry,' he says, looking at me and then the others. 'I got talking at the bar.'

'Where's Jenna?' Mandy asks as Rob sits down next to me and grabs his beer.

'Popped to the ladies, I think,' Rob says. 'Thanks for introducing me, Mandy. She's an incredibly interesting woman.'

I try not to feel jealous as Rob talks about Jenna and what she does over in the States. Apparently she's some sort of talent scout – which is why she was at the Cambridge Footlights review this year. She came over for her nephew Jonathan's wedding early so she could see a few shows around the UK and hopefully spot some new talent.

'So are you going to be the next big thing then, Rob?' Eddie asks, with what sounds like a smidgen of jealousy in his voice.

That makes two of us, Eddie, I think. *But for likely very different reasons.*

'Yeah, is she going to make you into the next Tom Hanks?' Suzy asks.

'More like the next Hugh Grant.' Mandy grins.

'No, don't be daft,' Rob says. 'I've got another year at

Cambridge yet. She's simply given me her card and said to call her if I'm interested in acting when I complete my studies – that's all. No big deal.' He shrugs and takes a sip of his beer again. 'Do you fancy a dance?' he asks me, listening to the music just beginning to play over the big speakers underneath the DJ. 'It's a song I think we both like.'

Wet Wet Wet's 'Love is All Around' was the previous song, so I have to listen carefully to the first few bars of the new song floating over the dance floor.

I nod.

Rob takes my hand and leads me onto the dance floor, then he wraps his arms around me and we begin to sway to Bon Jovi – 'Always'.

'Should we get out of here, do you think?' Rob murmurs into my ear when we've been swaying in time to the music for a few minutes, our bodies getting closer as the song plays. 'Find somewhere more private, perhaps?'

I look up at Rob. 'Yes,' I whisper. 'Let's do that.'

Rob takes my hand and begins to lead me away from the dance floor as Jon Bon Jovi finishes his ballad of love.

'Wait!' I say. 'Are we leaving the wedding?'

'Yes,' Rob says, looking puzzled. 'Why?'

'I need to say my goodbyes, then.' I look over towards the other mermaids.

'They'll understand.' He tugs on my hand again.

'Just give me a minute,' I say, pulling my hand away from his and dashing back across the dance floor to our table. 'Rob and I are going,' I blurt out as I reach the table.

I look at my friends sitting around the table sipping drinks. 'Oh, hello,' I say to an unfamiliar face sitting next to Mandy. 'You must be Jenna?'

'Hey, nice to meet you,' Jenna says in a Texan drawl, sounding like a cross between a character from *Dallas* – an American soap opera I used to sit and watch with my mum – and Jerry Hall, the model. She actually looks a little like Jerry Hall too as she stands up and reaches over the table to shake my hand. 'You must be Frankie?'

'Er . . . yes,' I say, taking her hand.

'Rob was telling me all about you earlier.'

'Was he?'

'Yeah.'

Rob appears next to me at the table. 'Hi again,' he says to Jenna.

'So, you two are getting out of here, are you?' Eddie asks, grinning at us.

I glance at the others. They all smile knowingly back. 'I didn't want to go without saying goodbye,' I say quickly. 'In case you're all heading off tomorrow?'

'Not until later,' Eddie says. 'What about you guys?' he asks Suzy and Mandy.

'No plans to dash off early,' Mandy says. 'Suzy?'

Suzy shakes her head. 'I'd like to get away in the afternoon if possible. Shall we have a coffee together in the morning?'

'Yes, great idea,' I say keenly. 'Let's do that. How about the café overlooking Morvoren? Say eleven . . . thirty,' I add, realising we will all probably be a little hungover in the morning.

We all agree to meet up tomorrow before we go our separate ways again.

I feel Rob take my hand. 'Right, see you all tomorrow, then,' he says, tugging my hand again. 'Nice to meet you, Jenna.'

'Call me if you change your mind!' Jenna says, smiling at him. 'I'm serious.'

Rob just nods.

'Don't forget your flowers!' Suzy says, and she lifts Claire's bouquet from the table and hands it to me.

'Thanks.' I take it from her. 'See you guys tomorrow.'

'Have fun!' Eddie winks.

Rob and I walk hand in hand across the dance floor towards the exit of the hotel.

'What did Jenna mean just now?' I ask as we emerge outside into the fresh night air once more. 'When she said call me if you change your mind?'

'Oh, nothing. Now, where should we go?'

'It must have been something?'

Rob sighs. 'She wants me to go across to the States and meet some casting directors and agents, that's all.'

'I know, you told me that before – after you finish your degree.'

Rob turns to me. 'No, not when I finish my degree. Now. Immediately. She reckons she can get me work.'

'As an actor?'

'No, as a tour guide. Yes, of course as an actor.'

'Wow – that's amazing.'

'It is a bit.'

'But you told her no? You told her you had to finish uni first, right?'

'Yeah . . .' Rob sounds a little hesitant.

'You are going to finish your degree, aren't you, Rob?

Rob looks confused as he gazes down into my eyes. 'I don't know, Frankie. It seems like such an opportunity.'

'Yes, it sounds like that. But is it really? What do you even know about this Jenna?'

Rob reaches into his pocket and removes a white card.

'It looks all above board, and she is a relation of Jonathan's, isn't she?'

I take the card from him.

Jenna Morgan, it reads. *Talent Scout.* Then there's a New York address and a US phone number and, oddly, the little logo at the bottom of her business card is a row of little pink shells.

'This means nothing,' I say, handing him back the card. 'It could all be a ruse.'

'A ruse for what?' Rob looks slightly irked now.

'I don't know. But you hear of these things . . . in the papers. People being lured overseas for all sorts.'

Rob smiles now. 'Are you saying you think this Jenna is going to lure me over to New York and sell me as a sex slave?'

'No, now you're just mocking me.'

'I'm not! I just don't see why this can't be above board, that's all. This conversation shouldn't be about if the offer is genuine, it should be about if I should do it or not. Or maybe you don't think I'm good enough to be a professional actor?'

'I've never seen you perform – I don't know how good you are?'

'Ain't that the truth,' Rob murmurs. 'And the way this is going right now, you probably never will.'

'Is that all you can think about?' I demand. 'I thought we were discussing your future, not whether you're going to get your leg over tonight!'

'Clearly you don't want me to have a future,' Rob says, also getting riled now. 'Or are you just jealous that I've been given this chance . . . hmm? What are you going to do after university, Frankie? Live in some squat trying to eke a living from being a tortured artist?'

I stare at Rob.

'I'm sorry!' he says with an anguished expression. 'I didn't mean that. I'm just really confused right now.'

'You and me both.'

Rob sighs. 'Look, I came here to Claire's wedding not expecting anything, only a fun time with my old friends. But now . . . ' His voice trails off.

'Now?' I ask.

'Now, I've got a talent scout offering me work as an actor in America, and you, Frankie, my first love, here in my arms again. It's like all my Christmases have come at once. All the things I've ever wanted.'

I stare at Rob again. But this time it's not a stare of anger, but one of astonishment.

'Really?' I ask quietly.

'To which one?' Rob gives me a quizzical look.

'I think you know.'

Rob nods. 'Frankie, I've thought about you so much over the last five years. Yes, I've had other girlfriends, but none of them were ever you. They just couldn't be. Have you thought about me?' he asks, almost hesitantly.

I nod.

'Then what are we waiting for?' he says, clutching my arms and pulling me to him so Claire's bouquet is almost crushed between us.

'Are you going to America?' I ask, in a voice that sounds like it's completely removed from me.

'I don't know – why does that matter right now?'

Why does it matter? I'm still so confused.

'Because it would be hard enough for us to have a relationship if I'm in Glasgow and you're in Cambridge,' I hear myself saying. 'Let alone if you're halfway across the world.' I pull away a little from Rob as I speak.

But my small movement seems to take on a greater meaning.

'I see,' Rob says. 'We're using that as an excuse, are we?'

'No. I just want to know.'

'What if I said I was? Does that mean we don't get a chance?'

'I . . . I don't know.'

'I think you do know. I think you're using Jenna as an excuse to push me away again. Just like you used Marnie as an excuse when we were at school.'

'I did not. That was – according to you, anyway – a genuine mistake.'

'What do you mean, according to me? That's the truth.' Rob lets out an exasperated sigh and steps back a little. 'Why are you doing this again, Frankie? Why are you scared of relationships? Do you push all your boyfriends away like this? Or do you save this particular treatment for me alone?'

I don't know how to respond. Mum said something very similar to me only a few days ago. Do I always do this? Are all my break-ups actually my fault? Or is it only Rob I'm scared to commit to, because even though I try really hard not to care about him . . . the truth is I care about him very much?

'I'm going to go now,' I hear myself saying in a clear voice, that is totally unlike the tangled, confused thoughts in my head. 'Perhaps when you've made your decision we can talk again. But if you want my opinion on whether you should give up everything you've worked so hard for at Cambridge to go to America on a whim . . . then I think you already know my answer.'

I turn swiftly away from Rob, so my shoes make a satisfying scrunching sound in the gravel, and as I do something drops out of Claire's bouquet.

Rob and I both go to pick the item up, but I get there first.

How did a shell get into Claire's bouquet? I briefly think as I quickly shove it into my bag to look at later. Maybe it was hidden in there as a lucky charm or something?

'Frankie ...' Rob calls out behind me as I begin to march purposefully down the driveway. 'Let's talk about this.'

But I don't turn back; I continue to walk away from the hotel, and away from Rob. And as I do, I think I can actually feel my heart breaking.

Fifteen

Early April 2004

As I sit on the last part of my very long train journey down to Cornwall, watching the passing scenery gradually change into the landscape I know so well, I don't feel the same joy I usually do as I approach St Felix.

Usually when I return home, it's for a holiday or an event of some kind – something cheerful, something to look forward to. But this time is different. This time, I know it's going to be anything but joyful.

I got the phone call about ten days ago. My mum called me one day when I was shopping for groceries – or messages as my Scottish friends and neighbours called them – in Glasgow city centre, before I went home to my flat.

Nothing unusual in that. Mum often rang me to pass on some local gossip, or to simply check how I am, even though I'm now thirty years old.

'You're still my little girl, Frankie,' she'd say. 'I still worry about you, especially since you still live so very far away from us.'

So there was nothing strange in Mum phoning – what was odd was she always rang on my home phone, never on my mobile.

'Mum?' I said with concern into my phone in the middle of the M&S food court. 'What's wrong?'

'Oh, Frankie,' she said, sounding quite tearful. 'Something dreadful has happened. You remember your friend Mandy?'

'Yes …' I murmured quietly, immediately imagining the worst.

'Oh, it's awful, it is. That poor woman …'

'Mum!' I snapped. 'What's happened? Tell me. Has something happened to Mandy?'

'No, love, not Mandy. It's her sister – Hetty.'

I stare out of the train window as rain begins to beat against the glass.

Great, that's all I need, for it to be raining when I arrive. I'll get soaked getting to Mum and Dad's house.

But I quickly chastise myself; a little bit of rain and a damp arrival is nothing compared to what Mandy and her family are going through right now.

Mandy's younger sister, Hetty, and her husband, David, had been killed in a skiing accident in the Swiss Alps when a freak avalanche happened as a result of a heavy snowstorm, and tomorrow was their funeral.

Even though Hetty and David lived in London with their young son, who thankfully wasn't with them on the trip, they both originated from St Felix, so that is where their funeral service is being held, and where they are going to be buried, in the cemetery up on the hill.

As far as I'm aware, all the mermaids are coming back to pay their respects and to support Mandy at the funeral.

160

After Claire's wedding it was difficult to keep in touch. We tried via a sort of chain-letter system for a while, where we'd all write one group letter, and then pass it on to another mermaid one by one until we all received and read it. Then it would be someone else's turn to write. This worked for a while, but as people became busier and their lives changed, the letters became less and less until they petered out altogether.

Claire and I spoke on the phone fairly regularly and to begin with, Eddie, Suzy, Mandy and I all rang each other in an attempt to keep in touch, but eventually that faded out too, for the same reason as the letters – busy lives and not enough time.

There were a few attempts to physically get everyone together, but often someone would have to drop out at the last minute, and we'd all agree to reorganise for another time. But then something would crop up to prevent that happening, and in the end we gave up even trying to arrange anything.

However, it was the popularity of the internet and mainly email, which as Mandy correctly predicted, completely changed how we kept in touch with each other.

We all joined Friends Reunited to keep up with our fellow schoolmates, but most importantly we were now able to email each other privately, and, most often, all the mermaids at once in what was called a 'group email'. We were even occasionally doing MSN Messenger, where we could all chat online together by typing messages to each other in real time. This completely revolutionised how we were able to keep in touch, and, instead of drift apart as I feared would happen, these days we spoke to each other using the internet more than at any time since we left school.

All except Rob, that was.

*

He went to America after Claire's wedding, stayed there and had not returned to university. I know he kept in touch with some of the others because they were the ones who would tell me what he was doing. The other mermaids think we've not spoken to each other since the night of Claire's wedding.

Which isn't exactly the truth ...

Because not only have Rob and I spoken to each other, last New Year's Eve we did a little bit more than just talk ...

Hogmanay is a big thing in Scotland. I didn't realise quite how big until I lived in Glasgow. I left art college with the degree I worked so hard for and lots of hope for the future. But it very quickly became clear that having an art degree and actually getting work as an artist were completely different ball games, ones I was not equipped to play at all well.

I took jobs in cafés and shops – always temporary positions, because I thought that my big break in the art world was going to be just around the corner. But when two years passed and the corner kept getting further and further away, I finally admitted to myself that not only did I need a more permanent job, but I also needed a place of my own. I was still house-sharing at the time and I was starting to crave my own space, some peace and quiet, and somewhere I could paint and create my own artwork. Not with a view to selling anything or creating a portfolio, but simply for me, without being constantly interrupted or watched over by my housemates.

I managed to get my first permanent job in one of the larger art galleries in Glasgow, and that is where I've been for the last five years. I started as a gallery assistant, and I've now progressed into more of a curator and managerial role.

So when friends of mine persuaded me to go to a fancy-dress party in Edinburgh for Hogmanay last year, I gladly accepted.

I had no ties, no current boyfriend, I was still relatively young, free and single.

I thought I'd have a fun night, that's all, and I'd see in 2004 in style in one of Edinburgh's elegant and expensive Georgian townhouses. I didn't think I'd be introduced to a Hollywood actor that night, and I especially didn't think that actor would be Rob.

When Rob first went to the States, he had a few minor roles in television commercials to begin with, and then he got a small, but regular job on a daytime American soap opera, which the writers made into a much bigger role as time went on. He was in a few low-budget movies too, but I never saw him in anything and, to be honest, at the time I wasn't too bothered if I ever did.

Rob was a schoolgirl crush and an almost-dalliance at my friend's wedding. He was nothing more than a distant memory. The only time I ever thought about him with any concern was for a few seconds when I heard about the 9/11 terror attacks in New York a few years ago, but I quickly remembered that, although Rob originally went to New York to meet Jenna, he was now based in Los Angeles.

But on New Year's Eve, for the movie-themed party, I was dressed as Catwoman, an outfit that didn't go unnoticed by many of the male guests at the party. When I'd just about had enough of men lusting after their own Catwoman fantasy, and I knocked back not only a stream of advances, but an even larger number of glasses of champagne too, one of my friends thought it would be hilarious if I was introduced to a guest dressed as Batman. This guy was not the cartoon-esque Batman of sixties TV with tights and a dodgy codpiece, but the full 'Dark Knight' Batman of the movies and even I had to admit as I prepared to give another kind but firm rejection, that he did look quite sexy in his all-black outfit and mask.

'Hey,' he said after we were pushed together. 'Nice outfit.'

I was about to reply the same, when I paused, looked closely at him then simply said, 'Rob?'

Rob, like me, drank a fair amount that night. And as the clock struck twelve, I expected to find myself batting away offers of a midnight kiss. But, instead, I found myself sneaking out of the party still dressed as Catwoman, running through the streets of Edinburgh hand in hand with Batman, towards one of the best five-star hotels in the city.

Where two superheroes spent a rather enjoyable New Year's Day together. Until Batman had to return to his Batcave in LA, and Catwoman had to get a train back to Glasgow, and neither of them has ever spoken of the event since.

I sigh as I look out of the train window. I know Rob is going to be at the funeral in a couple of days' time – Claire told me he was coming. But I really hope I won't have to speak to him that much, not for any length of time, anyway. What had happened in Edinburgh, although lovely at the time, quickly turned into something I now deeply regret.

The train pulls into St Felix station, and with the rain still pouring down I alight alongside all the other passengers.

As I'm debating whether my waterproof coat is going to be enough, or whether I'm going to need the addition of my umbrella, I hear a familiar voice calling my name from further along the platform.

'Frankie!'

'Eddie!' I say as a man wearing a bright yellow mackintosh comes charging up the platform towards me. 'Oh my God, were we on the same train?'

164

'It seems so. I can't believe it!'

We try to hug each other, but with all our waterproof clothing it's not easy, and quite squeaky.

'I see you've brought the rain down with you from Glasgow,' Eddie says, looking up at the grey clouds. 'It was fine when I left London – even some spring sunshine!'

'I can't deny we do have our fair share of rain up there,' I admit. 'This is crazy – what time was your train from Paddington?'

'Twelve thirty-five. What about you?'

'Same! Man, we could have travelled together and caught up. I can't believe we've been on two trains from London together and not seen each other until now.'

'Especially with me in this coat!' Eddie says. 'Are you blind?'

I grin. 'Come on, let's walk together. Where are you staying while you're here?'

'B and B at the Merry Mermaid,' Eddie says as we walk alongside each other, pulling our suitcases behind us.

'I didn't know it was a B and B now?'

'Yeah, Rob's mum and dad sold it last year and moved away. It has new owners now.'

'Oh, that's news to me.' It wasn't. Rob told me at New Year, but I didn't want to let on to the others we'd hooked up.

'Well, it would be, wouldn't it?'

'Why?' I ask casually as we leave the station and begin walking into the town.

'Because we don't share much news about Rob when you're on MSN.'

'Why on earth not?' I ask, playing along. I know I didn't mention Rob, for fear of letting our secret out. But I wasn't aware that the others held back when we were all chatting.

'Cos you're funny about it.'

'No, I'm not,' I reply a little too ferociously. 'And even if I was, how would you tell? You can't see me.'

Eddie shrugs and drops of water fly from his mackintosh like a wet dog shaking himself. 'We just get that vibe from you.'

'Well, you're wrong. I haven't been bothered about Rob for ten years now. Besides, you know I've had other boyfriends since then.'

'And how's that going for you?' Eddie asks calmly. 'Erm ... it's Oliver at the moment, isn't it?'

'Oliver was way before Christmas last year. Dougie is the most recent.'

'*Dougie*, sorry. I didn't know.'

'No need to worry about it. We just split up recently too.'

'Blimey, Frankie, you sure get through them. Who knew the art world was such a lovefest!'

'I can't speak for the whole of the art world, but I do seem to meet a lot of single men via my work at the gallery.'

'Please share some of them!' Eddie declares dramatically. 'Since I started running the restaurant, I barely have time to sleep, let alone for anything more exciting in bed!'

'Most of them aren't worth sharing,' I say honestly. 'Far too full of their own self-importance. There's just the odd one or two that I might take a shine to occasionally.'

'How's it going at the gallery? Are you still enjoying it?'

'Yes, I am. Especially the curator side of my job. I may not be displaying my own work, but I enjoy looking after other people's.'

'One day, perhaps?' Eddie says encouragingly.

'Nah, I think that ship has probably sailed now. Anyway, working with art rather than trying to sell your own is much more profitable. I've just moved into a new apartment – it's much bigger than my last flat, so I've much more space to paint for my own pleasure now.'

'Cool.'

'How's the restaurant game, then?' I ask.

Eddie, much to our surprise, gave up the theatre when he was twenty-two, retrained as a chef, then managed to nab himself a very junior position in the Ritz in London. After progressing through the ranks of the hotel's kitchen, Eddie is now managing a restaurant of his own not far from Covent Garden in London. It's owned by two well-known pop stars, but Eddie's in charge of the day-to-day running of the restaurant and all the menus.

'Exhausting!' Eddie says dramatically. 'But fabulous at the same time. I love it!'

'Sounds like you've found your niche in life,' I tell him. 'I never thought it would be food rather than performing, though.'

'I don't know. Have you seen behind the scenes in a chef's kitchen? It's full of drama and larger-than-life performers.'

'I can imagine.'

'I think this is where we part company,' Eddie says, pausing on the pavement. 'I assume you're going straight to your parents' house?'

'Yeah, I'd better go and see how they're getting on.'

'Not many of us left that have family here now, are there?' he says. 'My mum moved away ages ago, and Suzy and Rob's parents have gone now too. There's only you, Claire and Mandy, I think?'

'Yes.' I pause on hearing Mandy's name mentioned for the first time. 'Oh, God, Eddie, tomorrow is going to be awful, isn't it?'

Eddie nods. 'It is. I have no idea what I'm going to say to Mandy, or her parents.'

'I know. What can you say other than I'm so dreadfully sorry? It just sounds so banal. Without meaning. When really what we want to say is, "This is heartbreakingly awful. We all feel absolutely terrible, so we have no idea how you must be coping."'

'Perhaps we can say that to Mandy if we see her before?' Eddie says. 'Save the polite condolences for her parents. Mandy was always honest with us, wasn't she? Maybe we should be honest with her?'

I nod. 'Mandy was never one for polite chit-chat. She always got straight to the point.'

'Often with honest brutality.' Eddie smiles. 'But at least you knew where you stood with her. She never had anything to hide.'

'You're absolutely right. Mandy will appreciate us telling her how we really feel – not fudging over the truth with niceties.'

'What are you doing later?' Eddie asks. 'Fancy a drink at the pub?'

'I'd love one,' I reply eagerly. 'Can we get the others to come too? I mean, not Mandy, obviously; she'll want to be with her family. But I can ask Claire, and do we know what time Suzy is getting here?'

'She said evening, I think. Blair has some big function or something on today, so she couldn't get away early. But apparently, she's getting the train down as soon as she possibly can from Westminster tonight. I'll text her and tell her our plans.'

'Great. I'll text Claire too and see if she can come.'

'What about Rob?' Eddie asks. 'Do we know what time he's getting here?'

'Is he even coming?' I shrug, even though I know he is. 'Surely, he's too busy being famous in Hollywood, isn't he?'

'Claire said he was going to try to come.' Eddie raises his eyebrows at me. 'I think he was as shocked as the rest of us when he heard.'

I feel bad. 'Yeah, I guess so.'

'Right, I'm going to go before this raincoat stops being waterproof and I get soaked through! I just hope the Merry Mermaid rooms are centrally heated or I'll freeze to death.' Eddie stares at me and pulls an anguished expression. 'God, that was terribly bad taste in the circumstances.'

'Don't worry about it; it's only me. I guess we're all going to feel a little on edge during this visit. It's not quite like the old days, is it?'

He shakes his head. 'No, sadly. We've all grown up now, and we have to deal with grown-up things. Tomorrow is just one of those.'

The rain suddenly starts getting harder. 'Right, let's go and get dry; this rain isn't getting any better. I'll see you tonight in the bar at the Mermaid, say about eight o'clock?'

Eddie nods. 'I'll be there. We'll just have a quiet little drink, a bit of a catch-up.'

'Sounds perfect.'

But little do I know as I scurry along to my parents' house, dripping rainwater as I go, that our little drink tonight will be anything but quiet.

Sixteen

It's strange to see someone other than Rob's parents behind the bar of the Merry Mermaid but Rita and Richie, the new owners, seem jovial and efficient as they serve both us and the mix of early holidaymakers and locals out for a drink this evening.

Eddie and I are the first to arrive. We quickly find a table big enough to accommodate the others when they come, and we sit down with our drinks feeling like we've never been away, as the familiarity of the Merry Mermaid on a busy Thursday evening envelops us like a warm and comforting blanket.

'You know what you were saying earlier?' I ask Eddie as we sit on the same side of the table watching the comings and goings at the bar. 'About our parents all gradually moving away?'

'Uh-huh,' Eddie replies, sipping on his lager.

'Apparently my mum and dad are going to be next in the parental exodus of St Felix.'

'Really?' Eddie looks surprised. 'Are they selling up too?'

'It would seem so. They told me tonight over dinner they're going to put our house up for sale sometime this year.

Apparently, the property market is just too good in St Felix at the moment. Houses are going for way over the odds as people clamour to buy second homes, or holiday rentals. They're hoping to buy a bungalow somewhere and possibly take early retirement with the proceeds if all goes well.'

'How do you feel about it?' Eddie asks perceptively. 'By the tone of your voice, I assume not too happy.'

I shrug. 'It's always going to be hard when the home you grew up in is sold. It doesn't surprise me they're moving on; I just didn't expect it quite yet. But it's not just the selling of the house that bothers me, it's the fact I won't have any reason to come back here to St Felix if they don't live here any more.'

'Claire is still here. You could come and visit her if you need an excuse?'

'I suppose. Claire and I don't actually speak as much as we used to, though. What with her young family and everything, I get the feeling she's really busy these days. Have you noticed that?'

'Not really, but you two were always a lot closer. She doesn't always make our MSN chats on the rare occasion we can get everyone together these days, though, does she?'

'No, I've noticed that too. Or she's really late coming online.'

Eddie nods. 'Oh, talk of the devil ... Claire!' He starts waving madly in the direction of the pub entrance. 'Claire, over here!'

Claire smiles and raises her hand, then weaves her way through the busy bar to our table.

'It's so good to see you both,' she says, hugging Eddie and then me. 'So very good.'

Claire hugs me a little longer than feels comfortable.

'Are you OK?' I ask, smiling at her.

Each time I've seen Claire over the last ten years, she's looked a little bit more stressed, and a little bit older. Heartbreakingly she lost the baby she was pregnant with at her wedding. But fortunately for her and Jonathan, they managed to conceive again – and they now have three beautiful children between them: Alice, age eight, George, age six, and little Freddie, who is almost four. That's enough stress and worry for anyone!

At thirty we have all begun to age, of course we have – a few more lines around our mouths and eyes, a few more wrinkles on our foreheads that don't disappear quite as fast as they used to when we stop frowning. But Claire seems different. Her lines appear worn into her face rather than simply accrued by age, and she looks tired, exhausted even.

'Yes, of course I'm OK. Why do you ask?'

'No reason,' I say quickly, shaking my head. 'Come, sit down. What are you having to drink?'

For the next twenty minutes or so, it's just the three of us chatting about what's been going on in our lives and what's been going on in St Felix.

'Rita and Richie seem to have fitted in really well,' Claire says, looking up at the bar. 'It was sad when Rob's parents left, but his dad's health wasn't great, so it was becoming too much for them, I think. Have you guys heard Rob's news?'

I shake my head.

'He's only gone and got himself the lead role in a new superhero movie!'

'Blimey!' Eddie says. 'What superhero?'

'Er . . . he's going to be Danger Man or something like that. It's very exciting – it's going to be his first leading role.'

'Are you sure it isn't Danger Mouse?' I ask sarcastically, raising my eyebrows. 'It seems more apt.'

But my mind immediately casts back to Rob in his Batman outfit.

'Ooh, meow!' Eddie says. 'I don't know about mice, but someone's catty tonight!'

'Frankie,' Claire says reproachfully. 'That's mean. This is going to be Rob's big break. He's very excited about it.'

'How do you know all this?' I ask her. 'He never comes on chat any more.'

'My mum keeps in contact with his mum; they're still good friends even though they've moved away.'

'Oh,' I say quietly, slightly distracted as I glance behind Eddie's head. 'I see.'

'Are they giving him a bodysuit?' Eddie asks, still playing along. Since Claire arrived, his back is to the bar now. 'He was hardly buff the last time I saw him.' He attempts to flex his biceps. 'Superheroes need muscles, you know!'

'They do indeed!' a familiar voice says, making Eddie jump. Eddie spins around on his stool to find Rob standing behind him in a fitted navy T-shirt flexing very well-developed biceps.

'Rob!' Eddie stands up immediately. 'Good to see you, man! Wow, you have filled out ... ' Eddie says admiringly as they give each other a hug.

'Claire.' Rob smiles at her as Eddie releases him. 'Good to see you again.'

'Hello, Rob,' Claire says, looking pleased to see him. 'I'm glad you could make it.'

'Frankie.' Rob finally looks at me. 'How have you been?'

'Good, thanks,' I say quickly. 'Very well.'

'Good. Good.' Rob holds my gaze for a moment and annoyingly I feel my stomach do that silly thing it always used to do when I first knew Rob, taking me right back to my school days once more. 'Oh, sorry, mate,' he says to a man behind him who I've only just noticed standing there. 'I should introduce you.'

I look with interest at the man who steps forward. I'd guess he's about our age, tall like Rob, and fit-looking, with a healthy LA glow to his skin. A pair of piercing blue eyes smile from under a mop of dark glossy hair, which he runs his hand through to push it back off his face.

'This is Mack,' Rob says. 'He's a mate from the States. Mack used to live here in St Felix too. I bet none of you remember him?'

'I would definitely remember if we'd met before,' Eddie says, eagerly standing up to shake Mack's hand.

'Good to meet you, Eddie,' Mack says with a strong American accent as he firmly shakes Eddie's hand. 'And you, Claire, and, of course, Frankie.' He smiles at me. 'Rob's told me a lot about all of you.'

'I'll get the drinks in,' Rob says. 'Usual, Mack?'

Mack nods, pulling up a seat opposite me.

'Lager for you, Eddie?' Rob asks.

Eddie nods. 'Yes, please.'

'Claire – still a gin and tonic?'

'Well remembered, Rob, but, no, I'll have a glass of white wine, please.'

'Frankie?' Rob asks, looking at me. 'Still the same Jack and Coke?'

'No, I'm just on the orange juice tonight, thanks,' I tell him.

'Frankie's got a dodgy tummy,' Eddie says. 'Amazingly, she's not touched a drop all night.'

Rob looks surprised. 'Orange juice it is, then,' he says, holding my gaze again. 'Back in a mo.'

'You all make me sound like an alcoholic.' I shake my head. 'What will Mack think?'

Mack shrugs. 'Mack will think nothing of it,' he says. 'Because I am one.'

I stare in horror at Rob's friend.

'Oh my ... I'm so sorry!' I say quickly, absolutely mortified. 'I ... I didn't mean ... I mean, I did mean ... but I wasn't poking fun or anything like that.'

'Please,' Mack says quietly but firmly. 'I'm not in the least offended. So why should you be upset?'

I nod, but I feel myself blushing furiously.

'So,' Claire says quickly. 'Rob said you used to live here in St Felix, but you've clearly been in America a long time. What's your story?'

'Yeah, I lived here until 1989, the year I left school, in fact. My dad got a job over in the States so the whole family upped and left with him, and never looked back. It is quite odd to be here again now, though. It feels like I never left. It doesn't change all that much, does it?'

'No, not a lot.' Eddie nods, looking at Mack with wide eyes.

'I have to disagree,' Claire says. 'As a resident here, I think it does change. We try to move with the times, but people like the quaint timelessness of it all. That's why they holiday here year after year.'

'You're right, of course.' Mack smiles. 'A few of my friends were quite jealous when I said I was coming to Cornwall.'

I like how he says *Cornwall*. Drawing out the vowels to make them seem more important.

'Why are you here?' I ask. 'Did Rob just ask you to come with him?'

I'm desperate to know what their relationship is, and why Rob has brought Mack here for Hetty's funeral. It seems very strange.

'Ah, that's a funny one. No, funny is the wrong word. Strange is probably better. Rob and I know each other from the sports bar I run in LA. We have quite a lot of ex-pats who drink with us because we show British sport – English football, rugby, sometimes cricket, you know the stuff. Most of my rivals only show NBA, NFL and NHL. They're American sports,' he adds, in case we don't know.

Eddie nods, eagerly taking in every word, while Claire and I just listen.

'Rob's one of my regulars. To cut a very long story short, we were chatting one afternoon when the bar was quiet, and I discovered that Rob was going to be coming back here to England for a funeral. That's a coincidence, I said, I should be going back to England for a funeral too. When we both discovered that not only was it the same funeral, but that we'd both lived in the same Cornish town when we were younger, we couldn't quite believe it.'

'Did you know Hetty too?' I ask.

Mack shakes his head. 'Not that I remember. But I did know her husband, David. We were buddies at school. Played in the same rock band together. I was in the year above you guys. Terrible, isn't it, what happened?'

We all nod sadly.

'So, anyway, when Rob suggested we travel here to England together for their joint funeral, it didn't take much for me to agree. I thought as well as paying my respects, it would be cool to see the old place again.'

'You said you were in a rock band at school,' Eddie says,

still staring at Mack. 'Was it the band that played at the Enchantment Under the Sea dance, by any chance?'

'Yeah, that's us. We called ourselves the Friday Rock Project.' He rolls his eyes. 'We thought we were so cool and trendy with that name! We were the leavers the year you guys put on our entertainment. I remember you singing that Beach Boys song dressed as mermaids. You won, didn't you?'

Eddie visibly blushes. 'No, sadly we came runners-up. It was the band with the ringer singer that won.'

Mack frowns. 'Ringer singer?'

'Yeah, they found this supposed new pupil who could miraculously hold a tune extremely well, and they completely changed their act to accommodate her. We had no chance.'

Eddie is clearly still very peeved about that competition.

'Oh, yeah.' Mack nods as he remembers. 'They got her to sing with us too. The rest of my band were not at all happy when we had to accommodate a lead singer last minute, but the girl had some pipes on her that's for sure; it didn't do us any harm. Never saw her again afterwards, though.'

'Yeah, funny that,' Eddie says sourly. 'It's almost like she was never going to be a pupil at all . . . '

'Who was never gonna be a pupil?' Rob asks, coming back to the table with a tray of drinks.

'We were just talking about the Enchantment Under the Sea dance,' Claire says. 'And that girl, Marnie, who sang.'

Rob glances at me, but I pretend not to notice as I reach for my orange juice.

'Yeah, I was quite surprised when I ran around from backstage to see you guys play that night.' Rob glances at me again to check I'm listening. 'I was a huge fan of your band and very jealous I wasn't in it.'

Mack shrugs good-naturedly. 'That was all a very long time ago now. Funny how these things happen, though. What are the chances I'd bump into someone in LA who not only lived in the same place as me when I was young, but who actually went to school with me too – incredible!'

Rob lifts his pint of beer. 'Let's have a toast,' he says. 'To old friends.' He looks around at us all. 'And to new ones!' He gestures to Mack. 'May they all mingle into one big happy mess together. To our friends!'

'To our friends,' we all repeat. 'Old and new.'

As we all take a sip from our glasses, a voice calls out across the pub.

'Oi! You lot! I hope you haven't started without me?'

We all look up to see Mandy waving wildly at us from across the bar.

'Barman!' she calls, slamming her hand down on the bar as a worried-looking Richie comes towards her. 'Tonight needs to be a party, not a wake. What's everybody having? The drinks are on me!'

Seventeen

Mandy, good to her word, buys everyone in the pub a drink. It quickly becomes clear she's probably had a few drinks already, as she smiles and grins her way around the bar speaking to people and patting them on the back, before moving onto the next.

'Is she all right?' Claire whispers as we watch her. 'She's not behaving very ... well, very normally, is she?'

'Grief can be a funny thing,' Rob says. 'It affects everyone differently. I suspect this is Mandy's way of dealing with everything that's going on.'

We continue to watch Mandy until eventually she joins us in our corner of the bar.

'Well now,' she says, her eyes bright as she casts them around the table, 'How are we all – good, I hope?'

Claire is the first to speak. 'Mandy,' she says anxiously. 'I'm so very sorry for your loss. We all are.'

Mandy immediately looks down into her glass. She swirls what looks like a spirit of some kind around, so it swooshes over the ice cubes. 'Yes. Well. It is what it is.'

'How are you doing?' I ask gently. 'Is there anything we can do to help? You know for tomorrow?'

Mandy's head snaps up again. 'I'd really rather not talk about tomorrow,' she says, and I notice how drawn her face looks under her heavy make-up. 'I'm grateful you came and all that. But I'd rather hear all your news tonight if that's all right with you?'

'Yes, yes, of course,' we all hurriedly reply.

'And who might you be?' she asks, turning her gaze to Mack. 'We have a stranger in our midst!'

Mack quickly explains why he's here.

Mandy nods sombrely. 'I appreciate you coming all this way. Both of you,' she says, turning to Rob now. 'The journey from London is bad enough, let alone the USA!'

'It's the least we could do,' Rob says. 'Isn't it, Mack?'

Mack nods.

Mandy takes a gulp from her drink. 'So, what's your story?' she asks mischievously, looking at Rob and Mack. 'Are you batting for the other side now, Rob? Eddie will be over the moon, but my mate Frankie here will be extremely disappointed!'

Eddie looks horrified, and my cheeks flush incredibly hot, partly from embarrassment and partly from annoyance.

'No,' Rob says firmly. 'I am not, and neither is Mack. We're just mates. Mack has a wife.'

'I do indeed,' Mack says. 'Sarah.'

'Oops! Sorry,' Mandy says, not seeming in the least embarrassed, unlike myself and Eddie. 'My mistake! It does happen you know – the change, and I'm not talking the menopause. Still time for you and our Frankie to get it on then?'

I glare at Mandy now.

'What?' she asks, seeing me. 'You've always had the hots for him, as he has for you.' She takes another long gulp from her

180

glass, draining the remaining liquid. 'Another, you lot? No? Well, I need one. Back in a minute.'

Mandy gets up, steadies herself, then walks as competently as she can back over to the bar.

'She's grieving,' Claire says. 'Try not to be too cross with her, Frankie.'

'I'm going to get some air.' I stand up. 'It's very hot in here tonight. I'll be back in a bit.'

I hurry outside into the cool night air, where I immediately take a few cleansing breaths. Then I walk over to the harbour railings and lean on them. The earlier rain has now cleared, and it's a beautiful moonlit evening. Above the waves rolling into the harbour, I can see tiny stars dotted across the night sky. I look up at them, take another deep breath and sigh.

'Do you want to be on your own?' a voice behind me asks. 'I'll go back in if you do.'

I turn around to see Rob.

'It's fine,' I reply. 'I just needed some air. The pub is super busy this evening.'

'Yeah, Mum and Dad loved it on nights like this.' He moves forward to stand next to me.

'It must be strange for you not seeing them behind the bar?'

'It is. But the new owners seem to be making a good job of everything. The Merry Mermaid looks to be in safe hands.'

There's a moment of silence.

'I'm sorry for what Mandy said.' I say this at the same time as Rob says something similar.

We both smile.

'She's clearly had quite a lot to drink,' Rob says. 'Like Claire said, we shouldn't be too cross with her.'

'No, I know. But I don't want to embarrass you in front of your friend.'

'Mack's all right. He runs a bar, remember? He's used to people saying awkward and embarrassing things when drunk.'

'I suppose so. How odd you two bumping into each other like that, though, halfway across the world.'

'Funny thing is I wasn't even going to visit that particular bar, but the girl I was with at the time insisted we went there. The relationship didn't last long, but my patronage of that particular bar did. People always say it's a small world.'

I wonder if he's referring not only to him and Mack, but to our tryst in Edinburgh, too.

'So how are things going in La La Land, then?' I ask casually.

'Good. I've finally bagged my first lead role.'

'Yes, Claire was telling us about it. Congratulations, you're actually going to get paid to be a superhero this time,' I say with a wry smile.

'I am indeed. Not quite Batman . . . ' He raises his eyebrows. 'But I think it's going to be pretty big. They're putting a lot of money into it, that's for sure.'

'Good. I'm pleased for you.'

'You still taking the art world by storm?'

'Hardly. But I'm still enjoying working at the gallery if that's what you mean?'

'Good. Good.'

There's a pause in conversation, and all I can hear is the rather strange mix of the hum of people behind us in the pub, along with the clinking of their glasses. Versus in front, large waves splashing up against the harbour wall.

'Should we talk about what happened in Edinburgh?' Rob asks, looking out over the sea.

'Do you want to?'

'Only if you do.'

'I'd rather not. Look, it was a great evening and everything. But it was a one-off.'

'Yes, yes, of course. I know that. You don't regret it though, do you?'

Do I regret sleeping with Rob? Until about a month ago, no. But just recently I've had quite a few regrets.

'No, I don't regret it,' I reply as honestly as I can.

'Me neither. It was a good night.'

'Perhaps we should leave it at that, then – a good night enjoyed by us both.'

There's silence again.

'I think I might go back in.' Rob turns around so his back is to the railings. 'I'm getting the feeling you want to be on your own.'

'No, not at all. I'm just feeling a bit grouchy tonight, that's all.'

'Because of what Mandy said?'

'No ... well, maybe a little bit. It's mainly because I found out tonight that my parents are going to sell their house here. I'm feeling quite unsettled by that, and a few other things if I'm honest. I'm sorry if you thought it was because of you.'

'No apology needed. I felt a bit like that when my parents said they were selling the pub. But we hadn't lived there all my life, just a few years. Your parents have always lived in St Felix, haven't they?'

'Well remembered. Since I was born they have. I can't imagine them living anywhere else.' I look back out at the boats in the harbour. 'It's like my anchor is being taken away, and right now I really need that anchor.'

'Why right now?'

'Oh, no particular reason – maybe it's just my age – I feel I need roots somewhere.'

'Just because your parents don't live here any more doesn't mean you can't call St Felix your home.'

'I guess . . . '

To my surprise, Rob places his hand over mine on the railings. 'I still think of here as home, and I didn't live here anywhere near as long as you did.'

'Really?'

'Yeah, some of my happiest memories were spent here.'

He doesn't elaborate further, so I don't ask. Now is not the time to be dragging our past up again. I have enough to worry about in the future.

'Yes,' I admit. 'Mine too.'

We look at each other and, for a brief moment, all those old feelings come flooding to the surface once more as I gaze into Rob's eyes, but they're interrupted by a splashing sound in the harbour.

We both look down, then look back at each other, our previous wistful expressions now simply ones of acknowledgement at the all too familiar sound below.

Eighteen

We wander back inside the pub together, still talking about the fish's tail that once again appeared before us in the waves around St Felix.

There's a change at our table as Suzy is now sitting where Claire was, and Mandy has rejoined the group.

'Suz!' I rush over to greet her. 'You made it.'

'I did indeed.' Suzy smiles at me. 'Always one to make a dramatic late entrance, aren't I? Hello, Rob,' she says, looking behind me with interest at Rob. 'I saw you two outside when I arrived, but I didn't want to disturb you; you looked deep in conversation.'

'Just catching up,' I say quickly. 'Now, tell me all your news. I want to hear all the gossip from the Houses of Parliament.'

'Ha, you know I can't tell you any gossip,' she says, grinning at me. 'Not anything too juicy anyway!'

After we've all been sitting back down at the table for a few minutes, with Suzy telling us everything she is allowed to about her job working for Prime Minister Tony Blair, I begin to wonder where Claire is.

'Where's Claire?' I ask Eddie, now sitting next to me. 'When

I came back in, I thought she'd just popped to the loo, but she's been gone ages.'

'The husband called when you were outside with Rob. Claire left shortly after that.'

'Oh, that's a shame. I hope nothing is wrong at home.'

'I doubt it,' Eddie whispers, leaning in towards me. 'Nothing with the kids, anyway ...' He raises his eyebrows meaningfully.

'What do you mean?' I also lower my voice.

'I dunno,' Eddie says. 'I get the feeling something isn't right there.'

'With Claire?'

'With Jonathan, more like.'

'Eddie, what are you trying to say?' Eddie's serious tone, unusual for him, is worrying me.

'What are you two whispering about?' Mandy asks in a loud voice. 'No secrets allowed around this table!'

'Nothing,' Eddie says, sitting up again. 'Nothing for you to worry about, anyway.'

'We were just talking about Claire,' I reply honestly. 'I wondered where she'd gone.'

'Home to the hubby!' Mandy says, saluting. 'Like the good housewife she is.'

I frown. 'That's not fair, Mandy. Claire is a good mother to her children.'

'I never mentioned her children,' Mandy says. 'It's her husband you need to watch.'

I stare at Mandy. 'What's going on here?' I ask. Now Mandy is talking about Jonathan in a strange way too. 'Am I missing something?'

Mandy shakes her head. 'Just forget I said anything.'

186

'No,' I demand. 'I won't. Do you guys know something I don't?'

'Don't look at me.' Rob shrugs. 'I live in America. I have no idea what they're talking about.'

'Or me,' Suzy says. 'Has something happened?'

We all look at Mandy.

She sighs loudly. 'My mum said something to me tonight when I said I was going to be meeting you all. I didn't think much of it at the time. But when Claire rushed off like she did, it reminded me.'

'What?' I ask. 'What did she say?'

'She said she was surprised Claire was being allowed to go out to the pub on her own. From what she'd heard, Jonathan keeps a tight rein on her.'

'Tight rein? What's that supposed to mean?'

'I think he's quite possessive. Claire used to be on all sorts of committees – the school, the local women's guild, et cetera. But she's suddenly stopped all that now. My mum said Claire's mum is quite worried about her.'

I stare at Mandy, trying to take all this in. How did I not know any of this? Why didn't I notice? Claire used to be one of my best friends. Correction, she still is one of my best friends.

'Actually,' Rob says. 'Now you've mentioned it, my mum said something similar a while back too when I was on the phone to her. She's remained quite good friends with Claire's mum since the move, and she did say something about her mum being worried about her and did I know anything? I said no, I hadn't really spoken to any of you that recently – which I'm sorry to say is the truth. My mum had doubts about Jonathan from the start, though.'

'Why?' Suzy asks.

Rob shrugs. 'I don't know. But when I came down for their wedding, she said could I find out what Jonathan was really like. So I asked a few questions and you guys all seemed to think he was fine – do you remember me asking you, Frankie?'

'Not really,' I mutter, trying to take all this in and make sense of it. Claire looked particularly drawn and exhausted tonight. But she seemed fine once we sat down and got chatting – just like the old Claire, quiet, considered, full of concern for everyone.

Full of concern for everyone ... but herself. I tried several times to engage Claire in conversation about herself and her family, but she answered briefly and quickly changed the subject. Was that why? Because she didn't want to talk about her home life? Were things so awful that she'd rather talk about anything but herself?

'I'm going to her house,' I say, standing up suddenly. 'To make sure everything is all right.'

'Do you think that's a good idea?' Eddie asks. 'It might make things worse?'

'How can it make things worse? I want to check my friend is all right.'

'Frankie, Eddie might be right,' Suzy says calmly. 'If, and it's a big if right now ... we have nothing to go on, only a little bit of hearsay and gossip. If something is wrong at home, you turning up all guns blazing, full of alcohol, isn't going to help. It might make things worse.'

'Firstly, I am not full of alcohol,' I tell her. 'I've been on soft drinks all night, so I am perfectly compos mentis. And, secondly, I'm not going to cause a scene. I'm simply going to call in on my friend and check she's OK. What could possibly be wrong with that?'

'Should we all go?' Eddie asks. 'Safety in numbers and all that?'

'Yeah,' Mandy says, raising her fists in front of her. 'We'll sort him out. I'm in the mood for a fight!'

'No,' I say firmly. 'I don't think that's a good idea at all. You guys stay here. I'll be fine on my own. I don't want Jonathan to think we know anything.'

'If there's anything to know,' Suzy reminds me. 'Look,' she says to everyone, 'I work in politics, and I know how quickly a rumour can spread, whether it's true or not. We might make things worse if we all turn up throwing accusations around.'

'I'd offer to come with you,' Rob says, looking slightly shamefaced. 'But Jonathan and I aren't on the best of terms.'

'Why?' I ask. 'Something else I don't know about?'

'Well, yes. You see, Jonathan's sister came out to LA to work. She didn't know anyone there so Claire asked me to show her around.' He hesitates and glances at me. 'Things got a little heated, shall we say, one night, and Diana wasn't too happy when I didn't want to make it a more permanent arrangement.'

'Rob!' Mandy is grinning at him, 'You dog! No wonder Jonathan hates you. You bedded his sister then ditched her.'

'It wasn't quite like that.' Rob looks decidedly uncomfortable. 'But I'm not his favourite person in the world.'

'Would you like me to go?' Mack asks. I've almost forgotten Mack is here with all this going on. He of course remained silent throughout our discussions, not really knowing either party that well. 'I'm a neutral in all this.'

I turn away from Rob, trying not to think too much about what he's just told us. 'Yes, thank you, Mack. That might be a good idea. If you don't mind, that is? I don't want to drag you away from the pub?'

Mack smiles. 'Nah, I spend far too much of my time in a bar. Some fresh Cornish night air will do me good.'

'We'll come back when we've checked everything is OK,' I tell the others. 'We won't be long.'

Mack and I leave the pub together and begin to walk to Claire's house – one of the traditional fishermen's cottages in the old part of town.

'Thanks for coming,' I tell him as we walk.

'Not a problem,' Mack says. 'I'm glad to be of help.'

'So, what's your bar in LA like?' I ask to make conversation. 'A bit different from the Merry Mermaid, I bet.'

'It's big,' Mack says. 'And often real noisy when it's busy and there's games on. So this,' he holds out his arms as if he's willing as much fresh sea air to absorb into him as possible, 'this is wonderful. Here I can only hear the wind and the occasional gull who hasn't gone to bed yet – this is heaven. I'd forgotten how healing silence can be.'

I smile. It's lovely to see someone else enjoying the simple pleasures of St Felix.

'I'll be quiet then, shall I?' I ask. 'So you can really enjoy some peace and quiet?'

'You will not,' Mack says, smiling at me. 'Rob has told me so much about you and your friends that it's rather wonderful to hear you talk for yourselves.'

I'm surprised to hear Rob talks so much about us after all these years.

'Rob said you live up in Bonnie Scotland,' Mack continues. 'Which part?'

'Glasgow – I work in an art gallery there.'

'Cool. What sort of art?'

'Mostly fine art. We also have a couple of galleries with more modern stuff in too.'

'And what do you think to the modern stuff?' Mack asks, surprising me.

'It's all right, I suppose. It's not my personal speciality.'

'What is?'

I glance at Mack to see if he's simply making polite conversation. But he seems genuinely interested.

'Don't call me dull, but I really like impressionism of the late nineteenth century.'

'Why does that make you dull?'

'When I was at art college, it wasn't the done thing to like Monet, Renoir and the rest. Everyone was trying to be cool and different.'

'And you weren't?'

'I tried to be to begin with, but then I realised you just have to be yourself, whether yourself is the in thing or not.'

'Quite right.' Mack nods. 'What do you think to Cézanne?'

'Love Cézanne.'

'Cubist or post-impressionist?' Mack asks, and again I'm surprised.

'Post-impressionist,' I say. 'Cubism is Picasso to me, and I'm not really a fan.'

'Me either. Have you ever been to the Met Museum in New York?'

'No, sadly.'

'If you ever get the chance, I thoroughly recommend it. You'd love it there.'

'I'll be sure to check it out the next time I'm in New York.' And I can't help smiling to myself.

Mack turns and sees me. 'You've never been to New York, have you?' he says knowingly, but not judgementally.

I shake my head. 'No, but I'd like to one day.'

'You should. I think you'd like it there. New Yorkers are very much themselves at all times. Whereas in LA there are a lot of people trying very hard to be someone they're not.'

'It sounds perfect. I much prefer to surround myself with genuine people.'

Mack smiles.

'What does your wife do?' I ask. 'Sarah, isn't it?'

'Yes, Sarah's a doctor. She mainly works in primary care.'

'That's like a GP here?'

'Yes, only without your good old NHS. We have to pay for our healthcare over in the States.'

'It must be difficult with your hours in the bar – I assume she works mostly days and you nights?'

'I do afternoons too, but, yeah, it's not ideal. How about you – any sign of Mr Right yet?'

'Noo!' I probably say it a little too vehemently. 'Not yet. I'm not really looking though.'

'Why not?'

I shrug. 'Dunno, just a bit busy with work right now. We're here,' I say, pointing down the street. 'That one with the blue door – that's Claire's house.'

'Do you want me to hang back?' Mack asks.

'Might be for the best.'

Mack stops walking and allows me to continue. I stop in front of Claire's door and take a deep breath.

Then I knock.

I look back at Mack while I wait for someone to answer. He's leaning casually against a wall, as if it's the most natural thing in the world for him to be hanging around a narrow Cornish street late at night. He smiles at me, so I smile back.

'Frankie?' Claire says as she opens the door in her dressing gown. 'What are you doing here this late – has something happened?'

'No, nothing's happened. I wanted to check you were all right, that's all.'

'Why wouldn't I be all right?' Claire asks a bit too breezily.

'Er . . . ' I didn't really think about what I was going to say to Claire, I just knew that I needed to see her. 'It's just you left the pub quite quickly tonight,' I say as the thought occurs. 'It seemed a little odd. Is everything OK?' I glance behind her into the house, not really knowing what I'm looking for.

'Yes . . . ' Claire frowns. 'Why wouldn't it be? You're being very odd, Frankie, even for you. And considering I've known you since you were four years old, that's saying something.'

'How's Jonathan?' I try a different tack, knowing this conversation is going nowhere fast.

I see Claire stiffen just a little. She pulls the collar of her dressing gown a little tighter across her chest. 'He's fine.'

'Good. Everything is OK, then?'

'Frankie, why do you keep asking me that? Is there something I should know?'

I swallow, and glance quickly at Mack. He's still waiting patiently a little way down the street.

Claire sees me and leans out of her doorway. 'Is that Rob's friend, Mack – what is he doing here?'

'Nothing, he just walked me here. We . . . I just wanted to check you were OK.'

'And as I keep telling you I'm absolutely fine. The children are fine. Jonathan is fine.'

I nod hurriedly. 'Good ... that's good. It's just ...'

Claire waits for me to finish with a questioning expression.

'Rob said your mum is worried about you,' I say eventually.

'Rob said?'

'Yeah, he said when he was speaking to his mum, she asked if you were OK because your mum had told her she was worried about you.'

I know I'm starting to sound like we're back at school again with all the 'his mum, your mum said' stuff. But how else can I explain why I'm here?

'Did she?' Claire says with pursed lips.

'Yes, and Mandy said something similar too.'

'I see how it is. You're all in the pub getting drunk, you've run out of things to talk about, so you're discussing me, are you?'

'No, it wasn't like that. You just seemed to go off in a hurry, that's all.'

'Frankie,' Claire says in a voice that makes her sound like her mother. 'Unlike you, I have other people to think about in my life. I have a husband and a family who need me. When they call, I come, it's as simple as that. We don't all have the freedom you do to come and go as we please. You clearly like being single – perhaps it suits you, perhaps you aren't cut out to have a family. But I am and they will always come first.'

Claire finishes her speech and stares at me – defiantly to begin with, but then her face softens and she looks immediately apologetic. She's about to speak again when a voice behind her in the house calls out. 'Claire, who's at the door?'

Claire visibly stiffens.

'No one, Jonathan. Go back to the television. I'll be there in a minute to make the tea.'

'You'd better go,' she whispers.

'Why?' I ask, equally defiant. 'What's wrong with your friend calling on you?'

Jonathan clearly hasn't listened to Claire. He appears behind her, also wearing nightwear with a dressing gown over the top.

'Oh, it's you,' he says, seeing me. 'I should have known.'

'Jonathan,' Claire says reproachfully. 'Frankie was just worried about me because I left the pub without saying goodbye, that's all. She's going now I've told her everything is fine.'

Jonathan nods. 'You didn't bring that waste-of-space boyfriend of yours with you, did you?' he asks, leaning past Claire to look out into the street. He squints as he spots Mack's shadowy figure.

'No,' Claire says hurriedly. 'That's not Rob, that's someone else.'

'Dumped the movie star now, have you?' Jonathan asks, grinning. 'I'm not surprised.'

I stare hard at Jonathan. How have I never noticed what a loathsome man he is? Perhaps he's been very good at hiding it.

'Not that it's any of your business,' I reply calmly. 'But Rob and I have not been together since we were at school.' A lie of course, but what did it matter right now? What's important is finding out if Claire is all right. 'And if you don't mind, I've come here to check on Claire. Not to listen to you insult my other friends.'

Jonathan glares at me. But I simply stare back at him. I'm not going to let this excuse of a man bully me. Because it's becoming clearer by the minute that's what he's probably doing to Claire.

'Claire, I think it's time you came back in,' he says, putting his hand across her so it rests on the door frame, his arm now a visible barrier between us. 'I'm sure your friend has better things to do with her time than stand on our doorstep at night.'

I turn to Claire. But she simply looks beseechingly back at me. 'Please go, Frankie,' she says pleadingly. 'It's for the best. I'll see you tomorrow at the funeral.'

'That's tomorrow?' Jonathan asks. 'Is it not bad enough that you abandoned your family to spend tonight in a public house with your friends, but you expect to do the same again tomorrow?'

'Tomorrow is different,' Claire says quietly. 'It's Mandy's sister's funeral. It's hardly a day trip.'

'We'll see tomorrow,' Jonathan says in a cold voice.

'You can't stop her going to a funeral,' I blurt out. 'That's crazy. What do you think she's going to do, run away with the undertaker?'

I hear Mack snort with laughter down the road. But Jonathan doesn't find it quite as amusing. He steps forward in front of Claire and leans over me in a threatening manner, but only because he's still standing on the step. I know Jonathan is no taller than I am.

'Stay away from Claire,' he says quietly but firmly. 'Do you understand?'

'Or what?' I ask defiantly, folding my arms across my chest. I can feel myself shaking inside, but it's more from rage than intimidation. 'What will you do, Jonathan?'

'You little bitch. Who do you think you are?' He sneers and lunges towards me. As I swiftly sidestep his advance, he stumbles a few steps across the road, but he doesn't fall. He turns and is about to come towards me again when someone steps in between us.

'I don't think so, fella,' Mack says. Now Mack *is* much taller

196

than me, so he towers over Jonathan. Jonathan looks angrily up at him.

'What business is this of yours?' he snaps.

'None of my business whatsoever,' Mack says calmly. 'But I never appreciate seeing men attack women – physically or otherwise.' Mack glances at Claire. 'Are you all right?' he asks her gently. 'Would you like me to call anyone for you? Anyone at all?'

Jonathan sees his moment and lunges at Mack, but Mack quickly administers what looks like a martial art move on him so Jonathan lands firmly on his back.

'That's enough now,' Mack says firmly, looking down at him. 'I deal with guys three times the size of you several nights a week in my bar. Claire?' he asks again. 'What would you like to happen now?'

'I think you should both go,' Claire says, looking with pity at her husband lying on the cobbled street. 'I'll be fine, honestly.'

Jonathan pulls himself to his feet. He attempts to glare at us as he brushes himself down.

'Now,' Mack says, addressing Jonathan. 'We'll expect to see Claire at the funeral tomorrow. In fact, Frankie and I will personally be calling in the morning to escort her.'

Jonathan hobbles towards his front door and pushes past Claire.

'And Jonathan,' Mack calls after him as he tries to disappear down the hall.

Jonathan turns.

'If I see one bruise on Claire tomorrow. Just one. I won't be quite as polite when I come calling next time. Understand?'

Jonathan growls something and turns away again.

'Claire.' I go over to her. 'Are you—'

'You have no idea what you've done.' Claire looks tearful. 'Please just go. Thank you, Mack,' she says, turning to him. 'I'm sorry you've got dragged into this tonight.'

Mack just nods.

'Come on, Frankie,' he says gently, trying to guide me away. 'Let's do as Claire wants. We'll call for you tomorrow, Claire. Around ten-thirty, all right?'

Claire nods, then she backs through her doorway and closes the blue door.

I stand staring at the door for a moment.

'Frankie,' Mack repeats. 'We should go. We can't do anything more tonight.'

Reluctantly, I nod.

'Would you like to walk for a bit until you've cleared your head?' he asks. 'Or shall we go back to the pub?'

'A walk sounds like a good idea. I'm not ready to face the others' questions just yet.'

'Lead the way, then.'

We walk down the street a little further until it branches out into a car park and then into a large area of greenery, which in turn leads up a hill towards the cliff edge.

I'm grateful to Mack that he doesn't try to force the conversation. I'm still trying to process what just happened, and I need time to think.

It's breezy out, and my long hair blows around my face as we get nearer to the sea. I reach into my pocket, but I haven't brought a band with me.

'What are you thinking about?' Mack asks, after we've walked for a bit without saying an awful lot. 'Claire?'

'Yes, mostly. I was actually just thinking that I wished I'd brought a hairband with me,' I reply as yet again I'm forced to push my hair away from my face. 'I usually carry one, but I didn't expect to be walking out here tonight.'

Mack smiles. 'As you can see, I don't have that problem.' He gestures to his wavy brown hair, which seemed floppy in the pub, but now is blowing back off his face so I can see all his features in more detail. Mack is actually quite handsome, my mind registers momentarily, before my hair is blown across my face once again. But Mack reaches into his jacket pocket and produces, to my surprise, a hairband with a little pink bow on it, surrounded by three tiny shells.

'Why on earth do you have that?' I ask, staring at his hand. 'Do you have children?'

'No, two nieces. I often end up with all sorts in my pockets after a day spent with them. Although I don't actually remember how I came across this particular item?' He stares at it a little puzzled. 'Here, take it. You have more use for it than me.'

I take the band and tie it loosely into my hair to make a ponytail. 'Thank you.'

We stand for a moment looking out over the sea, the moon still lighting up the waves as they roll in over the sand.

'I should also thank you for earlier,' I say. 'For helping out with Jonathan.'

Mack shrugs. 'It's nothing. I've dealt with men like that before – too many times in fact.'

'I can't believe I didn't notice anything was wrong sooner. I know we don't see each other too often these days, but I've visited their house, spent time with both Jonathan and the children. Everything seemed fine.'

'In my experience, both parties involved in this type of relationship are desperately trying to hide it. The abuser is worried someone will find out about their behaviour, and then they'll lose the one thing they think they're trying to keep safe with their actions – the victim. And the victim is usually so embarrassed it's happening to them, they can't bear the thought of anyone knowing their relationship is anything but perfect.'

'How do you know so much about this?' I ask. 'Everything you're saying is absolutely spot on.'

'Ah, I've been around,' Mack says. 'I'm not talking from personal experience, I should add. The only abusive relationship I've overcome is with alcohol. But I've had friends in similar situations. These types of relationship don't always involve physical violence. Sometimes the abuse is simply about controlling the other person.'

'I hope that's the case with Claire. Not that mental abuse is any better, mind, but if I find out he's been hitting her.' My hand balls into a fist.

'What will you do?' Mack asks to my surprise. I expected he'd say something like, 'You mustn't get involved', or 'It's no good you steaming in with all guns blazing.' That's the sort of thing people usually said.

'I . . . I don't know. I'm just so worried about her. Especially after tonight. She must be so scared.'

'Conversely, the abuser is actually the one who's usually the most scared, even though he's the one doing the abusing. They're paranoid about losing the other person, and therefore behave with them in a way that isn't acceptable. I only met Claire tonight, but I'd say she's stronger than you think.'

I look at Mack. He really is saying all the right things, even if they aren't what I want to hear. 'Yes, you're probably right. I just wish there was something I could do, though.'

'Unpopular opinion, but, if you want my advice, there's

nothing much you can do. Not yet. Not until the person wants to be helped. But when she does . . . '

'I'll probably be hundreds of miles away up in Scotland.' I sigh.

'You can still be a sounding board, a friendly ear for her to unload all her problems.'

I smile at Mack. 'Who made you so wise?'

Mack shrugs. 'Worldly wise maybe. It comes from listening to many, many people unburden their problems to me over the years.'

'This is some trip back home, you know? If it's not bad enough that one of my best friends is burying her sister to-morrow, now I find out that my other friend's husband could be abusing her. As if I didn't have enough problems of my own right now.'

Mack doesn't enquire what those problems are. And I'm glad.

'I meant what I said,' he reminds me instead. 'We'll swing by and pick Claire up tomorrow. Check everything is all right.'

'Thank you. I think that's a great idea. I'm sorry you got dragged into all this, Mack. I'm sure the last thing you need on your vacation is to find yourself in the middle of a broken marriage.'

Mack is silent for moment, before he says, 'No worries at all. I'm kinda used to that as well.'

Nineteen

We decide to head back to the pub, and we get there just before last orders.

We don't spend too long telling the others what happened, because it's very clear straight away that Mandy has been knocking back the drinks faster than everyone else around the table, and her constant shouts of, 'Let's go get the bastard!' and, 'We'll use his testicles as bait when the fishing boats leave the harbour tomorrow!' are drawing far more attention to our table than we'd like. Especially when we're trying to discuss such a sensitive topic.

Eventually, we decide that at least one of our party has had enough drinking for one evening, and we call it a night.

'I'll walk Mandy home,' I tell the others. 'It's on my way.'

'Let me help you,' Rob says. 'I'm not sure you can manage her on your own.'

'Nah!' Mandy says, hearing us. 'We don't need men, do we, Frankie?' She throws her arm around my shoulders. 'Me and my mate Frankie here will be just fine together. Just like we always should have been, if you hadn't come along.' She pushes Rob away playfully at first, and then with a bit more force.

'All right. All right!' Rob says, holding up his hands in sur-render. 'I get the message!'

'Sure you'll be OK?' he asks me in a whisper when Mandy's attention is caught by something else for a moment.

'Yeah, I'll be fine. She can still walk … just,' I say as Mandy sways next to me.

Those of us who don't have rooms in the pub leave and go our separate ways, while Mandy and I stagger together towards Mandy's parents' house.

'Ah, Frankie,' Mandy says as we wobble along, her arm still around my shoulders. 'How did it come to this, eh?'

'Me making sure you get home all right?' I ask. 'I think it might have happened a few times before.'

'Yeah, you have, haven't you?' she says, stopping to look at me for a moment. 'You're a good friend. One of the best!'

'Thank you.' I move her along again.

'You know you've always been special to me,' Mandy says as we walk extremely slowly along the pavement together. 'And I'm sorry.'

'Sorry for what?'

'For what I did at that dance.'

'What dance? Do you mean the Enchantment Under the Sea dance?'

'Yeah, the enter …encha … that sea thing we all went to and sang. Do you remember?'

'Of course, I do,' I say, desperately trying to get her safely across the road before a car comes.

'Do you remember what I said to you that night … you know, in the toilets?'

'Er … vaguely, yes.' This journey back to Mandy's house is getting harder by the minute. Every time Mandy asks me a question, she stops walking, as though she can't cope with doing both at the same time.

'Well, I'm going to tell you something now you might not like.' Mandy pulls an overly sombre expression, which ends up looking quite comical.

'OK, can we keep walking though while you tell me? Otherwise you'll never get home, and neither will I.'

'Yes . . . ' Mandy waggles her finger at me. 'That is a genius idea. Let's do that.' She is silent while she tries to concentrate on walking for a few steps. 'Wait, the thing!' she says, suddenly remembering. She stops walking again.

'Right, I tell you what. You tell me the *thing*, and then we'll walk back quietly together. How about that?'

'Yes.' Mandy nods furiously. 'Again, a wonderful idea.' She stands swaying slightly in front of me. 'Do you remember what I told you about Rob that night?' she asks, surprising me.

'Kind of – why?'

'Well, I shouldn't have said it.' She nods matter-of-factly. 'I told you that because I was jealous. Not because it was the right thing to do.'

'OK . . . but what you said was great advice if I remember rightly. About your girlfriends being the most important thing.'

'And you not needing a man to make you happy. Yes, it was, wasn't it?' She thinks about this for a moment. But then just as quickly she shakes her head. 'No! No, it wasn't good advice. I only said it because I was jealous, Frankie.'

'Yes, you've said that already. But it really doesn't matter now if you were jealous of me having a boyfriend back then. It was a long time ago.'

'No!' she says, shaking her head again but much more ve-hemently this time. 'You've got it all wrong.' She pokes her finger into my chest. 'I wasn't jealous of you having Rob as a boyfriend. I was jealous of him having you as a girlfriend.'

'What do you mean?' I ask, not understanding. 'It's the same thing, isn't it?'

Mandy shakes her head, slowly this time, and then wobbles a little.

'You're not listening,' she says as she steadies herself. 'I didn't like you giving Rob all your attention, Frankie, I didn't like it at all. So I said what I did to try to break the two of you up. And I did it because ... because ... because I fancied you,' she finishes with a flourish of her hand. 'There, I've said it. *I fancied you*, Frankie. In fact,' she looks me up and down, 'I think I still do.'

I stare at Mandy for a moment trying to take this in. *Is she really saying what I think she is? She's clearly more drunk than I realised.*

'OK ... ' I say, not really knowing how to respond. 'Perhaps we should get going again.' I try to take hold of her once more.

'No!' She pushes me away like she did to Rob. 'You're not listening to me. I'm telling you, Frankie. I'm telling you I'm gay. I like girls and women. Not boys and men.'

Mandy's earnest face suggests this isn't something she's just decided to tell me on a drunken whim. It's something she's been storing up for years, waiting for the right moment.

'Let's sit down.' I gesture to a low brick wall that borders the garden behind us. There's a dense hedge the other side of the wall so I doubt the owners will notice us sitting there. And an added bonus, if Mandy should topple backwards off the wall, the hedge will stop her from falling. 'When did you first know?' I ask as we perch on the red-brick wall together. 'When we were at school?'

Mandy shrugs. 'Kind of. I wasn't really sure, though. I knew I felt differently about girls than boys, but it was when I met you that things began to change in my mind.'

'I'm flattered.'

Mandy grins. 'You should be.'

I notice that sitting on the cool brick wall seems to have sobered Mandy up a little. 'So all that stuff you used to spout about boys, that was all a front?'

'Yeah, sorry. I was very confused back then. I probably over-compensated for what I was really feeling.'

'Don't worry about it. Name a teenager who's got it all together at that age. I certainly hadn't.'

'That's true. Remember when you asked Rob if he wanted to be a mermaid?'

'How could I forget?' I roll my eyes.

'Even though you were my first crush, Frankie, I didn't have my first encounter, shall we call it, until I was twenty. And it was at, of all places, Claire's wedding reception.'

'No way! Really? Who with?'

'Remember that talent scout – the American who took our Rob over to the States?'

'Yes, of course I do. Wait, she was your first?'

Mandy nods. 'Jenna. She was older than me, obviously, but we got talking at the reception, and afterwards we stayed in the hotel bar drinking until quite late. One thing led to another and I've never looked back since. It seems both Rob and I have much to thank Jenna Morgan for.'

I think about this for a moment.

'Are you shocked?' Mandy asks earnestly. 'I don't mind if you are.'

'Shocked – no. Surprised – yes. Bothered – of course not!' I lean over and put my arms around Mandy's shoulder. 'If you're happy, then so am I. Oh, God, I didn't mean . . . of course you're not happy, what with tomorrow . . . Lord, I'm such a dunce!'

'Hey,' Mandy says, tapping my knee. 'Don't be daft. I have such a weight on my shoulders right now with Hetty, that telling you what I have tonight has lifted just a little of that weight away. You're the only one of the mermaids I've told, you know?'

I nod. 'I'm glad you have. Not because I want to pry or anything, I'm just pleased you wanted to confide in me.'

'Are you cross about Rob?' Mandy asks. 'That I tried to split you two up?'

'Not really. I think it would have happened anyway. Let's just say I got a few wires crossed that night. But it was probably all for the best. Look at where he is now. If we'd still been together, I wouldn't have fitted in that world at all.'

'You don't fancy starving yourself into frocks to go to awards ceremonies, or partying with the stars, then?'

'Definitely not. Rob has his life now, and I have mine. Never the twain shall meet.'

Not any more, anyway.

'That's a shame. Much as I hate to say it, I think you two are perfect for each other.'

'Well, that's something we do disagree on,' I say, standing up again. I hold my hand out to Mandy. 'Come on, you. I still need to get you home.'

Mandy nods reluctantly. 'I don't want tomorrow to come,' she says, still sitting. She looks down at the pavement. 'Because when it does, I have to say goodbye. And I'm not sure I can do that.' She looks up at me with such a harrowed expression, I feel my insides twist with compassion.

'I wish I could take away this pain you're feeling,' I tell her.

'But I can't, no one can. Tomorrow is something you have to do, Mandy. But you won't be alone. We'll all be there with you, supporting you, and helping you through it. Because that's what we've always done for each other. And that's what we always will do.'

I reach out my hand again, and this time Mandy takes it.

I pull her to her feet and then we give each other the biggest of hugs.

'Thank you,' Mandy whispers into my hair. 'I'm really gonna need you guys tomorrow.'

'We'll be there,' I repeat, thinking of Claire again. 'All of us – together.'

Twenty

The last time we were all here together was for Claire's wedding, I think sadly as we wait in the church for the funeral procession to arrive.

At the time that had seemed such a happy day, but, now, after last night, those memories seem a little tarnished.

I glance over at Claire, but she doesn't return my gaze. Instead, she stares straight ahead, listening intently to the sombre organ music that is wafting through the church.

Good to his word, Mack had called for me at my parents' house this morning, looking incredibly dapper in a smart black suit and shiny black shoes, and then we walked down through the town together to collect Claire. Contrary to my expectations, it went a lot more smoothly than I expected after the events of the previous evening.

Claire was polite as we all walked down to the church together, but quiet, even for her. I glanced with concern at Mack a couple of times after I tried to engage Claire in conversation and she answered my prompts with one-word answers. But he simply gave a small shake of his head – as if to say, 'Don't worry. Now's not the time.' And I felt immediately comforted by this small gesture. Mack being involved in this somehow managed to make me feel like everything was going to be all right.

I turn to my left and look across at him further along our pew, sitting next to Rob. He's reading the order of service, but he looks up at me and smiles. I smile back, at the same time as Rob looks up. He sees me smiling and mirrors my gesture, assuming I'm smiling at him.

Suzy, sitting in between us, notices our exchanges and smiles knowingly to herself.

Great! I face forward again. Now everyone is getting the wrong idea.

I glance at Eddie on my right to see if he has noticed any of this, but he's still sitting staring ahead, a bit like Claire, only he looks more upset.

'Are you OK?' I ask him.

Eddie turns his head. 'Yeah, I'm fine. I don't really like funerals.'

'I don't think anyone *likes* funerals,' I whisper. 'It's just one of those events you have to endure in life.'

'I mean, I don't like the whole dead-body thing. What do you think happens when we die?'

'I . . . I don't really know,' I say, surprised by his question. 'I'd like to think there's an afterlife of some sort. What about you?'

Eddie shrugs. 'That's the thing, I don't know. I'm in awe of these people that have faith. It must be very comforting at a time like this.'

'Yes, I suppose it must.'

The organist suddenly changes the music as the vicar appears at the doors of the church and begins to lead the procession down the aisle.

I've been lucky enough in my life that I've only had to attend a few funerals, so the sight of the coffin entering the church as we all stand is one I'm quite used to seeing. But witnessing two coffins following each other into the church, for some reason hits me harder than usual, and I have to stifle a gasp.

Eddie glances at me as the procession begins to pass us. 'You all right?' he mouths.

I nod, and then I see Mandy and her parents following behind the first of the two coffins, and I have to stifle another gasp, this time by putting my hand over my mouth.

Mandy looks paler than I've ever seen her before as she walks arm in arm between her mum and dad. The grief, anguish and torment etched on all their faces twists my heart so tightly that I can hardly bear to witness their pain, and I just want to hug all of them and tell them it's going to be all right.

Mandy looks across at us all lined up, and her red-rimmed eyes rest upon me.

Without thinking I blow her a kiss. I don't stop to think whether it's the most appropriate thing to do at a funeral, only that I want her know we're here with her, supporting her all the way.

She nods gratefully as she continues along the aisle.

Mandy and her parents are closely followed by the next coffin. Behind that walk two more grief-stricken parents arm in arm, as they attempt to support each other through the hardest thing they'll ever have to do – bury their own child.

As the two coffins are lined up at the front of the church side by side, I notice they both have matching wreaths of white flowers on top. One spells out *Mummy* and the other *Daddy*, and my heart breaks once more. Of course, Hetty and David had a young son.

The rest of the service is equally as moving. In between

the hymns and the vicar giving his eulogy, there are emotional tributes from both family and friends to the departed couple, and the tissues are passed frequently up and down our row as people who clearly thought they wouldn't need any are moved to tears, and those of us who knew we would need some use up far more paper hankies than we came prepared for.

When finally it's all over, and the close family have left to attend the internment at the nearby cemetery up on one of the hills in St Felix, we all step outside into the fresh air once more.

'That was pretty emotional,' Rob says, lighting up a cigarette as we stand outside the church.

I glance at him. *When did he start smoking?*

'Yes,' Suzy agrees. 'I think that's the most I've ever cried at a funeral. And we buried my grandad last year.'

'Anyone else?' Rob holds his cigarette packet out. 'Don't worry, I only smoke when I'm feeling stressed.'

We all shake our heads.

'Good job,' he says, grinning. 'Nasty habit to get into.'

'I thought superheroes were always fit and healthy, not full of nicotine,' I can't help saying.

Rob glances at me. 'They also have to look the part and, as we all know, these guys speed up your metabolism.' He holds up his lit cigarette. 'No good having the muscles if they're hidden under three layers of fat, is there?'

'I'm sure there's a better way than smoking,' I begin.

'Don't you think I've tried?' Rob snaps. 'Let me tell you there's a lot worse things you can use to shed the weight in LA. Eh, Mack?'

'Don't bring me into this,' Mack says lightly. 'You're the

212

movie star. I'm just the guy lining up another abusive substance for people to become addicted too – alcohol,' he adds in case we don't understand. 'I don't mean I deal drugs in my bar.'

I smile at him.

'Where's the wake being held?' Suzy asks. 'I'm sure someone told me, but I've forgotten.'

'The café by Morvoren Cove,' Eddie says.

'Really?' Suzy asks. 'That's an odd place for a wake, isn't it?'

'Apparently they do events and stuff now.'

'They've been doing events for some time now,' Claire says without emotion. 'Mandy's mum knows the owner. I think they're doing them a deal.'

'Shall we make our way over there, then?' Suzy says. 'I'm sure by the time we get there, Mandy and her family will already be on their way.'

'Seems like a plan,' Rob says. 'You coming, Claire?'

Claire looks around at us, all nervously awaiting her reply.

'Yes, of course. Why wouldn't I be?'

'Frankie?'

'Yes, I'm coming. I'm just going to catch up with someone first. I'll see you there, all right?'

I've just spotted my old boss, Rose, from the flower shop, talking to one of the other mourners. I take a deep breath and go over to her.

'Frankie!' she says as I walk up to them. 'How lovely to see you again.'

'I'm sorry to interrupt,' I say to Rose and her companion. 'But I just wanted to say hello.'

'I'll see you later, Rose,' the lady Rose has been talking to says. 'Beautiful flowers as always.'

'Thank you, Janet,' Rose says. 'Yes, I'll see you tomorrow.'

Janet walks away and Rose turns to me. 'So lovely to see you again, Frankie,' she says in her soft gentle voice, immediately transporting me back in time fifteen years. 'Sadly in such sad circumstances, though.'

'Yes. Did you know Hetty or David?'

'I'm friends with Doris, David's mother,' Rose says. 'She asked me to do the flowers today.'

'Of course. They looked beautiful – as always.' I know I have to say it, even though I don't want to. It's breaking my heart just thinking about it, let alone actually talking to Rose about it. 'I was so sorry to hear about Will,' I say quickly, ripping the plaster off the wound, knowing getting it out there in the fresh air is the best and only way for it to heal.

Rose's soft, kind face immediately twists with pain, and I feel terrible for making that happen.

'I ... I can't imagine what you must have gone through,' I continue when Rose doesn't immediately speak. 'What you must still be going through.'

'Thank you for both your letter and your flowers – they meant so much, Frankie,' Rose says. 'You were kind to think of me and remember Will.'

Rose's grandson collapsed suddenly at an outdoor concert in Penzance. He was there with his sister, Poppy and, incredibly sadly, the paramedics were not able to revive him, and Will died before he even reached the hospital.

When I heard, I felt so desperately sad for Rose and I didn't know what to do for the best. At the time, it was impossible for me to take the number of days off from work that would have been required to travel here and attend the funeral. So instead, I wrote Rose a long letter of condolence, and carefully chose the appropriate flowers to send to her.

'I tried really hard to get the meanings behind the flowers right. I hope I did.'

'They were perfect; thank you for putting that little bit of extra thought in.'

'How is Poppy?' I ask.

Rose wrinkles her nose. 'Not doing all that well to be honest. She's finding it quite difficult to cope.'

'Understandable – they were very close, weren't they?'

Rose nods. 'Inseparable. They argued like all siblings do. But they always made up quickly. I miss both of them so much. Since it happened, Poppy doesn't want to come here to St Felix any more. I understand that, of course I do. But I do miss her.'

'She's not been here in four years?' I ask, surprised to hear this. Poppy and Will used to visit Rose several times a year when they were children.

'Sadly no. I'm sure she'll return when the time is right, though.'

'Oh, Rose,' I say, and I can think of nothing other than giving her a hug, which Rose receives gratefully. 'I'm sure she'll come back.'

'Thank you, Frankie. Now.' She pats my hand. 'I mustn't hold you up. You must go after your friends. I saw them all leaving without you. It's lovely you all still keep in touch after all this time. Hold on to that, Frankie. Friends and family are all we have in life. And sometimes they're taken from us all too soon.'

The café on Morvoren Cove is already receiving guests when I arrive, and a bit like a wedding everyone is offered a drink as they go in – but unlike a wedding when it might be a glass of champagne we're offered from a silver tray, this time it's tea and coffee and soft drinks all laid out on a long table covered in a white cloth. The table is also laid with long plates of sandwiches, quiches, sausage rolls and other buffet food all wrapped tightly for the moment in layers of cling film.

Gradually, we are joined by the other mourners and eventually Mandy, her family and David's relatives and friends, and the little café – closed especially for the funeral – is packed full of people.

I watch Mack as he goes over to speak to David's mother and father.

'Life's funny, isn't it?' Suzy says, coming to stand next to me with a cup of tea in her hand. 'Imagine going halfway around the world and bumping into someone who not only used to live in the same small town as you, but who you also went to school with. Mack's all right, isn't he?'

'Yes, he seems like a good guy.'

'Sounds like it was just as well he went with you last night to see Claire from what you were saying.'

'Jonathan wasn't exactly friendly, that's for sure.'

'Claire's definitely very quiet today.'

'I think she's a bit embarrassed we all know what's been going on.'

'We think we all know. Nothing has been confirmed yet.'

'I'm not sure it ever will be unless Claire admits it to herself.'

'That's very wise.'

'Not my wisdom,' I say. 'Mack's. He said we can't help Claire until she wants to be helped. We just have to wait until she's ready.'

'And he's right.' Suzy looks over at Mack again. 'As well as being a smart guy, Mack's pretty easy on the eye, isn't he?'

I look at Suzy; her eyes are shining mischievously.

'If you think he's so hot, you go talk to him.' I know exactly what she's hinting at. 'But I warn you, he's married.'

'Sadly, I can't. I'm also spoken for.'

'Since when?' I ask in surprise. 'That's news to me.'

'Since about a month ago,' she says, the joy of new love radiating from her every pore. 'It's early days yet, but he seems like a keeper.'

'You kept that quiet last night,' I say, pleased for her. I knew how difficult Suzy found it to hold down a relationship and a high-powered job.

'I don't want to jinx it this time, that's why. Harry works in a similar job to me, but for the other side.' She grimaces. 'So although we have some very heated discussions about politics, we really do understand each other.'

'I'm so pleased for you, Suz.' I give her a hug. 'You deserve it.'

'Now, what about you?' Suzy asks earnestly. 'Or are you still holding a candle for our Rob?'

'Of course not. Rob and I were a long time ago now. A very long time ago. He'll always be special to me. But there's nothing like that between us.'

Not now, anyway. We had our moment in Glasgow. It was lovely at the time, but that felt like a lifetime ago now, and things changed. Rob and I would always be good friends. But that's all. Nothing more.

'You sure?' Suzy raises her eyebrows. 'Does he think that?'

'Why, what have you heard?'

'Nothing, I just get the feeling he might not be as over you as you are pretending to be him.'

'I'm not pretending . . . why would I be?'

Suzy shrugs. 'You tell me? If you're so over Rob, why haven't you met anyone else yet?'

'Why do I need to meet anyone? I'm perfectly happy as I am, thanks. I don't need a man to complete my life.'

'Now, I'd be impressed by that statement if I thought you were telling the truth. Something's going on with you, Frankie. I just haven't figured out what yet.'

'Oh, who's that?' I ask, quickly changing the subject as a small boy runs across the café towards Doris and Walter, David's parents.

'I think that might be Fisher, Hetty and David's son.'

We stare at the small dark-haired boy, who can't be more than four years old. Understandably, he hadn't been in the church for the funeral.

'Claire was telling me that Walter and Doris are going to bring him up here in St Felix,' Suzy says. 'Poor little soul losing both his parents so suddenly like that.'

Doris picks up the little boy and holds him close to her, while Walter strokes his hair.

'Perhaps it's some comfort to them that they still have Fisher,' I say quietly, still watching them. 'Mandy's parents must feel something similar too. At least little Fisher will grow up in St Felix near both sets of grandparents.'

'How are we all getting on?' Rob asks, coming over to us. 'A guy over there just told me they're opening up the bar in a few minutes for anyone who wants an alcoholic drink.'

He looks hopefully at us.

'Nice,' Suzy says. 'I could do with one.'

'Nah.' I look away. 'I'm not really in the mood today.'

The other two look quizzically at me.

'I want to keep an eye on Claire,' I say as an excuse. 'And I want a clear head for that.'

Rob shrugs, but Suzy looks suspicious.

'In fact, I think I'll go and look for her now. Back in a bit.' I walk over to where I last saw Claire heading towards the café's veranda, which overlooks the beach, an area very popular with visitors in the summer.

I'm going to have to be a bit more careful, I think as I walk towards some welcome fresh air. *Or those who know me well are going to guess. I've barely got my head around it myself; I'm not ready to share my secret with anyone. Not yet, anyway.*

Twenty-One

Claire is sitting outside at one of the wooden picnic tables that line the veranda. Her legs straddle the bench so she faces the sea.

'Mind if I join you?' I ask hesitantly, half expecting Claire to tell me to leave her alone.

Claire shrugs. 'Free country.'

I sit down opposite her.

'How are you?' I ask when she doesn't speak.

Claire turns slowly towards me. 'How do you think I am after last night?'

'I'm sorry, Claire. Perhaps I haven't dealt with this in the best way. But when I found out ... no, *suspected* that something might be wrong, I couldn't just stand by and do nothing. You're my friend. I want to help you.' Claire doesn't speak so I continue. 'Look, if I'm completely wrong about Jonathan then tell me and I'll back off. But if I'm right ...'

'You're right,' Claire says in such a low voice I can barely hear her over the sound of the waves rolling in. It's high tide so the sea isn't any more than twenty metres away from us right now.

She glances at me, a look of total humiliation on her face.

'Oh, Claire.' I take hold of her hand across the table. 'It's not your fault.'

'It feels like it is. He makes me feel like it is.'

'That's what they do, men like this. They twist everything so it seems like it's all you, but it's not you, it's them. It's Jonathan who's at fault here. Does he . . . ' I hesitate again. I can hardly bear to think it, let alone say it out loud. 'Is he physical with you?' I force myself to voice it.

'Do you mean, does he hit me? No, he doesn't. It's all up here.' She taps the side of her forehead. 'He gets inside my head. He twists everything and confuses me until I think it's me that's doing everything wrong.' She pauses for a moment as if she's trying to justify something to herself. 'I guess I should be grateful, really, that he doesn't hit me, so it's not real abuse.'

'Whoa!' I say. 'Stop right there. Just because it's not physical, it doesn't make it any less wrong.'

'Yes, but maybe he's just looking out for me, you know? He only wants what's best for me and the children. Maybe this is his way of showing that he loves us, that he cares. He just goes about it in a slightly different way than someone else might.'

'By trying to control you?' I ask aghast, but knowing I have to tread carefully or else I'll put Claire's back up again. 'I'm sure that Jonathan does love you and the children. But he doesn't have the right to control you, to stop you living your life. Why would someone who loves you want to stop you from seeing your friends? Or stop you from going to a funeral, for goodness' sake? Jonathan is a bully, Claire, and you need to get yourself far away from him as soon as you possibly can.'

Claire looks at me in astonishment. 'I can't do that,' she says. 'What about the children? What about our house? It's their home. I can't just uproot them from everything they know.'

'Claire, you have to, for your own sake.'

'I have to put the children first.'

'No, you have to put you first. You have to think about your safety *and* the children's. What if he does become physical with you, or with Alice, George or Freddie?'

'He wouldn't.' Claire shakes her head.

'He tried to with me last night.'

'No, that was just an accident. He didn't mean anything by it.'

'Claire! Listen to yourself. Stop making excuses for his behaviour. Wake up to what's going on here!'

'I am awake!' Claire says angrily. 'I wish I bloody wasn't. I wish this was all just a bad dream that I could wake up from. But it's not, is it? This is my life. *My* life, Frankie, not yours. You don't have a husband or children, so how could you possibly know what I'm going through? You live this wonderful, young, free and single life up in Scotland. You don't have any cares, nothing to worry about. You don't understand and you never will.'

I stare at Claire, and then very slowly I begin to nod.

'No, you're right. I don't have a husband and I don't have any children – not yet anyway.' I put my hand on my stomach in the same way Claire did back in 1994, when we were sitting outside a café, but in the sunshine this time. 'My life is certainly not carefree though. In fact, I've got many worries right now that are bothering me greatly.' And I begin to gently stroke my belly.

Now it's Claire's turn to stare at me.

'Frankie?' she asks quietly. 'Are you pregnant?'

I nod.

'Oh my, that's wonderful,' she says, happily this time. 'Why didn't you say before?'

222

'It's not been the right time. Also, it's early days. I haven't known myself all that long. I haven't told anyone else yet.'

'Not even your parents?'

I shake my head. 'Nope.'

'I'm the first?' Claire looks quite emotional.

'Yes.'

She gets up from her bench and comes around to my side of the table. Then, without speaking, she simply gives me a huge hug.

'I'm so sorry for what I said just now,' she says when she's let go of me. She sits back down again, this time on my side of the bench. 'It was rude and uncalled for.'

'Forget about it,' I tell her. 'You've got a lot going on.'

'Not as much as you,' she says, looking down at my stomach, as though at any moment it might suddenly start growing a baby bump. 'You are keeping this baby, aren't you?'

'Yes,' I say. 'I'm keeping it.'

'And what about the father?'

'Nah, I don't need him.'

'But you will tell him?'

'At some point, I suppose.'

'You're going to bring the baby up on your own?' Claire looks quite shocked by the thought.

'It has been done before, you know.'

'Of course, but it's harder than you think. I know, I've had three of my own, and although he's a shit,' Claire grimaces at her use of a swear word, 'Jonathan did help me a lot with the children when they were tiny.'

'I'll be fine.'

'You could move back in with your parents?'

'I don't think so! And, anyway, they're selling up soon and

moving on – probably to a little retirement bungalow if they get their way. The last thing they'll want is a new baby taking up all their space.'

'But still . . . ' Claire begins.

'Claire, I'll be fine. I have my job. I've just been promoted, haven't I? I won't be short of money.'

'But who will look after the baby when you're at work?'

'There's such a thing called day care.'

Claire looks shocked.

'You're so old-fashioned, Claire.' I smile at her. 'It's the modern way.'

'I know, but you might feel differently when the baby is born. You might be surprised at how you feel about leaving it with strangers.'

'Then I'll cross that bridge when I come to it. Now, this is still a secret,' I tell her seriously. 'I don't want the others knowing just yet.'

'Why not?'

'Because everyone will try to offer advice, and I especially don't want Rob to know.'

'Why not?'

'Because . . . he might look down on me from his Hollywood perch.' I hurriedly say the first thing that comes to mind.

'Rob wouldn't do that.'

'Maybe not, but this is my baby, and I'll tell everyone when the time is right for me, OK?'

Claire nods. 'I'll keep quiet.' She pretends to zip her mouth shut. 'Oh, Frankie,' she suddenly bursts out. 'This is so *exciting*. *You*, my best friend, having a baby.' She clutches her hands together. 'I'm so happy for you.'

'Congratulations!' An unfamiliar voice calls from down

below us, and a willowy figure wearing a long black dress begins to climb the steps from the beach at the side of the veranda. 'I'm sorry,' the woman says as she comes level with us and walks towards our table. 'I was sitting down on the beach before you arrived, just taking in some sea air. It's been a hell of a day with the funeral and everything,' she explains, tossing back her long, curly grey hair over her shoulder. 'And I couldn't help overhearing your conversation as I sat there on the rocks.'

Claire and I both stare at the woman, both of us wondering just how much she heard. She's tall and thin, and the plain black dress she's wearing is more than appropriate for a funeral, but on her feet she wears black flip-flops encrusted with crystals, and around her neck a necklace made up of more crystals interspersed with small seashells.

'Don't worry,' she says, looking at both of us in turn. 'I'll keep your secrets.' She puts her fingers to her lips. 'But can I just offer you both a tiny bit of advice?'

I half nod, more out of surprise than encouragement. If we thought someone was listening in on our conversation, I'm sure we wouldn't have been quite so honest about everything.

'Get help,' she says. 'Both of you. Get as much help as you can with your baby,' she says to me. 'You really will need it. And you, my darling,' she says to Claire. 'You must seek help with your problems too. Here,' she opens up a small clutch bag and tries to pass Claire a business card. 'This is a support group that meets every Monday night in Penzance. I know you won't want to go, but you must. They really will be able to help you. They helped me no end when I had my own relationship problems.'

Claire doesn't take the card, so the woman lays it down on the table in front of her and very oddly places a small shell on top of the card.

'Think about it,' she says, tapping the card. 'I only want to help you. Now.' She looks back through the café window. 'Have either of you seen Eddie?'

'Er, no ...' I say, still in a state of shock from this odd, very one-sided conversation we seem to be having with this stranger. 'He's here somewhere, though.'

'Then I'll simply have to go and look for him,' she says, smiling serenely. 'I have some news ...'

Claire and I sit open-mouthed as we watch the woman sashay away across the wooden boards of the veranda back into the café.

'Did that actually just happen?' I ask Claire, turning back towards her. 'Who was she? Was she even at the funeral earlier?'

'I vaguely remember seeing someone who looked a bit like her.' Claire looks puzzled. 'I think she was on the opposite side of the church to us. But she was wearing her hair pinned up then, and a little pillbox hat with a veil – a little over the top, I thought at the time.' She looks down at the card but doesn't pick it up.

'What does it say?' I lift it from the table myself. '"Shell Seekers. A Penzance Support Group for Women,"' I read. 'And there's a telephone number. It also says all calls are treated with the strictest confidence and there's no pressure within the group to share anything. They welcome observers who just want to sit, listen and take comfort from others who might be in the same situation. It might be worth you investigating it?' I say hopefully, holding out the card to Claire.

Claire stares hard at the card for a moment, and then to my surprise she takes it from me.

'I'll think about it.' She tosses it into her bag. 'That's all I'm saying. In fact,' she says, smiling as a thought occurs to her. 'I promise to think about all my problems, as long as you think about all yours. Namely how you're going to cope with a baby all on your own.' And in the same way as I passed her the card, she hands me the shell the woman left behind.

I take the shell and hold out my hand. 'Deal,' I say, and we shake hands, just before we pull each other inwards for a very welcome hug.

Twenty-Two

'Did that woman ever catch up with you?' I ask Eddie as we all sit on the rocks overlooking Morvoren Cove.

Most of the other mourners have departed, the café is beginning to close up and it's just us six mermaids and Mack who have stayed behind to enjoy the cool night air and the clear skies above us, affording us a beautiful view of both the moon and the stars as they light up the sand and the waves below.

Mandy has brought along some bottled beers from the café and some of the others are drinking them as we sit listening to the splashing of the waves.

'What woman?' Eddie asks, looking puzzled.

'There was a woman looking for you earlier. Tall, with long grey hair – she was wearing a long black dress and a seashell necklace. We think she was in the church earlier today.'

'But she was wearing a hat with a little veil then,' Claire adds. 'And her hair was pinned up.'

'Do you mean Marilyn?' Mandy asks. 'It sounds like her from the description. She's my aunt.'

'It might be. She spoke to Claire and me and said she was looking for Eddie.'

Mandy turns to Eddie. 'Was she now? How do you know her?'

Eddie still looks puzzled. 'I don't. Well, I didn't until today. A woman matching the description you're giving did come and talk to me, though.'

'What did she want?' I ask, intrigued.

'It's all a bit odd,' Eddie says. 'She asked me whether I liked living in London to begin with. I said it's all right, I guess.'

'I thought you loved living there?' I say, surprised to hear him say this.

'I do – well, I did. I don't know, I've been thinking for a bit whether it's actually for me.'

'Not another change of career, Eddie,' Rob says. 'How many is that now?'

'I didn't say I wasn't happy being a chef, I said I wasn't sure if London life is for me any more.'

Again, I'm surprised. Eddie always seemed so happy in the capital before.

'Funny thing is, it wasn't until I came back here this time that I realised how much I miss St Felix. Cornwall in general, really. So when this woman – Marilyn, did you say?' he asks Mandy.

She nods.

'When Marilyn asked me that question, I was surprised – shocked, even. I hadn't voiced those thoughts to anyone before.'

'What did she say next?' Suzy asks.

'She said that I should go to the estate agent on the high street tomorrow morning, and I should look in the window. She was very specific about the time. She said I should arrive at ten a.m., and wait.'

'How odd.' I'm trying to work out why this Marilyn would say this. 'Does it mean anything to you, Mand?'

'I think she does work in property in some way,' Mandy says. 'I'd have to ask my mum, though. That might explain the estate-agent part.'

'Are you thinking of moving, Eddie?' Claire asks.

'I wasn't before this trip,' Eddie says. 'But after the funeral today ... ' He glances at Mandy.

'Don't worry, it's fine,' Mandy says. 'You can talk about it.'

'After the funeral and realising how short life can be, I have to say it has crossed my mind. But again, I've told no one this. Not until now.'

'Will you go?' I ask Eddie. 'To the estate agent?'

'I think I will. If only to see what it's all about.'

'You'll have to tell us what happens – send us a group email or something.'

Eddie nods.

'While we're talking about secret hopes and dreams,' Mandy says, taking a swig of her bottle of beer. 'I have a secret to share with you all.' She glances quickly at me. 'I'm gay.'

There's silence on the rocks as the others process her sudden announcement.

'You never are?' Eddie says in astonishment. 'But you love men.'

'Used to, perhaps,' Mandy says. 'Not now.'

'Well, of all the things I thought you might say, Mand, that's certainly not one of them,' Rob says, grinning. He lifts his bottle of beer. 'Congratulations!'

'Thank you,' she says, doing the same to him.

'Gosh,' Suzy says, looking a bit shocked. 'I can't say it's not a surprise, Mandy. Is this something new, or have you known for a while?'

'A while,' Mandy says. 'Just took me a few years to accept it.'

'You've had ... partners, have you?' Suzy continues. 'Sorry, is that too personal?'

'No, not at all,' Mandy says. 'Yes, I've had partners. My first was at Claire's wedding.'

Claire looks surprised. 'Really? Who?'

'Rob knows her,' Mandy says, looking at him knowingly.

Rob thinks about this for a moment. 'Jenna?' he asks, getting it right first time.

Mandy nods. 'Yep, she was my first.'

'Wait, Jenna – that American talent scout?' Eddie asks as he remembers. 'No way.'

'It seems she was instrumental in changing both Rob's and my life – in different ways, of course.'

'Well, I never expected to hear that tonight,' Eddie says, blinking. 'Anyone else got anything they want to share with us?'

Claire glances at me. But I give a tiny shake of my head. Our secrets need to remain secret – for a while longer at least.

'Mack?' Eddie asks. 'Would you like to share anything? Since you're hearing all our secrets tonight.'

Mack has been quiet until now, and I wonder what he's making of all this. We've all known each other for years; Mack has known us approximately twenty-four hours.

'No, my life is an open book,' Mack says. 'Isn't that right, Rob?'

'I'd say so,' Rob nods. 'No secrets under the bed for Mack here. He's as straight as they come. Oh, no offence,' he says hurriedly to Mandy and Eddie. 'I meant straight as in straight as a die, not, well, you know?'

'Rob, you've been offending me for years with your heterosexual comments,' Eddie says, grinning. 'I'm not going to start taking offence now.'

'You're good, babe.' Mandy takes another swig of her beer. 'Ooh, I'm empty. Another, anyone? Claire?'

Claire, to all our surprise, takes the beer Mandy is offering her.

'What?' she asks innocently. 'I do drink, you know. Besides, tonight is a new start for me. Tomorrow things are going to change in my life.' She reaches for the bottle opener and pops the top off the beer. 'Here's to new beginnings!'

'To new beginnings!' we all agree, and those of us with a bottle lift them in a toast.

'Frankie?' Mandy asks. 'You sure you don't want a beer?'

I shake my head.

'Not pregnant, are you?' She grins.

I stare at her. 'No, of course not,' I say quickly. 'I've not felt great since I've been here, that's all. I haven't felt like drinking.'

I glance quickly at the others; they all seem happy with this explanation. But I can see Rob is thinking hard, so I turn away.

'Did anyone else just see that?' Mack says as he leans over the edge of the rockface as if he's trying to see something.

'See what?' Suzy asks.

'I don't know. It looked like a giant fish's tail flipping over in the waves.'

Rob and I glance at each other again.

'Ooh, remember the last time we saw that in this bay?' Eddie asks. 'The night of the mermaid's treasure.'

'Mermaid's treasure?' Mack asks, sounding intrigued. 'What's that?'

Eddie, Suzy and Claire give Mack a quick rundown on what happened the night we threw the whisky barrel back into the sea – including the part when we all made wishes. Rob, Mandy and myself all remain silent.

'Cool,' Mack says when they've finished. 'And have any of these wishes come true?'

'Yeah, mine,' Suzy says, holding up her hand.

'Tell me more?'

'I don't know what the others wished for that night,' Suzy says, sounding a tad embarrassed. 'But I wished that I could make a difference in my life – and I feel like I'm already doing that by working in politics. We have our first Labour government after eighteen years of Tory rule, and, even though I work behind the scenes, I feel like I really helped to make that change.'

Mack nods. 'Nice. What about the rest of you? Frankie?'

'Nothing yet,' I mumble.

'Me neither.' Rob reaches for another bottle of beer.

'Claire?'

'My wish sort of came true, I suppose,' Claire says. 'I wished I could have a family and a nice house of my own in St Felix. I have both of those things, even if there's a few ... issues with them at the moment. I ... I don't mean my children; they are perfect – everything I could and did indeed wish for. I think you all know what I'm referring to that's not quite so perfect?'

We all nod.

'But like I said before, that's going to change!' she says, lifting her beer again.

'Eddie?' Mack asks now. 'How about you?'

'Nope, not yet,' Eddie says, grinning. 'But then I did wish for something very specific. Something I can't see will ever happen, to be honest. That's why I did it – to really test the mermaid. Oh, it's never going to happen so I might as well tell you—'

'No!' Rob and I both cry out at the same time.

I look at Rob, wondering if he's thinking what I am. If Eddie reveals his un-granted wish, then we will have to reveal ours as well.

'You mustn't tell us, Eddie,' Claire says quickly, glancing at me. 'Or the wish won't come true. Keep it a secret and maybe the next time we all see each other, it will have come to fruition.'

Eddie looks less confident about that than Claire, but he nods.

'Mandy! Last but not least.' Mack smiles at her. 'Now tell us, did your wish come true?'

Mandy takes a very long swig of her beer. 'Sadly, Mack, yes, it did. And I'll never forgive myself for wishing it.'

We all stare at Mandy, wondering what she could mean.

'Blimey, what did you wish for, Mand?' Rob is the first to ask.

'Don't you all remember?' Mandy says. Her face that has just begun to recover some of its colour again is now ghostly white, and her expression is fraught with grief once more.

'We all wished secretly, didn't we?' I tell her gently, sensing something is very wrong. 'No one knew anyone else's wishes.'

'But you all heard mine,' Mandy says, her voice trembling. 'If you remember, I said, even before we threw that stupid barrel back in the sea, "Can I wish not to have a sister?" And, as you've all witnessed today, my wish certainly came true, in all its stupid gory detail!'

'Mandy, no!' I realise a beat quicker than the others what's happening. 'Don't be silly – you can't blame yourself for this.'

'Oh, I can,' Mandy says, drinking again. 'I have every day since Hetty died, and I probably will every day until *I* die. Which, if there's any justice in the world, will be very soon.'

I pull myself to my feet and rush over to her at the same time as Claire and Suzy do.

Mandy is shaking as I put my arms around her. 'It's my fault,' she murmurs as tears begin to stream down her face. 'It's my fault Hetty is dead.'

'No, Mandy.' Claire tightly grips Mandy's hand. 'Of course it's not your fault. It was an accident. A dreadful, but unforeseen accident caused by nothing more than some freak weather.'

'Claire is absolutely right,' Suzy says, desperately trying to reassure Mandy. 'That's not what you actually wished for, was it – not when we threw the barrel off the rocks?'

Mandy is silent except for her sobs.

'Is it?' Suzy asks. 'That was just a throwaway comment that any teenager might make about their younger sibling. The mermaid would have known that.'

I love how Suzy, probably the least likely one of us to believe in anything magical or spiritual, is talking like the mermaid is real. But then *her* wish had kind of come true, I suppose.

'Yes,' Claire says keenly. 'Suzy is spot on. What *did* you actually wish for? You don't have to tell us if it hasn't come true yet,' she adds. 'But it might help us and you to say it out loud.'

Mandy looks up at Claire, then around at us all. Eddie, Rob and even Mack are all now standing around her in a semi-circle of concern.

'I wished I could live my life as my true self,' Mandy says quietly. 'I didn't even know what that was back then – I was pretty messed up and confused. But that's what I wished for when we threw the barrel back.'

'But that's wonderful,' Claire says, putting the positive spin she always does on everything – good or bad. 'Because that's what's happening to you now. You are living your true life, Mandy. You've not only come out to yourself, but to us as well. Now, you can go on and live your life exactly as you should, not pretending to be someone you're not, but honestly and truthfully as the wonderful person you really are.'

Mandy looks gratefully up at Claire as more tears roll down her face. I pray they are tears of relief this time, and not sorrow.

'You really think it wasn't me that made it happen?' she asks in a tiny desperate voice, that sounds quite unlike the Mandy we're all used to.

'I *know* it wasn't you,' Claire says. 'We *all* know it wasn't you.'

As we all surround Mandy in an enormous group hug, I'm sure I can actually feel the love bursting from our tight-knit little group as we stand in the moonlight, under the stars, looking after one of our own. And, the wonderful thing is, in the process we now seem to have accrued one more, if unexpected member to our gang, as Mack joins in and therefore becomes one of us – a Misfit Mermaid.

And as we slowly release Mandy one by one, I'm sure I'm not the only mermaid who hears the all too familiar splash from the waves below us . . .

Twenty-Three

July 2014

My journey down to Cornwall today has been relatively easy and without incident.

We took the early morning train from Glasgow Central, changed once before we got to London, and then again a little while ago in Penzance, and now we are on the last – and by far the prettiest – part of the journey as we travel towards St Felix. We could have got a slightly more direct train, but it was a lot more expensive, so we took the cheaper, if a lot longer route.

But Rosie, as she always does, has taken it all in her stride and is now, as she's been for much of the journey, nose-deep in her latest paperback novel. I smile lovingly at my daughter; she always looks so utterly engrossed in her books and I often have to call her name several times before she hears me when she's reading at home in her bedroom.

Rosie has only visited St Felix twice before in her young life. Once when she was a baby, and I took her down to visit my parents before they moved to Norfolk. They moved almost eight years ago, are now happily retired and living in a little bungalow by the sea. And the second time, when she was five, and we went to stay with Claire and her children for a short holiday.

Rosie is now nine years old, and my whole life.

When I first had her, like Claire correctly predicted, I did need help, and a lot of it. I read so many baby books that I thought I had everything covered. But reading about having a baby is one thing – actually looking after one yourself is a completely different ball game. So when I first came out of hospital, my parents travelled up from Cornwall and stayed with us for a while to help out. Dad returned home for work after a few days, and Mum stayed for several weeks.

When it was time for her to go, part of me was pleased it was just going to be me and Rosie at last, but another part was petrified about looking after her on my own.

Mum offered us the opportunity to go and stay with them down in St Felix, but I declined. I had to get used to looking after Rosie on my own at some point, and I still had nearly five months of maternity leave left from the gallery. I figured that was going to be plenty of time to get all my ducks in a row before I went back to work.

But ducks have a funny way of not sitting all that neatly when you ask them to, and even if they do decide to rest for a while, there's often a lot of flapping of wings and quacking before they calm down, let alone getting them into anything like a straight row.

So, although I thought I had everything as together as it was going to get before I went back to work, I found out the hard way that the reality of looking after a young child and working full time is way more difficult, challenging and downright exhausting than anyone realises. Especially if you're doing it on your own.

'Nearly there,' I say to Rosie now. 'I'm sure you won't

remember when we came here last time, but on this final part of the journey you get a really lovely view of St Felix.'

Rosie looks up from her book. 'Actually I do remember. You go around a bend and then suddenly you see the sea, the beach and a harbour.'

'Wow, I'm surprised you remember that – you were only five when we came last time. Do you remember anything else from that trip?'

Rosie shrugs. 'Not a lot. Playing with some other kids on the beach, I think?'

'Claire's children. They're not really kids any more though.' I try to remember their ages. 'Alice is eighteen now, I think. George must be sixteen, and that makes little Freddie . . . wow, fourteen. I can hardly believe it.'

Rosie watches me in the way she often does, like she's trying to work me out.

'You're really excited about this trip, aren't you, Mum?'

'Yes and no,' I tell her honestly. I'm always honest with Rosie, even if it's to my detriment sometimes.

'Why yes and no?'

'Yes, I'm looking forward to seeing St Felix again and some of my friends. Most of them I haven't seen for ten years.'

My mind wanders to the other mermaids.

'And no?' Rosie prompts me.

'No . . . Now that's a little trickier to explain.'

The truth is I'm really looking forward to seeing the others again. It's been so long since we all last caught up properly. Other than Claire and Eddie briefly, I haven't really seen any of the others since before Rosie was born, and even though I follow what they are all up to these days via social media, mostly Facebook and more recently Instagram, knowing it, and actually seeing them again to talk about it, is a completely different thing.

Everyone is doing so well with their lives right now, and the truth is I feel left behind.

'It's been so long I wonder if we'll all have things to talk about.' I try to explain as truthfully as I can. 'We all lead such different lives now.'

'But you'll always be the mermaids,' Rosie says. 'Mum, I don't think I ever see you smile as much as when you tell me stories about what you got up to with your friends when you lived in St Felix. I'm sure you'll be fine once you're all together again.'

'Who made you so wise?' I ask, grinning at her. 'Not me, I'm sure of it!'

'Certainly wasn't Dad!' Rosie smiles now too. 'I love my dad, but he's not what I'd call wise.'

'No, he certainly isn't. But he's a good man and he does love you.'

I took Claire's advice and told Rosie's father that I was pregnant, but that I didn't want anything from him.

But to my surprise, after the initial shock, he stepped up immediately and made arrangements to pay me maintenance after Rosie was born. He was also very keen to be a part of her life, which, after a little reluctance on my part I agreed to, and I'm pleased I did. Because now at least Rosie has a father figure in her life, even if it's only occasionally.

As the train pulls into the station, I feel a strange mix of excitement and anxiety.

Excitement at being back here again, still one of my favourite places in the world, and anxiety at what's to come over the next few days.

We're here this time to celebrate Eddie's fortieth birthday. He's decided to have a big party in the café and restaurant in St Felix he now runs with his partner, Dexter.

Even though we have all turned forty this year, or are going to, Eddie is the only one of us who's having a party to celebrate. I assume he's the only one, I certainly haven't been invited to any other events. And to be honest I'm quite relieved – this trip has been costly enough and I don't think I could have managed visits to London to see Mandy and Suzy, and I definitely can't fly to Los Angeles should Rob decide he's having a birthday bash. Not that he'd probably invite me anyway – I'm sure he has lots of celebrity friends he'll be partying with come the end of August when his birthday falls.

And Mack, of course, being a year older than the rest of us celebrated his fortieth last year. Much to my surprise, Mack kept in touch when he returned to the US with Rob, not just with the group as a whole, but sometimes one-to-one with me, too.

When I finally announced to everyone that I was pregnant, he'd often send an email to check how I was getting on and then when Rosie arrived, he sent us a very cute pink fluffy rabbit perfect for a newborn, and also a basket full of lovely things for me. *Something to pamper yourself with*, was written on the notecard, which I couldn't help but notice had a Monet print on the front, and I wondered to myself if he remembered our conversation.

Our emails to each other became less as I coped with the day-to-day trials of being a single mother, and Mack, I assumed, was getting on with his own life. They continued on and off until a couple of years ago. I heard via Claire, who still kept in touch with Rob, that Mack had moved away from LA and bought his own bar in New York. Although I longed to hear from him again, I knew he must be really busy getting the bar off the ground, and I hoped it was going well for him.

'Have you got everything? I ask Rosie as we gather our luggage. 'You've picked everything up?'

'Yep.' Rosie puts her Harry Potter rucksack over her small shoulders. 'Do you want me to pull one of the suitcases?'

'No, I can manage them. Could you carry Eddie's gift, though?'

'Sure I can.'

'Be careful with it.'

'Yes, Mum.' Rosie sighs. 'I'm always careful with your paintings.'

I look anxiously at the painting wrapped in bubble wrap and brown paper.

'He's going to love it, Mum. Stopping looking so worried.'

'I hope you're right.'

'Of course he will!' Rosie says with the easy confidence of a nine-year-old. 'Now, have you got everything?' she asks, mimicking me.

I grin at her. 'Yes, now let's go!'

I'm pleased it's a dry sunny afternoon as we drag our bags and cases along the streets of St Felix towards Claire's house.

Claire moved out of the house she shared with Jonathan about a year after Hetty's funeral. They tried counselling, which I think from what Claire told me at the time actually only served to make Claire more aware of Jonathan's failings, and rather than make her want to keep trying, it simply gave her the strength to leave her marriage and take her children with her.

Claire moved in with her parents to begin with as a

temporary measure, but when her father died suddenly, she stayed to both look after and keep her mother company.

Recently, her mother became so ill with dementia that Claire was forced to find a nursing home for her, and her mother now resides in Camberley House in Bude, a specialist nursing home.

Claire's parents were older than mine but I was so grateful after hearing about Claire's experiences that my parents were still in fairly good health.

So Claire now lives in her old house, but with her own family. When we stayed with her before, her mother was still around, but this time it would just be us, Claire and her children.

'You're here!' Claire looks delighted to see us as we stand on her doorstep with all our luggage. 'It's so good to see you again, Frankie.' She gives me a hug, then turns her attention to Rosie. 'Oh my goodness, how big are you now? You'll be taller than me soon. Come in, come in. Let me help you with your things.'

Claire shows us to our room. Inside there's a double bed and by its side a small blow-up camp bed for Rosie with a My Little Pony duvet that I assume must have belonged to Alice at one point.

'We haven't put anyone out, have we?' I ask, looking around the room, which seems to be devoid of any personal possessions and looks very much like a guest room now. When we stayed last time, we had slept in the boys' room, while they slept in with Alice on camp beds.

'No, not at all. This used to be Mum's room,' Claire says, looking around wistfully. 'We took all her things with her to Camberley, so she'd feel more at home there.'

'How's she getting on?' I ask, while Rosie sits on the edge of the bed, bouncing up and down a little.

'Oh, all right – you know?' Claire sighs a little. 'She's much better there, but I do miss her being here with us.'

'I'm sure.'

'But at least I have you both for a few days. It will be nice to have some female company again. Alice is at uni most of the time now, and the boys are always out with their friends and girlfriend.' She grimaces.

'Which one has a girlfriend?' I ask. George and Freddie were just little boys the last time I saw them; I can't imagine them having girlfriends now.

'George. Her name is Lucy and, according to George, they just "hang out together".' Claire does the air quotes with her fingers.

I smile. 'George is actually a year older than I was when I,' I do the air quotes now, '"dated" Rob.'

'Gosh, yes, so he is. I hadn't thought about that. Goodness, where have those years gone?'

I shake my head. 'Beats me.'

'But it's lovely we're all still friends,' Claire says. 'Not many people can say they're still friends with the same people they were twenty-five years ago at school.'

'No, I suppose not.'

'Right, I'll leave you to unpack and get settled in. Dinner will be ready in about half an hour if that's OK?'

'That's lovely, Claire. Thank you for letting us stay with you.'

'The pleasure is all mine. Ooh, it really is so good to see you again, Frankie.' She gives me another hug. 'It's been too long. We have so much to catch up on.'

Twenty-Four

Claire and I sit in Claire's large kitchen diner, finishing off a bottle of red wine. We've all enjoyed a very tasty homemade lasagna with garlic bread and salad. Claire and I remained at the table while Alice – who is back home for the summer holidays – and Freddie took Rosie through to the lounge to play some computer games with her. George politely asked to be excused after dinner, so he could go and meet Lucy.

'Your children really are a credit to you, Claire,' I tell her, sipping on my wine. 'They are so polite and well mannered.'

'Thank you. Rosie is a delight too. I see so much of you in her, Frankie.'

'Really?'

Claire nods. 'She's quite laid back on the surface, but she's got a real determined streak running through her. Just like you had when you were younger.'

I smile. 'Yes, she has. I really hope she makes a better job of her life than I have.'

'What do you mean?'

I shrug. 'Oh, you know, something better than being a single parent, living on benefits in a tiny flat, with no garden, no view, and, most of the time, no hope either.'

Claire looks genuinely shocked. 'But you're not on benefits, are you? You have a job?'

'I have a part-time job that's topped up with benefits.'

'But I thought you worked at the gallery?'

It must be the wine. I've already said more than I planned to tell Claire about my life. I planned to fudge over the gorier details and focus on the things that sounded better. 'I used to work at the gallery. But I left a few years ago now. I work in a local corner shop part time these days.'

Claire stares at me, trying to piece together what I've just told her, and I know she wants to ask why. But I assume that she won't. The Claire I used to know wouldn't dare, but I've forgotten this is a new Claire now, one who *will* say boo to a goose. And today that goose is me.

'Why did you leave – you loved that job?'

'I had to,' I reply reluctantly. 'I got . . . ill, and I had to give it up. I've been working in the local corner shop for a while now. They're really good at working around Rosie and school hours – I can pick her up from school and not have to pay for childcare.'

'What do you mean you got ill?' Claire asks with concern. 'With what?'

I take another swig from my glass. 'Depression.'

'Depression?' Claire looks just as traumatised as my insides feel from telling her. 'Why didn't you tell me? Are you all right now?'

Depression crept up on me slowly. I didn't even know that was what was wrong with me until I saw a segment about it on daytime television, and everything both the TV doctor and the callers to the phone-in were saying struck a chord.

I sheepishly went to my GP with my symptoms – thinking she'd tell me not to worry and it was a phase or something. But to my surprise, she prescribed antidepressant medication immediately. I didn't think I was that bad, but my doctor seemed quite concerned and suggested many things to help, including therapy, but she was extremely keen for me to start on the medication immediately. Thinking she was being a little overdramatic, I put off taking it at first, thinking I might be able to shake it off if I tried. But after one particularly bad spell, when I couldn't even get to work, and could barely look after Rosie when she came home from school, let alone myself, eventually I gave in and took the pills, and I was shocked by how different I felt after only a few days.

Colours suddenly seemed brighter, the world seemed a lighter, friendlier place and, for the first time since Rosie's birth, I slept more than a few hours at a time. A dense fog, like the sea mists in St Felix that would settle over the waves and stay until the tide turned, lifted from both my brain and vision.

My own internal tide turned just after Rosie turned six years old. It took away the mist that was hanging over my life, and I'm happy to say so far it hasn't returned since.

'Yes, I'm fine now,' I try to say as reassuringly as I can. 'It's under control, anyway. I was on medication for a while, but now my main therapy is painting. When I have the time and the room to do it, that is.'

'Oh, Frankie, I'm cross you never told me, but I'm pleased you feel better now. That's such a shame you had to give up your job though.'

'Yeah, I just couldn't do it any more. They were good to start with, they tried to make it work. But the stress was too much.

People think working in an art gallery is a nice, relaxed job, but there's a bit more that goes on behind the scenes.'

'And you had to leave your nice apartment too?'

'Yes, sadly. I just couldn't afford it any more. But we're happy where we are now. And the people are nice around us. There's quite the community spirit in our block.'

'You live in a tower block?' Claire is trying to hide the fact she's horrified at the thought. 'Gosh, I'm sorry; that makes me sound quite snobby, doesn't it?'

I smile. 'It's fine, Claire. I'd have probably done the same a few years ago.'

'No, it's not fine. I shouldn't judge you. It could be a lovely place for all I know.'

'It's not, but thanks for trying.'

'Oh, Frankie.' Claire puts her hand over mine. 'I'm sorry you've been through all that. Depression is a horrible thing. There are ladies who come to my group who are terribly depressed with the state of their lives. Some of them are on medication too.'

Claire eventually attended the support group that Marilyn, Mandy's slightly odd relative, had suggested to her and, after a few years, when her life was back on track, Claire took over the running of it, which she still did voluntarily today.

'Doesn't surprise me. I've heard doctors deal out antidepressants like sweeties. But they helped me, so I can't complain too much.'

'It wouldn't surprise me if some of the others have been on antidepressants too,' Claire says. 'Mandy went through all that with her sister, didn't she? And Rob works in Hollywood – I bet drugs are as easy to get there as a Cornish pasty is to get here in St Felix.'

'Probably. How is Rob? Have you heard from him lately?'

'He's OK, I think, I haven't heard from him in a while, though, come to think of it. Have you seen his latest movie?'

I shake my head.

'Have you seen any of his movies?' Claire asks, almost reproachfully.

'Not really my thing.' I try to fob her off, along with, 'I've been busy, Claire,' when she raises her eyebrows at me.

'For the last ten years?' she asks.

'OK, maybe I could have tried a bit harder to watch them,' I say eventually.

'Still in love with him?' Claire asks bluntly.

'No! Why would you say that?'

Claire shrugs. 'I don't know, what other reason would you have for avoiding seeing him, if you're not still harbouring feelings for him?'

'I can assure you it's nothing like that,' I say firmly. 'Anyway, even if I was, there wouldn't be much point, would there? Isn't he getting married soon?'

'You know about that?' Claire grins. 'I think that's off now.'

'Really? Why?'

'Now that I don't know. Could be any reason knowing Rob. He seems to get through them, doesn't he?'

I nod. I did know that Rob had quite the reputation in the media as a ladies' man. None of his reported relationships ever last more than a few months, it seemed.

'We'll all find out tomorrow night at Eddie's party, won't we?' Claire continues.

'Is Rob coming to that?' I ask, shocked to hear this. 'I didn't think he would.'

'So Eddie says. Rob texted him the other day and said

would it still be all right for him to come. Eddie's delighted and Dexter is really excited to meet him. Apparently, he's a big fan of Rob's films.'

'He would be.' I smile. Dexter and Eddie have been together for the last ten years. They met the day Eddie went to the estate agent, after Marilyn suggested he go there. Dexter was looking in the window when Eddie arrived. The estate agent was late opening up, so they got chatting, realised they were both looking for a business in the area, and not only that but something in the catering line too.

And if all that wasn't strange enough, when the estate agent finally arrived, she told them that she had a brand-new listing – the café on Morvoren Cove was up for sale. Would either of them be interested in taking over the business?

So Eddie and Dexter, partners in both love and in business, run it together as a café in the day and a restaurant at night, and they seem to be making a wonderful job of it, if the reviews on Trip Advisor are anything to go by.

'Dexter's great, isn't he?' I ask Claire. 'So good for our Eddie.'

Claire nods. 'Sure is. I've never seen him happier than he's been in the last few years. I think getting the business off the ground took a lot out of them to begin with, but now it seems to be flying.'

'Good for them,' I say, meaning it, but at the same time feeling a pang of jealousy.

'What's up?' Claire asks perceptively.

'Nothing.' I lie.

'*Frankie?*'

It's no good, Claire has known me too long. Even though we don't see much of each other these days, she still knows me better than anyone.

'All right.' I sigh. 'It's just everyone seems to be doing so well these days. Eddie has Dexter and the café. Mandy is flying high with her own tech business – *and* she has a new partner. Suzy is an MP now, for goodness' sake, and her husband runs his own events firm. And I'm not even going to mention Rob! And before you ask – yes, I am jealous. Of all of them. They're successful, they've got their lives together, and I'm living in a tiny flat, working in a corner shop, and just about managing to get by.'

'What about Rosie?' Claire asks with concern. 'She must count for something good in your life?'

'Of course she does! I didn't mean that. Rosie is everything. She *is* my life. She's what I get out of bed every day for. She's the *only* reason most days.'

'But that's success right there,' Claire says. 'You've not only given birth to a beautiful human being, but you've nurtured her and helped her become the lovely little girl that she is today. You've done that, and you've done it all on your own, Frankie. That's a huge achievement in itself.'

Claire is right – of course she is.

'So have you,' I reply. 'And you've done it three times.'

'But I wasn't on my own. I had Jonathan to begin with, and then I had Mum helping me out. I don't think I could have coped if it was just me. I'm in awe of you, Frankie. You don't give yourself enough credit. And I don't exactly have a career, do I? I work in my friend's beach café.'

'But you have all this.' I wave my hand around the room. 'This is a beautiful house, Claire. You should be proud.'

'Yes, it is. But it was my parents' house,' Claire protests. 'I inherited it mortgage-free. If it wasn't for them, I wouldn't live here. I'm one of the lucky ones – when my marriage fell apart I had somewhere to go. So many women don't.'

251

We stare at each other for a moment, and then we smile.

'So what if all the others have great careers,' Claire says, refilling both our glasses with the last of the wine. 'We're the only ones who have children. Perhaps the others are jealous of us?'

'I doubt it,' I reply, grimacing. 'But for now, let's drink to everyone's successes in life, both monetary and . . . procreatory too!' I grin. 'That's not a word, I know. But I can't think of a better one right now.'

'To all of us!' Claire lifts her glass. 'Whatever we've been good at so far in life! May there be much more success and, more importantly, happiness to come!'

Twenty-Five

Claire is working the next day in the takeaway part of the café, while Eddie and Dexter set up the restaurant for the party tonight. So I spend the morning showing Rosie around St Felix once more.

We visit the harbour and the beaches. I show her where I used to live with her grandparents and then we walk back down into the town through Harbour Street. I'm hoping to stop in on Rose at the flower shop. I haven't seen her in ages, and the last time I was here she wasn't looking too well, although she insisted she was absolutely fine.

We call in at the bakery – now called the Blue Canary rather than Mr Bumbles – and meet the new owners, interestingly called Ant and Dec. Apparently Dec is the nephew of the previous owner, and he and his partner Ant now run the bakery together.

They've obviously inherited the old recipes too, because their pasties and cakes still look as delicious as ever.

'I used to know your uncle,' I tell Dec as I pay for our lunch. 'I used to come in here for my lunch when it was Mr Bumbles and I worked as a Saturday girl at the flower shop down the road – that was a long time ago now, though!'

But instead of smiling at my joke, Dec looks concerned.

253

'You knew Rose?' he asks.

'Yes, I was just going to pop in and visit her before we enjoy these.' I hold up the paper bags containing pasties and cakes. 'I haven't seen her in ages.'

'You don't know, then?' Dec asks, returning from the till with my change.

'Know what?'

'Rose is in hospital.'

'Hospital? Why, what's wrong with her?'

'I'm not really sure I can say – but we think it might be *cancer*.' He whispers this last word for some reason, as people often do. 'She was taken ill suddenly a few months ago and admitted to a local hospital. But her daughters quickly arranged for her to be transferred into a specialist hospital down in London. That's all I know, I'm afraid.'

I stare at Dec for a moment. Another piece of my St Felix rock has broken away. First it was my parents, and now Rose.

'You were obviously close to her?' Dec says, as Ant continues to serve the other customers.

'Yes, I always call in at the shop when I'm back in St Felix. Gosh,' I say as I think about Rose. 'I can't believe she won't be there making up her bouquets. Is the shop closed or is someone from her family running it for her?'

'It was closed for a while, but volunteers from the local women's guild have been running it for the last week or two to help Rose out and try to keep the business going.'

'That's good of them. But no one from Rose's family has been in touch? Her daughters are florists, aren't they? I remember Rose telling me it runs in the family.'

'I really don't know. But I do know how much we miss her in St Felix. She's a special lady, that one.'

'Yes, she is. Thank you for your help,' I tell him, still thinking about Rose.

'Enjoy your goodies,' Dec says. 'I hope they're as good as you remember them.'

'I'm sure they will be.'

Rosie is waiting outside the shop for me.

'Are you all right, Mum?' she asks, taking my hand as we walk down the street towards the harbour again. 'You look a bit white.'

'Yes, yes, I'm fine. I just had some bad news, that's all.'

'What news?'

'The lady who I used to work with in the flower shop. That flower shop over there,' I say, pointing as we pass on the opposite side of the street. 'The Daisy Chain. I just found out she's in hospital.'

'Oh, that's sad. I hope she gets better soon.'

'Yes, so do I. Do you know I chose the name Rosie for you partly because of her? She's called Rose too.'

'That's nice. What was the other part?'

'What do you mean?'

'You said you called me that *partly* because of the lady you used to work with – what was the other part?'

I smile at Rosie; she is so smart and on the ball all the time.

'Let's find somewhere to eat our lunch first, and I'll tell you. We'll go to one of the places I always liked to go when I was younger.'

We walk around to Morvoren Cove and climb up over the grass to the little viewing spot I always liked to go to on my lunchtimes. And I'm overjoyed to find that no one is already sitting there as we peep round the brow of the hill.

'This is amazing,' I tell Rosie as we sit looking out over

the sea. To our right is Eddie and Dexter's café, now called The Mermaid of Morvoren. Right now, it's busy with a queue of people waiting outside for drinks and sandwiches. 'I can't believe I'm sitting up here again after all this time, and I have my beautiful daughter sitting next to me.'

'It's a fab view, isn't it?' Rosie says as a breeze lifts up off the sea, blowing her long dark hair away from her face.

'It is that.' I sigh. 'I could sit and watch the sea for hours. It's always changing, and yet in another way, it never does. That reminds me, I was going to tell you about your name.'

'Yes, you were,' Rosie says before she takes her first bite of Cornish pasty. 'Ooh, this is good.'

'Even though you were partly named after Rose from the flower shop, I also chose it because your full name, Rosemary, means "dew of the sea". I wanted you to have a name that was related to St Felix in some way, because even though I've lived in Scotland for so long, I'll always think of here as home.'

'That's really nice, Mum,' Rosie says after she's swallowed her second mouthful of pasty. 'I like it here too. It's very ...' Her little face screws up in concentration as she tries hard to think of the right word, before deciding on one. 'Fresh.'

'Yes, it is fresh, isn't it? It's the air, I think.' I take a deep breath. 'It's very clean.'

Rosie does the same. 'I wish Grandma and Grandad still lived here,' she says. 'Then we could come back here and stay with them.'

I automatically assume Rosie means holiday with them.

'Yes, we could. But at least Claire is still here, so we've been able to stay with her on this holiday.'

'No, I mean *stay* with them – like live with them?'

It's always funny when I hear Rosie, who understandably has

picked up a slight accent, use a Scottish turn of phrase when I still hear the English use of the word.

'Oh, I thought you meant *stay* as in holiday.'

'No.' Rosie looks confused for a moment. 'Oh right, I get it. You heard the English stay.'

I nod. 'But you would have liked that, would you? To live here with Grandma and Grandad?'

'Oh, yes. I mean, I like the wee house they live in now. But I would have liked to stay, I mean, *live* in a big house here like Alice, George and Freddie do.'

'Yes, that would be lovely, wouldn't it? One day, maybe,' I say wistfully. 'Perhaps not right now, though. I mean, you have school and all your friends in Scotland. You'd miss them if we moved all the way down here.'

Rosie considers this. 'Yes, but I'd make new friends. And school is school.' She shrugs and tucks into her pasty again. 'Could I have these every day if we did move here?'

'Er, no. Pasties are an occasional treat only.' But as I begin to eat my own pasty, I can't help but dream as I look out over the waves, of what it might be like to move back here again to St Felix.

'Let's wish, Mum,' Rosie says, lowering her pasty for a moment.

'What for?'

'Let's wish that we can come and live here again one day.'

'All right.' I nod, knowing full well that is all it will ever be – a dream. Property is far too expensive now for me to be able to afford to buy or even rent anything in Cornwall, let alone St Felix.

'Close your eyes ... tightly!' Rosie tells me. 'Right, I'm doing the same. Now we wish!'

And as I sit in my favourite spot in all of St Felix, with my world sitting by my side gripping my hand tightly, I put all my sensible, realistic, even pessimistic thoughts to one side, and I wish. I wish really hard.

And as I do, I hear a sound I haven't heard in a decade.

The sound of a large tail splashing in the waves below us.

Twenty-Six

'You look beautiful, Mum.' Rosie comes up behind me and puts her arms around my waist while I stare into the long mirror in our room at Claire's house.

'No, you're the one who looks beautiful,' I tell her. 'This is such an old dress now, I'm not sure it suits me any more.'

I bought the dress I'm wearing tonight a number of years ago in a sale when we were having a gala event at the gallery. A three-quarter length, sleeveless black gown. It's fitted on the body, until the long chiffon skirt extends into loose waves around my calves. Tonight, I've teamed it with black velvet shoes with a small heel, and a black velvet clutch bag with colourful flowers embroidered on to the front – both of which I've also had in my wardrobe for several years.

'Of course it suits you,' Rosie says. 'You can wear anything.'

I kiss the top of Rosie's hair. 'I'm so pleased you're coming with me tonight. It's like having my own personal cheerleader boosting my confidence.'

Originally, I didn't realise that Rosie was invited to the party as well. Both Claire and I made arrangements for Alice to look after her this evening. But when Claire came back from the café this afternoon, she said that Eddie and Dexter were keen to make this a family affair, so suddenly both Rosie and Alice were joining us. The boys both passed on the invite, preferring to stay home and play computer games, rather than attend some 'old folks' do'.

But Alice was surprisingly keen.

'She's only coming so she can meet Rob,' Claire told me with a wink. 'All her friends are jealous that her mum knows a Hollywood movie star.'

'Isn't he a bit old for her?' I responded. Something about Alice liking Rob felt a bit weird.

'Of course he is – in real life. But superheroes don't age, do they? When Rob made his first Danger Man film, he was a lot younger. People remember him like that'.

'I suppose.'

If everyone remembers me as I was ten years ago, they're in for a shock, I thought. *The last few years haven't been kind to me.*

'Can I be your personal cheerleader too?' Claire asks now, popping her head around the door. 'You look great, Frankie. And I won't hear you say otherwise. You both do. I'm so pleased some of Alice's old clothes fit you, Rosie.'

'I love them,' Rosie says, spinning around. 'It's like nothing I have at home.'

Alice is of average height for an eighteen-year-old girl, but Rosie is tall for her age, so she fitted easily into some of Alice's clothes from a few years ago that Claire found stashed away in her attic.

In fact, there were so many that Rosie liked, that Claire promised to courier them up to us when we left, as there were just too many for us to manage in a suitcase.

'Thank you,' I told Claire quietly as we watched Rosie try

them on and then parade through Claire's house like a catwalk model. 'I could never afford to buy her clothes like this.'

'Don't be silly,' Claire said. 'You're doing me a favour. Now I don't have to find a charity shop that will take them.'

Claire is now frowning at me slightly. 'Will you be warm enough like that, Frankie?' she asks. 'It's all right out there at the moment, but it might get chilly later.'

'I'll be fine,' I say hurriedly. There is no way I'm putting on my Primark puffer jacket with this lovely outfit.

'Wait there.' Claire disappears again.

She reappears a few moments later with something in her hand in a deep shade of purple silk.

'It's a pashmina,' she says, handing it to me. 'Jonathan bought it for me years ago, so I never wear it – for obvious reasons.'

I open up the folded fabric, which is incredibly soft to touch, and place it around my shoulders. I don't want to wear it, knowing that Jonathan bought it, but I have to admit it does set the dress off beautifully.

'Perfect,' Claire says, smiling. 'I knew it would work. What do you think, Rosie? Isn't your mummy beautiful?'

Rosie nods. 'We'll be the belles of the ball,' she says, smiling at us both. '*Beauty and the Beast* is my favourite Disney film,' she tells Claire. 'And we're all just as beautiful as Belle is when she dances with the Beast. You too, Aunty Claire, you look *very* pretty tonight in your dress.'

Claire looks at Rosie and I'm sure I see her blink away a tear.

'Thank you, Rosie,' she says quietly. 'It's been a long time since anyone told me that.'

'Right then,' I say, feeling myself beginning to well up. I can't cry now – it's taken me far too long to do my make-up tonight to have to redo it all again. 'As long as there's no beasts tonight at Eddie's birthday party, then we'll all be quite safe, won't we?'

The café looks beautiful when we arrive at Morvoren Cove that evening.

The sun has just started to set, so the soft white twinkling lights that are hung all around the outside of the restaurant look even prettier as they light up not only the party venue, but the surrounding beach as well.

I hesitate as Claire, Alice and Rosie move forward to enter the party.

'Mum?' Rosie looks up at me.

'It's going to be fine, Frankie,' Claire says with a confidence I'm not feeling at all. 'You look fabulous tonight. Hold your head high. Our achievements are those accompanying us, remember?'

I nod and take a deep breath.

'Let's go.'

We walk together into the party. Inside there are already a lot of guests milling around. Most of them are holding drinks in their hands, chatting in small groups, or sitting at tables with pristine white cloths and small posies of flowers on the top. The dining tables that usually fill the restaurant space have been pushed back and a temporary wooden dance floor has been erected in the centre of the large room.

'Gosh, this is fancier than I expected,' I say, looking around. 'It looks more like a wedding than a fortieth birthday party.'

'Frankie!' Eddie comes bounding across the wooden floor. 'I'm so pleased you made it.'

He gives me a huge hug, then he kisses me on each cheek.

'You look fabulous, darling. As do you, my lovely Claire. And Alice . . . You got it goin' on, girl!' he says, waving his hand over her as Alice grins at him. 'And this must be little Rosie? Golly, not so little now. How are you, beautiful girl?' He shakes her hand formally. 'It's so lovely to see you again.'

'This is for you,' Rosie says solemnly, holding up my painting still wrapped in brown paper. 'Mum did it.'

'Let's just put it on the table over there with the other gifts,' I say hurriedly. 'I'm sure Eddie doesn't want to look at it now.'

'On the contrary! I do want to look at it now. A painting by the one and only Frances Harris? Come, let's put it over there on the table near the dance floor so I can see it in all its glory.'

Feeling like everyone is staring at us, I quickly follow Rosie and Eddie across the dance floor. Eddie places my painting on top of the white cloth and begins to carefully unwrap it, all the time talking about how he's always wanted one of my paintings to hang on his wall, and joking that if it's terrible he can just hang it in his downstairs toilet.

But when he finally gets all the protective paper off, Eddie is silent for once.

'Don't you like it?' Rosie asks, slicing through the silence like a knife through butter.

I close my eyes. I knew this would happen. Why couldn't Eddie have waited until he opened all his other gifts? Now everyone would know he hated it. I just want to drop through the floorboards and escape this embarrassment. I knew I should never have given Eddie this as a gift, I should have just brought a bottle of something like everyone else did by the look of all the bottle bags on the gift table.

But when I open them again. Eddie is holding up the painting so he can get a better look at it.

'It … it's wonderful,' he says, his voice quivering. 'It's everything I love. All there in one painting.'

My heart lifts from where it's been stuck in my black velvet shoes for the last few seconds. 'Do you really like it?' I ask quietly. 'You're not just saying that?'

'No, of course I'm not. Honestly, Frankie, it's amazing.'

The picture I've painted is of Morvoren Cove. The café features heavily in the foreground, against a backdrop of the beach and the sea.

'You even put Dexter in there serving a customer,' Eddie says, still examining the painting. 'And is that me clearing one of the outside tables?'

'It is.'

Eddie continues to examine the painting. 'Wait until Dexter sees this – he's going to be just as amazed and delighted as I am. Oh …' Eddie's eyes stop scanning my painting for a moment. 'Is that what I think it is in the sea?'

'Yes.'

'Oh, Frankie,' Eddie says. 'You have no idea how perfect this is.'

I thought long and hard about adding the addition of a mermaid's tail in the sea. In fact, I painted over it twice and then added it again when I changed my mind. The tail is small, and you have to look quite closely to see it poking out over the top of one of the waves. But it's there, and now I'm pleased I let it stay.

'It's like us, isn't it?' I tell him. 'The Mermaids of St Felix.'

'I thought you were called the Misfit Mermaids?' Rosie pipes up.

'We were, darling,' Eddie says. 'In fact, we always will be – won't we, Frankie?'

I nod.

'But that's not the only reason why that little detail is so important,' Eddie continues.

'Oh my goodness, is that our restaurant?' Dexter is hurrying over towards us.

'Tell you later,' Eddie whispers to me. 'It is!' he says to Dexter, holding up the painting for him to see. 'Isn't it wonderful?'

Dexter kisses me on each cheek and says hello to Rosie. Then he examines the painting. 'This is superb, Frankie,' he says. 'Why aren't you doing this professionally?'

I blush. 'Stop, please. It's not that good. It's just a hobby and I don't even do it that often.'

'*Au contraire!*' Dexter says. 'It's magnificent. You must stop doing whatever it is you do up in Bonnie Scotland and take up painting as a profession immediately!'

'Ha, the chance would be a fine thing,' I say, playing along. I assume Dexter is being his usual exuberant self. 'I don't think it would quite pay the bills, though.'

'Frankie, I'm serious, darling,' Dexter says, actually sounding serious for once. He's lowered his voice and he puts his hand on my arm. 'You have a talent. You must do something with it. Listen, I know a couple of people. I'll put in a word for you.'

'Thank you,' I reply lightly, sure that this will be the last I hear on the subject. 'I won't give up my job just yet, though, if you don't mind. I'm really pleased you both like the painting, but enough about me – let's talk about you two. You're both looking very smart this evening. Is something going on we don't know about? This place is set out like it's a wedding we're attending, not a fortieth birthday party, with you two in fancy suits and the flowers on the tables and everything.'

265

Eddie smiles secretively at Dexter. 'Shall we tell her?'

Dexter nods.

'It's not just a party for my fortieth,' Eddie whispers. 'We're going to be getting married tonight too.'

'What?' I exclaim loudly. 'Sorry,' I whisper hurriedly. 'You're getting married? That's amazing news.'

'Isn't it the best?' Eddie says, his eyes shining with joy. 'We didn't want to make a big fuss about it, because some people are still a bit funny about gay weddings. So we thought we'd get all our nearest and dearest together on the pretence of my birthday, and surprise everybody.'

'Wow, I can't believe it. This is incredible, Eddie. It's what you always wanted.'

Eddie nods. 'When they changed the law, I couldn't wait to propose to Dexter. Funny thing was, he was planning on doing exactly the same thing on the same night – we both had rings in little boxes tucked inside our jackets.'

'How lovely,' I say, smiling at them both. 'I'm so pleased I'm going to be here to witness it.'

'We're going to tell everyone in a little while,' Dexter says. 'Keep it a secret for now, won't you.'

'My lips are sealed.'

'About what, Mum?' Rosie has returned from her examination of the rest of the gift table.

'See you later,' Dexter says, as Eddie props my painting up in pride of place along with the other gifts. 'Eddie, some more people have just arrived. You'd best go see them.'

Eddie blows me a kiss, and then he and Dexter hurry across the dance floor to greet their guests.

'Eddie and Dexter are getting married tonight,' I tell Rosie. 'It's a secret, for now anyway. We mustn't say anything.'

'Why is it a secret?' Rosie asks.

'I think they wanted to surprise everyone. And some people are still a bit funny about gay weddings.'

'Why? Isn't that what you're supposed to do if you love someone – get married?'

'Er . . . ' I'm torn. 'You don't have to get married if you love someone, not if you don't want to. But until recently some people who have wanted to get married to each other haven't been able to.'

'Why?'

'Because it was against the law. It's only recently things have changed so that two men or two women are allowed to get married.'

Rosie thinks about this. 'What does it matter if it's a man and a woman or both the same? Love is love, isn't it?'

I put my arm around her shoulders and give her a squeeze. 'It is. Of course, it is. And it doesn't matter who you love – if they love you back, it's the most special feeling ever.'

'Have you ever been in love?' Rosie asks.

'I have.'

'But you didn't get married?'

'No.'

'Why?'

I sigh. I thought Rosie had grown out of the 'why?' stage years ago.

'Because we were far too young at the time. Now, shall we go and get a drink from the bar?' I say, hoping she'll forget about this line of enquiry.

'Do you ever get too old to fall in love?' Rosie continues as I guide her towards the bar.

'No, of course not.'

'I hope you fall in love one day, Mum, and that person loves you back. I'd like you to feel special again.'

I take a breath. *How could the words of one so young be so very powerful?*

'That's a lovely thought, my darling. But you are the only person I need to love right now. And as long as you love me back, that's all that I need.'

Relieved that Rosie has stopped asking me difficult questions for a while, we queue up at the bar to get some drinks, and, as we wait, I notice a bit of a kerfuffle at the entrance of the restaurant.

I glance over to see what's happening, and as I do I notice that everyone else in the room is looking too.

The other guests stare with excitement and interest at the famous film star who has just made an entrance to the party.

But all I see when I look at him – is Rob.

Twenty-Seven

Hurriedly, I turn back to the bar.

But all I can hear around me are whispers and low voices, interspersed with occasional words and phrases like, 'movies', 'superhero', 'Danger Man' and 'looking older these days'.

I quickly order our drinks and then Rosie and I carry them over to a table where Alice and Claire are sitting with Mandy and another woman.

'Mandy!' I say at the same time as Mandy calls out to me.

'Frankie, long time no see!'

Mandy stands up and after I've deposited our drinks carefully on the table, we give each other a hug.

'You're looking well,' I tell her. The last time I saw Mandy in the flesh was ten years ago at her sister's funeral, and understandably she looks a lot less fraught and worn today. In fact, she probably looks healthier than I think I've ever seen her before.

'So are you,' she says. 'Hello, Rosie. Goodness, don't you look like your mum did when she was younger.'

'Don't tell her that.' I smile. But Rosie is still at the age when looking like her mum is a compliment. So she too smiles at Mandy.

'Hello,' she says shyly. 'Mum has told me all about you, Mandy.'

Mandy grimaces. 'Oh dear. Hopefully she's told you to do the exact opposite of everything I did when I was young.'

Rosie looks confused. 'No, just how much fun you used to be.'

Mandy blushes and looks at me.

I laugh. 'What? It's the truth.'

'This is Jules,' Mandy says, introducing the other woman at the table. 'My girlfriend.'

'Hi.' I give Jules a sort of half-wave. 'Good to meet you.'

'Hello,' Jules says. 'It's great to meet the infamous Frankie at last. Like your daughter just said about Mandy, I've heard a lot of good things about you too, Frankie.'

'Thanks,' I reply, taking a seat and feeling just as uncomfortable receiving this praise as Mandy was.

Rosie sits next to Alice, but Alice's attention is already elsewhere.

'Mum, it's him!' she whispers loudly to Claire. 'Can you introduce me?'

We all follow her intense gaze across the dance floor.

Rob is standing chatting to both Eddie and Dexter, and I allow my gaze to rest on him for longer than when he first arrived.

The people at the bar were right – Rob does look older since I last saw him, but that was ten years ago so it was to be expected. And the only other time I saw him was when he occasionally popped up on TV in the UK.

I allowed myself to watch him being interviewed by Graham Norton one evening not that long ago, but I suppose he would have had heavy television make-up on then. He appeared happy and confident that night, plugging his latest movie. But tonight, not only does he look older, he also looks quite tired as well.

Eddie turns around and points to where we're all sitting. Rob raises his hand and waves. Some of the table acknowledge his wave. But I just turn away, trying desperately to ignore the stupid fluttery feeling in my stomach that always pops up when Rob is around – although I notice this time it's not anywhere near as strong as it once was.

'Who's that Rob's with?' Mandy asks, peering across the dance floor.

'That's probably his latest PA,' Claire says. 'This one's name is Nixie, I think?'

'Nixie?' I scoff. 'What sort of name is that?'

'I'd say a perfect one by the look of her,' Mandy says, grinning. We all stare at the slight, but buxom peroxide blonde on Rob's left, wearing a silver sequin mini dress and the highest heels I think I've ever seen any woman manage to balance on. I have to give Nixie some kudos for that mean feat alone. 'Is that what Rob is calling them now – his PA? She's as much a PA as I am Mary Poppins.'

'Even if she is, why would you need to bring your PA all the way to a birthday party in Cornwall?' I ask, trying not to look. 'Bit over the top, isn't it? Next thing he'll have a bodyguard with him as well.'

'There is someone else standing with them,' Claire says. 'He's being blocked by Dexter right now, so I can't quite see ... Oh!' She exclaims in delight. 'I think it's Mack.'

My head does turn now, and I look with everyone else.

'It is Mack,' Claire says as Dexter moves to the side a little. 'How lovely. I didn't know he was coming. Did you, Frankie?'

'No,' I say, still staring at Mack as he chats amiably with Eddie and Dexter.

'Why would Frankie know?' Mandy asks with interest.

'Frankie and Mack kept in touch for a while after ... well, after the funeral.'

'It's all right, Claire, you can say Hetty's name,' Mandy says. 'I won't get upset. I've had a lot of very expensive therapy over the last ten years that has helped me come to terms with what happened. And how I was dealing with it.'

I turn back to look at Mandy and she's looking at Jules, who squeezes her hand supportively.

'You and Mack kept in touch, did you?' Mandy asks, raising her eyebrows at me suggestively. 'I never knew that.'

'By email only,' I say firmly. 'Nothing else. I haven't spoken to him in quite a while though.' I turn around again, and I see Rob, Nixie and Mack making their way over to our table. So I swiftly turn back.

Alice shrieks. 'Oh my God! He's only coming over here!'

'Alice, calm down,' Claire says. 'It's only Rob.'

'Hey,' Rob says with a slight LA twang to his voice. 'How are we all?'

He goes around the table giving each of us a hug and kiss on the cheek, with Mack following. Nixie stands to the side watching them, looking a bit bored.

I smile as Rob gets to Alice. Her face turns a deep shade of beetroot and she looks like she might faint when Rob lightly kisses her cheek.

'I can't believe this is little Alice,' Rob says to Claire. 'The last time I saw you, you were twelve, I think, Alice. How are your brothers?'

'Good ... I think.' Alice stutters a little as she stares at Rob.

'I love your movies,' she blurts out suddenly, and immediately looks mortified.

Alice is usually so composed and confident, so seeing her turn into a quivering mess at meeting Rob is actually quite disconcerting.

'Thank you,' Rob says, obviously used to this. 'I appreciate that a lot.' He comes to Rosie next. 'And who is this lovely lady?'

'I'm Rosie,' Rosie says, not in the least bit starstruck like Alice. 'You're my mum's friend, Rob, aren't you?'

'I am indeed.' Rob smiles at her. 'Pleased to meet you, Rosie.' And he formally shakes Rosie's outstretched hand. 'I can see you've inherited your mum's beauty.' Rob looks at me over the top of Rosie's head. 'Hi, Frankie,' he says, leaning forward to kiss my cheek. 'How are you?' he whispers in my ear.

'Good, thanks,' I reply, trying to keep my voice steady. 'How are you?'

'Yeah, good.'

Rob moves on to Mandy and Jules, and suddenly Mack is next to me.

'Hey, Frankie. Long time,' Mack says, as he too kisses my cheek. 'It's good to see you again.'

'And you too,' I tell him. 'How's things? How's your family?'

'Well, thank you,' he says. 'And you must be Rosie. I feel I know you already, Rosie. Your mum has told me a lot about you.'

'Thanks,' Rosie says. 'Are you the one who bought me my pink rabbit?'

'I am!' Mack says, looking surprised. 'Do you still have it?'

'Yes, she sits with my other favourite cuddly toys in a hammock over my bed.'

Mack, looking quite moved, nods. 'I'm very pleased to hear that, Rosie, very pleased.' He turns to me again. 'I'm sorry we lost touch lately,' he whispers. 'Can we catch up properly later?'

'Yes, sure,' I say, smiling at him.

Rob, Mack and Nixie – who is very quickly introduced to everyone – all sit down at the table with us. But before we have time to start catching up, Suzy arrives with her husband and the greeting process begins all over again.

'Let's make this easy on us all, shall we?' Rob says as Suzy's husband, Harry, arrives back at the table with their drinks. 'Shall we all go round the table one at a time and share any news we have, so we're all caught up with each other's lives? Otherwise, we'll spend all night saying the same things time and time again.'

'Good idea,' Mandy says before I have a chance to object to this idea. 'I'll start, shall I? As some of you know, this is my partner, Jules. We've been together five years now and she is my rock.' Mandy reaches across and squeezes Jules's hand. 'She's one of the main reasons I'm still sitting here now. I was in a pretty bad place the last time you saw me. But with a lot of therapy and Jules's support, I'm now in a much better place in my life . . . I've been sober for almost five years now, and, most importantly, for once in my life I'm truly happy.'

'That's fantastic, Mandy,' Suzy says. 'I'm so pleased for you. And your business – how's that going?'

'Strength to strength,' Mandy says. 'It's doing incredibly well. I'm truly blessed in life right now.' And again, she gazes at Jules. 'Suzy – your turn?'

I glance at Claire and raise my eyebrows. *I knew this was going to happen.*

But Claire just gives a quick shake of her head.

'Well,' Suzy says. 'As most of you know I'm now an MP in a constituency that has been a Conservative seat for far too long. I was over the moon to be elected when there was a by-election last year. I'm also married to Harry here.' Like Mandy, Suzy squeezes Harry's hand. 'Apologies for not inviting any of you to our wedding a few years ago, but it was a very small, intimate affair abroad – wasn't it?'

Harry nods.

'Sadly, we've not been blessed with any children as yet, so we're preparing to begin IVF treatment in a few weeks.'

'Wow, that's amazing, Suzy,' Claire says. 'I hope it works for you – really I do.'

'How about you, Claire?' Suzy asks. 'Anything new to report?'

Claire firstly tells the table all about her children, then she goes on to talk about the women's groups she runs. Also, how much she enjoys working here at Eddie and Dexter's café. Then she gives a quick update on Eddie, because he and Dexter are still attending to their guests, and I wonder for the first time if she might know about the secret wedding.

'Rob,' she says at the end, and I'm grateful to her for not handing over to me. 'I think we all know about you professionally, but do you have any other news?'

Rob smiles. 'Thanks, Claire. Yes, I guess you all know about my movies. Acting is still going well – even though I'm getting a bit too old to play a superhero! It's not quite as easy to get myself into that sort of shape these days.'

Rob does look like he's lost some of the bulky muscle he was carrying the last time we saw him in St Felix. I hadn't noticed until now, but his physique is much slighter than it was before. More like he used to be when we were at school.

'But Rob is still getting lots of offers,' Nixie says, speaking to us directly for the first time. 'Hollywood still want you, don't they, Rob?'

Rob smiles gratefully at Nixie. 'Yeah, but does Rob still want Hollywood? That is the question,' he says with a sombre expression. To which Nixie simply blinks back at him. 'Of course he does!' He quickly follows through with when we all look confused. 'Guys, I'm only kidding with you.'

But there's something about Rob's grinning face that to me doesn't quite feel as genuine as he'd want us to believe.

'And I'm assuming Nixie is the current lady in your life?' Mandy asks, raising her eyebrows. 'You don't expect us to believe she's actually your PA.'

We all smile. But Rob looks a bit put out by Mandy's assumption.

'You can believe what you want, Amanda,' he says, lifting up his bottle of beer. 'But I can assure you that Nixie is employed as my personal assistant, aren't you, Nixie?'

'Yes,' she says proudly. 'I certainly am.' She pulls a notebook and a phone out from her silver bag. 'Is there anything you'd like me to do for you, sweetie?'

Rob shakes his head. 'Not right now, thank you. You can put that away. I'll let you know later.'

'Should I go next?' I ask reluctantly. I'm in absolutely no hurry to share what little news I have, but watching Rob and Nixie together is making me feel uncomfortable. 'I have very little to report. The best thing in my life is sitting right here next to me.' I put my arm around Rosie.

'What about your job at the gallery?' Suzy asks. 'Are you still working there?'

I shake my head. 'No, I left the gallery a while back.'

'Where are you now?' Suzy continues, obviously not realising this is something I don't want to discuss.

'I just have a little part-time job,' I say, trying to sound upbeat. 'It means I can spend more time with Rosie.'

'Mummy was sad for a while,' Rosie tells the table. 'But she's much better now.'

The others all look at me with various confused expressions, all except Claire and Mack.

'I'm glad to hear it,' Mack says, rescuing me like I did Rob. 'I know I'm not really a mermaid as such. But should I take a turn?'

'Of course you should, Mack,' Claire says hurriedly. 'Just because you were a lovely late addition to our group, we still want to hear your news.'

I look gratefully at Mack, and he gives me a reassuring wink.

But before Mack can speak, a loud noise comes through the speakers surrounding the dance floor, like someone tapping a microphone.

We all look round to see Eddie holding a microphone in the middle of the dance floor, and standing next to him is Dexter.

'Welcome everyone,' Eddie says, looking a little nervous. 'Thank you all for coming. It's wonderful to see so many friends and loved ones looking back at me right now. I know some of you have travelled a long way to be here tonight, and I can't tell you how much both myself and Dexter appreciate it. I hope you all have a wonderful time with us celebrating.'

There's applause and the odd whistle and cheer.

'But there's something I have to share with you all. A little secret that Dexter and I have managed to keep quiet. A secret until now, that is ...'

The room falls silent.

'Tonight, you are not simply here to help me celebrate my fortieth birthday ... you are also here to both witness and help us celebrate the occasion of our wedding!'

There's the sound of a room of people gasping in surprise, followed by applause and more cheers.

'I know this might come as a shock to some of you.' Eddie looks around the room. 'But there is no one I would rather spend the rest of my life with than the man standing next to me right now.' Eddie reaches for Dexter's hand. 'And there are no other people we would rather say our vows in front of than you all!'

Again, more cheering and clapping.

'So, I ask that you all make your way down onto the beach in the next few minutes, because our wedding ceremony is going to take place on the sand in ...' He looks at his watch. 'Approximately ten minutes from now!'

'Then afterwards it's back here for party time!' Dexter says, grabbing the microphone from Eddie. He then hands it back to the DJ, who has been playing music quietly over the speakers since we arrived. Then they both exit swiftly through a door before anyone can talk to them.

I turn back to face the table and the others, all of whom have various expressions of shock and delight on their faces.

'I can't believe we didn't know!' Mandy exclaims first. 'Did any of you guys know they were getting married tonight – Claire?'

Claire shakes her head. 'No, I didn't know either. I had a feeling this was something more than simply a birthday party. Eddie was being very secretive about some of the things to do with it. But I had no idea this was the secret.'

'We knew, didn't we, Mum?' Rosie says.

'Did you, Frankie?' Suzy asks.

'We only found out when we arrived tonight,' I say hurriedly. 'I didn't know before then.'

'I thought the room was decorated fancily for a birthday party,' Mack says. 'I know you English do things differently than us in the States, but I didn't think this differently.'

'I'm pleased we're going to be here for it – all of us,' I say. 'It's so rare for us all to be together now that to be back here in St Felix for something so special is rather wonderful.'

'Agreed!' Rob lifts his glass. 'Here's to Eddie and Dexter! Let's do everything we can to make sure tonight is a wonderful evening for both them and for us all!'

Twenty-Eight

The ceremony is just perfect.

It's held down on the sand outside the restaurant. There are no chairs, but all the guests stand on either side of a red carpet that is laid on the sand for Eddie and Dexter to walk to the end of, where they then say their wedding vows in front of the celebrant. We later discover they have already had a legal ceremony a few days ago in a registry office in Penzance.

The intimate service, performed in the moonlight under the stars, is so moving that I find myself sobbing through most of it – especially when Rosie is chosen by Eddie and Dexter to throw rose petals from a little basket over the red carpet in front of them as they make their entrance.

I'm supported throughout the ceremony by Rosie, who has her basket in one hand, while her other hand tightly holds mine. And Mack on my other side, who passes me a clean white handkerchief to dab my eyes with.

When the service is over, we all head back up to the restaurant together, while Eddie and Dexter have a few more photos taken down on the sand, just the two of them.

'Are you all right?' Mack asks as we follow the others back up the beach.

'Yes, sorry about that. I didn't expect it to move me quite as much as it did, or I'd have come prepared with tissues.'

'Keep the handkerchief,' Mack says, looking at it covered in mascara and tears. 'I've got others.'

There's a bit of a queue as all the guests try to funnel in through the restaurant doors at the same time, so we stand back and wait.

'So how have you been?' I ask. 'How's your bar in New York?'

'I have several now,' Mack says without a hint of bragging in his voice. 'We've expanded.'

'How does your family like living in New York?' I ask.

'They don't,' Mack says again without any particular emotion in his voice. 'They stayed in LA.'

'Oh.' I don't really know how to respond to this. 'Do you commute back and forth?'

Mack smiles. 'Hardly, it's five hours plus flight time.'

'Really? I had no idea. Can't you fly from London to New York in a similar amount of time?'

'You can indeed. The US is one big country! But to answer your question, my kids come and visit – they love NY, and I go back to see them sometimes too.'

The question is hovering in the air. So Mack answers it before I have to ask it.

'My wife and I split up a couple of years ago, just before I bought the first bar, and our divorce came through almost twelve months to the day.'

'Oh, Mack, I'm sorry,' I say, meaning it.

Mack shrugs. 'It happens. I can't say I miss my wife all that

281

much, but I do miss my kids. The twins are a similar age to your Rosie.' Mack looks over to where Rosie is drawing in the sand with a piece of driftwood, and then colouring her outline in by scattering rose petals over the top.

'Samuel and Benjamin, right?' I say, impressed not only by my own memory for once, but by Rosie's creativity too.

'Yes, well remembered. I take my hat off to you looking after a baby all on your own. It was hard enough with two of us.'

'But you had two babies, so I guess that's one each.' I smile. 'Makes us even, I reckon.'

'Perhaps. I wouldn't have fancied it all on my own, though.'

'You do what you have to.'

'Yes, that's one of the reasons I moved to New York. My marriage was over, but I still needed to support my boys. When a pal of mine offered me the chance to come in with him on the purchase of a bar it was just too good an opportunity to turn down. I knew I'd be able to provide for the boys and give them a better life – and it's proved to be true. That's why we've been able to expand our brand to several bars across the city.'

'Well done you. I'm sorry you're not nearer your children, but you seem to be doing very well with your businesses.'

Mack nods. 'Did you ever visit New York? I don't suppose you remember, but we discussed you visiting the Met Museum when I was last here?'

'I do remember. But, no, I haven't ever got there ... yet. There's still time, especially now Rosie is older. I'd love to take her one day.'

'Make sure you look me up when you do,' Mack says, smiling. 'It would be my pleasure to show the two of you around the city.'

'Don't you worry, I'll be banging on your door the minute we get off the flight.'

'Hey, you two!' Eddie and Dexter are making their way past us with Rosie in tow. She's looking up in awe at both of them as she skips along between them, holding their hands. 'Stop whispering sweet nothings to each other and get yourselves inside. We've got some serious partying to do!'

I blush at Eddie's words – even though I know he's only joking.

'Shall we?' Mack asks, holding out his arm.

'Let's,' I say, taking it, and we follow the three of them inside to the immediate warmth of the birthday party that's now a wedding celebration too.

'Can I get you two a drink?' Mack asks as we sit back down again at the table with the others. There's currently ten of us sitting here – Nixie seems to have deserted Rob for now and he has been joined instead by Alice, who looks like she's hanging on every word he says.

Rob glances at us as we return to the table.

'That would be lovely, thank you,' I reply. 'Rosie will probably have a Coke in a bottle if they have them, and I'll have a gin and tonic, please.'

'Alice, don't bother Rob too much,' Claire says, looking with concern across the table at her daughter.

'I'm not bothering him, Mum. He's telling me all about making movies – it's incredibly interesting.'

'She's not bothering me in the slightest, Claire.' Rob smiles. 'I'm more than happy to share what little knowledge I have.'

Alice gazes at Rob in a similar way I would have gazed at my posters of Bon Jovi when I was a teenager and I have to smile.

'Where's Rosie?' Mandy asks, sitting down next to me as Mack goes to get our drinks.

'Over there with Eddie and Dexter – she seems to be taking her role as flower girl pretty seriously. She can't leave them alone now – and they seem to be loving it.'

Eddie is currently giving Rosie a piggyback while he talks to one of his guests.

'Good. I wanted to talk to you.'

'Oh, yes?'

'Are you all right?' Mandy asks with a serious expression.

'Yes ...' I reply a little hesitantly. 'Why?'

'What you said before ... you know ... about being depressed. Are you all right now? Because I know some really good people who can help you if you're not. I'm talking the best – Harley Street, you know? They don't come cheap – I should know, I've had far too many sessions with them over the last ten years. I'll pay for you to see them. And before you say anything, it's a gift from me to you. It's not charity.'

I smile at Mandy. 'That's really kind of you to offer, Mandy, but I'm fine right now. Really. I had some pills for a while, but now my main therapy is painting.'

'Painting?' Mandy screws up her nose. 'Really?'

'Yes, really. I'm sure you can't imagine it ever helping you with your troubles. But I find it really helps me. Some of my stuff can be a bit dark when I'm having rough days, but for the most part I find it lightens the load, and on occasion I produce some canvases I actually quite like.'

'Whatever works for you,' Mandy says, nodding. 'You're right, it would never have been my bag when I was having therapy, but I can see it's doing you good. You always did like a bit of art and craft.'

284

I feel like pointing out it was more than a bit of 'art and craft'. I did do a degree in fine art and art history. But I choose not to.

'But if you ever need a little more help,' Mandy adds, 'the offer is there, all right? You only have to ask.'

'Sure, and thank you.'

Mandy looks over at Rob, with Alice still hanging off his every word, and laughs. 'Who would have put money on Claire's daughter sitting there with your Rob twenty-five years ago? She's about the age you were when you went out with him, isn't she?'

'A few years older, actually. It is odd, though. How things change, eh?'

'Just a bit. Are you all right, though, in other ways I mean? You said earlier you had to give up your job?'

'Yes, it wasn't really working out when I had my problems. But I have my part-time job now, and of course Rosie's father helps out with some money, so Rosie never goes without.'

'But do you have enough money?' Mandy asks, as always not beating about the bush. 'Claire said she thought you might be struggling a bit.'

'Did she?' I say, eyeing Claire for a moment.

'She wasn't saying anything wrong, Frankie. She's just a little worried about you, that's all. She's your friend – we're all your friends. If you need help—'

'I don't.'

'I know. But if you do, you only have to say.' Mandy puts her hand over mine. 'You've been there for all of us at one time or another. Especially me and Claire. If there's any way we can give you something in return, then we *want* to.'

'I know.' I tap her hand so it's clasped in between mine. 'I know, and if there is anything I'll let you know, all right?'

'Promise?'

'Promise.'

Mack comes over with our drinks. 'Hey, Mandy,' he says. putting two glasses and a glass bottle of Coke with a straw down on the table. 'How's things?'

'Good, thanks, Mack. Very good, in fact. And yourself?'

'Can't complain,' he says amiably. 'It's good to be back here again.'

'Is it?' Mandy looks around. 'Don't get me wrong, I'm thrilled to be here for Eddie's fortieth and his wedding – that was one big surprise, eh?'

We both nod.

'But I don't think I'd be here otherwise.'

'Really?' I ask in surprise. 'I love coming back here.'

'Nah,' Mandy says. 'Not really my cup of tea these days. Now most of my family isn't here there's not really any reason for me to come back. Except for my nephew of course, he's still living here with his grandparents. But Fisher is sixteen now, he doesn't want to spend time with his Aunt Mandy any more.'

'Oh Mand,' I say putting my hand over hers again 'That's a shame about Fisher. But completely understandable you'd find it difficult coming home. I guess we all move on. We all change.'

'Don't we just?' Mandy pulls a face. 'Mainly in the number of wrinkles we all have! Although Rob over there is looking far too smooth for someone approaching forty – I might have to ask him where he gets his fillers done.'

'Do you think he's had Botox?' I ask, surprised again.

'Yeah, course he has. Mack will tell you – won't you, Mack?'

'I'm staying out of this,' Mack says diplomatically. 'Not my business what Rob does or doesn't do with his face.'

'Did I hear my name mentioned?' Rob asks, looking across

286

at us. 'Do you want me to come around to that side of the table?' He looks at us hopefully, like he's searching for an excuse to get away from Alice for a while.

'No ...' Mandy says with a straight face. 'I don't think we mentioned Rob's name, did we, Frankie?'

I shake my head solemnly. 'No, Mandy, I don't think we did.'

'Mack?' Rob asks desperately.

'No, buddy. You're on your own.' Mack winks.

Rob shakes his head good-naturedly and rolls his eyes. 'Thanks. Talk about friends helping friends. I must go and take a look at your painting, Frankie,' he says, looking over at the gift table, where a few people are already viewing my painting. 'It looks like it's attracting quite a crowd.' He makes his excuses to Alice, then comes over to me. 'Why don't you come and tell me all about it, Frankie? Explain where you got your inspiration from?'

'Er ... all right, then. See you in a bit,' I say to Mack.

Rob and I walk across the dance floor together. Even though the DJ is doing his best to attract people onto the dance floor by playing a mixture of appropriate tunes, he's not getting many takers just yet. But as we weave our way through the few children that are sliding around on the shiny floor, I'm very aware of many pairs of eyes upon us.

'Do you get this all the time?' I whisper to him as we walk.

'Get what?' Rob asks.

'People staring at you wherever you go?'

Rob glances around, and everyone immediately pretends not to be watching at him. 'Oh, that? Yeah, you sort of get used to it. I hardly notice it now, to be honest.'

I don't know how you could ever get used to people looking at you wherever you went. It feels a bit creepy.

'So this is the masterpiece?' Rob says as we stand in front of my painting. The group that had been there previously moved on when they saw Rob approaching.

It's funny – instead of people gravitating towards him, as I'd expect might happen, they actually run away, as if they can't possibly speak to someone as famous as Rob.

'I didn't expect Eddie to display it for everyone to see. I just hoped he might like it, that's all.'

Rob gazes at the painting. 'You don't change, do you?'

For a moment I think he's talking about my painting, then I realise he means me.

'Don't I? What makes you say that?'

'You're still so unpretentious, so modest, so unassuming, even.'

'Did you swallow a thesaurus?' I ask, smiling.

'I mean it. I spend all my time in Hollywood with people who are full of themselves. It makes a nice change to listen to someone who is actually talented but doesn't realise it.'

'Er . . . thanks,' I reply, stunned by his words. I turn back to my painting. 'It's just a hobby, really. I enjoy it, I just don't get all that much time to do it these days.'

'I'd like to see some of your other paintings sometime. Maybe buy one or two. I could do with something to remind me of home.'

Rob stares at the painting again.

'I'm surprised to hear you say that. Call St Felix home, I mean. It's a long time since you lived here.'

'I know. I still think of it as that, though – don't you?'

'Yes, very much so. Funnily enough, Rosie and I were talking about how much we'd like to come and live here again.'

'Why don't you, then?' Robs asks, as if it's the easiest thing in the world.

'Because it's expensive for one. Have you seen the house prices here recently?'

'No, not really.'

Of course he hasn't.

'And I have Rosie to think about too,' I add hurriedly, in case Rob thinks my lack of funds is the only reason.

'But you just said she would like to live here?'

'Yes ... but there's her school. And ... her friends. I can't just make her leave all that. And what about my job – I have to earn money somehow. I can't just live on fresh air.'

Rob just looks at me, and I know he's seeing right through all my feeble excuses.

'If you had the money, would you move back here?' he asks, looking me straight in the eye, so I have no choice but to tell the truth.

'Yes, in a heartbeat,' I answer totally honestly for the first time.

'Then let me give you the money,' Rob says, making me physically jump.

'What?'

'Let me buy a house for you here – for you and Rosie. Hollywood pays pretty well when you're at the top of your game. We'd have to be talking millionaires' mansions for it to put more than a small dent in my bank accounts, so I'm sure I could run to a little cottage by the sea. What do you say?'

Twenty-Nine

I stare at Rob.

'What?' he asks. 'I mean it, you know. I'm not joking.'

'No, I know you're not. But I simply can't accept.'

'Why ever not?'

'Because I want to be – no, I *need* to be – independent, that's why. I've brought my daughter up myself for nearly ten years now. I can't say I haven't struggled at times, but I've done it alone and I'm proud of that.'

'What about Rosie's father? Isn't he involved?'

'Yes, he contributes what he can.'

'And your parents, haven't they helped you out at all?'

'Of course they have. But they're getting older now, and they've retired to Norfolk. I'm sure even you remember it's a long way from Glasgow to Norfolk.'

'Yes ... but what I mean is you've allowed them to help you; why not me?'

'Because it's different.'

'Why is it? We all care about you and Rosie. You know it wasn't all that long ago I wondered if she might be mine ...'

I stare at Rob. Just him saying he still cared is enough to

make my stupid stomach jump. And now, as I always knew he would, he's talking about Rosie.

I'm also very aware that people are likely still watching us – correction – watching Rob.

'Not here, all right?' I say, glancing casually around. I see a lot of heads immediately turn the other way.

Rob notices too. 'Outside, then?'

I nod.

I check where Rosie is, and I see she's now playing with some of the other children sliding across the dance floor.

Suzy passes by on her way back from the ladies.

'Suz, can you just watch Rosie for me?' I ask.

'Sure,' she says, looking across at Rob. 'Where are you going?'

'Just outside for a bit.'

Suzy raises her eyebrows.

'No, it's not like that,' I insist.

'Darling, it's always like that when it comes to you and Rob. Sure, I'll keep an eye on Rosie. You do what you have to.'

Rob and I hurry outside together before someone decides to brave asking Rob for a selfie or an autograph.

The night air has cooled significantly since I was last out here, so I pull Claire's pashmina a little tighter around my shoulders while we walk down onto the beach together.

'I'm going to be honest with you, Rob,' I tell him, not wasting any time. 'I wondered for a while if Rosie might be yours too.'

Rob looks hopeful for a moment.

'But she's not,' I say firmly.

'How do you know? The dates match. You can't have forgotten Edinburgh.'

'Of course, I haven't forgotten. And to be honest, when she was born, I still wasn't one hundred per cent sure. But the dates

291

matched just that little bit better with Dougie – that's my ex – rather than you. It wasn't until we both had to have some blood tests when they thought Rosie might have a genetic disease that I knew for sure he was her father.'

'Rosie's all right, though?' Rob asks, looking worried.

'Yes, she's absolutely fine now. We were lucky she didn't have anything wrong in the end.'

'Good.' Rob glances back up at the café. 'I wish she had been mine.'

'Do you?'

He nods. 'Yeah, maybe then I'd have done something right in my life.'

The wind whips in off the sea and I shiver.

'Are you cold – do you want my jacket?' Rob asks, making me smile.

'Do you remember the last time you asked me that when we were looking out over this beach?'

'Of course I do. I've told you before I've never forgotten anything to do with you, Frankie,' he says as he places his jacket over my shoulders. 'I really would like to help you and Rosie, even if she isn't my child.'

'Why?'

'Because you're my friend. My oldest friend.'

'If you really are my friend then you should understand why I can't let you do this. Who offers to buy someone else a house, for goodness' sake? You really must have more money than sense.' I smile at him, trying to make light of this. I don't want to fall out with Rob. Not tonight.

'You're not far wrong there,' Rob says, kicking a pebble across the sand.

'What do you mean?'

292

Rob shrugs. 'Look at me, Frankie. I'm an ageing actor who made it big by playing a superhero. But superheroes don't really age, do they? And I am right now – badly.'

'You look OK to me.'

'I look OK because I've had work done,' Rob says, pulling at his face. 'A necessary evil, I'm afraid, to keep getting the lead roles.'

'You don't have to do that.'

'No, I don't have to. But people remember me like I looked in my early movies. Young, handsome, chiselled, even. Most of them, apart from my most ardent fans, aren't keen on seeing me the way I really am now. I'm tired, Frankie. I just don't have energy like I used to, the energy to get into the sort of shape big movie roles require, and to be honest I'm also tired of the sort of life I live in Hollywood.'

I've never seen Rob like this before – weary of life. He's always had so much get up and go.

'Don't go for the big roles then. Try something different in-stead. You just told me you have plenty of money, so you don't necessarily need big-budget movies. You could try something like TV . . . or theatre, perhaps?'

Rob smiles at me. 'You make it sound so easy.'

'It is. Everything is easier when you've got options. It's when you haven't, the decisions are that much harder.'

'Then let me help you,' Rob says again, but this time he turns to me and takes my hand in his. 'I want to do something good with my money.'

'I'm sorry, Rob. But I can't.' I gently extract my hands from his. 'Why don't you give some to a charity if you want to do something good with it?'

'I already do that.'

'Then start your own charity. I'm sure your PA up there will be more than expert at helping you do that.'

Rob grimaces. 'Nixie is expert in many things. But I feel setting up a charity might be a little out of her remit.'

I smile.

'Are you happy?' I suddenly ask.

'With Nixie?'

I shake my head. 'No, with life. *Your* life?'

Rob shrugs. 'I guess. I mean, I can't complain, can I?'

'No, you shouldn't complain – not about how famous you are, or how much you get paid to pretend to be someone else. I mean, are you happy outside of that? When you go back to whatever fancy penthouse you're living in this week and close the door. Are you happy then?'

Rob doesn't even hesitate. 'No, not when I'm on my own I'm not.'

'Then do something about it. Life is too short not to be happy. Especially if you're lucky enough to have the option to make changes.'

Rob gazes at me, and then to my horror suddenly leans in towards me.

'What are you doing?' I say, pushing him away.

Rob shakes his head. 'Sorry,' he says, looking confused. 'I don't know what came over me. Looking at you then felt like looking at you twenty-five years ago. I just wanted to kiss you like I did back then and hold you in my arms.'

I stare at Rob, my stomach suddenly remarkably calm as the penny finally drops.

'Rob, I love you,' I tell him earnestly. 'You know I do. But I realise now, for the first time, that I love you like all my other mermaids – as a friend. Our time was long ago.'

Rob nods sadly. 'You're right. But I'll always feel like there's still that tiny spark between us . . . do you feel it too, or is it just my imagination?'

'I feel it,' I reply honestly. 'Sometimes I'm annoyed I feel it, but, yes, it's still there.'

'There's something about your first love that never truly fades away. And that's what you were, Frankie, my first and *only* true love.'

As I'm about to try to voice something equally as heartfelt, Rob sways a bit in front of me.

'Are you all right?' I ask.

'Yeah,' Rob says, blinking hard but still swaying. 'I think so.'

'Do you want to sit down?' I look around and spy a cluster of rocks, the same ones we often used to sit on when we came down here as teenagers.

I guide Rob over to the rocks and we perch on one of the smooth edges.

'Have you had a lot to drink?' I ask, realising that might explain his slightly odd behaviour.

Rob shakes his head. 'No, I'm completely sober. I don't drink any more. Gave it up a few months ago. I was getting too many headaches with the booze.'

'Right . . . Have you felt like this before, then?'

Rob shrugs. 'Occasionally. I just assumed I was doing a bit too much. Burning the candle at both ends, you know?'

'Yeah, I know the feeling. I didn't sleep that well either when I was in the worst of my depression. Lack of sleep can mess with your mind.'

'Are you all right now? I mean, I know depression doesn't ever truly go away, but you're on top of it at the moment?'

'Yes, I'm in a good place right now. My painting helps me a lot. It's like my therapy.'

'You're really good. You should do more of it.'

'I probably would if I had the chance.'

'Move here and become a painter,' Rob says. 'That would answer all your problems in one go.'

'Ha ha, yes. I'm sure I could make enough money to live on doing that!'

'You never know?'

'Sadly, I can't take that chance. I have a daughter to support, I need steady and regular income. I'll figure it out,' I add, before Rob starts suggesting he support me or something equally as mad. 'If *you* figure out what you want to do next with your career. Something that doesn't involve filling your face with Botox!'

'Deal.' Rob holds out his hand.

'Deal,' I reply, shaking it. 'Now, we'd better be getting back to the party, or people will wonder where we are.'

'Anyone in particular?' Robs asks, looking back at the café.

'No?' I'm a little puzzled by his question. 'I just meant Claire and the other mermaids. It's really good to see everyone again, isn't it?'

'Yeah.' Rob turns back to me. 'The best.'

The rest of the party is a lot of fun.

We all dance, drink and enjoy the huge buffet of food that Eddie and Dexter have laid on for their guests.

'I think I'm going to head back to Claire's soon,' I say, leaning across towards Mack, who has spent a lot of the evening sitting close to Rosie and me.

The more people drank tonight, the more the dance floor filled, and the more people that danced, the louder the music got, until you couldn't really hear anyone else other than the person sitting close to you. So I almost have to shout into Mack's ear to get him to hear me.

'Rosie is getting tired,' I say, looking down at Rosie who is snuggled next to me leaning against my side. About twenty minutes ago she was dancing to a medley of One Direction songs with Eddie and Mandy.

'Would you like me to walk you back?' Mack asks. 'I could do with the fresh air to be honest.'

'Sure, if you don't mind. That would be great. Thanks.'

Before we go, I excuse myself to visit the ladies. Carefully, I lean Rosie against Mack, so she's propped up by him instead of me. 'Back in a minute,' I tell Mack, looking at Rosie snuggling into Mack's side as if she's done it many times before.

As I'm washing my hands in one of the sinks in the ladies' toilet, one of the cubicles opens behind me and another woman comes up to the sink next to me. 'Hi,' she says, smiling at me as she turns on the tap and runs her hands under the water.

'Hi.' I turn off the tap at my sink and head across to dry my hands.

'Are you Frankie?' she says over the noise of the electric hand-dryer.

'Yes, I am,' I reply, wondering why she's asking.

'The painting you did for Eddie is amazing.'

'Thank you.' The dryer has stopped, so I return to the mirror to tidy up my hair and redo my lipstick.

'I mean it,' the woman continues. 'You have a very distinct, and I'd go so far as to say unusual, style.'

'Thank you,' I say again, feeling embarrassed by her praise. 'It's kind of you to say.'

'Do you paint a lot?'

'When I can. I've been doing it on and off since I was a teenager.'

'Do you know much about art in general?' she asks suddenly.

'A bit,' I reply, a little thrown by her question. 'I used to work in a large art gallery in Glasgow, as a curator.'

'Nice.' The woman looks impressed, and I notice for the first time her attire. She's wearing a floaty dress in many shades of turquoise, green and blue. She wears several long, beaded necklaces in matching colours to her dress, including one with seashells interspersed with the beads, and in her long red hair she wears a comb with a small starfish attached, pulling her hair up on one side. 'Are you looking for a job by any chance?'

'I'm sorry, what?'

'A job? I should introduce myself. My name is Cordelia Delmare and I'm the manager of the Lyle art gallery here in St Felix. And I think you might be just what I'm looking for. An artist such as yourself can only be an asset to a gallery such as ours.'

I stare in the mirror at Cordelia, completely confused. *The Lyle Gallery is huge, by far the biggest gallery in St Felix. What would they want with me?*

'Are you offering to display some of my work?'

Cordelia smiles. 'Oh, I'm sorry, I should have been clearer. Your work, although amazing, isn't quite right for our gallery. We specialise in more … avant garde works of art – modern art, some would call it, although some of our work does come from as early as the 1950s. We have a lot of Ben Nicholson's work and some Barbara Hepworth sculptures too.'

I nod. I've heard of these artists, of course. Even if some of their work is a little too modernist for me.

'So, sadly, I'm not offering to display your work, Frankie. But I do have a vacancy at the gallery I'm desperately trying to fill with the right person. And I think that person might be you.'

Thirty

Mack and I walk back to Claire's house, with Rosie half asleep in between us.

'Are you all right?' Mack asks. 'You're very quiet.'

'Sorry.' I shake my head. 'Yes, I'm fine. I had a funny encounter in the ladies' toilet before we left, that's all.'

'Oh, really?' Mack says, raising his eyebrows.

'Nothing weird. I mean someone randomly offered me a job. Well, they offered me an interview anyway. But I got the feeling the job was mine if I wanted it.'

'In a public bathroom?' Mack asks, sounding every inch the American he is.

'Yes – pretty odd, isn't it?'

'What kind of a job?'

'Working in the art gallery here in St Felix.'

'Golly. And do you want to move back here again?'

'Actually, I do. We both do.' I look down at Rosie. She's so tired she's just about putting one foot in front of the other. I'm sure she isn't listening to what I'm saying to Mack above her. 'We were only talking about it yesterday. Oh,' I say, suddenly remembering. 'We both wished for it too . . .'

'Seems like you might have got your wish. It's not often someone says their wish came true. Not unless you're in Magic Kingdom in Disney World, of course.' He smiles.

'I haven't actually got the job yet. And even if I do get it, I haven't decided if I want to move. It's a big decision.'

'Of course.'

'What do you think?' I suddenly ask. For some reason, Mack's opinions matter to me.

'Me?' Mack sounds surprised.

'Yes, I'd like to know.'

'I think you should do what your heart tells you to.'

'But what if my heart is fighting with my much more realistic and practical head?'

'Still listen to it. The heart is a very good judge of everything, I find. It gives you truthful guidance on most things. Even if it makes you fall in love with the wrong person, the feeling isn't wrong, only the practicality of doing something about it.'

'Are we still talking about the same thing?' I ask, frowning.

'Do you think we are?'

Rosie suddenly stumbles between us, but fortunately we're both holding on to her, so she doesn't slip.

'Luckily we're nearly at Claire's,' I tell her. 'We'll soon have you tucked up in bed.'

We arrive at Claire's house and I invite Mack in – it seems like the polite thing to do. While I'm upstairs getting Rosie into her pyjamas and into bed, Mack is down in Claire's kitchen making me a cup of tea, and himself a coffee.

'Is she all right?' Mack asks as I return back downstairs.

'Yes, she's out for the count. Tonight has really worn her out.'

'She's not the only one. I think my partying days are over. I'm getting too old.'

300

'You and me both.' I smile at him as I take the mug of tea he's holding out.

'Nonsense, you look great for forty,' Mack says.

'You lie. But thank you for the compliment.'

'I only tell the truth.'

Shyly I glance at Mack to see if he really means this or is just messing.

His earnest face suggests the former.

'Shall we go through to the lounge?' I say hurriedly, already heading for the door.

'Sure.' Mack follows me and sits down on Claire's huge comfy sofa, so I automatically sit in one of the armchairs.

'How long are you here for?' I ask before sipping on my tea. 'Ooh, you make a good cuppa – well done!'

'For an American, you mean?' Mack winks. 'I fly back on Monday, sadly. Shame, I'd have liked to stay a bit longer this time. But work commitments said otherwise. You're not the only one who misses St Felix.'

'Really? Even after all this time?'

'Yeah, it gets worse as I get older. I don't think popping back like I seem to keep doing helps too much, either.'

'I guess it's so very different from New York – maybe that's the fascination?'

'Maybe. Maybe it's because you're here every time I visit as well.'

'Yeah, right,' I say quickly, brushing off this compliment like I had the first. 'Is that why you want me to move here, so you have an excuse to come and visit?' I grin, trying to make a joke.

'It would definitely be an added bonus.' Mack is smiling, but his eyes show he means every word.

'Maybe I should use you living in New York as an excuse

to fly over there?' I continue, still trying to keep it light. Mack was saying things I wasn't expecting him to, and, although I'm secretly quite enjoying it, I'm also quite confused.

'If you like? You know I was going to suggest you came over to visit one day – you and Rosie.'

'I'm sure Rosie would love that. But I don't think our finances are quite up to flights and hotels. Not right now, anyway.'

'You could stay with me,' Mack says. 'My apartment has two bedrooms. I'll sleep on the couch.'

I smile. 'That's very kind of you, but Rosie and I would share, of course. I'll keep it in mind should I win the lottery or something.'

'I'm serious.' Mack puts his coffee down on the table. 'I'd love it if the pair of you would come over sometime. I'd offer to pay for your flights, but I know you'd turn me down.'

'I would, you're right. Do you know Rob offered to buy me and Rosie a cottage here in St Felix earlier?'

'Did he?' Mack says with a wry smile. 'I should have known he'd outdo me.'

'It's not a competition.'

'What did you say?'

'About the house? No, of course.'

'Is that what the two of you were talking about earlier on the beach?'

I'm surprised Mack knows about the beach.

'That and other things.'

'You seemed pretty close.'

'Were you watching us?'

'No, of course not. I happened to see you through the window, that's all. Rob's told me all about your past. I know the two of you were close once.'

'Once being the important word there. Rob and I are just friends, good friends, in the same way as I'm still friends with all the other mermaids.'

'Does he know that?'

Why is Mack asking me all these questions. Has Rob asked him to?

'Yes, definitely after tonight. I was very clear. Well, I hope I was. Has he asked you to question me?'

'No.'

'Why are you, then?'

'Don't you know?' Mack asks with an anguished expression.

'Not really.'

Mack nods slowly, then he stares straight ahead. 'I thought you might, that's all,' he says quietly.

'Know what?'

'Why I care what Rob is saying to you, what Rob is thinking about you. I don't want to step on anyone's toes. I don't want to come between two people who have known each other since school, and who clearly still have feelings for each other.'

'Even if that was the case, which it's not – not those sorts of feelings anyway – why would you come between us?'

Mack turns his head and looks me straight in the eyes.

'Because I have feelings for you, Frankie. In fact, I might even go so far as to say . . . I'm in love with you.'

Thirty-One

I walk back from the Lyle art gallery on Monday afternoon with my head full of thoughts, each jostling for attention.

My interview went extremely well, and Cordelia offered me the position there and then if I wanted it. The gallery houses many fine works of art – mainly modern, which isn't exactly to my taste, but the job, the benefits, and most importantly the salary, are so good that dealing with a bit of modern art would to be a small price to pay.

I hesitate at a junction in the road. One cobbled street leads back to Claire's house, where I know everyone is waiting for me to hear what happened at my interview. The other tarmac path leads up towards Morvoren Cove, where I know, if I'm lucky, I can spend a bit of time on my own for a while just thinking. And, boy, do I have a lot to think about.

Decision made, I quickly text Claire, telling her the interview has gone well, and I'll be back soon to tell her more. Then I hurry along a narrow street that leads down towards the harbour.

As I walk quickly along Harbour Street, I pause for a moment at the deserted flower shop. It's so sad to see it like this, abandoned and empty. No buckets of flowers outside, calling to people as they pass by. No bouquets being made up inside, and then tied with one of Rose's special white ribbons.

I hope you're all right, Rose, I think as I stand gazing into the blank window. *You've been through so much over the last few years.* Then I think about William, Rose's late grandson, and her granddaughter, Poppy. *Life can be so cruel. Maybe I should take my chances while they're being offered to me. You just never know what's round the corner.*

I stand in front of the flower shop for another minute or so, before I decide I really must leave if I want some time alone up in my favourite spot. I'm about to walk away and continue on towards the hill, when I spot something on the wooden window ledge of the shop. I stare at it for a moment, before calmly picking it up and carefully placing it in my pocket.

Then I carry on my way, along the harbour and up the grassy hill, where I climb even higher before reaching my special place, which I'm overjoyed to see is just being vacated by an elderly couple wearing hiking boots and carrying rucksacks. They smile at me as I pass them.

Finally, I sit down, and as I do I let out a long sigh. But then I replace it by inhaling a deep breath of fresh sea air, and I immediately begin to feel calmer.

What a thirty-six hours it's been. How do I even begin to process it all?

Let's start with the easy stuff, I tell myself.

The easy stuff is the job offer. It sounds great. Perfect, even. Absolutely nothing to complain about there. It's almost too good to be true, so I spend the next few minutes trying to find a loophole or a drawback, something to make me decide to stay in Glasgow. But I can't.

Before yesterday, my other worry would have been where we were going to live if we did move back here. But when I told Claire about my job offer, she went into overdrive.

'Oh my goodness! That's amazing. It would be so lovely to have you back here again. You can stay with me,' she continued when I mentioned accommodation. 'For as long as you like. You can have the room you're in now, and we can clear the box room for Rosie. It needs decorating and we can do it in whatever colour she likes. I say box room – it's easily big enough for a single bed and some furniture. One of the boys was going to have it at one stage, but they decided they liked sharing and playing their computer games and the like. So we left it like that, but it would be perfect for Rosie.'

'Claire, take a breath,' I said, trying to calm her down. 'I haven't got the job yet.'

'Oh, you will! I know you will – it's written in the stars. Talking of which, we've even got a little studio outside where you could paint in your spare time. I say studio, it was actually my dad's shed, but it's not really a shed, more of an outhouse. I can just see you in there creating your works of art – maybe you could sell some of them? You know how much the holidaymakers here love to buy a painting of St Felix to take home with them.'

'I think we're getting a little carried away now.'

'Nonsense, you're good and you know you are. Please say you'll come and stay, Frankie. Alice will be off to uni soon and I'll be so lonely here on my own with only the boys. I'd love to have some female company to even it out a little.'

So I agreed, if only to calm her down, that *if* I got the job, and I decided to take it, I would temporarily come and stay with Claire until I was able to get my own place for Rosie and me.

Right, that was the easy stuff; now to something a little more complex that needed my attention.

Mack.

After Mack's declaration in the early minutes of Sunday morning, I was lost for words for a moment or two, just sitting there and staring at him.

'I should go,' he said, standing up. 'I shouldn't have said that. I'm sorry.'

But, as he made a move for the door, for once in my life I didn't wait for my brain to OK something. I did as Mack suggested I should do, and followed my heart.

Seeing him leaving, I jumped up and rushed over to him, grabbing his hand. Then, as he turned back towards me, his face full of sorrow and regret, I simply kissed him.

The look of surprise mixed with joy on Mack's face is one I think I'll never forget. And as I think about it now, I smile.

And what happened next, as we both followed our hearts and not our heads, and way before anyone else returned to the house, is something I don't think I'll ever forget either.

But Mack was due to fly back to New York late this afternoon from Heathrow. He left with Rob and Nixie early this morning, with the promise of calling as soon as he got back so we could sort something out.

That was another funny thing to happen – Nixie.

Cordelia left me in the ladies' toilet on Saturday night, staring at my reflection in the sink mirror in a state of complete shock. As I stood there, Rob's PA, Nixie, had exited the third of the cubicles behind me.

'Hi,' she said, smiling at me.

'Hello,' I replied.

'I hope you don't mind but I couldn't help overhearing

just now,' she said as she washed her hands next to me. 'That sounds like a great offer – you should take it.'

'Sadly, it's not quite that simple.'

'Why isn't it?' she asked, moving over to the hand-dryer but not putting her hands underneath.

'Just lots of stuff to consider.'

'Isn't there always?'

'Probably.'

'Rob talks a lot about you, you know?' Her beautiful set of perfect white teeth formed into a warm and genuine smile.

'Sorry.'

'Why are you apologising?'

I shrugged. 'Well, you and he must be . . .' I waved my hand awkwardly at her. 'You know?'

'Sleeping together?'

I feel embarrassed now as I remember.

'Most people assume that,' Nixie replied calmly. 'But we're not. Our relationship is totally a professional one.'

'Sorry.'

'Stop apologising. What is it with you English and your apologies? Is it like queuing? Do you just enjoy doing it?'

'Not really. We moan about it mostly – queuing, that is.'

'And the weather.' Nixie winked.

'Yes.' I grinned. 'We moan a lot about the weather too.'

Nixie smiled again, before becoming serious. And I saw in her sharp eyes she was definitely no bimbo. Underneath all her Botox and bleach, Nixie was one smart cookie. 'You only get one life, Frankie. You never know how long it will last. Do what you think is right for you and for your daughter. Don't go worrying about anyone else. Life has a funny way of showing you the right path to take. It might not be the path you've chosen for yourself – but know that whatever happens, life has got your back – eventually.'

And then without needing to dry her hands, she left.

'Life has got my back?' I repeat now. *I sure hope so, because this next path already seems to have so many obstacles and I've not set off along it yet.*

Realistically, what are Mack and I going to sort out when he phones? He lives halfway across the world in a huge busy metropolitan city. And I'm currently considering moving even further away from him, to a tiny, if beautiful, Cornish fishing town.

How are we supposed to have a relationship with that distance between us? Right now, it seems totally impossible.

But even just the memory of last night puts a huge smile on my face.

'Life, I really hope you've got my back this time,' I say into the wind, which picks up my words and carries them off into the sea. 'Because this is definitely not the path I expected to be on – in fact, my whole life has suddenly become a huge, great detour.'

I reach into one of my pockets and pull out what I picked up from the shop window ledge.

It's a beautiful conch shell. I probably wouldn't have thought much of it if I found the shell anywhere else. But finding it so prominently on the flower shop windowsill made me think.

You never know what's going to happen next . . .

'If this is a sign from you, I get it,' I say into the wind again, as it carries my words out onto the waves once more. 'I have to make the most of every opportunity, because you never know when it might be your last.'

I reach into my other pocket, and then I look at what's in my hand.

Two small shells rest in my palm – a cockle shell and a horn shell. Both of them in delicate shades of pink and cream.

The cockle shell, I found on the sink when Nixie left the restaurant toilets, and the horn shell had been on my seat when I stood to shake Cordelia's hand after I accepted the job at the gallery. How I didn't feel it when I sat down, I still couldn't figure, but now it doesn't seem to matter.

'If that's what you want, life, then that's what I'll do!' I call out to the sea. I look down at the beach and then behind me at the town. 'St Felix!' I declare. 'At long last it looks like ...' My voice breaks. 'I'm coming home!'

A tear runs down my face. As I brush it away and turn back, I hear the familiar, and for the first-time, comforting sound of splashing down below.

As I look down a tail flips over in the waves below me – its scales shimmering in the bright afternoon sunlight. I watch totally mesmerised as the tail splashes around below me not once, but several times. And suddenly I realise that the tail, and whatever it belongs to, is giving me its unique seal of approval.

Thirty-Two

May 2024

'Thanks, Jack!' I call as I leave the art shop on the high street. 'You're my saviour!'

'No problem,' Jack calls from his wheelchair as he manoeuvres swiftly around his shop, adding more stock to the shelves already packed with art equipment. 'Any time.'

I love Jack's art shop. Formerly a butcher's, it opened in the summer of 2020 and now, some four years later, it is still thriving, and I am one of its most frequent customers.

Before Jack opened his shop, I had to buy the majority of my art equipment online. There was the little craft shop in St Felix that Jack's other half, Kate, owned, but she only stocked a small amount of painting equipment, aimed at the amateur artist. Which these days – and it still astonishes me to say it – I am no longer.

I walk back down the high street clutching my precious tube of Prussian-blue oil paint, and onwards towards Harbour Street. The town, as always, is bustling with tourists on this beautiful May morning.

I call in on Ant and Dec at the Blue Canary bakery and

pick up a tuna salad roll for my lunch, and I treat myself to a Belgian bun while I'm there. Then I carry on down towards the harbour, passing the flower shop as I go.

'Hi, Poppy,' I call to a woman placing some rose stems in a metal bucket outside the shop.

She spins around. 'Oh, hi, Frankie. How are you?'

'Good, thanks.' I hold up the tube of paint. 'Jack has saved me once more.'

Poppy smiles. 'How's the latest masterpiece going?'

'I wouldn't call it that. But it's coming on . . . gradually!'

'All great works of art take time – I imagine so, anyway. You know I'm not the most artistic of people even though I run this place. Amber is the creative one.'

Poppy, Rose's granddaughter, who I first met when she was just a small girl, took on the running of the flower shop in 2015 when Rose sadly passed away.

I went to Rose's funeral, feeling as if a huge part of my life had been removed quite forcibly from my memories, and also feeling incredibly guilty that I never made the effort to visit Rose in hospital down in London when she was alive. But I'd just moved back here to St Felix, and I simply didn't have the spare money after our move to spend on long and expensive train journeys to the capital.

However, Poppy arrived in St Felix not long afterwards, and, with the help of Amber, her assistant and friend, made a huge success of the shop once more.

'I'm sure you both do your bit,' I reply, smiling at Poppy. 'Your grandmother would be very proud.'

'Thank you, Frankie. Coming from you, that means a lot.'

'You're very welcome. Right, I'd better be getting back; the painting won't finish itself.'

'Good luck!'

I leave Poppy and continue down to the harbour, then I cut up a side road that leads towards my little studio.

Yes, I actually have my own art studio and shop now. I still can't believe it.

After Rosie and I moved back here, I worked in the Lyle gallery for five years, but during that time I painted a lot in the outhouse in Claire's garden.

Claire really has been so kind to both Rosie and me. Before we even moved in with her, she emptied her little box room and had it redecorated in pink emulsion, and the very specific Cath Kidston wallpaper Rosie had always wanted, but I had never been able to afford to buy for her. Claire had redecorated the little workshop too – painting it in pure white – so it made the perfect studio for me to create my own works of art.

Over the next few years, we were extremely happy living with Claire. Rosie absolutely thrived living by the sea, and every day I could see her becoming a little healthier as she spent more time outside and breathed in the clean and bracing coastal air of St Felix. She made friends, had boyfriends and I watched my daughter blossom from a little girl to a shy and gawky teenager, and finally into the beautiful young woman she is today, just about to complete her first year at the University of East Anglia in Norwich.

I missed her, of course I did. But over the years, as I watched Claire cope with the departure of first Alice, and then George, and finally Freddie, I realised that letting Rosie go out into the world to find her own way, and learn her own lessons, was just as difficult, if not harder than actually parenting her when she was young. As each of Claire's children left the house to go to university or start their first job, Claire would be bereft for a while, but then as her children settled into whatever new place they had departed for, and she witnessed them growing in confidence and happiness, she would settle, and become happier herself, until it all began again with the next one.

So when it came to Rosie's turn to leave, I knew what to expect. I allowed myself to grieve her departure, telling myself that I'd soon feel better. It took a while but, eventually, just like Claire, as I saw her changing, so did I.

A car horn toots behind me, and I realise that I've been dawdling along in the middle of the road lost in my own thoughts.

I turn and realise the person tooting is not annoyed or angry with me, but simply saying hello.

'Sorry!' I call to Ana as I move to the side, and she pulls her red vintage camper van alongside me. 'I was lost in thought.'

I know Ana well. Her husband, Noah, owns the antique shop not far from my studio.

'I could see,' Ana says through the open window. 'Good thoughts, I hope?'

'So, so.' I smile. 'Are you on your way out or back home?'

'Home,' Ana says. 'I was just showing Daisy-Rose to a prospective client.'

Daisy-Rose is the name of Ana's VW camper van. Ana runs a very successful business renting Daisy-Rose out for weddings, graduations and the like.

'Any luck?'

'Of course. Once they see her in all her glory they can't resist.' She winks. 'Oops,' she says, looking in her rear-view mirror. 'Looks like I'm the one causing the traffic jam now. I'd better go. See you soon!'

I wave as she drives off, and then I continue to stand to the side of the narrow road while three more vehicles pass me. Then I carry on my way.

My studio and shop is not that far from Morvoren Cove, along a fairly busy thoroughfare in St Felix. It wasn't in among all the hustle and bustle of Harbour Street like the flower shop and the bakery. But it had enough passing footfall to make it visible to the many tourists and holidaymakers who came to St Felix wanting to buy a souvenir of their trip – and luckily for me that was often a painting or a print of their holiday destination.

As I unlock the door to my studio, I marvel, as I often do, at how I'm this lucky.

I've never regretted for a moment moving back to St Felix and, even though the last ten years feel like they've flashed by in a few moments most days, it's been quite the eventful decade, and not just for myself and Rosie.

After a few minutes of pottering about, I settle myself down into my seat in front of my easel at the back of the shop and I begin to paint. Painting still soothes me, as it always has. The rhythmical process of placing a brush in paint and applying it to a canvas calms me in a way nothing else does, and it allows me time to process my thoughts.

I'll always be disturbed by someone coming into the shop to browse and, if I'm lucky, to buy one of my paintings. But I don't mind at all. I'm still so grateful that I'm able to make a living this way. I've continued living with Claire; it's only the two of us in the house now and we split all the bills between us. When Claire's mother sadly passed away, Claire inherited what was left of her parents' estate, and that included a mortgage-free house. So now all our children have moved to pastures new, our monthly bills are incredibly reasonable for two people living in such a large house in St Felix. Claire and I have been friends for nearly forty years now, and we're still more than happy to be in each other's company.

I spend the next couple of hours happily painting. Currently, I'm working on a private commission – a painting of Morvoren Cove. The customer was very specific in what they wanted and, as always, I was happy to oblige.

One of the most interesting things about the commission is what I learnt while discussing it over the phone with Muriel, the lovely old lady who asked me to create an artwork that summed up her lifelong love of both St Felix and in particular of Morvoren Cove.

How I never knew this before, I really couldn't understand once Muriel told me – but apparently the word 'morvoren' is Cornish for mermaid.

'Did you know that?' I asked Claire when I came back from the studio that evening.

'Of course!' Claire said, smiling. ' "Mor" is the Cornish word for sea, and "moren" for maiden. And there's the mermaid myth that goes with that particular cove. I told you about it when we were at school. Do you remember?'

'Of course I remember,' I replied. *I've never been allowed to forget it over the years.*

'That seems like a long time ago now, doesn't it?' Claire said wistfully. 'I wonder how many of those wishes we made ever came true?'

Luckily for me, an Amazon courier knocked on Claire's door at that moment, so I didn't have to answer any more questions on the subject. The less said about those wishes, the better in my opinion, especially in light of recent events.

But as I lock up the studio that night, I pause at my desk and stare at the items displayed on the windowsill. They're nothing unusual, especially not for a windowsill in a Cornish seaside town. But the ornate shells that I have on my windowsill are special, to me anyway. Because they're the same shells that have been collected at very special moments over four decades of my life.

Thirty-Three

'What are you up to today?' I ask Claire as we sit down for breakfast on Saturday morning.

'I've got a meeting about the school reunion,' Claire says, sipping on her cup of tea.

'Oh, right,' I reply, trying not to sound too dismissive. Claire already knew what I thought about the reunion she was organising for the 'Class of 1990.'

'It's happening, Frankie, whether you like it or not. I know a lot of people are looking forward to it, even if you aren't.'

Claire originally tried to organise a reunion for the thirtieth anniversary of us leaving school in the summer of 2020. But unfortunately for Claire, this momentous anniversary also coincided with another momentous event – one that spread a little further around the world than our ex-classmates – a global pandemic on a scale no one had ever witnessed before.

The reunion had to be postponed when a second wave of Covid-19 broke out, and then again when the school decided to have some renovation work done over the course of one summer. So here we are now in 2024, and finally Claire has decided to try one last time to reorganise the event – the occasion,

318

2024 is the year the majority of the class will be celebrating their fiftieth birthdays.

'Claire, you know that's not fair. I said I'd come, didn't I? And that I'd help you out on the night with everything. Forgive me if I'm not super excited to see a load of people I haven't spoken to in over thirty years.'

'You have spoken to them. What about the other mermaids – they are all coming.'

'Four of us already live here! One never left,' I say, winking at Claire. 'And the other three have gradually made their way back over the years.'

Claire, Eddie and I are not the only ones of our original group who have found their way back to St Felix. Rob now lives here as well.

Part of me was shocked when Rob said he was coming back to St Felix in 2023. But part of me wasn't at all surprised.

My life has only changed for the good during the last decade, but the last ten years haven't been kind to Rob at all.

I first learnt that Rob had cancer when I was in a doctor's surgery. It was pre-pandemic, so surgeries still had magazines for you to thumb through while you were waiting for your appointment. When I read that Hollywood heartthrob Rob Matthews had a brain tumour, I nearly dropped the copy of *Hello!* on the waiting room floor. But I quickly read the short article that said he was getting treatment, and his prognosis was good. But they had to call my name three times over the surgery tannoy before I registered they were calling me for my appointment.

When I got back to Claire's and told her, we tried to contact Rob. But his mobile kept going straight to answerphone, so in the end we emailed instead.

A few days later we got a reply from Rob saying not to worry and he was getting treatment from the best oncologist in LA. And his prognosis was very good.

That was in January 2020, and of course we did worry, but not just about Rob. Very quickly everyone was worried as Covid-19 gradually locked down the world bit by bit.

St Felix was very strange during the pandemic. During the first lockdown we went from a bustling seaside resort to a ghost town in a matter of days. Even in the winter months the town was usually still busy, with holidaymakers taking refreshing brisk walks on the beaches and warming themselves afterwards with a coffee or a hot chocolate.

But suddenly, when we were all told to 'Stay at Home', that stopped. The streets were deserted, the shops closed, the takeaways shut.

Claire and I had each other, Rosie, and Claire's youngest, Freddie, who was still living at home then, for company. The children were homeschooled, which Claire and I took turns to attempt to try to help with, and to keep busy I painted a lot, because of course the Lyle gallery was closed too.

To begin with, we couldn't even see Eddie and Dexter, who also couldn't work because their café and restaurant had to close down. Eventually they were able to reopen as takeaway only, and then, with huge restrictions due to the number of diners they could accommodate with social distancing, their restaurant opened again too. It was an incredibly difficult time for them, but they managed to survive – just – and only now were they beginning to make a profit again, so their little business could thrive, not simply survive.

But, after a couple of false starts, eventually the world began to open up again, and by the spring and summer of 2021 St Felix was gradually getting fully back on its feet.

'Exactly, so it's not like you won't know anyone.'

'Claire, calm down. I know you're worried about it all going smoothly, but with you in charge it can't fail. You're one of the most organised people I know.'

These days, Claire runs her own very successful therapy business. She took some time out after her mother died to think about what she wanted to do with the rest of her life and quickly decided that she wanted to build on what she already did with her self-help groups. She went back to college part time, trained and subsequently qualified as a therapist and counsellor. Much of this was done online during the pandemic years, after which Claire converted the children's old games room into a comfortable and relaxing space to see her clients in. This, along with her self-help groups, keeps Claire super busy, but she still always seems to have the time to pitch in with good causes that need her help, or in this case school reunions that need organising.

'Hmm ... perhaps,' Claire says, but secretly she looks pleased. 'So what are you doing today – the usual?'

'Yep, heading to the gallery first to open up. But Jessica is in today, so if it's not too busy I might finish up early and head to the pub. Rob said he wanted to speak to me about something.'

Jessica is my part-time assistant in the gallery. Much like Rose took me on when I was at school as some extra help, Jessica came along just at the right time when the shop was getting busier and I needed someone to look after customers, so I could be left in peace to get on with creating my artwork behind the scenes. Jessica worked Saturday and Sunday, and occasionally weekday afternoons in the busier summer months. She was lovely, and even though she was only seventeen, I trusted her completely to look after my gallery and shop.

'What does Rob want to talk to you about?' Claire asks with interest.

'No idea. But I said I'd pop in after the lunchtime rush and have a word.'

'Can you check with him if he got my email about the re-union? I need him to confirm in writing if the pub can do the bar for us. And I have to get a special licence for the school.'

'Will do!' I say, saluting. 'Email and licence.'

'Thank God it was Rob who took over the pub. I'm sure Rita and Richie would have been fine with helping out. But what if it had been someone less helpful who'd bought it when it went up for sale? It's one less thing to worry about knowing Rob will be in charge on the night. I know he won't let me down.'

Rob decided to give up Hollywood after the pandemic and, to our surprise, bought the Merry Mermaid when it went up for sale last year. His cancer diagnosis and subsequent battle with it during the pandemic, when he was immunocompromised and had to be super careful, meant he became incredibly iso-lated and as a result incredibly lonely too. So, after he got the all-clear, Rob decided that it was time for a new chapter of his life. And he couldn't think of anywhere better to begin that new chapter than here in St Felix.

Just like his parents before him, he now owns and runs the Merry Mermaid. At first, he wasn't here all the time as he had some contracted acting jobs he needed to complete, so he brought in a temporary manager to work alongside the few remaining part-time staff the pub already had.

But now he is here the majority of the time and, aside from the press tour he was contractually obliged to take part in over in New York recently, is now finished with Hollywood. He spends most of his time behind the bar, and I don't think I've ever seen him happier.

I glance at my watch, 'I'd better go, or I'll be late opening up. Takeaway for dinner later?'

'Of course!' Claire says, smiling. 'What movie is it tonight?'

Claire and I had a Saturday evening routine – which like many other people was takeaway and a movie. We mixed the movies up, and we were currently going through an eighties phase – taking us back to our school days.

'*Back to the Future*,' I reply, carrying my plate and mug across to the kitchen sink and rinsing them. 'Kind of appropriate really with you organising the school reunion right now.'

Claire looks puzzled.

'The Enchantment Under the Sea dance?' I say. 'It's from that movie, isn't it?'

'Of course! How could I forget? Ooh, do you think I should give the reunion a theme like that?'

I hold up my hand. 'Claire, I think you've got enough on your plate without overcomplicating things with a theme. You'll have us all dressing up as mermaids again next. And before you even think about it – no way!'

Claire grins. 'You know me too well. All right, I'll keep it simple ... probably.'

I shake my head as I load my breakfast things into the dish-washer. 'That will be the day!'

After a busy morning and afternoon in my gallery, where we sell five paintings – a great day for me – I leave Jessica to close up and I head down towards the harbour and the pub at around four o'clock. I know the Merry Mermaid will still be busy, but late afternoon is usually its quietest time.

Having an ex-Hollywood movie star as a landlord has increased the pull of the already popular pub, so along with all the usual holidaymakers keen to drink in the ancient building, there is now a constant stream of Rob's fans making the pilgrimage down to Cornwall just to have a drink there and the chance of spotting him behind the bar.

It was strange at first to have Rob back here again. It took me long enough to get used to living here again myself, but to have another blast from the past with my teenage boyfriend in the same town was disconcerting at first, but now I was used to it, it was kind of nice as well.

The familiar benches outside the pub are packed on this sunny spring afternoon as I head past them and in through the open door into the bar.

Rob, as he is often found, is leaning over the bar having a selfie with two customers. Their grins and flushed faces as they take their drinks from him and head outside are nothing unusual. I've witnessed it hundreds of times since Rob came back to St Felix.

He looks up as I walk towards the bar and smiles.

My stomach, so long at the mercy of a Rob Matthews smile, is these days much more in control of its actions. Rob and I are now simply very good friends, nothing more, nothing less. When I first found out he was coming back here, I was worried. Especially after Eddie's party. But the Rob who arrived back in St Felix, post-pandemic and post-cancer, was a different Rob; a changed man, many would call him. I just call him my old mate, Rob.

'Hey,' he says, smiling, still with a perfect set of white Hollywood veneers. But these days the Botox is long gone from his face, and in its place, the usual lines and wrinkles of a nearly fifty-year-old man. 'Thanks for coming over.'

'No problem,' I say, pulling up a stool at the end of the bar ready to perch on. 'How was your trip?'

'So, so,' Rob says, moving along towards the end of the bar with me. 'No, don't sit down here; there's no way I'll be able to talk to you if we try in the bar – you know what it's like.'

I nod. I long ago gave up trying to have a conversation with Rob in public, because we'd always be disturbed by a fan wanting a selfie, or, more rarely these days, an autograph scrawled in black marker over a photo of Rob.

'Where do you want to go, then?' I ask. 'The town is pretty busy this afternoon.'

'Give me a minute,' Rob says. 'I'll be right with you.'

Rob disappears out back and reappears a few moments later in the disguise of many a celebrity – dark glasses and a baseball hat, which, surprisingly, usually works for him. Particularly in the summer months, when he blends in easily with many other men wearing something similar. In the winter months, Rob would usually pull on either another baseball cap alongside a thick anorak, or a tweed cap with a wax jacket, in an effort to go unnoticed.

'Ready?' he asks, pulling the peak of the cap well down.

'Sure, where shall we go?'

'I have an idea . . .'

We walk up away from the busy harbour towards the grassy hill.

'We've no chance of the viewing area being empty today if that's where you're thinking of going?' I tell him. 'The beautiful weather means everywhere is heaving with people.'

'We could at least check? I know we won't be disturbed there.'

'All right.' I shrug, wondering what it is Rob wants to talk about that matters so much if we're disturbed.

We walk up the hill and over the grass, and just as I suspected there is already a young couple sitting up on the little wooden bench that has recently been added to the viewing area.

But as we approach, they see us and stand up. Rob lifts his hand and they wave back.

'Do you know them?' I ask. This isn't the usual sort of reaction Rob's fans give if they recognise him. Usually it's disbelief, mixed with excitement or panic on their faces, but this couple is remarkably calm.

'I may have asked them to reserve the bench for us,' Rob says with a half-smile.

'But why?' I ask, not as surprised by this as I once would have been. Even after buying the pub, Rob still has a very healthy bank account – which he had no qualms at all about admitting to me one day – and it would seem that money can buy you almost anything in life. Including, on this occasion, a reservation on a bench with a view.

'I told you – I don't want us to be disturbed. Come on.'

We climb the final part of the hill and sit down on the bench.

'Remember when this was just rock,' Rob says, taking off his shades and looking at the little bench. 'It's much better now, isn't it?'

'Yes. I'm surprised the council forked out for it, though. They've been pretty strapped for cash since the pandemic.'

'Would it shock you to know I paid for it?' Rob says.

I look at him for a moment. 'No, actually it wouldn't. It's lovely of you, of course, and much more comfortable to sit here now. But why?'

'This place is special to me – it always has been since we came here on our first date all those years ago.'

I nod, but hurriedly gaze out at the sea wondering again what Rob has brought me here for. He's behaving a bit oddly, and I wonder again why it's so important that we're not disturbed? Suddenly a horrible feeling begins to form in the pit of my stomach. Rob isn't going to tell me he has feelings for me again, is he? Or worse ...

I turn my head slowly, fearing I might find Rob down on one knee, but he is just sitting like I am, looking out at the view.

'Do you feel the same about it, Frankie?' he asks, still gazing outwards.

'Yes,' I reply, a sense of relief seeping slowly through me. Of course Rob wasn't going to propose – why would he, when we're just friends? 'This place has always held a special place in my heart, and not only because we had our first date here. I remember a time that Rosie and I sat here together before Eddie's fortieth birthday, actually his wedding as it turned out. I realised for the first time that day how much Rosie loved St Felix too. We actually sat and wished we could come back and live here. It seemed like such a remote pipe dream that day, but somehow it did actually happen.'

'Do you miss her?'

'Of course. Every day. But she's happy, and that is all you ever want for your children – for them to be happy.'

'I wish I'd had a child,' Rob says. 'I've left it a bit late now, though.'

'Are you sure you haven't got one tucked away somewhere?' I grin. 'All the girlfriends you've had over the years.'

But Rob doesn't see the funny side, as he usually does to a joke made about his many exes.

'Perhaps I have, but what's the point if you never know them?'

'It's not too late, you know? I mean it is for me, of course, but for a man approaching his fifties it's nothing these days. You're still considered a viable baby-making machine, whereas I'm just old and menopausal!'

Again, to my surprise Rob is silent. Usually I'd have expected a witty retort from him. That's the type of relationship we have these days – we can laugh and joke with each other, each of us knowing it's always meant in a friendly, light-hearted way.

I look across at him. 'All right, what's wrong? And before you say nothing, don't bother, I know you too well.'

Rob turns towards me now and even under the peak of his cap I can see he's ashen-faced. 'It's the cancer, Frankie,' he says in a low voice. 'It's back.'

Thirty-Four

'How bad?' I ask quietly, when I've got over the shock of Rob's statement. By the look on his face, I am in no doubt his reply is not going to be positive.

'Bad. And it's spread this time apparently. I found out last week when I was over in New York. I'd had some symptoms, so I went back to see my oncologist and they did some tests. It's not looking good.'

'But there must be something they can do? Some treatment. Can't they do what they did before?'

Rob shakes his head. 'Too late for that. It's progressed too far. It's more a matter of when, rather than if this time.'

I shake my head in disbelief. 'No, that can't be right. You should get a second opinion – you of all people can afford that, can't you? Find a different specialist. One who will help you!'

Rob takes hold of my hands and turns me towards him.

'Don't you think I've thought of that? Problem is they will all say the same. My guy is the top in his field. If he says there's nothing they can do, then . . . ' Rob hesitates, and he swallows hard. 'Then there's nothing they can do.' He looks at me, his eyes swimming with tears. 'I wanted you to be the first to know,' he says, trying to keep it together. 'In fact, I want you to be the only one who knows here in St Felix.'

I have to pull my hands away to wipe the tears from my own eyes. I scrabble about in my bag for the pack of tissues I know is always in there. I pull two from the pack, pass Rob one, and then I dab my eyes on the second, while Rob wipes his own eyes.

'When you say you want me to be the only one who knows,' I say when I've composed myself. 'I can tell Claire though, can't I?'

Rob shakes his head. 'No, only you.'

'I can't keep this a secret from Claire! We live together for goodness' sake.'

'Claire mustn't know, Frankie. No one must. I don't want people treating me differently. The time I've spent back here in St Felix has been like a breath of fresh air. Yes, I get the occasional request for a photo or an autograph, but in between that I'm able to be myself. I haven't been able to do that for a very long time. It's meant the world.'

I nod. 'But still ... people will begin to notice, won't they? I don't know much about ... ' I can't even say it. 'What you're going through. But surely there will be signs as you ... well, as you progress.'

'Stop beating about the bush, Frankie. Just say it. "As I die."'

'I don't want to! Because if I say it, then it's real. And it can't be real, Rob. It just can't.'

I take hold of his hands this time.

'You can't die,' I say as the tears begin to flow again. 'You've always been here. Not here as in St Felix. But here.' I place his hand over my heart, with my hand covering it. 'You've been here since I was fifteen, Rob, and as we both know that's a very long time.'

Rob smiles and blinks back his tears.

'And you've been here all that time too, Frankie.' Rob does the same as I did, and places my other hand over his heart, so we're both now touching each other's chests. 'And you always will be.'

We both let go then, desperate to wrap the other in the tightest embrace possible.

'I never stopped loving you, Frankie,' Rob whispers into my hair. 'And I never will.'

'Oh, Rob.' Sobbing, I pull him as close as I possibly can to me. 'I'll always love you and whatever happens I'll never ever forget you.'

Thirty-Five

Spring turns to summer and life continues in St Felix.

The town becomes busier as we enter the first months of summer. Claire's school reunion moves ever closer, and Rob still won't let me tell anyone what's happening to him.

I became so quiet and withdrawn for a while after Rob's shock confession, that Claire began to wonder if my depression was rearing its ugly head again. But when she questioned me about it, I lied – well, partly lied. I said I wasn't depressed, just feeling a little low lately. Which was the truth. Rob's news knocked me for six.

But luckily Claire was knee-deep in both her work and organising the reunion, so, for the time being at least, I was managing to hide my true feelings from her.

One Wednesday afternoon in mid-June, I'm sitting at the back of my shop finishing off the painting I've been commissioned to do by Muriel, the lovely old lady who got in touch with me before the terrible afternoon that Rob told me his news.

I've got behind with my painting over the last few weeks, and I'd had to telephone Muriel to apologise for the delay. But she was perfectly lovely, and said there was no hurry, she wasn't due down in Cornwall until early July anyway, so I had plenty of time before she needed to collect it.

The shop bell rings, so I look up expecting to see a customer, but I almost drop my paintbrush when I see the person standing there looking a little lost among all the paintings.

It's Mack.

I haven't seen Mack in person since 2019. After I moved back here to St Felix with Rosie, it took me a year or two before I got fully back on my feet again, both financially and mentally. Claire was great, helping us out, and as soon as I could start paying her rent, I did. As time went by, not only was I able to pay Claire money to help out with the monthly bills, and provide for myself and Rosie, but I was able to save some money as well. And in 2019, for Rosie's fifteenth birthday, I surprised her with a trip to New York in the autumn, or as it's called in America – the fall.

The gallery needed someone to go over and sweet talk a local Cornish artist who lived over there, and persuade her into allowing us to display her work. This, if I could pull it off, would be huge kudos for both the gallery and for me. Not only did I manage to do just that, I swung an extended holiday out of it for both myself and Rosie, and of course while we were there, we spent some time with Mack.

We didn't stay with him, as Mack suggested we might way back in 2014. We stayed in a hotel on the Upper West Side, partly funded by my employer and partly by me. But we did manage to spend quite a lot of time with Mack while we were there, which Rosie and I both enjoyed immensely.

After we did all the touristy things like the Empire State Building and the Statue of Liberty, Mack showed us around other places like parks and galleries, including the Metropolitan Museum of Art, which I absolutely adored, just as Mack knew I would.

One evening after dinner – a takeout from a Chinese restaurant a few blocks away from Mack's apartment in Brooklyn – white boxes sat empty on Mack's coffee table with disposable chopsticks still resting inside. Rosie was asleep on one of Mack's two sofas, overcome by a day spent walking the Brooklyn Bridge and shopping in Bloomingdale's and Macy's.

Mack quietly re-entered the sitting room carrying two cups of coffee, which he placed down among the takeaway boxes on the coffee table, before sitting next to me on the other sofa.

'She's tuckered out,' he said, looking at Rosie sound asleep.

'Must be all that shopping! Can't say I blame her – it's all I can do to stay awake myself. I really need this coffee, thank you.'

'My pleasure. In fact, these last few days have been my pleasure too. It's been wonderful to have you here at last – both of you. It's been some time coming, eh?'

'Yes, it has. But we're here now and I'm so grateful to you for taking time out to show us around.'

Mack looked at me a little oddly. 'When I said it's been my pleasure, Frankie, it really has. I feel guilty now for not coming back to St Felix again. But you know with my dad and all.'

'Please don't apologise. Your family comes first. It must have been incredibly difficult for all your family to deal with. Alzheimer's is a horrible disease.'

Mack nodded. 'His passing has been a blessing to be honest – both for us children and my mom. He didn't know us at all towards the end.'

I put my hand on Mack's arm to comfort him. And Mack stared at my hand.

I was about to remove it, wondering if I shouldn't have done that, when slowly he raised his head.

'I wanted to, you know,' he said quietly. 'To come back and see you. But as time ticked by, I wondered if ... well, if I'd dreamt some of it up.'

'Some of what?' I asked innocently, wondering if he was thinking the same thing as me right now, which was how much I wanted to kiss his gorgeous, soft mouth and run my fingers through his dark wavy hair.

'This ...' Mack gestured with his hand between us. 'This feeling I get when I'm with you. Do you know what I'm talking about, Frankie?'

'Yes,' I said. 'I know ... exactly what you mean.' I'd always thought Mack was an attractive man, but this trip made me realise he wasn't simply attractive, he was *incredibly* attractive ... especially to me. 'Are you feeling it right now?' I asked him, in what I hoped was a suitably seductive voice. I felt very rusty. I hadn't been in this kind of situation for a very long time.

Mack nodded his head slowly and then he glanced over at Rosie. 'Would it be wrong to kiss you when your daughter is asleep on my sofa over there?' he whispered.

'Not if we don't wake her, it isn't ... '

Mack leant across on his green velvet sofa and kissed me ever so quietly, and ever so gently, and it was one of the sexiest kisses that I'd ever had the pleasure of enjoying ...

'Mack?' I say now, in a voice almost as quiet as that evening in New York. I clear my throat. 'Mack?' I say again. 'What are you doing here?'

He turns towards my voice. 'This is your gallery, then?' He smiles. 'I thought the paintings looked good.'

'I can't believe you're here?' I stumble to my feet and hurry towards him. Then I stop myself. I haven't seen him in nearly five years; his feelings might not be the same as mine any more.

But the look on his face suggests otherwise.

He moves towards me too, and without saying anything else he pulls me into his arms and kisses me, and it's every bit as wonderful as the first time.

'Mack is here?' Claire asks, as I breathlessly tell her what happened this afternoon in my shop. 'Why?'

The huge, dopey smile, which hasn't left my face since Mack walked through the door a few hours ago, immediately drops.

'I don't really know,' I say, hating having to lie to Claire like this. 'I think he's come to see Rob.'

This isn't exactly a lie. Mack is here to see Rob. He's also here to see the pub Rob has asked him to buy.

'You're going to buy the Merry Mermaid?' I asked when Mack told me why he was actually here. 'Why?'

I closed the shop as soon as Mack and I could finally bear to pull ourselves away from each other. I tidied myself up a little, washed away the day's paint from my hands, and we went for a walk. Partly so we could talk, and partly in an effort to suppress our feelings, as my little shop, on a busy street in St Felix, perhaps wasn't the most private of places to resurrect our relationship, and I think we both knew if we'd stayed there then things would have got very steamy indeed.

'I know you know why,' Mack said as we paused high up on

one of the cliffs to look out over the beach and the sea. 'Rob told me he'd told you everything.'

I breathed a huge sigh of relief. 'Oh, thank goodness you know. I couldn't bear to keep this a secret from you as well.'

'I know. It's the pits, isn't it? But Rob seems to be bearing up quite well.'

'You've seen him then?'

'Yes, he was the one who told me where your shop was.' Mack looked at me and frowned. 'Frankie? What is it?'

'I feel guilty,' I replied, tired of telling fibs and white lies over the last weeks. 'Guilty for feeling like I do about you when Rob is going through what he is.'

'I feel exactly the same,' Mack said, turning towards me. 'I've always known how Rob feels about you, Frankie. I feel like I'm doing the dirty on him by feeling like I do.' He paused, and I got the sense he didn't want to ask his next question. 'What I need to know is . . . how do you feel about Rob?'

I'm jolted back into the present by Claire's voice. 'He's come all this way again just to see Rob? Frankie, are you listening to me?'

'Yes.'

'Has he then?'

I look at Claire.

She sighs. 'Has he come all this way just to see Rob?

I shake my head. 'No, Mack is buying the Merry Mermaid.'

'What?' Claire looks even more confused. 'Why? Rob's only been here five minutes. Don't tell me he's bored with it already.'

I shrug. It's getting harder and harder not to tell Claire anything. I'd have to speak to Rob about it. I can't keep lying to her like this – she's my best friend.

'What's happened, Frankie?' She narrows her eyes. 'Something has. In the same way you know me, I know you too well.'

'I'm in love with Mack,' I burst out, desperate to at least share one secret with Claire. 'And I have been since Rosie and I visited New York in 2019.'

After our trip to New York, Mack and I promised to stay in touch, with Mack announcing he would definitely be coming over to England early next year.

But then the thing happened. The thing that had so much of an effect, not only on my life, but on the lives of so many.

The pandemic kickstarted me back into serious painting again, and as a result allowed me the chance to give up my job at the Lyle gallery and paint full time, something I'd always dreamed of. But at the same time, it also stopped me from seeing Mack.

At first, we jumped on the new trend for video calling, and we spent many hours on Zoom chatting to each other at times when it wasn't the middle of the night for either of us. But as the pandemic continued and New York closed down altogether, Mack not only had himself and his family to worry about keeping safe, but he also had the responsibility of keeping his business afloat and the jobs of his many staff. So our chats became less frequent and when we did finally manage to arrange a call, it was clear Mack often had other more pressing things on his mind.

Realising he wasn't quite himself, he of course apologised and said maybe we should wait until it was all over, and he could go back to being the happy-go-lucky chap I was used to him being.

I agreed, reluctantly. And I missed our chats desperately.

But what could I do? I was halfway around the world, I couldn't exactly pop over there – there were no passenger flights between the UK and the US for some time, and even when the world began to open up again, both Mack and I had so much on our respective plates – me with starting my own business and he with saving his – it just wasn't the right time to try to resurrect what little relationship we had. So, like many things when you don't put effort in, eventually it simply wilted away.

But now things are different. We have a chance at a new beginning. The problem is, Rob has exactly the opposite.

'I know you love Mack,' Claire says without surprise. 'I've known that for a long time. Perhaps even before you did?'

'Really?' I ask.

She nods. 'You two are great together. Your problems have been caused by external influences, not by something either of you has done. And Rosie agrees with me.'

'She does?'

'Yep, we've talked about it a few times.'

'When?'

'When you returned from New York I think was the first time. She told me she'd seen the two of you kissing and holding hands when you thought she wasn't looking.'

I should have known my daughter was a bit too sharp for us to hide that from her.

'And then a few times over the years since, I suppose. Mainly when you were video calling each other a lot during the pandemic. Rosie really likes Mack. She's sad the two of you never properly got it together. You didn't get it together, did you?'

'Maybe a couple of times . . . ' I say, smiling coyly. 'And if we hadn't been in my shop today, it might have happened again. It got pretty steamy for a while.'

'Enough!' Claire holds up her hands in mock horror but is smiling at the same time. 'What is it the young folks say? YGTF?'

'What does that mean?'

'You've gone too far? Isn't that right?'

'No!' I laugh. 'You mean TMI. Too much information. Oh dear, we are getting old, Claire.'

'I am. It sounds like you've still got some fire in you, though. I say good on you. If you and Mack have got another chance after all this time, then go for it. Is he going to move here then if he's buying the pub? Or is it in name only and he's going to remain in New York?'

'He's talking about moving.'

'Great! So what's the problem, then?'

'Rob is,' I reply, knowing I have to tell her. 'Rob is the problem.'

Thirty-Six

'How's it going then?' Rob asks as we walk along together one morning up to our special viewing area. 'With Mack, I mean, before you start talking about your work.'

I stare at Rob for a moment.

'I know all about the two of you,' he says, not sounding in the least angry. 'I've known for some time.'

Mack has been back and forth over the last month between New York and St Felix – two bigger contrasts you couldn't get.

He now officially owns the Merry Mermaid, even though it's completely hush hush and everyone else thinks nothing has changed and Rob is still the owner.

We also resurrected our relationship on a more permanent basis, so even though Mack isn't here all the time, our separations only make our reunions all the sweeter.

'That makes two of you who knew before me then,' I say, trying to keep it light. We are about to have a conversation I've been dreading since Mack returned to St Felix.

'Who's the other one? Wait, don't tell me – Claire. You tell her everything. I also know you told her about me.'

'I had to. I couldn't lie to her any longer. It was killing me.'

'It's fine. I forgive you. We don't want two of us going at the same time now, do we?'

'Oh, Rob,' I say, clamping my hand over my mouth. 'I'm so sorry. I didn't think.'

'Not a problem. I've made my peace with it now.'

'Have you – really?'

Rob nods. 'It comes to us all eventually. Perhaps this is a little bit earlier than I'd expected, but when it happens, I'm ready. That's why I wanted to talk to you, to let you know I'm happy for you and Mack.'

We seat ourselves on the little bench and I turn to him to see if he means it.

'Are you? Honestly?'

Rob nods. 'Mack is a good man – one of the best. If I can't be with you for much longer, then I'm pleased he will be.'

'Don't say that. You don't know how long you've got left – it could be ages yet.'

'Or it could be any day.'

'Really, so soon? But you seem so well.'

'Good meds,' Rob says quickly. 'I told you I was with one of the best.'

'But still . . . '

'Frankie, when it happens, it happens. And I don't want you being miserable for longer than you have to be. By all means, mourn me for the appropriate amount of time . . . ' He winks. 'But then get on with the rest of your life – with Mack. My two best friends owe me that at least.'

I nod. But it's so hard hearing Rob talk like this. I can't bear it.

'You will always be my first love,' I say, trying to control the wobble in my voice. 'Always – like the song. Remember?'

'Bon Jovi – of course I remember.' Rob takes my hand. 'That's when I first knew how special you were when I saw your T-shirt that night.' He squeezes my hand, and I have to dig my nails into the palm of my other hand to try to stop myself from crying.

'I may have been the first, Frankie, but I was never going to be *the one*. I think we both know that. Sometimes it takes people a long time to find the one, but I think you have now. Keep each other safe, and love each other as if each day is your last. Because you never know if it might be.'

And as we gaze out at a view we've looked upon so many times together over the years, we both hear the familiar splash in the water below. But this time, we don't need to look down. We simply gaze at each other.

Thirty-Seven

'I'm so pleased you like it,' I say happily, as later that afternoon I'm back in my shop showing Muriel, the lovely old lady who commissioned me to paint Morvoren Cove for her, her new piece of art.

'It's exactly like I asked you to do it,' she says, gazing up in awe at the painting from the chair I found for her to sit on. 'The detail is amazing, and I see you've put all the mermaids in there for me.'

Muriel had been at Eddie and Dexter's wedding, although I can't remember seeing her there. Apparently, she used to work at the café with them as a waitress many years ago before she retired and moved away. She admired my painting, as many of the other guests had that night, so when she decided she wanted a painting of her own, she got my number from Eddie.

Although she was quite loose about how she wanted me to depict the cove, she was very specific about the placement of several mermaids she wanted in the painting. They were partly hidden, so you had to look quite hard at the painting to find them, just as in Eddie's picture. But if you knew where to look, you could find them easily.

'Of course, just like you asked.'

'Do you know much about mermaids, Frankie?' she asks, turning away from the painting to look at me. 'They're very interesting creatures.'

'Not a lot,' I reply. 'But me and my friends called ourselves the mermaids when we were at school.'

'Did you? How interesting. Why did you choose that name?'

'I don't know really. Probably something to do with a show we put on when we were dressed as mermaids. It was a very long time ago now, though.'

'How lovely. I imagine you looked wonderful.'

'I wouldn't go that far.' I smile. 'But we had a fun time.'

'I bet you did. I've always been fascinated by mermaids. I used to sit and watch for them in the cove when I was a girl.'

'And did you ever see any?' I ask, playing along. I should really be shutting up the shop now, but I get the feeling Muriel wants to chat, and she's been so lovely about the painting I haven't the heart to try to move her on just yet.

'Oh, yes, many times,' Muriel says to my surprise. 'Very enigmatic creatures they are. You know some people say they are the sea's version of angels.'

I want to stop Muriel and ask her more about seeing mermaids, but she's already moved on. 'But whereas angels leave white feathers as their calling cards, it's said a mermaid will leave a shell when they've visited you.'

I stare at her now. *What did she just say?*

'Are you all right, dear?' she asks. 'You look a little pale. Do you want to sit down?' She goes to stand up, but I stop her.

'No, no, please, you stay seated. A shell, you say?'

'Yes, like a calling card. You must know the story of St Felix's mermaid?'

'Oh, yes, my friend told me when we were at school. Erm . . . it's something to do with a maid who stole some jewellery from Tregarlan Castle and tried to pass it on to smugglers in a barrel, I think. But she got very drunk before she was able to send the jewellery out into the waves, fell into the sea and drowned, and that's why the pub in St Felix is called the Merry Mermaid, because of the myth.'

Muriel smiles. 'Yes, that's the story that's developed over time. I feel that's a lot to do with marketing the pub to unsuspecting holidaymakers, though, and less to do with the real mermaids of Morvoren Cove.'

'Mermaids? You think there's more than one?'

'I know there is. I've seen them.'

I'm about to ask what they look like, and did she ever see more than a tail, when she continues. 'The reason I know that story is made up is because a mermaid's treasure would never be a set of fancy jewels, as is depicted in that version. Mermaids live a much simpler life. Their treasure is always made up of natural objects – like shells, and items found in the sea.'

'Like *The Little Mermaid*?' I suggest. 'I used to watch that movie a lot with my daughter, Rosie, when she was young. Ariel's treasure was things she'd found in the ocean.'

'Ah, you are referring to the animated film.' Muriel gives a little shrug. 'A good attempt, but about as true a tale as the drunken maid version is.'

'What is the true story, then? And how do you know so much about this, anyway?'

'I don't suppose you have a kettle here, do you?' Muriel asks, looking towards the back room where I do all my painting. 'I'd love a cup of tea if you could spare one?'

'Of course,' I say. 'Give me a couple of minutes.'

I make Muriel and me both a cup of tea and then I pull up another chair and sit down next to her in front of the painting.

'Lovely name your daughter has,' Muriel says as she admires the painting again while sipping her tea.

'Thank you. I named her partly after someone I used to know, and partly because Rosemary, which it's short for, means "dew of the sea". When she was born I lived in Glasgow, so I felt a long way from my home here by the sea.'

'That's lovely,' Muriel says. 'It's surprising how many names have a sea meaning, isn't it? My own does too. Muriel means "of the bright sea". It's a little old fashioned now, though. You chose well with Rosemary or Rosie. I'm sure it suits her much better. Now,' she says after another sip of her tea. 'Let me tell you some more about mermaids. That's if you're still interested?'

'Yes, of course I am.'

Muriel looks pleased. 'Right then, I have been studying mermaids and the stories that surround them for many years. It's quite the passion of mine.'

'That's why you wanted all the mermaids in the painting?'

'Partly. The true story of the St Felix Mermaids, I believe, is as follows – Mermaids are said to live for hundreds, sometimes even thousands of years. Again, to use the angelic realms for comparison – an angel needs to earn their wings by looking after humans for a certain amount of time. A mermaid needs to do the same, but instead of wings they try to earn their legs.'

I'm about to use *The Little Mermaid* again for reference, but I think better of it.

'To become human?' I ask instead.

'Oh, no, why would something as beautiful as a mermaid

want to become human? No offence to you, but humans are considered much lower beings in terms of the universe as a whole, than say something like an angel or a mermaid.'

'But you said they want to earn their legs. What would be the point in having legs if you were going to carry on living in the sea?'

'Earning your legs isn't about becoming something else, it's about having the option to.'

'I don't really follow . . .'

'It's quite common knowledge that mermaids are often able to shapeshift. That means they are able to take on the form of another living being. But to do that they have to earn their "legs", i.e. the gift of shapeshifting.'

This conversation is getting stranger by the minute. But I'm finding it incredibly compelling too. Muriel doesn't seem particularly eccentric or batty, she just seems very knowledge-able about her passion – which is clearly mermaids in all their guises.

'How do they do that?'

'When a mermaid, or a merman for that matter, reaches a certain age, it's their chance to prove themselves. To move up the echelons of merpeople so to speak. A bit like when a human reaches eighteen, or twenty-one as it used to be, they become an adult. Humans are bestowed with certain privileges in life at that age, and we hope they use those privileges sensibly and to the best of their ability. Many however do not, and they are often the ones that need the most help. That's when the more experienced beings are needed – your winged angels and the like. But whatever type of being you are, when you are just starting out on your spiritual journey, you need to choose humans to help that have slightly easier problems to fix. But the more you can help, the more you build up credit – let's call it – so eventually the gift of wings, or the ability to shapeshift is yours as often as you need it.'

I drink my tea while I listen to Muriel speak, part of me thinking I should be finding everything she says totally beyond belief, and simply the words of a little old lady who clearly takes great comfort from her own notions and beliefs. But she speaks with such confidence and total conviction, that I feel myself completely drawn to her every word.

'Go on,' I say when she pauses to have a drink.

'I'm glad you're so interested.' She smiles at me. 'There's many folks who would simply put my thoughts and observations down as the fantasies of a silly old woman.'

'I am interested – genuinely. I might have seen something strange too when I've been in the cove.'

'Oh, yes?' Muriel pricks her ears up. 'What sort of things?'

I tell Muriel all about my experiences in St Felix with what may have been a mermaid. From our first encounter with the barrel full of supposed treasure, to our wishes, and the splashing and huge fishes' tails we've witnessed over the years.

'Is there anything else?' she asks when I've finished.

'Isn't that enough?' I smile, feeling like a huge weight has been lifted from me now I've told someone.

'It's plenty to be going on with. And have you found any of the mermaid's treasure by any chance?'

'I thought you said the treasure wasn't real?'

'Not that treasure. I said a mermaid's treasure is much more likely to be something natural. There have been stories about a mermaid giving their necklace to a human piece by piece until they've collected it all. If they keep it, so it can be repaired and put together again, then they know the human they've helped

349

is truly worthy. But if the human loses or discards the pieces they've presented to them, then they've failed and chosen badly.'

'So what are these mermaid's necklaces likely to be made of?' I ask, although I'm pretty sure I know what Muriel is going to say.

'Shells,' she says, looking at my collection on the windowsill. 'Very much like the ones you have over there.'

'I met a really interesting woman today,' I tell Claire that evening.

'Really, who?' Claire asks. Claire is currently running around looking for her phone before she heads out to a meeting of her organising committee for the school reunion. Which is only a couple of weeks away now.

'It was the lady I told you about who commissioned the painting of Morvoren Cove. She came to collect it today.'

'Oh, yes, the one with all the mermaids hidden in it. What was she like?'

I choose my words carefully. 'Intriguing.'

'How so? Oh, there it is!' Claire finds her phone, where it often is when it goes missing, behind one of the cushions on the sofa.

'She just was. Look, you're in a hurry. I'll tell you about her later. Oh, Claire, just before you go, you don't happen to have a book of baby names lying around somewhere, do you?'

'Why, you're not pregnant are you?' Claire grins as she pulls on her jacket. 'Oh God, you're not, are you? I mean, I know you and Mack are . . .'

'No!' I say firmly. 'I am not pregnant. Menopausal, perhaps. But not pregnant.'

'Why do you want a baby book, then?'

'I want to look up some names and their meanings, that's all.'

Claire glances at the bookshelves stuffed with books. 'No, I don't think I have any more. I had one when the children were born, but I think we gave it to a charity shop. Why don't you just look on the internet? There's bound to be loads of websites full of names on there. Right, I have to go. See you later.'

'Bye!' I call as Claire dashes out of the door.

Why had I not thought of looking online? It was so easy these days, compared to when we were all at school and had to use encyclopaedias and the school library to find anything out. These days, all the information you could ever need was at the touch of a button.

I grab my phone and Google baby names.

Then I enter several very specific names into the search box, and I find exactly what I'm looking for . . .

Thirty-Eight

I awake the next morning to someone banging hard on our front door. After my internet search of baby names and their meanings, and what I subsequently discovered, it had taken me a while to fall asleep last night, so I'm not really with it as the prospect of a new day dawns.

It takes me a moment to realise that it is someone banging on the door, and not some workman or other doing repair work down the street.

Assuming Claire is up and probably answering the door, I lie back down again. But then I hear thundering again, but this time it's the sound of someone rapidly climbing the stairs with purpose.

Claire doesn't knock like she usually would. She simply flings opens the door, so I sit up.

'Oh, Frankie,' she says, and the look of total devastation on her face tells me before she says any more that something awful has happened. 'That was Eddie at the door ...' She looks at me and her lips begin to quiver. 'It's Rob. He's ... he's dead.'

It's amazing how your body responds in times of crisis. In all our many years it would nearly always be Claire who would be the sensible one. The one who was calm and in control when people around her were panicking and falling apart. But today it's me.

It's not until much later that I remember that odd fact, because at the time I simply went into automatic pilot.

After Claire's words sink in, I leap out of bed and get dressed as quickly as I can, finding out as I go what little Claire knows.

Rob's body was found washed up on the beach at Morvoren Cove early this morning by a dog walker, who immediately called the police.

When Eddie and Dexter arrived to open up the café for breakfast, the police and the ambulance were already there, and there was one of those yellow tape cordons around the sand. When Eddie asked what happened, he was simply told there was body on the beach. He only realised it was Rob when he heard some people standing around the police cordon gossiping. Even though the police would not confirm or deny who was found, the rumour that it was Rob Matthews the movie star began to spread around the town.

Eddie then dashed up here to tell Claire and me, so by the time we get down to the cove we can hardly get past all the people to find out what's going on.

'Can I see the body?' I ask the police officer in charge of keeping people away.

'No, I'm sorry,' he says firmly. 'We need to formally identify who it is first.'

'But I know him. Knew him. He was my boyfriend.' I'm babbling.

The police officer looks at me with narrowed eyes. 'Recently?' he enquires perceptively.

'No, when we were at school. But we were still friends. Please?'

'I'm sorry. I can't let you through, Madam. Please stand aside now.'

I do as he asks, and I'm about to head back over to Claire and Eddie who are talking to some of the St Felix residents who have gathered, when another police officer, a woman this time, beckons me over.

'Did I hear you say you were next of kin?' she asks quietly.

'Er, no, not really. But we were close.'

She nods, looks either side of her in a dramatic way that reminds me of an old-fashioned comedy sketch, then quick as a flash she lifts the tape up for me to duck under. Which I immediately do, then she pulls me to one side so no one else can see us.

'Hold out your hand,' she says in a low voice.

'Why?'

'Please, I don't have much time.'

I do as she asks.

'This was found clasped in his hand when he was washed ashore,' she continues, still whispering, and she places something cold and hard on my palm.

I look down to see a beautiful shell. But not the sort you'd usually find on a Cornish beach, it's one much more at home on the Caribbean or Mediterranean sand.

'No idea how it got there,' she says. 'But I think it might mean something to someone. Do you agree?'

I stare at the shell.

'Yes. Yes, I do.'

'You keep it,' she says, looking around again. 'I had a feeling you might know what it meant.'

'Thank you ...' I look for her name badge, but I can't see one.

'My name is Marina,' she says. 'Just so there's no doubt this time.'

'Thank you, Marina.' I look down at the shell again. 'But how . . .' As I look up again, she's gone. I turn sharply around to try to spot her, but there's so many people gathering now behind the cordon it's difficult to pick anyone out.

'Madam, move back behind the tape, please.' The police officer I spoke to a few minutes ago is waving his hands at me like he's directing traffic.

'But your colleague just told me to come under.'

'Which one?'

'The woman, er . . .' I look around again. 'She said her name was . . .' But I stop.

Of course she did . . .

'Said her name was what?' he asks. 'As far as I'm aware there are only male police officers here right now, so if someone is impersonating a member of the force . . .' He looks around angrily. 'I bet it's journalists – they'd do anything for a story.'

'My mistake,' I say, hurriedly ducking back under the tape again and tucking the shell in my pocket. 'You carry on, Officer.' And I hurry over to where Claire, Eddie and Dexter are standing.

As we watch Rob's body, covered in a long, zipped bag, being carried up the beach to the waiting ambulance, I hold on tightly to the shell in my pocket.

And as the ambulance drives away with Rob's body inside, the shell, so cold when it was placed in the palm of my hand, glows with warmth.

The day is filled with even more shocks and surprises.

Not too long after the ambulance departs, we sit in Eddie's

café drinking coffees laced with whisky – medicinal, Eddie says – in a state of total and utter shock.

But someone breaks our silence by knocking firmly on the café door. Eddie gets up, mumbling something about it better not be press sniffing around for a story already. But when he returns, it's with a familiar and very welcome face.

'Mack!' I jump up and run over to him. 'Oh, Mack.'

Only after Mack and I hold each other for a few precious moments, does it occur to me to ask how he got here so quickly. He isn't due back in St Felix until next week.

'I was already here,' Mack says, still holding me as he looks down into my face, his blue eyes full of sadness. 'I'm staying at the pub. I arrived late last night. I didn't even see Rob. I went straight to bed assuming I'd see him in the morning. God, I wish I hadn't now.'

'You weren't to know what was going to happen,' I tell him. 'None of us did. But why didn't you tell me you were coming? You usually do.'

'Rob suggested it,' Mack says. 'He said not to tell you. He said it would be a nice surprise for you.'

I look at Mack and Mack looks at me, both of us suddenly realising something isn't right.

'And he was found on the beach?' Mack asks. 'What was he doing there so early?'

I look around at the others, but they all just look blankly back at us.

'He wasn't just found on the beach,' I tell him. 'He was found washed up by the edge of the waves ... The man said he'd been in the water.'

'He drowned?' Eddie looks puzzled. 'But he can swim, can't he?'

'Yes,' Claire says. 'Rob could definitely swim.'

'If he was able to,' Dexter says.

'What do you mean?' Claire asks.

'Perhaps he was under the influence?' Dexter says bravely. 'What?' he adds to Claire and Eddie who glare at him. 'It's possible.'

'You don't think . . . ' I trail off. 'No.' I shake my head and look up at Mack.

'Think what?' Eddie asks. 'What? Why are you all looking at each other like that?'

'They're wondering if he did it deliberately,' Dexter says. 'Aren't you?'

I don't want to, but I have to agree.

'Why would he do it deliberately?' Eddie asks. 'He wasn't depressed, was he?'

'No, he wasn't depressed,' Claire says. 'But he did have cancer.'

Eddie frowns. 'I know he had cancer . . . oh . . . wait, was it back again?'

I nod. 'It was terminal this time. I'm sorry, Eddie, he didn't want anyone to know.'

'Did you know, Claire?' Eddie looks upset.

'Yes, but I only found out a few weeks ago. Frankie was the only one he told when he first came back here.'

'And Mack,' I add.

'I thought he was doing OK, though?' Mack says. 'I mean, I know it was terminal, but he seemed so well.'

My head drops.

'What is it, Frankie?' Mack asks. 'Do you know something?'

'He told me yesterday he didn't have long.' I look around at them all with wide, red-rimmed eyes. 'He said that's what the doctor told him on his last visit. But Rob wouldn't ... He just wouldn't. Would he?'

'Perhaps he thought it was easier this way,' Claire says. 'Perhaps he didn't want to go through a long, slow death.'

'So he jumped off a cliff?' Dexter asks. 'Why do you all keep looking at me like that? It's what you're all thinking. And so what if he did? If the man only had days or weeks to live and he wanted to end it himself with dignity, then good on him, I say.'

The rest of us all look at each other.

'Whatever happens,' Mack says. 'Whatever they find, we must keep what we've just discussed within these four walls, OK? The press will be all over this. There will be a post-mortem and possibly an inquest too. If they find Rob's death to be accidental, then that's what we go with. And if they find any other cause ... then we deal with that in the best way we can. But whatever happens, we must protect our friend's memory at all costs. Agreed?'

'Agreed.' We all say this at the same time.

'Rob may be gone from our lives,' Mack says. 'But his memory will live on for ever.

Thirty-Nine

Three weeks later ...

August 2024

Today is the first time we've all met up for ten years, but it won't be all of us this time. Sadly, there is one mermaid missing.

Rob's post-mortem results came back, to the immense relief of us all, with the result of accidental death.

It said that he had a high level of drugs in his body the night he died, but because he was on so much medication for his cancer, it wasn't clear whether the drugs or drowning had been the cause of his death.

The truth is no one will ever know why Rob died that night. He may have taken more pills than he needed, he may have slipped while taking a nighttime walk on the cliffs – he told me he often couldn't sleep and went for a walk at night when it was quiet and calm, so he could have stumbled and fallen, I suppose. But I was pretty sure I knew the truth.

The way Rob talked to me earlier that day. He told me he didn't have long; I think now he was trying to warn me. That last walk we took together; the things he said – I think he was trying to say goodbye. And the fact that he cleverly arranged for Mack to come back that night, so he would be here when we first heard . . .

There was a memorial service for Rob in LA.

Mack attended, but Claire and I didn't. We stayed at home and watched as it was streamed over the internet for anyone who wanted to be a part of it but couldn't be there in person. Claire and I watched amazed as tens of thousands of people tuned in with us. At the service, fellow actors and celebrities attended, and some stood up and spoke with both love and humour about working with him. Mack told us Rob's manager and his agent were also in attendance, and they told Mack afterwards how much happier Rob seemed to them after retiring to Cornwall. Rob's parents hadn't been able to attend due to ill health, but his sisters had, and they had also taken the time to tell us that the happiest times of Rob's life were definitely those he spent in St Felix, both before he became famous and during the last part of his life.

Claire and I organised our own memorial for Rob in St Felix. But instead of calling it a memorial, we chose instead to call it a celebration of his life.

Immediately following Rob's death, Claire of course wanted to cancel the reunion. But after some thought, we both decided that since a lot of people that knew Rob would be there that weekend, it would be the perfect time to hold the celebration.

So that's what we did. And today, along with our fellow mermaids, we attended the same church where we've stood together over the years for school carol concerts, Claire's wedding and Mandy's sister's funeral. We wore bright clothing, sung songs of celebration, not mourning, and spoke with love and often passion about the Rob we knew. The church was packed out, not only with people that Rob knew in St Felix, but with our fellow schoolmates too, and it was one of the most amazing things I've ever experienced. Mack even managed to reform his old rock band and they played a medley of rock tunes mainly from the eighties.

I hope you know how much you were loved, Rob? I think, looking up as we all stand to begin filing out of the church. *Not only by all these people here today. But by me especially.*

A song begins to play as we begin walking down the aisle towards the doors of the church.

'Why is this song playing?' I whisper to Claire. 'This isn't what we arranged?'

'Isn't it?' Claire whispers back. 'I thought we were having Bon Jovi?'

'Yes, we were. But it was supposed to be "It's My Life", not this song.'

Claire listens for a moment. 'I agree it's not as upbeat as we wanted to keep this. But it's fine, Frankie. Don't worry. Everything else has gone to plan. Rob would have loved it.'

I don't blame Claire for not understanding. No one else knew what the song playing meant. No one except Rob and me. Because playing all around us as we begin to walk out of the church is Bon Jovi's 'Always'.

Afterwards the vicar – also a fan, apparently – apologises to me for playing the wrong song. 'I don't know how it happened,' she says. 'I didn't think it was even on the playlist you'd given me.'

But I know.

Rob let me know that day on the cliff, what was going to happen, and he'd let me know today there would be a special place in both our hearts for the other . . . Always.

*

'He was pretty organised, wasn't he?' Mandy says as we sit on the rocks overlooking Morvoren Cove. The last of our guests finally departed after a wonderful evening spent in Eddie and Dexter's restaurant, celebrating Rob's life. Eddie and Dexter were the perfect hosts, and I think everyone left with feelings of warmth and contentment, rather than sadness, which is what we set out to achieve all along.

Currently, Suzy's husband, Harry, and their twin boys, Lucas and Edward, are sitting up in the restaurant with Mandy's partner, Jules. Claire's children are also there, along with Rosie and her new boyfriend. They are all having a last drink with Dexter while the six of us have our own private vigil for Rob. We've tucked ourselves away in the rocks, just like we used to, and we've opened a bottle of champagne to toast our friend.

'I mean, to leave everything so organised,' Mandy continues. 'With handwritten letters for all of us; he must have known he hadn't got long?' She looks questioningly at me.

I take a sip of my champagne. 'Rob knew it was terminal this time. I think he just wanted to get everything in order, before the end.'

'He certainly did that,' Claire says, giving me a brief glance as she skilfully moves the conversation along. 'It's been such a weight off my mind that you all know the truth now.'

I nod gratefully at Claire.

Even though there were several of us there that day in the restaurant after Rob's death, I only told Mack about my last conversation with Rob.

Mack and I discussed between ourselves what we thought might have taken place on the beach, but then we agreed that we'd never truly know, and we should simply let Rob rest in peace.

'How did he keep it all so secret?' Suzy says. 'He was like the Rick Stein of St Felix, owning all those buildings.'

'Who's Rick Stein?' Mack asks.

'He's quite a famous restaurateur,' Eddie explains. 'He owns a lot of buildings in and around Padstow, where he has a famous fish restaurant.'

Mack nods. 'It does ring a bell.'

'I had no idea Rob owned the building our restaurant is in,' Eddie says. 'I just paid the rent every month. To you as it turns out, Claire.'

'I only looked after it all for Rob,' Claire says. 'It was all his idea. He knew if he offered to help any of you, you'd be too proud to accept. Especially you, Frankie.'

'And he was right.' I smile. 'There was no way I'd have allowed Rob to buy me my gallery. It was bad enough when he wanted to buy me and Rosie a house.'

'He was going to buy you a house!' Mandy exclaims. 'And you said no?'

'I did. You also offered to help me that same night, if you remember? It was the night of Eddie and Dexter's wedding. I said no to that as well. I was very proud back then. Maybe a little too proud. I should have accepted help from my friends.'

Mack squeezes my hand. 'But if you had, things might have turned out differently.'

'That is true.'

'So, Eddie now owns all of his restaurant instead of paying rent on it,' Mandy says. 'You own the building your gallery is in, Frankie, and you, Mack, own the pub.'

Mack nods. 'Rob gave me a great deal on the place. As always, he was very generous.'

'Well, me and Suzy should be feeling left out,' Mandy says,

grinning. 'We didn't get anything! Nah, I'm kidding, of course. Rob made a very large donation to my favourite charity. He knew I didn't need any of his money. And he said some very sweet things to me in his letter. I was quite touched by it.'

'Actually,' Suzy says, 'Rob did help me out. David and I were offered money for our IVF from a benefactor who wanted to remain anonymous. I talked a lot at the time on various TV shows about my battles with infertility, so it wasn't a secret by any means. But Rob told me in his letter – the mysterious benefactor was him. I have Rob to thank for my darling boys up there.' Suzy looks up to the restaurant and waves to her family.

'I think we should make a toast!' Mack says, standing up. 'To Rob.'

We all stand up with him.

'To Rob,' he says. 'Our very famous, but also *very* generous, friend.'

'To Rob,' we all repeat, lifting our glasses, and we are silent for a few moments as we each remember him in our own way.

We all sit down again and I seize the opportunity to attempt to confirm some things that have been bothering me for the last few weeks.

'Do you remember the first time we were all here like this?' I ask. 'The night we threw the barrel back in the waves and made our wishes.'

Everyone nods.

'I've been wondering lately if what you actually wished for came true. I know some of you have mentioned it over the years. But maybe now is the time to say what we actually wished for that night?'

'Oh, fun!' Suzy says first. 'All right, yes. I've sort of mentioned this a bit before, but my wish was to be more confident and make a change. I certainly did that after I sang that night with that girl, Marnie Morrissey. You remember, she was only in our school for one night, but she certainly changed my life. First I had my singing career – which definitely helped me to gain confidence in myself. But as a result of that I found another voice – my political voice, and I've definitely brought about change during my political career. So, yes, my wish really did come true.' She looks across at Mandy. 'Mandy, do you want to go next?'

'All right, why not?' Mandy says. 'You all know mine already. I thought I'd wished not to have a sister. But at the time of throwing the barrel, not only did I wish I could live my life as my true self, which I've told you about before, but I also wished I could be rich and successful in life. And guess what – I'm both those things! I am definitely successful,' she says without any embarrassment. 'But, more importantly, I'm also very rich . . . in love.' She lifts her glass up towards the restaurant and Jules. 'So, like Suzy, it seems my wish, if you can call it that, did come true. More coincidence and a lot of hard work if you ask me, but I'll go along with it, since it's you lot.' She winks.

'But you said it was Rob's first agent who set you on the path to becoming your true self, didn't you?' I ask. 'What was her name again? Jenna?'

'Yes,' Mandy says, remembering. 'Jenna Morgan. She was my first; I'd almost forgotten . . . '

I tick the name off mentally in my mind.

Just as I thought, for Suzy, it was Marnie Morrissey who changed her life, and for Mandy it was Jenna Morgan. So far, so good – my theory is working out.

'Claire?' I ask. 'You next?'

'My wish as you all know was to get married, have a family and make people happy. I definitely, if disastrously, did the first one.' She grimaces. 'The second . . . well, I actually have two families now – my children and now Frankie and her family too.' She smiles at me. 'And the last . . . I think I do that with my therapy and counselling groups – people usually leave much happier than when they first arrive. But to make others happy, I didn't realise I had to be happy myself. And I would never have achieved that if I hadn't met Mandy's aunt, Marilyn. Her help was invaluable in giving me the confidence to leave Jonathan and step out on my own. She really was my saviour.'

Mandy smiles. 'It's funny, I mentioned that to Marilyn once at a family event, and she didn't recall meeting you the night of the funeral at all. She only remembers you turning up at her counselling group.'

Makes sense, I think to myself. Even though this was still so hard for me to believe, the evidence was all there and like a detective, as I piece each clue together, they are all fitting together perfectly – all except one.

'I wonder if Marilyn remembers me?' Eddie says. 'She was the one who came to me that night and suggested I go to the estate agent the next morning. Not only did I decide to rent our little café that day, but I met Dexter there too.'

'And was that your wish?' Claire asks. I can see the others becoming more and more intrigued by this conversation as we go along.

'Yes, exactly. I wished I could do lots of different things in my life – which I did. I wanted to have my own business.' He gestures up towards the café. 'And I wanted to be in love and – the big one – I wanted to get married. Remember, when I made that wish it was still impossible and illegal for gay couples to marry. I never thought it would actually come true, that's why I wished it – to test the system, so to speak.'

'It sounds like you were testing the mermaid, or maybe the myth?' Mack says, smiling. 'I'm glad it came true for you, Eddie.'

Eddie nods at Mack.

So that's another, I think, piecing this together in my mind – *Marilyn*.

'What is your aunt's surname, Mandy?' I ask. Forgetting that no one else knows why I need to know this.

'Why?' Mandy asks.

'I was just wondering if I'd seen her around here lately?'

'I doubt it,' Mandy says. 'She lives in an old folks' home in Cardiff these days. It was Irving, I think.'

I can't remember if that fits. But I'm certain it will. I'll check it later.

'Sadly, we'll never know Rob's wish,' Suzy says. 'I bet it was something to do with you, Frankie.'

I blush and reach for my glass.

'Do you know?' Mandy asks. 'You've gone awfully quiet.'

'Rob did tell me – in his letter,' I say quietly. 'It was partly to do with me, but he also wanted to run the Merry Mermaid, like his parents had.'

'Ah, that's nice.' Claire smiles. 'He got to do that.'

'Do you want to tell us what he wished that was to do with you, Frankie?' Suzy asks gently. 'Or would you rather keep it private?' She glances at Mack.

'I'm easy if you want to share?' Mack says. 'We all know you two were close.'

Mack squeezes my hand again and I nod.

'Rob wished that I would be a part of his life, for ever,' I tell the others, as my heart squeezes tightly as I think about Rob again. 'Which I was, even if it wasn't quite in the way he hoped when we were fifteen.'

Everyone is silent now as they think about Rob once more.

'That is actually really lovely,' Mandy says, and she looks quite tearful. 'Blimey, you've even pierced my tough old heart with that one.'

'And what about you?' Mack asks me. 'We've heard everyone else's wish – what did you wish for, Frankie?'

'Ah me,' I say knowing it would be my turn eventually. 'I wished for multiple things as well – like we all did actually.' I smile at the others. 'Not like we were greedy or anything?' I wink at them. 'I wished I could be a professional artist one day with my own gallery – which of course after many years I now am, and also have – thanks to Rob.'

'And?' Claire asks perceptively. 'What were the other things?'

'There was only one other thing. When Rob and I were together, one day Rob took a piece of driftwood and used it to draw a huge heart on the sand. Inside that heart he wrote "FH 4 RM for ever". I thought it was really cute at the time, so when I made my wish, I asked that FH would fall in love with RM for ever, and RM would fall in love with FH for ever too.'

'Aw, that's so special,' Eddie says. 'And he did fall in love with you, Frankie. I think Rob always secretly held a candle for you.'

'That's what I always thought it meant too,' I say, hardly daring to look at Mack. I can already feel his hand has loosened its grip a little on mine. 'But the other day I realised maybe it meant something else too.'

'What?' Claire asks.

'Remember when I went to see you at the pub the other day?' I ask, turning to Mack.

He nods, but still looks worried.

'You had just had your name put above the door, hadn't you?'

'Yes, it's the law here. You have to display your licence to sell alcohol.'

'I know, but it was the first time I'd seen your name – your full name.'

Mack looks confused. But then he gets what I'm hinting at, and he smiles.

'And you didn't know before then?' he asks, his smile getting broader by the moment.

I shake my head. 'But I do now.'

Mack leans forward, about to kiss me.

'Whoa!' I hear Mandy shout. 'An explanation, please, for the rest of us?'

'Sorry.' I turn back to them. 'Mack's full name is ... ' I look at Mack. 'You tell them.'

'My name is Robert Mackenzie,' he says, looking at all the other mermaids to see if they understand. 'My nickname has always been Mack, since I was at school. There were far too many Roberts around in the eighties, so I got called something different and it stuck.'

I grin at the others. 'His initials are RM. I didn't wish I could fall in love with Rob for ever, I wished I could fall in love with RM and, I'm very happy to say that's exactly what I have done.' I turn to Mack and I do kiss him this time.

'My mermaid wish came true,' I say, addressing my oldest and dearest friends. 'Just like all of our wishes did. I can't believe I'm about to say this, but it seems we are not the only mermaids of St Felix. There are a few more out there too, and at least one of them has been helping us all out since 1989.'

Epilogue

'If a mermaid's treasure washes up on the shore
Return it to the waves and be happy forevermore.'

Two months (and thirty-five years!) later

It never really changes does it – the sea?

The seasons change, the weather changes; the light that bounces on the waves and makes them look either an inviting turquoise blue or a bitterly cold grey – that changes. But the sea, with its rhythmical waves washing in over the sand, time and time again – it doesn't change. It simply remains a constant. You can rely on the sea to do its thing, day after day, year after year without any fuss or worry. It's always there – just like it always will be.

As I sit up on the little viewing area that I've sat on so many times during my half a century on this earth, and I look out over Morvoren Cove, the weather may be a little grey and overcast, but it is October, and the temperatures are just beginning to drop as autumn sets in.

But sitting up here today, I feel incredibly content with life, because now I know. I know that everything I've gone through over the years, both good and bad, has brought me here to this point, and I'm happier than I've ever been before.

Of course, I miss Rosie when she's away at university, and I'll always miss Rob – that goes without saying. I can't walk around St Felix without thinking of him, or remembering places we'd go, or things he'd say. But I think of him with joy and happiness now, instead of sadness and sorrow as I did for the first couple of months after he passed away.

Rob and I were never meant to be. I know that now. Marnie and perhaps one or two others did us a favour in trying to keep us apart.

Mack was who I was supposed to be with all along, but if it wasn't for Rob I never would have met him, and for that I'll always be grateful.

The night after Rob's memorial, as we all sat on the rocks together talking about our lives, I didn't go into too much detail about my suspicions. I wasn't sure any of the others would really believe it if I started talking about shapeshifting mermaids leaving me a calling card in the form of a shell. It sounded crazy even to me, yet I knew it was true. I just left it that our wishes were all granted one way or another, and the others seemed happy to accept that explanation.

But I know that all the women who helped set us all on the right paths in life had sea-based names. I checked and double-checked them all. Each of those women left a shell behind, and after what had happened to Rob, I was pretty sure that a mermaid was involved in that too. How else could I explain the exotic shell clutched in his hand when he was brought ashore, and the female police officer with another sea-inspired name who pressed it into my hand and then disappeared? We were told because the tide was going out, Rob's body should have been taken out to sea, not washed ashore. How did that happen if he wasn't helped back onto the sand in some way?

None of it really made any sense, and yet so much did.

Muriel, of course, never took the painting from my studio. She paid for it and said she'd come back and collect it when her holiday ended. But a note arrived for me some days later.

Frankie,

I love the painting. You know I do.

But I don't think it's quite the right fit (or should I say waterproof enough!) for where I live.

You keep it. I want you to be reminded every day of the magic that can live in and by the sea.

As you know, there are six mermaids hidden in the picture, with a seventh floating above in one of the clouds.

I asked you to paint it like this. And I hope now you understand why.

It's been a pleasure knowing you, Frankie, and all your friends.

Have a good life, and remember, some mermaids will be with you ...

Always.

'A perfect, sparkling, summer read' Cathy Bramley

Ali McNamara

Cornish Clouds
and
Silver Lining
Skies

This uplifting summer novel from Ali McNamara
will make you laugh, cry and feel like you
have your toes in the Cornish sand ...

Frankie's Mermaid Name Research...

1989   Marnie (of the sea) Morrissey (sea valour)

1994   Jenna (white wave) Morgan (sea-born)

2004   Marilyn (star of the sea) Irving (sea friend)

2014   Nixie (water nymph) and Cordelia (heart or daughter of the sea) Delmare (of the sea)

2024   Muriel (of the bright sea) Murphy (sea warrior) and Marina (from the sea)